First published 2021

First printed edition published 2024 by Drollery Ltd.

Copyright © Alice Coldbreath, 2021

ISBN 978-1-916736-09-2

More books available by Alice Coldbreath:

The Vawdrey Brothers Series:

Book 1: Her Baseborn Bridegroom

Book 2: His Forsaken Bride

Book 3: An Ill-Made Match

The Brides of Karadok Series:

Book 1: Wed By Proxy

Book 2: The Unlovely Bride

Book 3: The Consolation Prize

Book 4: Her Bridegroom, Bought and Paid For

Book 5: An Inconvenient Vow

Book 6: The Favourite

The Victorian Prizefighter Series:

Book 1: A Bride for the Prizefighter

Book 2: A Substitute Wife for the Prizefighter

Book 3: A Contracted Spouse for the Prizefighter

October

Kellingford Tournament

If anyone had asked her, Aimee could have told them the precise moment she had fallen in love with Lord Kentigern. She and her sister had been sat in the stands at Kellingford, enjoying the rare treat their father had secured for them. Since his star was ascending, Gerold Ankatel had vowed his daughters, too, must become accustomed to the finer things in life. They would dress like ladies in gowns of silk and satin, wear dainty slippers upon their feet, and chains of gold about their throats.

The sisters had sat, arm in arm, awaiting the joust with mounting excitement. Aimee had been wholly unaware at the time that she had been about to lose her heart to another. Up until that point, she and her sister had been in perfect accord in their tastes. This was only the second tournament they had ever attended, and at the first, they had spotted the young and boyishly handsome Sir Renlow d'Avenant. He had quickly captured their admiration. His humble manners and his headful of curls would have been enough, but when they spied his tattered standard, dented armor, and faded shield, their sympathies had been firmly secured to his cause. Seeing him once again at Kellingford, they were quick to name him their favorite.

"What a truly estimable young man he seems," Ursula had whispered shyly. "I do so hope he performs well here."

"Not puffed up with his own consequence like that odious Sir Jeffree!" Aimee had agreed, thinking of the arrogant Sir Jeffree de Crecy, who they had watched triumph in the melee that morning.

Ursula's eyes widened. "Aimee! Sister, you must not talk so!" Her sister had looked around nervously, lest any of the mixed company had overheard her.

Aimee sighed. "None heard me but you!" She greatly esteemed her older sister, but she did wish Ursula was not quite so proper and correct at all times.

"Oh no!" Ursula gasped in dismay, raising her fine cambric scarf to her mouth and covering it. The crowd groaned along with her in collective sympathy.

"What is it?" asked Aimee, looking up from where she had been trying to retrieve a sticky date from her own kerchief.

"You won't believe who poor Sir Renlow has drawn for the joust," Ursula said, tears starting to form in her eyes.

"Who?" Aimee asked, twisting in her seat to see who was entering the stadium. Her own mouth fell open at the sight that confronted her as the huge charger lumbered in, bearing its dread master. He looked like a demon from some terrifying text, promising dire punishment in the afterlife.

Had anyone asked Aimee to imagine what a knight of hell would look like, without a doubt, she would have thought of Lord Kentigern. With his horned helmet and black armor, he looked like some powerful creature of the underworld, come to drag his opponent to hell. Watching him in action only cemented this impression.

At their previous tournament, she and Ursula had sat in terrified silence, watching him reduce some unfortunate knight to a

2

helpless victim in what seemed like mere minutes. He had wielded his freakish strength with brutal and destructive intent. At his win, the crowd had sat in complete silence, staring as he had drawn off his helmet to salute the royal box. For removing his helmet had revealed an even more terrifying sight—his disfigured features. He could not have failed to hear the audience's reaction.

Ursula had hidden her face in her scarf, but Aimee had been unable to look away from the cruel and heavy scarring which covered the left side of his face. The eye on that side had to be blind, for it was completely white. At the King's acknowledgment of his win, the crowd had broken out in a hasty smattering of polite applause. Kentigern had barely seemed to notice, exiting the arena as imposing and intractable as when he had stalked into it.

Watching him enter the field now, Aimee was filled with misgiving. "'Tis Lord Kentigern!" she breathed with dismay. "He'll destroy him!" She glanced back at Sir Renlow, who was manfully squaring his shoulders and leading his horse to the starting position.

Ursula twisted her scarf. "That poor young man!" she moaned. "To be cut down in the prime of his life!"

"I don't think they are actually permitted to kill one another," Aimee said uncertainly, glancing about. All around her she could see the audience tutting and shaking their heads. They, too, felt bad for the handsome young knight who was seemingly doomed in the first round of the joust. *It really was too bad!*

"I don't think I can watch," Ursula said, lifting her scarf to shield her eyes. "Tell me when it's over."

Aimee nodded, only too familiar with her sister's squeamishness. She straightened her own spine. Sir Renlow was facing his cruel fate so manfully that the least she could do was bear witness to his valor. She kept her eyes on his upright figure as he lowered his visor, poised ready for the off. She did not see the signal given but watched as his white destrier lurched forward. The thunderous barrage of the horse's hooves seemed almost deafening as they pelted down the length of the field.

Despite her resolve, Aimee found her eyes squeezing shut of their own accord as the inevitable collision occurred. She heard the crash and splinter of lances, the heavy thud of a fallen body as it hit the ground.

"Is it over?" Ursula mumbled.

Aimee started to nod before she realized that it was the black horse that was riderless and not the white. She gave a squeak. "No!" she breathed. "I can scarce believe it!" All around, hushed sounds of wonderment were breaking forth from other spectators as they beheld the fallen figure of Lord Kentigern lying prone in the dust.

"What has happened?" Ursula asked urgently. "Is he dead?"

"I shouldn't think so," Aimee said, though to her eye, it seemed Lord Kentigern was entirely insensible, he lay so still. She nudged her sister. "It's not what you think! Sir Renlow has triumphed, sister!"

Ursula lowered her scarf and gaped at Sir Renlow, who remained in his saddle as though he, too, were frozen in disbelief. Ursula drew in a shocked and ragged breath as Sir Renlow dismounted and a page darted forward to throw a bucket of water over the stricken Kentigern. "No! Do not revive him!" Ursula burst out anxiously. "He will surely be furious!"

Sure enough, Lord Kentigern stirred and suddenly sat up, causing a buzz of consternation from the crowd. "'E'll kill 'im!" someone opined from Aimee's right. "Rip out 'is guts wiv 'is bare 'ands, you see if 'e don't!"

To everyone's horror, Sir Renlow started toward his fallen foe, a smile of singular sweetness spreading over his face. The arena fell into horrified silence at such foolhardiness. Lord Kentigern wrenched off his helmet, exposing his ferocious features, and clambered to his feet. "Boy!" he roared, and the crowd flinched.

Suddenly, the two opponents were embracing, or a rough approximation of an embrace that involved jarring blows to each other's backs and a sort of grasping of each other's shoulders. Sir Renlow had so wide a grin across his face that it looked like it would almost split in two. He was laughing, and Aimee could see Lord Kentigern's beard moving as he spoke in what she could only surmise was a congratulatory speech, for she could not hear the actual words.

"I don't believe it," Ursula uttered in stunned accents, fluttering her scarf against Aimee's shoulder. "Do you see that, Aimee? Lord Kentigern is happy for him! Actually happy!"

But Aimee could not answer. Her gaze was riveted to Lord Kentigern's dirt-streaked face. She felt love's arrow pierce her to the quick as tears flowed from her eyes and cascaded down her cheeks unchecked. *Most noble Lord Kentigern!*

Finally, she, Aimee Ankatel, knew what it was that poets wrote of in their rhyming couplets and celebratory verse. The clouds rolled back. Trumpets blasted. Birds sang. She had fallen in love, suddenly, wildly, madly in love. Not with handsome Sir Renlow, but with the mighty Lord Kentigern.

She had spent the rest of the day in a daze. She did not even remember her sister leading her out of the bustling crowds to meet up with their sponsor, Lady Wycliffe, for some refreshment. She could not have told anyone what she ate or drank or even what they had sat and watched for the rest of the afternoon.

The sisters had been transported back to Wycliffe Hall, and Aimee had been strangely silent as Ursula regaled their father and Sir Maurice at supper with the tales of the knightly prowess they had seen that day. Sir Renlow featured heavily in her sister's narrative, and Ursula's shining eyes and flushed cheeks were not lost on Aimee as she praised that knight's impressive victory. It was not like her sister to gush or speak so freely, especially in front of a table full of strangers. Sir Renlow's performance had evidently moved her greatly.

"And you, Aimee? Did you enjoy the tournament also?" her father asked, turning to her. "You are quiet, my child. It is not like you to fall silent as your sister chatters away like a bird."

"Father!" Ursula protested, coloring hotly.

"I would think the two of you had swapped temperaments this day!" Gerold Ankatel joked.

"Nay, Father," Aimee hurried to reassure him. "I am only thinking of—of some household matter I have left neglected at home." She saw her sister's surprise at this, for it was Ursula and not Aimee who was the conscientious one when it came to keeping house for their father.

Her father, however, saw nothing amiss with her hasty reply. "Well, well," he had said kindly, patting her arm. "You must not fret about that now. We will soon return to Caer-Lyoness, but I want you to make the most of your opportunities here. You are meeting many fine people, good nobles all, yes? You remember what Papa said about how our prospects are changing?"

6

"Yes, Papa," Aimee quickly assured him. She noticed the pointed look Lady Wycliffe exchanged with her husband. To mention such things in public was considered vulgar by people like the Wycliffes, even though they were happy enough to take Gerold Ankatel's money in exchange for introducing his daughters to their circles. Seeing Ursula bite her lip, Aimee realized her sister was also aware of their hosts' disapproval of their father's frankness.

"Good, good." Gerold Ankatel beamed at his daughters as they bade him good night and climbed up the stairs to the guest bedroom they were sharing at present. "That's my good girls, making Papa proud."

As she and Ursula had undressed for bed, Aimee cast many looks her sister's way. Ursula washed and brushed her hair, sweetly oblivious to Aimee's regard. As soon as the servant withdrew, Aimee sat on the edge of the bed, braiding her own long black hair. She asked lightly, "Do you suppose that Papa meant it? What he said about our being able to look in high places now for friends and acquaintances?"

Ursula set down the silver-backed brush. "I believe so," she said gravely. "For you must realize, Aimee—you better than anyone—that Papa is now…"

"Immensely wealthy," Aimee finished off for her.

Ursula nodded. "It hardly seems possible," she continued in an awed voice. "But as you know, Papa now even boasts connections at court."

"Yes, but—" Aimee bit off what she had been about to say, selecting her words carefully. "Money is not…everything."

Ursula looked up quickly. "To be sure," she agreed. "Papa may sponsor even the King himself, but…"

"He is still a merchant," Aimee finished off heavily.

"Yes. And that is nothing for us to be ashamed of," Ursula said in a rush of words. "For he came by his fortune honestly and is moreover an excellent man of business."

"Oh, I agree! Wholeheartedly!" Aimee concurred hastily. "It is just that, to people like the Wycliffes, we will never be palatable company." She hesitated. "It never occurred to me to enquire before, but why does Papa not accompany us on the visits we make with Lady Wycliffe?"

Ursula hesitated. "He does not want to ruin your chances, Aimee. Father intends a fine match for you," Ursula said softly. "You are young and beautiful and will be heavily dowered. You can have your pick of all the land for husbands." Her sister rose and crossed the room to climb into the canopied bed they were sharing.

Aimee fastened the end of her braid and did not speak the words that hovered on her lips. *What of you, sister?* Instead, she flung her braid over her shoulder and made her way around to the other side of the bed, climbing under the covers to lie beside her.

Once she was settled, Ursula leaned over and blew out the candle, plunging the room into darkness.

"What of you, Ursa?" Aimee asked, using the pet name from childhood. "Why should you not take your pick of husbands also?" It was somehow easier to ask that question in the dark.

"I am better at home with Papa," Ursula answered swiftly without pause. "You know that when I was younger, I worked at Papa's spice stall in the marketplace."

"But Papa has so many assistants now. You have not had to serve spices in ever such a long time."

8

"That is true," Ursula agreed mildly. "But I still keep his books for him and make sure his home is comfortably run."

"Papa could take a steward now and a bookkeeper," Aimee persisted. "There is no longer any need for you to sacrifice yourself and run things for him."

"I am happy to do it," her sister said simply. "You must never imagine that I am not. Besides, I am good at it."

Aimee frowned into the darkness. "And what about when I have left and am settled into my own house? Will you not be lonely without my companionship, sister? When Father is sat with his cronies, drinking wine, and sends you to bed so that they may speak freely?"

Ursula was silent a moment, seemingly pondering her answer to this. "You will want me to come and visit with you, I am sure," her sister rallied stoutly. "And give me plenty of nephews and nieces to spoil. I will spend my evenings writing you long letters and practicing my lute."

Aimee sighed, giving up on this approach. Her sister was too complacent in her role as the prop of their father's old age. "What if Father were to remarry?" she flung out into the darkness. "What then? You would not even be mistress of your own home! His new wife could bring him stepchildren who would supplant you and steal your portion on his death."

Ursula gasped, propping herself up on one elbow to look at Aimee even though she would not be able to make out her features in the dark. "Aimee, where is this coming from?" her sister asked in troubled accents. "Father has never indicated that he is looking to take a second wife. Indeed, the way he speaks of Mama, I cannot imagine—"

"Oh fie, Ursula!" Aimee burst out. "He is so rich these days, he even pours coins into the King's coffers! Do you imagine some canny widow will not soon have him in her sights! You are not blind; you must know that the Widow Hemmings has set her cap at him these past three years—"

"Aimee!" Ursula's shocked tones sounded deeply grieved. "This is not a proper subject for us to be speaking of."

"Ursa—"

"No, Aimee!" her sister cut her off resolutely, and her voice shook with emotion. "Please do not wound me by giving voice to such matters. It is not our place to judge Papa and—" Ursula broke off with a suppressed sob, and Aimee guessed her sister had dropped back onto her pillows and rolled away from her.

Aimee bit her lip. Upsetting her sister was the last thing she wanted to do. Any discussion of Mama always brought Ursula to tears. She remembered their sainted mother so much better than Aimee, who was younger and had really been raised by her sister. "I did not mean to wound you, Ursula," she said in a small voice. "It is my sincere attachment to you that brings me to raise such matters."

"I know, Aimee," her sister's tearful voice replied after a heavy pause. "I do not mean to be vexed with you. You have always been warm of heart and impetuous of speech. It is one of the things that makes you so lovable." Aimee felt her sister's hand groping for hers in the darkness, and they clutched each other's fingers tightly.

Aimee lay wondering if she should try a different approach. "Sir Renlow seems to be in dire financial straits," she ventured and heard her sister's softly indrawn breath.

"To be sure," Ursula replied, sounding slightly strained.

"It seems likely, then, that he might welcome patronage from one such as Papa?" Ursula did not answer for a full minute, and Aimee thought as usual her sister was likely measuring her words carefully before speaking them aloud. Taking a deep breath, she continued. "Do you know of any existing attachment or betrothal with regards to that knight?"

The pillow rustled, and Aimee guessed her sister was shaking her head. "I have never made enquiry," Ursula said at last. "But I think…that is, I am sure that it would be a good match for you, sister. Would you like me to approach Papa on your behalf?"

Aimee lay silent a moment with astonishment, both that Ursula could think she intended Renlow for herself, and also that Ursula should suggest herself as an intermediary on such a matter. Ursula was so reticent that picturing her in the role of emissary was hard to imagine. "I was not thinking of myself," she said at last, "but of you."

This time, Ursula's gasp was audible. "Me?" she said in stunned accents, the bedsheets rustling as she sat up in bed. "Aimee, what can you mean?"

Aimee looked in the direction of her sister's dim white form. She wished she had not blown out the candle now. "I was thinking of Sir Renlow for you," she said simply.

Ursula sat very still. "Aimee…" she said at last in wobbly tones. "Y-you must not think that I—"

"I can tell you admire him," Aimee rushed on. "And I think you would suit him admirably."

"No, no, dear sister," Ursula protested. "He would be far better suited to you! You are so much closer to him in both age and beauty—"

11

"Just how old is Sir Renlow?" Aimee demanded, thinking of his youthful appearance with sudden misgiving. Ursula was rather on the shelf, in truth. She had turned down the only offer she had ever received and made herself too indispensable to their father, so he had been loath to part with her when she had reached marriageable age.

"I believe he numbers some two and twenty," Ursula stammered. "The same age as yourself."

"Well, but you are only seven and twenty. What does a couple of years signify when it comes to such matters?"

"Five years, dear," Ursula corrected her painstakingly.

"After all, what is five years?" Aimee asked practically. "There are five years between us, but were ever any two sisters as close as we? Five years is hardly an insurmountable barrier to love."

"Love?" Ursula echoed. "Aimee, my dear…"

"What is wrong?" Aimee asked patiently. Ursula was ever a worrier. It came of the fact she had been expected to pick up so many of their late mother's responsibilities too young.

"You must understand," Ursula said with some difficulty, "that among these nobles, love does not enter into such matches. It is other, more practical considerations that take precedence."

Aimee waved a hand which her sister would not even see. "Oh yes, to be sure!" she agreed airily. "Very well, let us look at it from that angle. You are a very wealthy heiress—" Ursula spluttered, but Aimee ignored her, plunging on. "And Sir Renlow is an impoverished knight in much need of funds."

"Aimee—"

"You have so many sterling qualities and would make him an admirable wife quite apart from the wealth you would bring him."

"I hardly think—"

"You are capable, kind, and honest, and—"

"I am not beautiful like you, Aimee," Ursula interrupted her.

Aimee thought of Ursula's dear face and felt her heart contract. "You *are* beautiful!" she insisted.

"No," her sister contradicted her simply. "I have a looking glass, Aimee. As Papa has always said, you are his little beauty, and I am his capable one."

"Oh, curse Father!"

"Aimee!"

"Oh well! I hardly think Papa is a judge," Aimee huffed, thinking of the Widow Hemmings's double chin and rather prominent nose. "He just thinks plump women are pretty. I wish I was as slender as you are, Ursula. I daresay I will be quite stout before I am thirty. In any case, I will speak to Father on the morrow."

"Don't you dare, Aimee!" Ursula gasped. "Besides," she added in a stronger voice. "Besides, it is not just these considerations which convince me I am ill-suited for such a match."

"What, then?" asked Aimee, her ears pricking up.

Ursula lay back down on the mattress and let out a sigh. "I am not blessed with your sunny nature. I do not have your resilience."

"What does that have to do with it?" Aimee wondered aloud. For no one knew Ursula's retiring nature as well as she.

"Anyone who"—Ursula's voice faltered—"who marries outside the rank they were born into," she carried on painstakingly, "would need to be hardy of nature indeed and…and able to withstand the judgment and censure of others. You are strong of will, and such things would not affect you as much as me. Oh, Aimee," Ursa confessed in a rush. "Ever since we have been staying under this roof, I have felt I am walking on eggshells, miserably aware of…"

"Every glance Lady Wycliffe sends our father's way," Aimee supplied for her and heard Ursula's head turn on her pillow.

"You have noticed it too, sister?" Ursula sounded astonished.

"Of course. She winces and grimaces whenever Father speaks at their table. No doubt, she thinks he should sit there quiet as a mouse, profoundly grateful to find himself in such exalted company." Aimee's voice dripped with sarcasm.

"That is just what she thinks," Ursula agreed hollowly.

"Golda says Lord Wycliffe has drunk and gambled away their fortune, and they haven't a pot to piss in."

"Aimee!"

Aimee laughed. "I think of what Golda said every time I see Lady Wycliffe shudder, and it brings the serenest smile to my face. You should try it, sister." She reached out and patted Ursula's arm. "Now, try not to worry yourself to distraction. I will speak to Father on the morrow, and all will be well."

"Aimee, you must not," her sister murmured, but Aimee's mind was made up. She could not concentrate on her own love for

14

Lord Kentigern when her older sister's future was not provided for. Something would have to be done.

Ursula deserved to have what she wanted for once, instead of putting her younger sister or father first. Ursula admired Sir Renlow, and therefore, she would have Sir Renlow. By hook or by crook, Aimee vowed she would make it so.

The Following July

Caer-Lyoness, the Summer Capital

The right honorable Konrad Bartree, otherwise known as fifth Baron Kentigern, was in a vile mood. The ferocious glare he bent on the landlord at The Jennet Tree was enough to make the man take an involuntary step backward. Even as he opened his mouth to blast the wretch into oblivion, his manservant, Jakeman, stepped hastily into the fray.

"His lordship requires a room for the next two weeks," he interjected swiftly. "If you cannot accommodate me as well, then I am sure I can find alternative accommodation nearby. Lord Kentigern has been a patron of your inn these past three years, good master Johnson, as I'm sure you'll remember."

The landlord's shoulders came down a notch. "One room I can manage, right willingly," he agreed, casting a nervous look in Konrad's direction. "And I only 'ope 'is lordship can pardon the fact I must ask his servant to put up elsewhere. Caer-Lyoness has been overrun these past two weeks, and I've never known it so busy!"

Jakeman made all the right replies, tutting at the influx of strangers who had poured into the city and nodding his head sympathetically as the older man vented his woes. Soon the landlord had calmed sufficiently to have Konrad's bags carried up the narrow stairs to a bedchamber and a table set up below for his lordship's refreshment.

Konrad flung himself down on the bench and took a large swig of his foaming tankard. The pleasant taste of the ale soothed him and reminded him why he always put up at The Jennet Tree whenever he was forced to come to the accursed southern capital. He glanced about at the busy room. The landlord had not lied. Within was busy, just as busy as the teeming streets without.

Most of them must have flocked to the city for the same reason as he—the royal summer tournament. Unlike the hawkers, pickpockets, and tourists, he actually had a relevant role to play in the proceedings, he reflected sourly.

The tournaments this year had not thus far covered him with glory. He had not lifted the victor's trophy since Roget's Ford in March. Even that win had not been as sweet as it should, for he had wanted a rematch with the so-called King's Champion, Roland Vawdrey, to regain his honor. Instead, the bastard had ducked out to dance attendance on his pregnant wife! Konrad shook his head and slammed his tankard down on the table.

They didn't make competitors like they used to. Even Orde, who had been as grim and cheerless as you could wish in an opponent, had now taken to parading his wife about the tournaments like she was attached to his hip. He turned to Jakeman, who was refilling his cup. "You'd better do the rounds," he growled. "Find out who's arrived and who's rumored as a no-show this year."

Jakeman gave a murmur of agreement. In truth, he didn't need the direction. He'd been with Konrad for nearly five years now. The fellow was efficient, discreet, and unfailingly polite. Sometimes Konrad wondered how he could stand to be around such a perfect paragon of a servant, but there was a lot to be said for employing someone who had never known him before the war.

As far as Jakeman was concerned, his employer had always borne his grievous scars and been blind in his left eye. Old family retainers were wont to flinch and wince when they saw what the fifth Baron Kentigern had been reduced to. The sensation prompted by their horrified glances flayed his temper and put him in a worse humor than even nature intended.

His pilgrimages back to Vettel were few and far between, avoided wherever possible. Only the Solstice would see him drag his carcass all the way north to the ruined spot where his estate once stood. Confiscated now by the Crown for their family's role in the late war, Bartree Castle stood a blasted and blackened shell. Some might say its master was a similar ruin of his former self.

His elder sister, Magnatrude, lived there still in the old lodge house, and Konrad was forced to pay a handsome sum for the privilege. It mattered not what he said; she would not budge an inch from the spot where the degradation of their old home would be ever present in her mind. Trude wrote him long letters filled with bitter recriminations, and small wonder, for she was forced to bear witness every time another piece of masonry fell from the roof of Bartree Castle and shattered on what was left of the flagstone floors below.

He had another such letter in his pack even now and had it these past two days without so much as breaking the seal. He knew what it would contain, nothing but misery and woe. Trude would become a bitter old woman with a mouth full of nothing but ashes. There was nothing he could do to stop the rot. Last Winter Solstice, he had sat opposite her at table and realized she took a strange sort of pleasure in the sharp misery of her life.

Kentigern scowled and banished all thought of family and home. Bad enough that he was back in Caer-Lyoness. The summer capital always put him in a foul mood. The prosperity

18

of the winning side struck a pointed contrast with the hardship and deprivation still experienced in parts of the north. He didn't *want* to think about what had once been.

Tonight, he would fling Trude's letter onto the fire and drink himself into oblivion. Battle, winning, lifting the victor's cup— that was what got him through his days, and he needed for nothing else.

Konrad spent the next two days settling into his new routine. He arranged the care of his destrier, Actaeon, with the ostlers at The Jennet Tree and spent both days training in the extensive palace grounds. The southern field had been roped out and set up with training equipment, quintains, and blunted lances. Everything had been made ready for the best knights in all the land.

Having finished his exercise on the second day, he stripped Actaeon of his trappings and rubbed the horse briskly down. The bond between them was strong, and even though his manservant was more than capable, Konrad still liked to do this himself on occasion. Only once he had finished did he relinquish him to Jakeman to lead him away to feed and water.

Konrad unbuckled his chest plate and leaned against a convenient stall. Squires ran about the place giving it a bustling air, though he did not spot many of his fellow knights as yet. One young sprig passed by in brand-new armor which did not bear so much as a dent. He gave Konrad a wary nod, and Konrad returned the gesture. For a minute he had thought it was Farleigh, who for some unaccountable reason had taken of late to seeking out his company.

In fairness, Farleigh had been on the circuit for nearly two years now, and his armor did not look as pristine as all that. Most of the knights competing would take up quarters at the palace, but he could never bring himself to do this. Even when he had gladly bowed his knee to the king in the north, he had been no courtier.

Old King Magnur was dead, the last king from the royal house of Blechmarsh. The Argent King had rendered his only heir, the Princess Una, powerless by marrying her off to a southern scoundrel of low repute. Konrad had not had the stomach to attend the tournament two months ago that had seen her hand bestowed so disgracefully on that dog, Armand de Bussell, but he had heard of what had transpired. The news had made him sick to his stomach.

His sister had written to him imploring him to enter the May Day festival and save "the rightful queen of all Karadok" from a fate worse than death. Konrad had thrown her letter into the fire, wondering if his sister desired them both to perish a traitor's death. If that letter had been intercepted, it would have been considered evidence of treason. Had Trude really not seen enough bloodshed in the northern cause?

In any case, he wondered impatiently, how could she have expected him to marry a princess of the blood when he had precisely nothing to offer her? His lands and monies were all gone, confiscated by the Crown. His face disfigured, half his vision gone, only his name and reputation were left to him these days. How could any woman be expected to share such a fate? Let alone an ill-omened princess. His sister must be mad.

Instead of attending, he had retreated to a bolt-hole to lick his wounds. He couldn't even seek oblivion in the arms of a woman these days, not since the terrible scars the Battle of Adarva had given him. What woman would want his face looming over her in the dark? He would give her nightmares.

He glanced toward the mellow stone edifice of the summer palace, with its soaring towers standing proudly against a blue sky. Had it been on a day such as this that Princess Una had watched as her future was thrown away on a whim of King Wymer's? He was roused from his thoughts by a discreet cough behind him.

Konrad swung around and saw a stout figure dressed in a sage green robe stood nearby with his hands folded neatly in front of him. He looked rather like a friar, though the gold clasp that fastened his tunic looked too fancy for one under vows of poverty.

"If you will pardon my forwardness," the man said politely. "May I make so bold as to enquire if I am addressing Lord Kentigern?"

Konrad regarded him stonily. "You are," he answered shortly. He failed to see how anyone could mistake him. Southerners were always so fussy about their address.

"My name is Bryce," the other continued mildly. "I wonder if I might be permitted to have a moment's private conversation with you, my lord?"

Konrad felt himself stiffen with irritation. "If this is some administrative matter, my servant Jakeman will see to it."

"It is not," Bryce answered swiftly. "It is of a far more personal matter that I wish to speak with you, my lord, and not one for which you can deputize." He hesitated before drawing some missive from his wide sleeve and holding it out to him.

Konrad lowered his brows, regarding the newcomer balefully. "What is all this?" he asked with a glower.

Bryce coughed. "My lord, it is an invitation for you to dine with the King and some other select few guests for the feast of St. Drogo."

Konrad could not have been more surprised if it had been a challenge to arms. "Why does this southern king invite me to his table?" he demanded.

This was a step too far even for the polite messenger. "King Wymer is sovereign of *all* Karadok," he pointed out primly.

He had guts to say that to him, and Kentigern was forced to concede, looking over the plump little man in his monkish robes. "What was your name again?" he rumbled.

"It is Bryce, my lord."

"You come from the palace? Whose man are you?"

Bryce's chest swelled. "Earl Vawdrey's," he answered with pride. "His lordship has entrusted this delicate matter entirely to my hands. It is my first solo diplomatic mission."

Konrad's suspicions sharpened. "Mission?" he echoed. "What delicate matter?"

Bryce's face fell. "Oh, I, er, meant the celebration of the feast," he said lamely.

Konrad shrugged a mighty shoulder. "It is not my custom to celebrate feast days," he said with a curl of his lip. "I must respectfully decline."

"My lord!" Bryce's cry was dismayed. "You surely do not mean to decline the King's express invitation!"

"I am sure there are at least a dozen of my rank who could dance attendance in my stead."

"You misunderstand His Majesty's intent!" Bryce protested. "He does you great honor!"

Konrad threw him a scowl so fierce it made the ambassador wince. "I believe I will forego the honor, however it was intended."

"My lord." Bryce was so moved by this rejection that he went so far as to thrust the written invitation in Konrad's face. So startled was Lord Kentigern by this act of boldness that he froze. The little man's double chin shook. "I am persuaded you would not pass up so advantageous an opportunity as this gathering affords you," Bryce hissed, looking around nervously.

What was this? Konrad pushed the paper away, but not as roughly as such impudence deserved. "What do you mean?" he demanded, narrowing his eyes. He turned over what he knew about Oswald Vawdrey in his mind. The man was well known to be the King's right-hand man and spymaster, but what could he want with him? "I doubt I would make an effective spy. Not with a face like mine," he pointed out dryly.

Bryce sucked in his chubby cheeks. "I assure you—" he began hotly.

Kentigern waved a hand. "Never mind all that. Just get to the meat of the matter, or I will fling this 'advantageous opportunity' back in Wymer's face, never doubt it. I'm no diplomat," he finished gruffly.

Bryce appeared in the throes of some internal struggle. His face grew pink and shiny. "You put me in a very difficult position, my lord," he complained fretfully. "Oh, very well!" he huffed when he saw the other's dire expression. "Only, let us walk a little way off so we may not be overheard at least."

There was no one within hearing, but Konrad suffered himself to be led some ten steps away before he came to an abrupt halt. "Well?"

Bryce glanced fussily left and right, his face assuming an expression of painful earnestness. "I don't suppose you have heard tell of the rich spice merchant Gerold Ankatel?"

"Merchant?" Konrad repeated irritably, so far none the wiser. "I know of no merchants."

"Over the past ten years, he has amassed quite a fortune. Some would go so far as to say he has established a spice empire, with trade routes encompassing all of Karadok, Samare, and the Western Isles."

"Very enterprising. What of it?"

Bryce pursed his lips. "His success is such it hath garnered the attention even of the King himself."

"By which," Konrad cut in dryly, "you mean that some of his gold has found its way into the King's money chests."

Bryce coughed again. "Alas, the King's coffers have been much depleted these past few years," Bryce said sadly. "The late war took its toll…" Kentigern could tell the precise moment the little clerk realized he had blundered. A panicked look entered his eye. "O-of course," he stammered, "the cost on human life was far higher than mere economic concerns."

"Do not trouble yourself," Kentigern's cool words cut across Bryce's embarrassed babble. "It is all water under the bridge now."

Bryce paused a moment to catch his breath. "In short, Ankatel has been in a position to finance the King in certain ventures. He has been an invaluable ally to His Majesty of late, and—"

"What has all this to do with me?"

"He has two daughters of marriageable age!" Bryce blurted. The silence stretched as Konrad eyed him with growing incredulity.

"And?" he prompted sharply.

Bryce's gaze fell. "M-my lord, I am sure I do not need to explain to you that a man whose fortunes have dramatically risen in the world will look to better his offspring's standing in life." Bryce's cheeks were stained scarlet by this point, and Konrad took pity on the stammering fool.

"He means to marry them off," he replied shortly.

Bryce nodded his head, looking relieved he had caught his meaning. "Yes, my lord. He wishes to secure for his daughters the best possible matches he can."

"He wants titles for them, you mean," Kentigern reflected coldly. Otherwise, they would surely not have approached him. He had nothing else to offer a wife. They must be plain specimens indeed if the King thought to fob one of them off on a scarred and penniless northern nobleman without lands or seat.

"Not necessarily," Bryce answered cautiously. "The second party I am to approach is a mere third son without the prospect of a title."

Kentigern regarded him a moment in silence. "I am sure you have a promising career at court," he said heavily. "So, there is little need for me to explain to you why my involvement in such a scheme is impossible. I have no intention of taking a wife."

"My lord, I have not yet told you her dowry." Bryce paused. "It would be a fantastic sum indeed. And in addition," he added when Kentigern's eye refused to spark, "Gerold Ankatel would be willing to purchase the Bartree estate back from the Crown."

Konrad, who had started to walk away, abruptly halted. "What did you say?" he asked harshly.

"All that you once lost could be returned to you," Bryce said simply.

So flabbergasted was Konrad, fifth Baron Kentigern, by this piece of news that he stood stock-still, utterly staggered. Then he swung around, dry-mouthed. "Bartree?" he repeated hoarsely. The land of his forefathers, entrusted to him on the death of his father. The prized estate his family had been custodians of for generations. "You lie!"

Bryce folded his hands in front of him. "No, my lord," he uttered calmly. "And a substantial fortune to go with it on the occasion of your marriage."

The vision of Bartree's turrets that rose before him abruptly vanished from his mind's eye to be replaced with the appalling reality of how he had last seen it. "The place is a mere blackened shell, falling to wrack and ruin," Konrad forced himself to point out through numb lip. "The roof was set alight, and its contents sacked. Your king has invested precious little in its upkeep these past four years." Even if its ownership returned to him, what could he do with it as it stood now?

"As to that, my lord, Master Ankatel has already pledged the funds to restore your seat to its former glory," Bryce said, robbing Konrad of all words.

Bartree would be restored and returned to its rightful owner? Was such a thing even possible? It was almost too much to contemplate. He started to shake his head. "But that would cost—"

"A king's ransom," Bryce concluded for him. "Luckily, Ankatel has that kind of money at his disposal." He allowed himself a

26

small smile. "That is the sole reason why he is now acquainted with a King."

The blood had rushed to Konrad's face so fast, he almost imagined the scars across his cheek throbbed, even though they no longer held any sensation. He had no words. No hope of stringing together a reply.

"I can see I have given you much to ponder," Bryce said with a small smile of understanding. "Might I suggest our meeting again in two days' time?"

Konrad struggled with his response, before giving a nod.

"That is your man stood yonder, by the water trough?" Bryce gestured.

Konrad managed to make some reply of the affirmative, and Bryce bowed neatly and tottered in Jakeman's direction to make the arrangements.

3

Aimee checked her appearance one more time in her glass, turning full on and then to the side. She wished she were not so plump, or that she could grow a few inches taller to gain some stature. Her figure was short and sadly dumpy, she thought with a sigh. There was nothing she could do about it now, but mayhap Golda was right, and she should fast for one day a week for religious observance. She had surely grown as tall as ever she would by the age of two and twenty.

Hurrying from her own room into her sister's, which was across the corridor, she came to an abrupt halt as she beheld its sole occupant. As she had suspected, Ursula was sat braiding her hair into its usual neat arrangement.

"Sister, why is Golda not preparing your hair?" Aimee demanded. "Father employed her for that very purpose."

Ursula glanced up at Aimee's elaborate arrangement of beribboned braids looped about a gold circlet. "Golda has done yours very nicely, sister. As for myself, I look much better with a plainer arraignment."

"Nonsense!"

"I should feel foolish," Ursula said, pressing her lips together. "Done up with ribbons and presented as some marriageable maiden at the feast!"

"You are *not* wearing this tonight," Aimee said, whisking a heavy linen veil off Ursula's lap. "You are an unmarried lady and will not cover your crowning glory."

Ursula set down her comb, but even as she opened her mouth to protest, Aimee called loudly for Golda. "You have very nice hair, Ursa, and you are to let Golda dress it." When her sister looked set to argue the point, Aimee fixed a stern gaze on her. "Do you wish to make me look ridiculous? A nice sister I should look with you sat there like a poor relation! What would our guests think to see your younger sister finely arraigned while you sit plain and unadorned?"

Ursula flushed. "I'm sure they would not think anything of the sort!" But Aimee could see the fight had gone out of her sister. She had clearly not considered the contrast they would present.

Golda came in with her heavy tread, and Ursula meekly handed over her comb.

"Which gown were you planning to wear?" She walked about the bed and saw the pale blue garment Ursula had set on the bed. "*Not* this one, Ursula!" She rolled her eyes. "Why, you've owned it above a twelvemonth, and it never displayed you to advantage!"

Ursula threw up her hands. "Oh, very well, Aimee!" she cried. "Dress me however you will."

"The royal blue houppelande," Golda suggested. "Miss Ursula has never even worn it, and it's a very fine gown."

"The very thing!" Aimee flung open a trunk in the corner and drew the gown from within. "And underneath the gold robe, I think."

Ursula half turned on her chair. "Oh no, Aimee! That one is for very best. I was saving it in case Father should ever have the opportunity to take us to court."

"He would buy us new dresses for that," Aimee answered blithely. She carried the gown reverently to the bed. There was so much fabric in the skirts and long scalloped sleeves that she had to walk slowly so she did not trip over it. "This is truly beautiful, Ursa. You will look like a duchess in this."

Ursula started to shake her head, but Golda exclaimed and yanked on her hair. "Don't you disturb my handiwork, Miss Ursula. You keep your head still, now do!"

Aimee sighed with relief as the capable servant wove a gold ribbon through Ursula's brown locks. With Ursula seen to, she smoothed down her own over-gown of rose damask, decorated with silver thread. A deep V shape descended from her shoulders to her waist, revealing her under-robe of finest green silk. It was the fanciest outfit she had ever possessed, and she felt a thrill of excitement every time she caught sight of herself in a looking glass.

If their father were a nobleman, their gowns would be trimmed with ermine or fur of softest white and they would wear ropes of pearls and diamonds at their throats and waists. Among their class, however, such a thing was not permitted. Not in public anyway. One was supposed to observe the distinctions of rank and keep to the sumptuary laws.

Still, Aimee did not see anything amiss with their appearance as the two sisters stood before the tall mirror at the top of the stairs. She wound her arm about Ursula's slender waist. "You look lovely, sister," she said, placing a kiss on her sister's cheek.

Ursula flushed. "*You* look lovely, Aimee," she sighed, her eyes veering away from their reflection.

"We both do," Aimee insisted. "Father will be very proud."

Ursula made no response. Aimee seized her hand, and they descended the staircase together. Only by the greatest exertion of self-discipline did Aimee prevent herself from mentioning

30

Sir Renlow to her sister. She could feel Ursula's cold fingers trembling beneath her own and squeezed them hard. Where she was filled with excitement at the prospect of meeting with their prospective suitors, Ursula was struck with terror.

Getting to this point had taken so much persuasion on Aimee's behalf that she was still giddy with triumph that she had finally reached it. Not only had she had to bring her sister around, but their incredulous father also. Gerold Ankatel had found it hard to believe that his eldest daughter should want a husband of her own. Not when she had so resolutely refused Willard Hemmings's proposal six years previously.

Aimee had by turn cajoled, flattered, flounced, and even bullied until their resistance had finally caved. Her father had never been able to deny her for long, but Aimee felt unaccountably jittery with nerves as they descended the steps down to where their father awaited them.

Her father had already met once with Lord Kentigern in the King's presence at a formal banquet. He had returned home filled with the conviction the wrong nobleman had been summoned. "For I am persuaded you cannot mean the man the King presented to me, daughter!" he had said, looking shaken. "I make no mention of his disfigurement, though his face is alarming enough, but his age and his brusque manner! Both make him highly unsuitable for you, my child."

"His age?" Aimee repeated. "I do not understand. There can be no more than some ten or so years between us. Was there not some fifteen between yourself and my mother?"

Gerold Ankatel stifled an exclamation. "He is that young?" he burst out incredulously. "I had thought him older than that, I confess." He lapsed into thoughtful silence a moment. "Perhaps it was the beard that misled me."

"In any case, Father. I am two and twenty and fully old enough for marriage. Why, your friend Master Walter's daughters were both married at seventeen! And you said Anne Masterson was lucky to marry a man quite twenty years her senior!"

Her father waved this away impatiently. "Yes, yes, but they were not *my* daughters."

"Ursula and I both know we are treasured in your house, Father, and consider ourselves most fortunate that you were in no hurry to rid yourself of us."

Aimee had spent the next week persuading her father that, no, she did not find Lord Kentigern's manner off-putting and, no, the excessive scarring down the one side of his face did not trouble her in the slightest, nor the unruly beard, nor the blind eye. By degrees, she had managed to bring her father around to the idea. "Only think, Papa, how Lord Kentigern's manner must have been soured by the cruelty of what he endured during the late war and how I can make reparation for that, by being a kind and attentive wife to him now."

Her father had never been able to withstand Aimee's wheedling, and her words worked on him like a charm. He looked forward to tonight's meeting under his own roof with a good deal more equanimity than even she had dared hoped for in her sunniest mood.

"I am filled with pride at the sight of my two girls," he said, beaming as they reached the bottom step. "Aimee, my Aimee." He held out his arms to her, and she embraced him warmly. "My little beauty, so like your mother. And, Ursula," he said with surprise, turning to his eldest daughter. "You look very well also, daughter, though you could do with a little more color in your cheeks."

Aimee was opening her mouth to make up for this faint praise when a knock at the door had them all freezing. Ursula turned so pale, Aimee feared for a moment her sister might faint. "Quick, let us repair to the front chamber!" Aimee blurted, gathering up her skirts. "Burchard must bring them in to us."

Burchard, who had served their father ever since he had taken this big fine house, nodded and drew himself up very tall before starting a ponderous walk to the door. Aimee, Ursula, and their father hastened into the large-timbered room at the front, set about with benches and cushions and elaborate wall hangings. A fire blazed in the large hearth, and their father stood before it, clearing his throat and adopting a wide-legged stance as he adjusted the brooch that fastened his purple tunic.

Aimee snatched up her new symphonia and fiddled with the strings as though fully absorbed in her instrument. Ursula sank down onto a seat beside her and made a half-hearted grab for her lute. They would be expected to play to entertain their guests, and Aimee hoped devoutly that their singing voices could mask the fact that both sisters were mere beginners in the art.

There was a discreet knock on the door before Burchard flung it open. "Lord Kentigern and Sir Renlow d'Avenant!" he announced loudly and stepped to the side. Two figures entered the room, and Aimee drew in a deep breath, feeling her color heighten. Finally, the opportunity had arrived for her to secure Lord Kentigern's admiration! Her heart was beating so hard, she almost felt it would burst out of her chest and take flight.

4

Konrad sat back with a sigh, his trencher finally empty. If he had learned one thing this evening, it was that Gerold Ankatel kept a sumptuous table, with an array of surprising and fragrant dishes a million miles away from usual roasted boar's head and game stews.

Instead, they had started with seasoned minced meats, which had been fried with vegetables and rolled up into balls. These were served with a sticky glaze and sprinkled with some sort of shredded orange spice, the like of which he had never tasted.

This was followed by a dish of capons served in an orange sauce with a crisp, tart salad of leaves, onions, and vinegar. After this had been small pies with many layers of flaked pastry flavored with sage and pepper and stuffed with bacon and pork.

To finish, they had been served with fresh white bread, two wheels of different cheeses, and a large platter of heart-shaped tarts filled with a rich cherry sauce.

Konrad told himself the delicate tarts were too sweet, but he found himself eating three of them, one after the other, before he'd even realized it. At least when he was eating, nothing else could be expected of him. Renlow and the younger daughter had kept up a fairly even flow of conversation while the meal progressed, but it grew a little stilted toward the end of the fourth course when polite topics seemed to have been fully exhausted.

After the meal, they were ushered once more into the sitting room, and Ankatel's daughters had taken up their instruments to exhibit their talent. Konrad was not surprised to find neither excelled at this. He wasn't sure how adept merchant's daughters were expected to be in ladylike accomplishments, but their mingled voices were pleasing enough. Rather wisely, they kept their selection to simple country ballads and did not attempt anything sophisticated.

The livelier of the two sisters was a beauty with dark hair, a curvy figure, and dimples that appeared in her rosy cheeks when she smiled, which was often. He watched her a moment as she enthusiastically cranked the handle on her symphonia. Catching her sister's eye, she gave her a determinedly cheerful smile, from which the other averted her gaze, looking pained.

Obviously, the beauty was intended for Renlow, so he turned his attention instead to the elder and plainer sister. She wasn't so bad looking in truth, though she did seem a poor, spineless creature with her trembling lips and dull eyes. Her hair was several shades lighter than her sister's and was a sort of middling brown. Where her sister was bonny, with sparkling eyes and a healthy bloom, this one had barely any color to her face and looked listless and wan.

She'd barely lifted her eyes from her plate at supper, and he'd scarcely heard a murmur fall from her lips despite encouragement from her father and sister to join the conversation. Konrad couldn't say as he blamed her for being horrified at the prospect of him for a bridegroom, but still, the thought of taking her to his bed was not an enticing one. If the mere prospect of looking at him across a table made her faint at heart, she'd likely pass out with terror when it came to their wedding night. He grimaced at the thought.

She'd make a puling, wretched bedmate. He could not help but think that after six long years of abstinence he deserved something a bit more appetizing. Then again, he reflected, stroking the mangled side of his face, likely she felt the same way. He was no maiden's dream, and for all he knew, she could have had her heart set on another before her father's startling rise in fortune. The lower classes tended to marry where their fancy took them. Likely, this development was not one that Mistress Ankatel had foreseen.

"My lord, you will take another drink with me?" Ankatel urged, already refilling his goblet. Konrad accepted the cup and drank deeply. If he wasn't mistaken, this was where the bartering would start. His lip curled. He certainly wasn't going to be pleading his cause. He knew well enough what Gerold Ankatel wanted from him.

"I'm a baron," he stated abruptly. "If your daughter weds me, she will be a baroness, our son the sixth Baron Kentigern. What I want to know is, did that shuffling clerk speak true about your terms?" Out of the corner of his eye, Konrad saw Renlow start violently at his blunt speech, but the appraising look that Ankatel leveled his way gleamed with appreciation.

"There speaks a man after my own heart," Ankatel said heartily. "I commend you, my lord. I am not ashamed to speak in open and honest terms about the business. That's how I made my fortune, and it's clearly husbands I want for both my girls now and to see them settled. Why should I obscure my purpose to you gentlemen? Is it indelicate to speak the truth? Given the choice, I'll choose good plain speech between men over smooth-faced knavery any day!"

Renlow's mouth fell open, but Konrad's brows snapped together. "You speak of honest speech, yet you make no reply to my question."

The older man was silent a moment, though a smile lurked in his eyes still. "The King's messenger spoke no word of a lie," he said after a pause. "I am a very rich man these days. I can make marriage to my daughters worth your while." The

36

womenfolk started up another song with a slightly slower tempo. Gerold glanced meaningfully toward them.

"They are good girls both, even if I do say it myself, and these past two years I've not stinted on their instruction. I had them put up and squired about by Lady Wycliffe for a couple of months last year. They have mixed in some high circles. They know enough not to put their husbands to blush with any missteps." He sat back in his seat and gazed at them expectantly.

Konrad found himself at a loss how to respond. The only misstep he could think of in a wife was barrenness, and no father, however fond, could guarantee against that.

"I'm sure they are both models of feminine grace and propriety," Renlow responded hurriedly to fill the awkward silence.

Ankatel beamed on him. "You are a third son, are you not, Sir Renlow?" he said with a faint pucker between his brows. "Did your father never intend you for the holy life?"

Renlow shook his head. "No, for my second brother took up that mantle. It left me free to pursue my own course."

Ankatel nodded, stroking his neat gray beard. "That is fortunate indeed. A dutiful son is not always free to follow the path he chooses. Of course, a rich wife might make that path smoother," he reflected, and Konrad almost laughed to see how discomforted poor Renlow looked by such a comment. "Perhaps I should have invited your father to the table, Sir Renlow?" Ankatel pondered, seeing how tongue-tied the young knight looked by his frankness.

"He is of age," Konrad rumbled. "And his own man. Is that not so?" He directed a pointed look at Renlow, who cleared his throat.

"It is," Renlow responded quietly. "I will be fully three and twenty in one month's time, and it is now two years since I quit my father's roof."

Gerold Ankatel nodded and shrugged, seemingly satisfied with this. "And you, my lord," he said after taking a fortifying swig of his wine. "Might I ask your age? It is hard to determine in a countenance such as yours." Renlow uttered an exclamation, and when Konrad glanced at him, he saw his young friend had spilled wine down his front.

Konrad gave a grim smile as an attendant darted forward to mop the wine stain from Renlow's faded tunic. "I am one and thirty years of age," he answered briefly. Strange to say, Gerold Ankatel's words did not give him offence. He eyed the merchant speculatively. "And not unwilling to take a wife."

"I should think not indeed!" Gerold exclaimed in surprise. "It is high time you did so, my lord! I quite thought such things were arranged by nobles when their offspring were still babes in their cots."

Konrad shrugged. "The late war…" he murmured evasively.

"Your father did not see fit to play matchmaker?"

Konrad paused in the act of setting down his empty goblet. "There was once some such arrangement in place," he admitted, given no other option. "But that lady ended up wedding another." He looked Ankatel full in the face, daring the old man to ask him why his intended had cried off.

Gerold cleared his throat. "These agreements often fall by the wayside, so I hear," he said easily enough, though Konrad could see that Renlow's face was bright red with an embarrassment he felt quite unmoved by.

After the evening had ended, the two prospective suitors walked in a thoughtful silence together back along the side streets towards the center of Caer-Lyoness. Renlow, who usually fetched up near the bottom of the lists, was not automatically guaranteed quarters at the palace and usually stayed in the cheapest quarters of town. No matter how rough his surroundings, he always seemed strangely impervious to the dangers around him.

He was a strange lad, but for all that, not unpopular, especially among the squires who would run to help him beat the dents out of his old armor or mend his spears. It was almost like some spirit of *future* greatness seemed to cling to him. His cheerfulness and gameness won over even the sternest of critics, Konrad concluded.

Not only was Renlow undaunted by his losses, but he would stand up against any opponent with the self-same fearlessness and spirit of fair play. He was unfailingly good-natured and accorded the same respect to both the mightiest competitor and the lowliest pageboy.

Last winter, the talk of the royal tournament had been how Renlow had woken up one morning in a shared room in Aphrany to find its other five inhabitants lying with their throats cut and the sixth man absconded with all their valuables. The only reason he could give for his own uninterrupted sleep was that he had shared his loaf of bread with the murderer the night before and lent him his spare blanket. The same blanket which had been carefully folded and laid next to Renlow's sleeping head.

That said everything you needed to know about Renlow, or so Roland Vawdrey had said when he retold the tale to the King.

"Even murderers like him." Wymer had roared with laughter and the next day had summoned Renlow to court to make him tell him the tale again before an audience. The Queen had called him "A fair youth, that even the worst villain could not harden his heart against."

Konrad wasn't so sure about that, but he knew Renlow had flashes of undeniable brilliance in the joust. He had even defeated him once. But when it came to the melee and hand-to-hand combat, the boy was hampered by the fact he followed a code of chivalry which no knight in his right mind would ever subscribe to.

Konrad wondered if these same scruples would now prevent him taking one of the wealthy merchant's daughters to wife. He cleared his throat, and Renlow looked up. "You think you'll see your way clear to taking one of them?" he asked.

Renlow didn't answer for a moment. "It's a better marital prospect than I could ever have hoped for," he admitted. Considering Renlow's hand-to-mouth existence, Konrad found he did not doubt it. "What about you?"

"With a face like mine, you have to ask?" Konrad snorted, and when Renlow made as though to speak, he waved his words away. "The old man has made me an offer I can't refuse, and I'm not talking about his daughter." He paused heavily. "Ankatel's offered to buy me back everything I've ever lost: my home, my lands, my fortune." Renlow nodded wordlessly. "So, whatever he's offered you, I'd ask him to triple it before you take her to wife." Even though Renlow was getting the beauty, Konrad felt honor bound to tell the lad just how well he was doing out of the bargain.

Renlow just smiled. "I never had that much in the first place," he admitted.

40

"You'd be a fool not to drive up your price. Who's to say the King won't bleed him like a leech from now till he drops dead," Konrad warned him. "You may get nothing more out of the old man, even at his death."

Renlow frowned. "The greatest treasure he has to bestow is surely his daughter's hand."

Konrad shook his head. After all, what could one say to such naivety? "I turn left here."

"And I right," Renlow said. "Farewell, Lord Kentigern. I'll see thee anon."

Konrad grunted, listening to the light footfalls moving away down the cobbled street. That way led to the narrowest and most squalid of the city's streets. That boy would sleep tonight surrounded by the worst society Caer-Lyoness had to offer, and yet he would sleep the deep sleep of the blameless. He could never decide if Renlow's biggest character trait was saintliness or foolhardiness.

For a moment, Konrad spared a thought for Gerold Ankatel's rosy-cheeked daughter. What kind of a husband would Renlow make her when he made so little provision for his own safety? How could someone so wholly unaware of life's dangers protect another? Hopefully, the vivacious Mistress Ankatel had enough about her to look out for herself. Of her quieter sister, he did not think even once.

5

It was not until fully a week later that Gerold Ankatel informed his daughters he had met for a third time with their suitors.

Aimee looked up eagerly from her soup. "You have, Father?" she asked excitedly as Ursula dropped her spoon.

"Suitors?" Ursula repeated faintly. "You mean—?"

"It is all settled," he told them with satisfaction. "Did I not tell you girls your father would see to it?"

"You have settled on a wedding date?" Aimee asked breathlessly, clasping her hands in front of her.

"I have," he replied sagely. "Three weeks from this very day."

"Three weeks?" Ursula moaned, swaying in her seat.

Aimee jumped up and rounded the table to squeeze her father's shoulders. "That's wonderful, Father! We are to be wed on the same day?"

Gerold Ankatel patted her hand. "Yes, yes," he agreed, looking pleased with himself. "One after the other at the chapel of St. Genesius."

"You are the best and greatest of all fathers in the world!" Aimee praised him, leaning over to kiss his cheek.

Gerold chuckled as Aimee drifted back to her seat as though she was walking on air. In truth, she had been a little worried following the meal Lord Kentigern had taken at their house. He had barely seemed to notice her, despite the fact she had decked herself out in her most impressive finery, had sung like a linnet, and played her most impressive pieces on the symphonia.

Afterward, she had worried that she had expended too much energy trying to draw Ursa out of her shell that night. Her sister had sat like a stock while poor Sir Renlow tried to engage her in polite conversation. Aimee had been forced to take the lead. Though Ursa had endeavored to reply to the leading questions thrown her way, she did so in a joyless, wooden fashion.

As such, Aimee had not been able to devote her attention adequately to the object of her own affection. She did not blame Lord Kentigern for the fact they had exchanged no meaningful conversation. From everything she had heard about his reputation, his social skills were likely rusty as he was not used to mixing much in company.

Still, she thought as she sat back down, everything had turned out as it ought. A blissful smile spread over her face. She could not have left such an underwhelming impression on Lord Kentigern as she had feared. Glancing across at Ursula, she saw her sister push her bowl of soup away half-eaten.

"What is this, Ursula?" their father asked. "You have lost your appetite?"

Aimee reached across to touch her sister's cold hand. "She will likely be a bundle of nerves from now until three weeks hence."

Ursula's lips trembled. "Oh, don't, Aimee!" she whispered, turning her face away from them.

Gerold's brow crinkled. "I can scarcely understand you, daughter," he said, sounding aggrieved. "Is this Renlow not the young man who captured your fancy? I would have thought, if anything, your reactions would have been the other way around." He shot a troubled look at Aimee. "No doubt you have determined a title will do for you and nothing else, but this Lord Kentigern is not the manner of man I would have chosen for you, my child."

43

"Please, Father, I have already explained to you—"

Her father waved her protestations away. "Yes, yes, I know. He is a mighty champion, but if Ursula does not favor this young knight, then mayhap the two of you should exchange bridegrooms. Their respective ages would suit far better if you swapped and—"

"Father!" Aimee and Ursula exchanged startled glances, for both of them had burst out hotly at this.

Gerold Ankatel spread his hands wide. "I was only remarking that if Ursula is going to take this attitude, then she might as well be given a reason for it!"

Aimee's chin came up. "I fail to see why Lord Kentigern's bride should have any reason to repine."

Her father looked as though he disagreed but kept his own counsel. "Well, well, if you are determined on this course, daughter," he sighed resignedly. "Then there is nothing more for me to say."

Aimee glanced across at Ursula, but her sister refused to meet her eyes and was gazing sightlessly ahead of her. She hoped Ursula wasn't going to balk at the final fence. Three more weeks she would have to bolster her up for. Aimee almost sighed aloud. She could scarcely enjoy her own excitement when she was constantly having to soothe Ursula's nerves.

After supper, when Aimee would have escaped upstairs to snatch an hour to herself, her father summoned her instead to his private study and, after shutting the door behind them, informed her he had that morning purchased Bartree Castle from the Crown.

"Bartree Castle?" she repeated.

44

"Lord Kentigern's seat." He drew a map across his desk and tapped a finger against it. "The estate lies here at the top left corner of Karadok."

Aimee peered at the map and felt a strange lurch of her stomach to see how remote the spot looked and how far from Caer-Lyoness. "Vettel," Aimee read aloud, seeing the name of the biggest town thereabouts.

Her father nodded. "Apparently, his estate lies some eight miles from thence."

"I've never heard of it." Her eyes wandered to the town below. "Adarva," she read aloud. "Now that does sound familiar. It is a place of some fame or repute?"

"You are thinking of the Battle of Adarva, my child," her father told her ruefully. "There was fierce fighting there, and some do say it was the turning point in the war. Many northern standards fell there, and many noble lines were ended that day." He paused heavily. "I believe it was at that place that your betrothed suffered his grievous wounds."

With a shiver, Aimee cast about for something else to focus on. "Vettel lies on the coast," she murmured. "It looks even closer to the sea than we are here at Caer-Lyoness."

Her father murmured in agreement. "Though you must not expect the summers there that we have here in the south," he warned. "A cold, bitter place is the north." He shivered. "We must hope that your husband prefers to spend most of his days at the fine town residence I have bought you instead."

Aimee looked up quickly. "Father, you have not bought us a house here in town as well?" she asked with a gasp.

He nodded, his eyes twinkling. "The townhouse will be your wedding present, daughter. Bartree Castle is"—he broke off

45

with a wince—"more of a condition to the marriage taking place. From what my agents tell me, it is in poor repair and not currently fit for habitation." Her father gestured to a chair before the fire, and Aimee, rather warily, sat herself in it. Why did she feel suddenly apprehensive about what her father wanted to say?

"I had heard that the King's forces leveled Lord Kentigern's home," she began slowly. "Was it reduced to mere rubble, then?"

"The outer structure is somewhat intact," her father admitted. "But the roof was burned and the place sacked. No one lives there now, though he has kinswomen installed in the lodge house still."

Aimee looked up quickly at this. "He does? Kinswomen?" Her father nodded. Aimee wondered if her bridegroom would invite these kinswomen to their wedding.

"It will take a lot of work to restore the place to its former glory," her father said ruefully. "Luckily for Lord Kentigern, his father-in-law has very deep coffers."

Aimee reached across to clasp her father's hand. "How happy he must be at the place being returned both to him and its former glory," she said fervently. "And all thanks to you, Father."

Her father nodded and pursed his lips. "It is times like these that I most miss your mother," he sighed. "You and your sister won't remain for long under my roof now."

Aimee found herself a little choked at the thought. "Will you be lonely, Father?"

He gave a startled chuckle. "Lonely? Oh, I shouldn't think so. Always plenty of company willing to eat at an old widower's table."

Aimee knew full well her father never lacked for company and eyed him shrewdly. "Have you never thought of remarrying?" she asked, thinking of the Widow Hemmings, whose society he often enjoyed.

Gerold Ankatel immediately looked evasive. "I have never given it much thought," he said, blowing out his cheeks. "A new broom always sweeps clean, is that not what they always say? Well, I'm vastly comfortable in my own house with my own ways. I doubt Burchard would like a new mistress. Very gently and respectfully Ursula has always treated him."

Aimee snorted. "That's because she's afraid of him!"

Her father chuckled. "Well, Burchard's previous master was a very learned man. They do say as he was once tutor to the prince before the old man retired."

"And Burchard's current master is sponsor to a king," Aimee reminded him. "And equally bragworthy."

Gerold Ankatel laughed, though he looked gratified by his daughter's words. "It is true, the King has been good enough to meet with me now some half dozen times," he reflected. Aimee held her tongue between her teeth. Surely, granting an audience was the least the King could do for the privilege of dipping into her father's funds!

Her father frowned. "I had hoped to take you girls to court with me before you were married," he admitted. "But alas, thus far I have only attended one banquet and the other times were in His Majesty's private chambers." Aimee nodded, but made no reply. "Still," her father brightened considerably. "When you

47

are the wife of a baron, no doubt you will attend court on your own merit and will not need an introduction from your old father."

Aimee smiled, though she did not think Lord Kentigern looked very much like a polished courtier. Then again, her only experience of such things had been the two months she had spent with the Wycliffes over the summer. They had been a very cultured family who applied themselves diligently to the study of literature, art, and music.

Even mealtimes at the Wycliffes' had been accompanied by earnest discussions of these topics and a new guest invited each night to supper who would provide some fresh point of view or lecture them on some subject of interest. Lady Wycliffe had been most shocked to hear neither girl could play an instrument and had insisted that both Aimee and Ursula take up lessons immediately.

"What did you think of our playing the other evening, Father?" Aimee asked now, with a trace of unease. She knew full well her fingers had fumbled over the notes in the middle section of her solo and shrank with embarrassment to think of it. She had neglected practicing now Lady Wycliffe was not there to insist on it. Lord Kentigern was sure to have noticed that Ursula's playing was far superior to her own. Ursula never shirked her duty.

"Very pretty, my dear," her father assured her. "Only I much prefer it when you stick to the old country tunes. Why did you not sing that one your mother taught you? About the tree, the moon, and the lover's promise."

"Lady Wycliffe did not think that one suitable for mixed company," Aimee admitted.

Her father looked startled. "Eh?"

48

"She explained that there is—um—a hidden meaning behind the absent lover and the tree that bursts into blossom and then bears fruit with the waxing and waning of the moon," Aimee said, turning red.

Her father scratched his gray hair. "Ah," he said, clearing his throat. "But the young man returns in the last verse and weds the wench, so where's the harm in it?"

"I do not know," Aimee answered. "But Lady Wycliffe said Ursula and I were not to sing it anymore."

Her father blew out his cheeks and grumbled something under his breath. "Well, well," he said after a moment. "I suppose sacrifices must be made if my girls are to be fine ladies."

Aimee eyed him uncertainly. "We could still sing it for you, Father. When no one else is around to be shocked, I mean."

He reached across and patted her hand. "Rest assured, child. I am not so easily offended. I know full well what manner of man I am, and you and Ursula must not fear I will embarrass you once you are set up in your new lives."

"Whatever can you mean, Father?" Aimee cried, looking up. "Such a thought never entered my mind!"

He shook his head ruefully. "I know that, Aimee, but you must learn to feel differently when you are a baroness."

"I hope I shall never grow ashamed of where I come from!" she argued hotly.

"Not ashamed, no," her father agreed painstakingly. "But there is no denying these nobles feel differently about such things than plain folk like myself. You will need to heed their ways in future and be led by them in such matters."

Aimee gazed at her father in consternation. She had not considered before that marrying her true love could have such repercussions. "Father…"

Gerold Ankatel blew his nose. "There now, I've said enough," he said stoutly. "Do not let it trouble you. You girls have plenty to see to over the next three weeks. Gowns to be made up and your dowry items to be picked out. Those wedding chests I commissioned were delivered this morning. All that remains is for you to fill them with your trousseau items."

"They have been delivered already?" Aimee asked, startled. "I did not realize."

"Fit for a king they are too," her father said proudly. "Painted and glazed all over and gilded with gold leaf."

Aimee clapped her hands. "I cannot wait to see them, Father!"

He nodded sagely. "You are good girls, you and your sister both. You deserve the best."

Aimee rose impulsively from her chair and embraced her father. "You are so very good to us, Father," she said, feeling choked.

He patted her back. "And now you must go and rouse your sister from her mopes. Tell her she may have first choice of whichever of the chests takes her fancy. Maybe that will put a smile on her face."

Aimee found Ursula sat in the front room, staring distractedly into the fire.

"The wedding chests have arrived," she told her sister excitedly. "Shall we go down and view them? Father said you are to have the first pick as you are the elder."

Her sister rose to her feet with a slight frown. "I am sure they will all be lovely," she murmured, and together they proceeded

50

down to the entrance hall where they found the chests had been placed to one side. Aimee drew back the cloth which had been thrown over them and gasped at the grandeur of the lavishly decorated trunks.

"Oh, they are beautiful!" she sighed, kneeling down to examine the intricately painted scenes that decorated the sides. "These two depict a bridal procession," she exclaimed, tracing the glossy figures with a careful finger. "See, here are musicians and guests in all their finery. Look, Ursa! The finest artist must have worked on these scenes." When she glanced up, she saw a frown on Ursula's face. "What is it, sister? You do not care for them?"

"No, no," her sister said quickly. "It is not that. Only…" She bit her lip.

"Only what?" Aimee looked at her, mystified. She straightened up when Ursula did not speak and moved to the second pair. "If these ones are not to your liking, then perhaps these two will be more to your taste."

She drew the cloth away, revealing another pair of matching trunks, this time decorated with fruit trees, birds, and beasts all bathed in gold leaf. "Oh, these are beautiful too!" Aimee could not help but burst out. She could hardly decide which pair she thought the more lovely. When Ursula continued silent, Aimee felt a rush of impatience. "What is it?" she asked. "Why do you stand there so still and sulky?"

Ursula started at this. "I am not!" she protested, and indeed, Aimee knew deep down her claim was unjust. "I never sulk!"

"Tell me, then, why you stand there as dull and stiff as a stock at the sight of our father's fine gift."

Ursula fidgeted, staring down at her hands. "'Tis only that…
Well, they do not much resemble the wedding chests that Lady
Wycliffe showed us at Wycliffe Hall," she mumbled.

Aimee cast her mind back. In truth, she could scarcely
remember the gloomy furnishings at Wycliffe Hall. "They do
not?" she asked uncertainly. Ursula shook her head. "How do
they not?"

"Those were not painted and gilded," said Ursula in a small
voice. "But only carved about with borders of fruits."

Aimee gazed first at her sister and then at the dazzling chests.
"What are you saying?"

"I'm not saying anything!" Ursula responded quickly. "I am
sure these chests are perfectly adequate."

"*Adequate*," Aimee repeated in dazed accents. "Ursula, these
chests are *exquisite* and must have cost Father by far in excess
of what a pair of plain carved chests would have."

"I know that, Aimee," her sister answered impatiently. "You do
not understand!"

"No," Aimee answered, raising her chin. "I do not." Seeing the
martial gleam in her younger sister's eyes, Ursula reached
across and captured her hand.

"It was nothing, naught but a piece of foolishness. Do not let us
quarrel, sister dear," Ursula urged. "For I have just had a very
good idea."

"Oh? What is that?" Aimee asked, still feeling ruffled by her
sister's attitude.

"We will not each have a matched pair but split them, so we
both have one of each."

52

Aimee brightened at that notion. "That *is* a very good idea," she approved, gazing back down at the golden trunks.

The next couple of weeks passed quickly with tradesmen coming to the house every day to display their wares. She and Ursula selected fine linens, wall hangings, and every household item they could think of for the new townhouses their father had promised would be theirs on the occasion of their marriages.

"I do not think all of these items can possibly fit in our trunks," Ursula observed in consternation as they looked about at the growing piles.

Aimee agreed. "Can we not ask Father if the furnishings and linens could not be installed in our new houses ahead of time, so they are ready for us?"

"You know Father does not wish us to see them ahead of time," her sister reminded her. "He wants the houses to be a surprise."

"Yes, but they still will be," Aimee pointed out. "If others hang the tapestries and place the furnishings in the rooms for us." When Ursula hesitated, Aimee sprang to her feet. "Let me talk to Father," she said decisively.

For once, though, Gerold could not be persuaded by his youngest daughter, for he was convinced the dowry should be paraded through the streets in a procession accompanied by musicians and the bridal party.

"But, Father…" Aimee protested. "I do not think our friends and neighbors will enjoy carting so many wares before them, especially after they have sat down to such a lavish meal!" She tried and failed to imagine her father's business friends hobbling through the streets carrying chairs and tables over their heads.

Her father waved this away. "Nonsense, Aimee! I have employed many attendants along with the musicians and entertainers. When you and your sister leave my house, it will be to the accompaniment of great celebration and pomp. No one shall think I have not acted handsomely by you both."

Aimee regarded her father with sudden misgiving. "I thought you were inviting only fifty of your closest friends and acquaintances to the wedding banquet," she reminded him.

"Yes," he agreed. "That is correct."

"And how many paid attendants have you engaged?"

"One hundred and fifty," he answered grandly.

"One hundred and fifty?" Aimee squeaked. "Then the attendants shall outnumber the guests some threefold! However shall we fit them all in the supper chamber?"

"Well, we shall squeeze them in somehow, I daresay." Her father shrugged. "We can leave fifty outside to dance and play for the crowds."

"Crowds?" Aimee's heart sank.

"I am the richest merchant in all Karadok," he reminded her. "The wedding of my only daughters will not be some paltry affair!"

Aimee gulped and wondered how to break the news to Ursula that their wedding would now include a street show. Everything their father had said before had led them to believe the wedding feast would be a wholly modest affair, attended only by people she and her sister had known for years.

As such, she and Ursula had not ordered much by way of decoration for their father's house. Lilies and roses had been ordered to be strewn among the rushes underfoot and matching wreaths to adorn the mantel and door. Now Aimee wondered if this was going to be enough by way of adornment when one hundred and fifty attendants were trampling all over the flowers and filling their father's house to overflowing! Not to mention a baying crowd outside who would be expecting entertainment and spectacle to brighten their day.

Rather than focusing on the feast, which the sisters had imagined would be a quiet and intimate affair, they had concentrated their efforts instead on items to furnish their new homes. Aimee made her way slowly back her sister. She would have to tell Ursula, and once again, her sister would go into a quake.

Ursula hated being the center of attention. Aimee knew her sister was already dreading her role as bride, and this would make everything ten times worse. Perhaps heavy veiling might be a good suggestion? As usual, though, Ursula rose bravely to the challenge. She turned pale, it is true, but then she immediately fetched ink and a quill and started making lists.

"We will need favors for the crowd," she said, biting her thumbnail. "Treats to distribute and additional casks of ale."

"It is too bad of Father not to have warned us," Aimee grumbled as Ursula's pen scratched over the parchment.

Her sister smiled wanly. "Father is a man and never thinks of such things."

"These attendants will all need something to eat and drink throughout the day as well. Did Father think to neglect them all day?"

"Purses of pennies, too, to give out," Ursula mused aloud. "It is too late to get commemorative tokens made up now."

Privately, Aimee thought the crowd would prefer money in any case than some trumpery token that would be worthless hereafter. "What about decoration?" Aimee asked. "I do not think two floral wreaths will now be enough."

"No indeed," her sister agreed. "We will increase the order and have a quantity of garlands made up as well. I suppose we could order swathes of fabric to decorate the house." Her eyes glazed over. "Maybe the attendants could all wear a ribbon sash?" she suggested with a hopeless shrug.

"Yes, very good," Aimee enthused.

"Green?" Ursula suggested.

"The very thing," Aimee agreed aloud, then privately she wished the colors could be blue and yellow which were the colors of Lord Kentigern's shield. Still, it was a joint wedding celebration, and she could hardly expect to take over when Sir Renlow's crest was, if memory served, a very faded red and muddy brown.

"We had better don our cloaks and set about putting in our orders now," Ursula sighed. "The sooner we do so, the better the chance they can actually fulfill it."

6

Konrad was surprised to find the bridal party already assembled at the porch on the south side of the chapel. He almost took a step back when he observed the number of people loitering there. Clearly, he and Ankatel had vastly differing ideas of what "a small gathering" meant.

"There you are, my lord!" the merchant cried heartily, coming forward to clasp his hand.

Konrad returned his welcome and turned to his sister, who stood a tall, imposing figure in her burgundy velvet gown. He wondered if she might not be too hot in her formal garb before long, for Caer-Lyoness grew very warm in July. "This is my sister," he said, introducing her. "Magnatrude, this is Gerold Ankatel, whose daughter will be joining our family this morn."

As his sister condescended to shake the amiable merchant's hand, Konrad noticed the watery blue eyes of her attendant turned on him in reproach. "And our cousin Freda, who acts as her chaperone," he added belatedly.

Freda fluttered forward in a robe of faded green satin which had plainly seen better days. She was far from an impressive figure, tall like all Bartrees, but with a wiry, awkward frame and a good quantity of frizzy light brown hair. She simpered girlishly as Ankatel bowed over her hand instead of shaking it, and Konrad tried to reckon how old Freda must be by now. She must be forty-five if she was a day! She and his older sister were much the same age, and Trude had fifteen years on him at least.

Both women wore their braided hair coiled about their ears and bundled into hairnets on either side of their heads. It was not a style you saw much in the south these days, but his kinswomen had worn their hair this way since they had achieved womanhood.

"Charmed!" Ankatel murmured as he straightened up. To Konrad's surprise, he noticed his cousin blush. Out of the corner of his eye he saw his sister's features sharpen and guessed she would be giving Freda a stern talking-to later.

"So very kind," Freda twittered and retreated to his sister's side.

"Your bride awaits," Ankatel said, turning to him and gesturing toward the crowd gathered around the studded door of the porch.

"I do not see the priest," Konrad commented. He was in no great hurry to move up to the front where all eyes would be trained on him.

"The hour approaches, and he must surely be due any moment now," Ankatel responded, and without waiting for Konrad's response, he headed determinedly for the crowd. "Make way!" he cried. "The groom's party must come through." The crowd hurriedly made way for them, and Konrad cleared his throat and plunged into the heart of them, his sister and cousin on his heels.

So distracted was he by the unexpected hubbub that he scarcely gave more than a passing glance to his heavily veiled bride. When the priest appeared in the doorway, he felt her pluck at his sleeve and realized she wanted his hand. With some surprise, he extended it and found it grasped at once. For some reason, he had imagined her fingers would be cold and would shrink from his touch, but her hand was warm and her grip firm.

That was not to be his greatest shock either, for with her other hand she drew back her veil and revealed not the pale visage he

58

had been expecting but the radiant face of Ankatel's youngest daughter. He would have dropped her hand if she had not hold of his so tightly. Turning toward him, she beamed at him, and Konrad just about managed to stop his jaw from dropping.

Why was she here? What had happened to the other? He turned his head to look at Ankatel, and the older man nodded and smiled as though for all the world this was in fact his intended. So distracted was he that for a moment he did not realize the priest had started to speak.

"I am willing," he heard his bride return heartily, and he turned his head to find the priest regarding him expectantly.

"I—er—am also willing," he responded awkwardly after a moment. After all, what else could he do? The priest trotted out a few more phrases, and once more his bride tugged on his hand until he extended it, still clasped in hers. The priest held up a green ribbon, and then after speaking a few words over it, he deftly wound it about their two wrists and bound them together.

"Your lives are now entwined together, and henceforth from this point you will be as one," the priest intoned gravely.

"Thank you so much, Father Amos," his bride said earnestly and then turned to Konrad, lowering her voice. "We shall have to turn about so that we can head back up the other way," she advised, and Konrad dumbly allowed her to shepherd him about until they were facing in the opposite direction.

He felt wrong-footed by the scattered applause. Did people usually clap at weddings? Then there was a surge of people toward them, and Konrad found his shoulder clasped and his back patted. Gerold Ankatel embraced him, and he had little choice about the matter as he could hardly sidestep him without trampling his bride.

59

He noticed his sister standing aloof from the milling crowd, though his cousin was chattering excitedly to a matronly looking woman who was carrying a small infant. Before he could gather his wits, his bride was tugging resolutely on his hand once again and standing on her tiptoes to address him. "We need to move around to the west porch now," she explained loudly so that he could hear her above the tumult.

"The west porch?" he repeated blankly.

"For Ursula's ceremony to Sir Renlow," she explained cheerfully.

Following her promptings, he made his way like a sleepwalker and found himself in the midst of the crowd this time as Sir Renlow was bound in turn to the whey-faced sister. Konrad half expected Renlow to object to the bridal exchange, but the young knight showed no sign of surprise or discomfiture when the veil was drawn back to show the older sister stood at his side.

Knowing the strict code of chivalry Renlow adhered to, Konrad told himself he should not have been surprised by this, even though he was. He found himself glancing distractedly down at the woman he was bound to. What the fuck was her name? He had not troubled about their names, he acknowledged belatedly, and felt an uncomfortable prickling of something he had thought long gone.

As if aware of his regard, his bride lifted her face, and she flashed her dimples at him. He was still recovering from this when a cheer went up, and he turned to find Renlow and his new wife were now making their way back through the crowd and holding their bound wrists aloft. Even the older sister was smiling for once. Doubtless she was relieved at her last-minute reprieve, he thought grimly. Had she balked at the eleventh hour and her sister agreed to trade places with her?

He glanced down uneasily again and found his wife cheering and waving like the rest. She squeezed his hand. "Where is your party?" she asked him, gazing about. He stared back at her blankly. "Your kinswomen," she prompted. Konrad glanced around and saw Magnatrude still lurking on the edges, wearing her frozen look as Freda conversed freely with a minstrel carrying a lute.

"Over there." He nodded in their direction.

"I would love an introduction," she told him hopefully, and Konrad realized his manners were sadly lacking. He waved and caught Freda's attention. Magnatrude appeared to be staring in horror at some capering jesters. He beckoned, and Freda caught hold of his sister's sleeve. Immediately, Magnatrude shrugged her off, clearly in a disagreeable and prickly mood.

He watched Freda go through the pantomime of pointing and yelling in Magnatrude's ear. His sister still looked frosty, but they started to move toward them. When they had maneuvered their way through the milling crowd, Freda sank into an obliging curtsey, but Magnatrude remained standing tall and proud.

"Allow me to introduce my wife, Baroness Kentigern," he said pointedly. "My sister, the honorable Magnatrude Bartree, and my cousin, Mistress Fredagunde Bartree." The significance of his words was not lost on Magnatrude, who flushed and dropped into a stiff curtsey.

His wife curtseyed also, and he was pleased to see it was not obsequiously low but merely a good, plain curtsey. "I am very happy to meet you both," she said warmly. "I cannot tell you how pleased I was when I heard that my husband had sent for you to attend our wedding." Her bright eyes sent him a quick, brimming look when she said the words *my husband* which gave him pause. If he didn't know any better, he would almost think she took pleasure in them! "We go now to my father's house for the wedding feast," she explained. "Where you will be made very welcome."

"How very kind," Freda murmured. Magnatrude inclined her head, then jumped almost out of her skin when someone close by threw back his head and started gustily singing a ballad.

"I think that is our signal to start making our way toward my father's," the bride said excitedly. "We must follow that man in the red and yellow costume who is carrying the decorated pole." She pointed at an extraordinary figure in long scalloped sleeves who was carrying a beribboned staff decorated with bells and who had started marching forward in a high-stepped manner.

Konrad shrugged and they started forward, and Magnatrude and Freda fell in behind them. A good deal of the assembled company was now singing and strumming or plucking away on some instrument or other.

"It feels like quite a procession, does it not?" his new wife chirruped away beside him. "What a merry company we shall be!" The bustling townsfolk stopped whatever they were doing that morn and stared as they passed them. A raggle-taggle crowd of children and beggars started to follow along behind.

People crowded into the windows and balconies above to watch as they walked by, and Konrad realized a good number he had taken for Ankatel's guests must have been hired entertainers. Some were even walking on their hands and turning somersaults alongside them. His wife waved and smiled and showed every enjoyment of being part of the spectacle.

It took a good quarter of an hour to reach the street where the Ankatel's large black and white timbered townhouse resided. Though his bride still stepped lightly and quickly beside him, Konrad noticed that Magnatrude and Freda were looking rather harried by this point, more from the bustle and hubbub than the exercise.

"This is the house," he threw over his shoulder at them. To his surprise, two attendants stood at the door to pipe them across the threshold. "Welcome!" they cried. "All hail the bride and groom!"

Konrad ducked his head and walked inside. His bride, given little opportunity to tarry, accompanied him up the stairs to the main chamber where the benches and tables had been laid out for banqueting.

"We're to sit at this table on my father's right," she said in a hurried undertone, gesturing toward the head of the table where her father was already engaged in conversation. "Ursula and Sir Renlow will sit to his left, and your sister and cousin can sit on the other side of us."

Konrad gave a brisk nod and beckoned to Freda, who was still stood flustered and uncertain in the doorway. "What a fine, large room!" he heard her exclaim nervously as she hurried forward. "And so prettily decorated!" His sister made no response, though she looked glad to be directed to a seat.

It was only once he had sat down that Konrad had the chance to take in his surroundings. He found he scarcely recognized the room from the previous occasion, so heavily was it swathed in festoons and hung about with garlands and wreathes. There were even flowers underfoot, he noticed.

A flood of people clattered up the stairs and spilled through the doorway, though it seemed to Konrad that only a small number of them would fit onto the two long tables that had been set out for the guests. As if deducing his thoughts, his bride leaned forward. "Father hired a lot of entertainers for our meal," she explained with a smile.

He nodded as the attendants started to line up around the four walls of the chamber, and it seemed to Konrad that they would need to stand two-deep to fit them all in. Houses like this one did not include a gallery for the minstrels to set up in.

Seeing a tall figure amid the rabble, Konrad was glad to recognize his fellow bridegroom, Renlow, who drifted in with an amiable smile. His bride's smile looked rather strained as they joined them at the table.

"Father," she said as Gerold Ankatel greeted the newcomers with a kiss to their cheeks.

Konrad braced himself as the older man repeated the gesture to his own bride and then, perhaps seeing him tense, chose to clasp his shoulder instead. "Welcome, welcome!" their host enthused before raising his voice to encompass everyone else. "You are heartily welcome, all!" he assured the revelers. "If I might propose a toast to the married couples for their happy futures. Baron Kentigern and my Aimee," he said, looking first toward them. "Sir Renlow and my Ursula," he continued, turning to the other couple. "I wish you all that is bright and happy."

Aimee, thought Konrad. So that was her name. Only half of the table had been served with drinks, but Konrad reached for his goblet with his free hand, and his bride did likewise. They raised their cups aloft and echoed the toast. "Bright and happy!" A confused cheer went up from the half of the guests who had heard the toast. Ankatel clearly considered himself absolved of all hosting duties by this point, for he dropped back into his seat and gulped his drink as the room about them descended into chaos.

It was not so much the wedding guests that were causing the clamor as the musicians and players who capered around the table, getting in the way of the servers who were bringing out platters of breads and wine. Konrad heard a servant curse as something fell with a clatter behind them, though he did not look to see what it was. An acrobat overbalanced and went crashing down into the fragranced rushes.

Aimee cleared her throat. "It is very lively, is it not?" she commented to the table at large.

"Very," Konrad heard himself concur heavily when no one else replied.

She flashed him a grateful smile, and mercifully at that moment, a trencher of roast meats was placed on the table so he could tear his gaze away. Platters of wild boar and venison were followed by dishes of salmon and pike and a huge golden pie the size of which made even him blink. Seeing the direction of his stare, his bride leaned toward him.

"It is filled with twelve chickens, twenty-four hard-boiled eggs, and flavored with saffron and cloves," she said not without pride and surveyed him expectantly for his reaction.

"That's a lot of poultry," he managed after a pause.

This seemingly pleased her, for she beamed at him again. "You must try some of everything here, for my father has hired the best cooks to be found in all of Caer-Lyoness."

He nodded and was pleased to see his new wife had a good appetite, for she partook freely of all the dishes, making noises of appreciation when she sampled something she found particularly good.

"These gilded sugar plums are truly delicious," she confided in him. "You must try some."

He shook his head. "I dislike sweet things."

"Oh, but you enjoyed those cherry tarts so much at that supper last month!" she exclaimed. "I saw you eat several with my own eyes!" So surprised was he that she had been watching him that night that he could not think of any answer to make. "Why not try just one?" she coaxed and had already spooned it onto his plate before he could refuse outright. When he glared at it balefully, she looked crestfallen. "I had them made just for you, as I thought sweetened fruits must be your favorite."

A cough to the left of him had him turning his head, for that was his blind side. He found his cousin regarding him with interest, though his sister still looked like a carved edifice.

"When you were a boy, you always liked candied fruits," Freda observed, cocking her head to one side rather like a bird.

"I have been a man for many years now," he pointed out.

"'Tis of no matter," his bride hastened to assure him, and when she would have removed the plum from his plate, he stayed her hand.

"I'll eat it, now you've put it there," he said gruffly and proceeded to do so.

"How does it taste?" she asked anxiously.

"Sweet." He winced.

Her face fell. "Oh. Well—er—mayhap this fish cooked in parsley and vinegar with powdered ginger will be more to your taste?" she suggested, gesturing to a dish that had just been placed down.

He had no sooner nodded his willingness to partake of it than she was ladling it onto his plate. She was a little clumsy about it, spilling a few drops onto the fine linen cloth that covered the table. Seeing her frown of concentration, he guessed she did not customarily use her left hand.

"Should we cut the binding?" he asked, glancing down at their still bound wrists.

Instead of looking pleased, she looked dismayed at the prospect. "Oh, but—that would be far too soon, surely?"

Konrad glanced across at Renlow and Ursula and saw they had already removed their ribbon. Instead of pointing this out, he merely shrugged.

"Perhaps we could remove it at the end of the feast?" she suggested.

He gave a brief nod of acquiescence and, again, was the recipient of her smile. She seemed easily pleased in any event.

"There are certainly plenty of spices in this beef stew," Gerold Ankatel observed, removing his velvet cap. He wiped his brow and gestured for a servant. "Throw open these casement windows," he requested. "'Tis growing damnably warm in here, now the noonday sun shines down upon us."

There was some bustle before the musicians and players could be ushered aside to make way for the servants to open the windows, and then the musicians could plainly be heard in the street below. Unfortunately, instead of taking a coordinated approach to the tunes they played, they seemed instead to be trying to drown each other out.

For the first time, he felt some sympathy for Ursula Ankatel, who raised a hand to her brow with a pained expression. "It's very noisy in here," he heard her say.

Her father leaned across toward her. "What's that you say, daughter?" he boomed.

"The musicians, they are so loud, Father."

"Nonsense!" he replied, sounding aggrieved. "What you need to do is eat more. Why, you've scarcely touched a thing!"

Glancing across, Konrad could see her plate contained not even a smear of gravy and the merest token presence of a pile of herbs and greens. His own father had recommended that wives should be selected with much the same criteria as horseflesh. A lustrous mane, good-sized chest, well-turned limbs, and a fine pair of buttocks.

The fourth baron would not have approved of Ursula Ankatel for a wife. Konrad spared a moment's pity for Renlow to be saddled with so unpromising a mare before reflecting on his own unexpected good fortune.

"Perhaps a plain chicken broth could be sent up from the kitchen, Father," he heard Aimee suggest urgently. "This food is very rich and likely disagrees with my sister."

"Pshaw!" their father returned in irritation. "A daughter of mine who does not like good, flavorful fare!"

"It is not that," Aimee started to argue, but at that moment, Ursula staggered to her feet and stood swaying a moment, her upper lip and forehead beaded with sweat. "Ursa!" Aimee cried.

Renlow sprang to his feet and caught Ursula just as she fainted clean away. Mercifully, the music in the room abruptly stopped, save for one harp plucker who was speedily elbowed by a passing servant. Murmurs of consternation rose to the rafters instead as Renlow stood in bewilderment with his insensible bride clasped to his chest.

"Take her up to her bedchamber, my good sir!" Gerold Ankatel instructed. "Burchard shall show you the way."

A large, dependable-looking servant appeared at Renlow's side. "This way, sir," he intoned gravely.

Aimee started up from their bench before remembering she was still tied to her new spouse. "I must accompany her," she said agitatedly.

"Nonsense, Aimee!" her father said belligerently. "She will be very well, and Hilda may attend her directly."

"*Not* Hilda, Father." Aimee frowned. "She fusses so!"

Konrad reached for the knife in his belt and sliced through the binding. Aimee clearly took this as all the permission she needed, for she spun around and hastened after Renlow at once.

"Dear me!" Freda murmured. "Most inauspicious for *both* brides to leave the feast!" Konrad bent a stern look on her, and she looked contrite. "I only meant that—well—it does not seem a very happy omen."

"That's enough, Freda," he intoned, and she lapsed at once into silence, her cheeks turning pink.

"Ursula likely did not take enough nourishment at supper last night," Gerold said irritably. "Maidens can be fretful about their wedding day, or so they tell me," he added, still looking put out.

Konrad wondered if that was why the elder sister had been allowed to switch places with the younger but did not voice his suspicion.

"The prospect of marrying a complete stranger has likely put her in a flutter," a hook-nosed dame from further down the table piped up. She glanced significantly at the young man sat beside her.

"Perhaps Miss Ursula would benefit from the company of an old friend right now," the young man who was her companion suggested, picking up on her hint with an ingratiating smile.

Gerold Ankatel cast down his napkin in disgust. "You think your company would be more palatable than that of her own sister, do you, Willard?"

The young man flushed, and the older woman beside him bristled. "My son was only trying—"

"To ingratiate himself!" Ankatel snapped. "That ship has sailed, Elspeth. She refused your son, and he would do well to remember that fact!"

It was at this point that Konrad wondered if the musicians ceasing their playing had been such a good thing after all. He turned to consider his sister, whose lips had barely uttered a word in the past hour.

"Well, Magnatrude, and how are you finding your meal?" he asked, making an effort.

"The meat is well-seasoned," she replied coolly. "But I find this room a good deal too warm."

"I told you not to wear that heavy velvet," he reminded her.

"It is the only formal gown I possess that is not moth-eaten," she retorted, sounding stung.

That was likely true, he conceded. There had been precious little call or coins for fine dresses in Magnatrude's life these past ten years. "You will have to get some new gowns made up during our two-month stay in the southern capital."

"Two months!" she repeated at once with displeasure. "I surely did not hear you correctly, Konrad!"

"I do not think your sense of hearing is lacking, whatever else may be."

His sister bit back the words that sprang to her lips and sat a moment in seething silence. "You will not incense me into some vulgar display of temper, Konrad," she said at last in words that quivered slightly, despite her even tones. "However much it might suit our present company for me to do so!"

"I can well believe you," he replied. "Matching the mood of the occasion does not seem to have been high on your list of priorities this day."

"Oh look!" Freda interrupted them quickly. She lifted her voice. "Sir Renlow returns. What news of your bride, good sir?"

Renlow paused a moment before seating himself. "She is feeling a little delicate and will rest now until our departure." He flashed an apologetic look at his father-in-law, who was breathing heavily through his nostrils.

"And what of Baroness Kentigern?" the old man asked sharply. Konrad felt his sister stiffen beside him. It was the first time someone other than he had used Aimee's new title.

Renlow looked across at Konrad. "She begs leave to attend her sister—" he began.

"Well, she does not have it!" Gerold responded promptly, clearly forgetting that her husband now held sway over his daughter's actions. "Aimee can come back down here directly! At once!" He turned to the nearest servant. "Fetch her down, I say! She has a husband to attend now and new responsibilities!"

Well, perhaps he had not forgotten altogether, Konrad acknowledged. He glanced across at Renlow, who was looking rather awkward.

"I've never heard of such a thing!" Gerold Ankatel muttered, a heavy frown darkening his brow.

71

In spite of himself, Konrad found himself casting about for something to say to lighten the mood. "Perhaps some more music?" he suggested and felt rather than saw the startled looks his sister and cousin cast his way.

Ankatel snapped his fingers. "Music!" he demanded, casting a look behind his chair. "What the devil am I paying you fellows for?" The musicians struck up hastily, and the room was once more plunged into a mood of forced gaiety. As she approached from his blind side, Konrad did not realize Aimee had reappeared until she was clambering once more onto the bench beside him. She sent him a contrite look as she tidied her skirts about her.

"I am sorry, husband," she murmured, leaning toward him so he could hear her above the music. "I did not think. 'Tis only, I did not like to leave my sister to Hilda, but I did not mean to neglect you so."

He considered this startling statement a moment in silence. "Who is Hilda?" he heard himself ask rather grudgingly.

"Hilda? Why, she is a servant who has attended us for many years."

"Why, then, do you not trust your sister to her tender mercies?"

Aimee was silent a moment before shuffling even closer to him. "Well, you see," she said, angling her face to his ear so he could hear her confidentially lowered voice. "Hilda *will* try to coddle Ursula so. She does not try to bolster her up or encourage her as she ought. And now I am so vexed, for I find that Father has said that Ursula can take Hilda with her into her new household, and I am to have Golda."

"You do not care for this Golda?"

"Oh no, 'tis not that at all!" she hurried to assure him. "Golda is *very* capable and able. It is only that Ursa will not put Hilda in her place." Her expression darkened. "I fear that it is Hilda who will be running my sister's household before she even realizes it!"

He considered Aimee's expression a moment. Even when put out, she was animated and lively. The two sisters could not be more dissimilar, he thought.

"Ursula is not really ill," Aimee continued, sounding aggrieved. "She is only overwhelmed by everything, but by this evening, Hilda will have her convinced she must be put to bed with a posset and no visitors."

Konrad snorted. "On her wedding night? Her husband might have something to say about that."

Aimee turned her head to look across the table at Renlow. "Do you think so?" she asked doubtfully. "Only, Sir Renlow seems to me…"

"Yes?" he asked, rather more sharply than the occasion warranted.

"A rather considerate sort of man," she said flatly.

Konrad opened his mouth to argue that even a considerate man would hardly stand for such a thing when it struck him that if anyone would abide by such nonsense it would be Renlow. "Who is that?" he asked instead, nodding toward the commanding-looking woman Gerold Ankatel had been exchanging words with moments earlier.

Aimee's eyes widened. "The Widow Hemmings?" she whispered with sudden misgiving. "Why? What has she said?"

"She wanted to send her son up to sit with your sister," he explained dryly.

Two pink spots appeared on Aimee's cheeks. "The impertinence!" she spluttered.

"Did some previous attachment exist between them?" he guessed shrewdly.

"Certainly not!" Aimee responded hotly. "'Tis only that her late husband was a friend and acquaintance of our father's. When he came of age, Willard felt compelled to offer for one of us. The Hemmingses owned the premises next door when Father had property on the wharf. We have known each other's family for years." She looked as though she would say more but pressed her lips together instead.

It occurred to him that before her father had accumulated his wealth, a fellow merchant's son would have been viewed as a decent match for one of his daughters. He cast a look of consideration at Willard Hemmings and found his gaze resting on Aimee. As if growing aware of eyes upon him, Willard shifted his gaze to Kentigern before the young man visibly blanched, turning hurriedly toward his mother.

"He offered for Ursula or for you?" Konrad heard himself enquire in a growl.

"I'm not sure he really had a preference," Aimee admitted frankly. "As it was our father's fortune that was his object after all."

As this drew a rather unwelcome parallel between himself and Willard Hemmings, Konrad shifted in his seat. He wanted to ask how it was that Aimee had ended up as his bride, but this was probably not the time or place for such a question. He fancied he knew the answer in any case. Her chicken-hearted sister would likely have expired on the spot rather than join her lot in life to his.

Instead, he turned to contemplate the platters the servers were now bringing out of small pastry tarts both sweet and savory and many large cheeses. This must surely be the final course, and the banquet would soon be drawing to its close. Then he could hustle his kinswomen, his new bride included, back to their rooms at The Jennet Tree, where he could take off this damned tunic with its uncomfortable embellishments which stuck in him every way he turned, and take his ease.

It did not dawn on him until the remains of the meal were being cleared away that the celebrations were far from over and done with. His father-in-law cleared his throat and rose from his seat with an air of ceremonial gravity. He and Renlow in turn were solemnly presented, first one and then the other, with large keys. Konrad stared down at his palm and the key a moment and then back at Ankatel.

"Well, well," the old man said, rocking back on his heels and tucking his hands into his belt. "I was thinking you young people will need somewhere to set up your households here in Caer-Lyoness, so I've bought you both a fine house in the best part of town." He beamed at them and nodded his head, looking vastly pleased with himself.

Set up home here? Konrad thought blankly. He looked from Ankatel to the large key and then, slowly, to his bride. Her lips were curved into a smile, and she was gazing back at him, happy and expectant. Konrad cleared his throat. "I had not—" he started, then stopped himself from uttering anything undiplomatic. "I did not expect such a gift," he said gruffly. "When you have already done so much for me already, restoring my former home and lands to my possession."

Ankatel waved this aside. "A man who travels the country so much as you do will need more than one base," he pointed out jovially. "Thanks to my daughters, I have been hearing all about the life of a knight who follows the tournaments. And I must say, I do not think it becomes your dignity to be dragging a wife from pillar to post."

Konrad shot a startled look at Aimee. She had attended the tournaments? Her face was poppy red now.

"Father!" she remonstrated in a strangled voice.

Since he had not had the smallest intention of taking any wife of his to the tournaments, Konrad hardly knew what reply to make to this. Fortunately, Renlow took over at this point, stammering out his profuse thanks.

Konrad turned to his bride. "You knew about the house already?" he asked.

"I did," she answered, her gaze clear and open. "Though I have not yet seen it. Father let me pick out the furnishings for it."

"Furnishings?" He didn't know why he was startled by this point.

She nodded and her smile wavered. "I hope you don't think I took too much upon myself—"

"Of course not," he cut her off abruptly. "That is entirely your province. I know nothing whatsoever of setting up households."

7

It was not until they were making their way through the streets toward their new home that Aimee's excitement started to wane. She and Lord Kentigern were following along behind the first lot of attendants who, with many arms, supported her two wedding chests above their heads.

Trooping along behind them were at least eighty men carrying mattresses and chairs and tables and goodness only knew what else she had chosen in the last month for their comfort. She was far from a sensitive soul like Ursula, but even Aimee felt more than a twinge of embarrassment at these proceedings.

It felt rather as though she was flaunting her father's wealth with all the fine new items being paraded through the capital for all and sundry to see. She felt her cheeks start to turn hotter and hotter at the shouts and calls of the people who stopped to stare at their progress as the minstrels piped them on their way.

Originally, of course, her wedding procession was not intended to be this long, for half of the followers would have been for Ursula. Her sister's indisposition meant that Renlow and his bride would now spend the night under her father's roof and so avoid the clamor and fuss that Ursula found so abhorrent.

This meant that all the acrobats and musicians had now accompanied Aimee and Kentigern from her father's house and out into the streets. It was now late afternoon, and the sun was blazing down from the blue sky. Aimee's heavy veil did not so much as shield her from the sun as smother her. She clung to Lord Kentigern's arm and wondered if the house would be much further. She was surprised that her father had not picked a house nearer to his own, but they seemed to be heading away from the busy town center toward quieter quarters.

The second time her slippered feet stumbled on a cobble, Lord Kentigern's arm wrapped around her back, and she found herself hoisted up into his muscular arms. A cheer went up, and Aimee blinked up at him, her heart hammering in her breast. Finally, she knew what it felt like to be embraced in Lord Kentigern's arms!

Though she knew herself to be substantially built, the way he had swung her up had made her feel as light and dainty as any princess. For once, her ready tongue failed her, and she gazed at him, feeling quite tongue-tied and shy.

"It will be quicker if I just carry you," he told her coolly, somewhat dampening her enjoyment of the experience.

"Oh, I quite agree," she answered rather breathlessly as she tried to get her rioting senses under control. Her new husband seemed to have tidied his beard a good deal for the occasion which distracted her at closer quarters. His one eye, she noticed, was a sort of green which turned amber near the center. Hazel, she believed the phenomenon was called.

"What is it?" he asked abruptly, and she thought he tensed under her gaze.

"Who trimmed your beard?" she asked impulsively.

He looked surprised by the question. "Jakeman," he responded.

"Jakeman?"

"My manservant."

"Oh. Well, he made a very nice job of it. It was a good deal bushier when you came to dine with us before. I can actually see your jawline today. You look so much younger."

He frowned at her and grunted. Realizing her scrutiny at such close quarters was making him uneasy, Aimee turned her gaze to look back over his shoulder instead. Her new vantage point meant she could see her sister-in-law's haughty expression of disdain as she picked along the route.

"I think your sister must be quite fatigued," she commented anxiously. "It has been rather a long day, has it not? And the sun is rather fierce to go traipsing now through the streets." He made no comment, and Aimee's gaze wandered over to his cousin Freda, who had an absent smile on her face as she hummed along with the musician playing at her elbow.

"Your cousin seems a most amiable woman." He made a rumbling noise which she decided to take for assent. "It will be nice to have female relatives about the house in any event." His expression turned decidedly skeptical at this. "Why do you look like that?" she asked. "I am used to the company of my sister, you recollect."

"You and your sister do not seem much alike," he commented after a heavy pause.

"In looks, do you mean? Or temperament?"

"Both," he answered abruptly.

"Well, I *look* like my mother," she explained. "But apparently, her nature and ways were more akin to Ursula's."

"Hmm."

When he made no rejoinder, she felt a stab of disappointment which was blunted when she realized the men in front of them had come to a halt.

"Have we arrived?" Aimee asked, turning her head to face forward and take in the large gabled townhouse before them.

Her new husband pushed forward with her still in his arms until he had reached the front of the group. "Is this the house?" he asked the pole-bearer.

"It is, my lord," he responded promptly.

Lord Kentigern grunted and reached for the key which was about his neck on a string. Unlocking the door, he threw it wide open and stepped through. Aimee wasn't entirely sure if he was complying with tradition of crossing the threshold with her in his arms, or if this was just a happy circumstance. Either way, she rejoiced at her good fortune and gazed about at the well-appointed entryway.

"It has handsome proportions," she commented.

Again, Lord Kentigern merely grunted and then threw open another door to peer inside. After glancing about at the empty reception rooms, he made for the staircase and set Aimee down on the bottom step.

Reaching into his tunic, he extracted a purse of coins and handed it to her. "Get rid of them," he said succinctly. "Do not let any of them above stairs." He then turned about and went striding back out of the door. Aimee stared after him a moment before rousing herself to untie the strings of the purse. Luckily, she had one her father had given her, for there were surely not enough pennies in this one alone. Not when there were at least eighty bodies crowding their front door!

"Thank you so much," she enthused, seeing three men struggle into the hallway bearing the first of her wedding chests. "Could you please set that down in that room over yonder?" She pointed to the first of the doors. "I would be so grateful."

She had just directed the second chest in the same direction when Lord Kentigern reappeared with his sister and cousin on either side of him. Without another word to Aimee, he swept past her, escorting his kinswomen up the staircase toward the private chambers on the first floor.

Aimee's spirits faltered a moment, but she could not think she had done anything to cause him displeasure. Likely, he just wished to get his womenfolk away from the general tumult, she reasoned. Taking heart, she asked the ceremonial pole-bearer to unbolt the back door and to direct the thoroughfare out through that exit.

Then she stood smiling and nodding and dispensing with her pennies as their well-wishers trooped in through the front door of their new dwelling and then out of the back. Any bearers of furniture were directed to place the items in one of the two empty storerooms off the passageway whose true purpose she fancied were the pantry and buttery. Aimee saw with some trepidation that both rooms were soon full to bursting.

"Thank you," she said loudly and repeatedly. "Lord Kentigern and I are so grateful for your well wishes. You are very kind," she said firmly, stepping in front of one reveler who would have been happy to take his harp upstairs. "But I'm afraid the celebrations are now over for the day."

If, during the first twenty or so times she repeated this, she thought her bridegroom would soon reappear, by the time she had dealt with forty or so, she had given up on that forlorn hope. No, he had left her here to dispense with the alms alone. She did her best to manage the stab of disappointment she felt at being thus abandoned on her wedding day.

She was being unreasonable, she told herself heartily. His sister and cousin must have traveled at least a week to reach Caer-Lyoness. They had probably been wearied before the day had even commenced. It was only right that he should now see to their comfort as his first concern.

As for herself, she was no shrinking maiden who needed to be forever propped up by her spouse. She could see to this side of things very well alone. He paid her a compliment, she told herself staunchly, in recognizing that she, Aimee, was a capable wife who could deal with household matters without aid.

She was reaching the bottom of the second purse by the time the last of the attendants trooped through. She was just watching the disappearing back of one fellow in blue and wondering if she had not already paid him a penny once before, when the pole-bearer shut the back door after him and threw the bolt across. "That's the last of them, my lady," he said. "You must now bar your door after me or the first will be sprinting back around to the front for readmittance."

Aimee accompanied him to the front door without voicing her suspicion this had already happened at least once. "Wait," she called after him as he stepped out the door. She emptied the last of her pennies into her palm before extending her hand to him. "Thank you kindly, good sir, for your services. You must allow me to give you some payment."

He shook his head. "Your father hath already paid me," he said. "I return there now to let him know you have safely arrived." He nodded to her and turned with a stern frown to address the latecomers now approaching her door.

"Nay, you must not send these away, for it is my maid," Aimee said, pushing the door open and greeting Golda, who was weighed down with baggage and accompanied by a young lad of about ten years. "I am right glad to see you, Golda," she hailed her servant as she shut the door behind her. "And who have we here?" she asked, turning to the young boy.

"This is Unwin," Golda explained briefly. "He is the nephew of one of your father's groomsmen and in need of a situation."

82

"Which one?" Aimee asked with interest. Unwin shot a frightened look at Golda.

"Dickon," Golda said, naming the worst-tempered of her father's stable hands.

"Well, I am sure we can find you plenty to do here, Unwin," Aimee said, her sympathies engaged at once. She could not imagine that Dickon was a fond uncle. Wordlessly, she passed the boy the three leftover pennies with a wink. Unwin's eyes widened, but he clutched them in his palm without a murmur. "He seems a bright boy. I am sure he will do well here."

"He'd better," Golda said direly, and Unwin lowered his face, his shaggy brown hair falling across his eyes and hiding his expression. "Which way is the kitchen?"

"I think it's through here," Aimee said, feeling foolishly ignorant about her own residence. Together, they discovered the kitchen with its large fireplace and wide table. Golda set some sacks down on it at once and set Unwin to untie the strings.

"We've brought food and drink for supper. Your father's engaged a cook and a servant for you, but they won't come along until tomorrow." Aimee nodded. "Where's his lordship?" Golda added as an afterthought.

"He has gone to explore upstairs and assign rooms for his sister and cousin," Aimee responded.

"Oh." Golda looked askance. "He let you pick out which room you wanted first?" she asked. "After all, it is your house."

"I'm sure there are plenty of rooms for all of us," Aimee murmured, avoiding her servant's shrewd eye.

Golda sniffed but directed Unwin to go out to the back in search of the well. "For all it's so warm, we need to get the fire lit and get some water on for washing. I see we've one good-sized pot at least," she said, glancing around the bare kitchen. "You'd better get along upstairs, miss," Golda urged. "I mean, *milady*," she corrected herself with emphasis. "I'll send Unwin up with some refreshment for you presently."

Aimee's feet dragged as she crossed the kitchen to reenter the passageway. Almost, she wanted to stay below stairs with Golda. It wasn't like her to be so faint-hearted, she thought with surprise. Still, she could not help but reflect that her errant bridegroom had not once come in search of her. Banishing such melancholy thoughts, she peered curiously into the large dining chamber with its high ceiling and huge fireplace. It was a fine, big room. In the center, a long-carved table sat ready and waiting for use, while the rest of the room remained bare.

Walking back along the passageway, she noticed the front door was now unbolted. Aimee reflected that at one point when she and Golda were talking, she had thought she had heard the front door open and close. On impulse, she tried the door and found it was locked. Did that mean her husband had gone out somewhere? As far as she knew, the two of them possessed the only keys. Her father had given her her own without any attendant ceremony that morning.

Mounting the staircase with slow, thoughtful steps, Aimee reached the first floor and peered into a front-facing parlor which looked a pleasant room, for all it appeared rather bare, containing no wall-hangings or so much as a stick of furniture. There was a fine window seat looking out onto the street below which would do very well with some cushions on it.

Passing down the corridor, her steps slowed as her ears picked up the murmur of conversation.

"Such pleasant, airy rooms," a voice was prattling on. "So kind of dear Konrad to see us settled in."

That was the cousin, Aimee thought, recognizing her tones. She could not hear Magnatrude's replies, but her new sister-in-law had a low, deep voice that likely did not carry so well as the more shrill-voiced Freda. Guessing that the next two doors down this corridor were their bedchambers, she passed swiftly on without disturbing them.

She had seen no beds carried through the front door, so she hoped her father had had them at least delivered directly to the house. Trying the fourth door along the corridor, she was pleased to find an empty bedchamber that did indeed include a bed. It looked a little forlorn though, stood in the center of the room without any bedclothes.

Quietly closing that door, Aimee passed on to the final door and found it concealed a staircase which carried up to a third floor. After climbing this flight, Aimee was pleasantly surprised to find another floor of large-sized chambers. She had thought it would be attic rooms for the servants.

Then again, she had been too busy gawking at her husband on their approach to take a good look at her new house. It must be four stories high, she realized. Her father had done them proud. Only the best for Gerold Ankatel's daughter.

The first room she came across was a large bedchamber which looked down directly onto the street below. Aimee thought this would be a good candidate for Lord Kentigern's chamber. The bed was large and set high on a platform. Above it, a wooden frame hung suspended from the ceiling ready for the curtains to be hung from it.

The next room was smaller and would perhaps do for storing his clothing, armor, and swords, she thought vaguely. Or did knights keep such things elsewhere, such as near the stable? Surely, they would be at risk of being stolen if they were left unsecured in an outhouse. Dismissing these ruminations, she drifted on and found two more good-sized rooms.

One of these would do well for her own use, she thought, as both contained beds and would be near to her husband's. When Lady Wycliffe had given them a tour of Wycliffe Hall, she and Ursula had learned that husbands and wives of the nobility usually maintained their own bedchambers and did not share as commonfolk did. Still, she would like to be on the same floor as her husband at least. That way, if he should decide to come in search of her company, she would not be too hard to find.

Aimee idled a moment at the window, gazing down at the passersby in the street below. Watching them scurry by on their business, she reflected how funny it was that none of them had the first clue it was her wedding day today. A noise at the door had her wheeling around with a hopeful look on her face, but it was not Lord Kentigern. Instead, Golda stood at the doorway with her arms full of linen.

"This the room you picked out for yourself?" her servant asked, looking about critically. "Well, it's nice enough, but it's not the biggest of the bunch, is it?"

"No," Aimee agreed. "But the largest on this floor should go to his lordship."

Golda shrugged and turned back to look over her shoulder. "Don't dawdle there, child. Fetch in those bedclothes." Unwin sidled into the room, one spindly shank after the other, his skinny arms wrapped around a bundle of bed linens and red damask.

"Set them down on the bed," Golda instructed him, but here Aimee interrupted.

"Not those ones," she said hurriedly, crossing the room to where Unwin stood. "Those are intended for Lord Kentigern's bedchamber."

"What?" Golda squawked. "But those are the finest of the lot! Why would my lady squander those on one such as his lordship? He won't appreciate such quality linens, I assure you!"

Aimee eyed her maidservant in exasperation. "I embroidered those ones with his crest especially, Golda," she pointed out feeling a little self-conscious.

"I know that, milady," Golda replied, plunking one hand on her ample hip. "But now you'm married, that's *your* crest now too!"

How funny, she had not really considered that. "Well, yes," she agreed. "But I can always embroider my own at some later point. These are my wedding gift to him." Well, one of them anyway, she amended silently. She made no mention of the many other items she had picked out for him which were tucked away in one of the chests.

Golda pursed her lips but said no more as Aimee took the large pile of bedlinens from Unwin. "You can help me set up the master's bed now, Unwin," she said to the boy. "Follow me." She noticed the boy looked first to Golda before falling in step behind her. Golda jerked her chin at the boy, and he scurried after Aimee at once.

"Shall you miss the stable work, Unwin?" she asked conversationally as they proceeded down the passageway. When he did not answer, she turned back to give him a smile. "You must not be so shy around me, for I am sure we will see a lot of each other. In a townhouse such as this one, there is not much room for stables or a garden," she persisted. "I do not think there is even a central courtyard like the one in my father's house. No doubt my husband will keep his destrier elsewhere, so it will be housework you will be expected to help out with."

Unwin gulped and did the trick of letting his hair fall forward over his face again. Aimee swung open the bedchamber door and led the way inside. "I suppose you are not used to working in the house with women," Aimee observed as she threw the first sheet over the mattress. "But you will soon grow accustomed to us. Catch that corner and pull it over." The boy scrambled to help smooth out the creases and tuck the cloth under.

"Did my father's grooms not expect an answer when they spoke to you, Unwin?" she asked gently as she fetched the next sheet. The boy's lips quivered, and he seemed to grow short of breath. Aimee frowned, for he seemed almost afraid of her questioning. "Catch that side," she said, flinging out the scarlet damask covering. He was obliging enough in any case, she thought as she watched him catch the bedspread and bring it down over the mattress.

"We will need to stand on chairs to hang the canopy and curtains," she commented, gazing up at the canopy frame. "Neither of us will ever reach it otherwise." Unwin looked about the room, noting the lack of chairs. "There are plenty stacked in the storeroom downstairs off the passageway."

The boy did not need telling twice. As he darted from the room, Aimee set about pulling the scarlet cloth straight, smoothing it flat, and folding over the sheet to display the embroidered insignia of the Kentigerns. She had spent many hours toiling over the tiny stitches until they looked as perfect as she could ever achieve. She ran her fingertip lightly over the intricate gold stitches of the portcullis motif and smiled. She hoped such small attentions would persuade her new husband of her sincere attachment and hopes for their union.

Next, she laid the fine white pillow bearers at the head of the bed. These, too, were delicately embroidered. Indeed, so many times had she repeated the process that she fancied she could surely produce that gold portcullis perfectly now, even blindfolded.

When Unwin appeared with two chairs, they set about fixing the damask drapes about the hanging structure. Aimee felt herself break into a sweat as she craned, pushed, and pulled the fabric until it hung just as it ought. When she finally hopped down from her chair and surveyed the results, she felt deeply gratified.

"Does it not look quite splendid, Unwin?" she asked, clapping her hands together. "Why, it is already quite ten times as magnificent as the Wycliffes' best bedchamber." Unwin nodded obligingly as though he knew who the Wycliffes were. "And the rest of the furniture has not even been fetched up yet. Only imagine how it will look when it is fully furnished."

She would even have one of the magnificent wedding chests set down in his bedchamber, she reflected happily as they made their way back to her room. After all, it would hardly be fair of her to hog them both for her sole enjoyment.

When they reached her bedchamber, they found Golda was putting the finishing touches to her bed with pretty coverings of green and gold. Golda looked up as they entered the room. "We can't hang the curtains until you get a canopy set up," she said with dissatisfaction, nodding to where the curtains lay folded on the floor. "I reckon as that room on the floor below was meant to be yours, not this 'un."

"It is of no matter," Aimee assured her. "We can send for a carpenter on the morrow. This will do very well for now, Golda."

"The water really should be getting hot by now," Golda observed. "You'll need to wash up before taking your supper. Unwin," she said, addressing the boy. "You'll need to light this fire too before it starts going off cold." She nodded toward the fireplace, and the boy scuttled from the room.

A sudden thought occurring to her, Aimee turned impulsively toward Golda. "The boy *can* speak, can he not?"

Golda gave a short laugh. "Aye, miss, he speaks. It takes him a while to warm up to a body, that's all."

"He was not ill-treated in my father's stables, surely?"

Golda shook her head. "Put that out of your head," she said, gathering up the leftover curtains. "Nothing ails him, and he will be right enough, given time."

Relieved on that score, Aimee turned toward the window where the sun was hanging low in the sky. "You will need to take some bedclothes along to Miss Magnatrude and Freda also," she said conscientiously. "They will need their beds made up before long and water also to wash."

"Oh, you don't need to worry about them." Golda pulled a face. "His lordship brought their servants along not half an hour ago. They've been seeing to their comfort alright. They've had the first lot of the hot water already."

"Did he?" Aimee asked in astonishment. "Oh, I had no notion." She remembered the unbolted door and realized that must have been his errand. "Should I go and check they are settled in, I wonder?"

Golda pursed her lips. "You're the bride, Miss Aimee, and this is your wedding day. All you need worry about is taking your comfort now." She walked to the door. "I'll send Unwin up with a glass of wine for you and some hot water presently."

"Thank you," Aimee responded, but her capable servant had already closed the door after her.

Aimee sighed, and climbing the steps to the platformed bed, she sat on the feather mattress and reached up to the remove the jeweled pins that secured her veil to her head. She made a small pile of them on top of the bed coverings and then carefully folded the intricately decorated veil and set it down next to them.

Next, she removed the simple gold chain from about her throat and placed it on top of the veil, along with the engraved silver ring that had been her mother's. Now she was a baroness she could wear more extravagant jewelry, she reflected, and remembered the gifts she had bought for her new kinswomen. Her spirits brightened. She would set about winning their good opinion on the morrow.

A knock on the door had her starting up from the bed, but it was merely Unwin, carrying a small table into the room. Golda followed on his heels with a basin of water. She set it down on the table and removed a cloth from her shoulder to put next to it. "Come and wash, milady," she said. "Unwin will light your fire as I fetch your supper."

As Aimee vigorously washed her face and neck, Unwin set about laying the fire in her hearth. She was just drying her neck when Golda reentered with wine and a tray of foods.

"Shall I take down your hair, Miss Aimee?" Golda asked. "I mean, *milady*," she corrected herself painstakingly.

Aimee touched the elaborate arrangement of her hair. She felt oddly reluctant to lose the last vestiges of her bridal appearance. "Not just yet, Golda," she prevaricated. "It is not so very late after all."

Golda lifted an eyebrow at her but held her tongue. "It's a shame we can't drag your trunk up them stairs," she said after a moment's silence. "But it's more'n the boy and I can manage between us."

"You are not to even try," Aimee responded at once. "I can do without it this eve."

"Is there anything I can fetch from it that you might want?" Golda asked. "A comb? A clean shift?"

Aimee thought of how lovingly she had packed her bridal trunks and felt a pang at the thought of Golda rifling through it for her essentials. "No, thank you, Golda. I can unpack my trunks soon enough. Please do not fret on my account."

The maid pressed her lips together and said no more. She and Unwin moved the table to position it nearer to the fire. As Golda set out the food, Unwin carried Aimee's goblet of wine to her, and she took it from him with a smile. "Thank you, Unwin." He bobbed his head and retreated.

"Will there be anything else, milady?" Golda asked, crossing to the window and glancing briefly out before she emptied the basin of water out of the window.

"No, that will be all, thank you both."

When they had departed, Aimee moved to the window and drank her wine as she watched the sun go down on her wedding day. She wondered what Ursula was doing right now. Was she taking supper with her husband? Aimee glanced over her shoulder at the table which had been set with enough for two. And where oh where was her own errant bridegroom?

8

It was not until some two hours later when she had quite given up on him that Aimee heard the heavy rap on her door. Hearing it now, she marveled that she could have ever mistaken Golda's or Unwin's knock for her husband's. She sat up as the door opened and watched him enter before closing it behind him.

He stood a moment in silence, surveying her so grimly that Aimee felt a tingle of alarm spread through her body. Then she decided the coldness of his glare must surely be a trick of the shifting shadows from the firelight.

"Shall I light more candles?" she heard herself say in a quavering voice. "Only it has turned rather dark in here." When he said nothing, she asked, "Have you yet eaten?"

He gave a brusque nod and turned his back to her as he drew his tunic up over his head, and the words she had been about to utter withered and died on her lips. She sat as though paralyzed, watching the muscles in his back ripple. Flinging his tunic on the floor, he turned next to unlacing his crotch, and Aimee turned her head sharply to face forward, her breath coming fast.

She had long since shed her best gown and was clad now only in her shift. There was nothing more she could do to prepare, so she simply lay back down and tried not to panic. Old Janet, her father's oldest servant, had told her how babies were made when she had turned thirteen. Merchant's daughters were not generally sheltered against the facts of life.

Aimee reminded herself she was eager for the next part. She had anticipated Lord Kentigern's embrace for months now, so it was no good shrinking from him now like some terrified virgin, even if that was what she was. Hearing her husband's heavy footfalls against the floorboards as he approached the bed, Aimee braced herself and did not flinch when he reached for her.

When he rolled off her panting ten minutes later, she was reeling. The consummation had been jarring in its physicality, and for the first time, Aimee had not found Lord Kentigern's size to be a source of wonder and awe. Underneath her husband, she had realized the act was one of shocking intimacy.

The rapport she had established—or failed to establish with her husband—made her feel very alone as he had rolled off her. He had not been rough with her; far from it. Instead, he had handled her with a sort of calculated and studied care that had chilled her somehow quite to the bone. He had known what he was doing, and he had done it with the cool and detached patience of an impartial stranger.

Her touch had not made him tremble or blush or show any outward sign of pleasure. Instead, he had turned very still beneath her fingers, his face turning blank, his eyes shuttered. She was struck with an awful suspicion that he was simply suffering her, as one who felt honor bound to be in her bed rather than a lover who desired to be there.

And, gods, she thought with horror, that was the truth of the matter, wasn't it? At the end of the day, she had pointed him out and had her father buy him for her. To her horror, the empty feeling that had been stealing over her all evening was replaced by one of dizzying loss and panic. Their wedding had meant she had kissed her dear father and sister goodbye. This man lying beside her was her family now. This cold and strangely passionless man.

For the first time, it occurred to her that maybe his terrifying appearance did not mask a heart of gold. That maybe the one in need of compassion and pity was herself. She felt herself begin to tremble as he climbed out of the bed. After realizing his aversion, she had let her arms drop and had given up her clumsy attempts to caress him. He did not want affection from her.

She felt terribly sore, and not just in that spot between her legs, but heartsore also. A heavy weight seemed to settle over down her chest, squeezing the breath right out of her. It left her unable to sit up or even gather the sheets and cover her nakedness.

"I'll leave you to your sleep," he rumbled at her as he tied his braies about his hips.

Aimee nodded dumbly. Not that he noticed, for he did not look her way at all. She felt winded. Shaken. As though she had been thrown from a bolting horse and trampled on. He walked from the room still half-naked, and she watched him go in a sort of stupor.

What if he never did turn toward her? The sudden and terrible certainty of it washed over her like an icy wave, shocking her out of her insensibility. Aimee fought down the tears that rushed to her eyes. There was no one to dry them for her now.

She had delivered herself up to this fate. Nay, she had rushed headlong into it like a little fool. Lord Kentigern was the one who had been snared in her trap. She was the foolish hunter who had thought to keep her prize as a pet, and she had no one to blame but herself. A knock at the door made her gasp and struggle into an upright position. It was some old woman she had never clapped eyes on before in her life. She gazed at her in stupefaction.

"T' master sent me," the woman said abruptly with a strong northern accent. "I've hot water for you here." She brandished a jug, and Aimee forced herself to nod as she drew the blankets up about her.

"Thank you."

"You'll be wanting the tub now, I suppose," the older woman said with withering disapproval. "I've set water to heat over the fire, but if you imagine my old bones can lug it up and down stairs, you've another think coming. You'll need to send for your own servants to minister to you—"

Aimee cut across her words. "There is no need for that."

The old woman's whiskered chin came up sharply. "His lordship said I'm to change the bedsheets and set you in a bath, but if you think—" she argued belligerently.

"And I said, you need not bother," Aimee responded bracingly. The woman's unfortunate manner, tiresome though it was, was at least rousing her from her self-pity. "This is my bedchamber, is it not?" she demanded briskly. "If his lordship wants his bedsheets changed then you had better go to *his* room and strip his bed."

When the old woman opened her mouth to argue, Aimee felt her backbone spark. "What is your name?" she demanded as it suddenly occurred to her that the woman had not addressed her as she ought. She supposed she should pull her up about that, though it was the least of her concerns right now.

The servant's mouth snapped shut before she forced it open again to mutter grudgingly "Ingrid" through gritted teeth.

"Well, Ingrid, do you imagine I need a clean bed changed for one measly spot of blood? I bleed more than this on my monthly courses! And I don't require a whole tub full of water to wash between my legs. I lay in a perfumed bath all morning, and I am certainly not repeating the process now. His lordship *vastly* overestimates himself!" Her cheeks turned poppy red at her own coarseness, but bluster was all she had right now to hold herself together. If her sister could hear her now, she thought, Ursula would surely swoon at the lack of delicacy!

To illustrate her point, she flung her bedclothes back and leaped from the bed to cross the room and snatch up a cloth. "Hurry and pour the water, Ingrid, and do not dawdle!" In truth, it was her thighs that were smeared with blood and not the sheets.

The old woman emitted a dry wheeze. "Well, you're not giving me the die-away airs I expected, I'll give you that much."

Aimee shot her a level look as she dunked her cloth into the warm water. "Well, as I am sure you are aware, I am no gently born damsel." She saw the servant's guilty start at her words. Yes, she thought decidedly, this Kentigern servant knew all about her own ignoble birth. Likely, his people had been discussing her commonness since their betrothal. "So, let us have no pretense about the matter now."

Ingrid bridled as though this plain speaking was going too far. "Ye're the mistress now—" she started, but Aimee had no patience for the family retainer by this point. She certainly had not addressed her as her mistress when she had barreled into her bedchamber with her insolence.

"That will be all, thank you," she responded smartly, running the cloth up and down her thighs. "Leave me now." Her voice cracked over the last three words, shaming her. Aimee bowed her head so her dark hair fell forward, hiding her face.

Ingrid froze for an instant, and Aimee braced herself for a barrage of words which did not come. Instead, she heard the servant's footsteps retreat, and Aimee had just tensed for the slam of the door, only for it to softly close after her. Aimee breathed out raggedly, finished her ablutions, and crept naked back into the bed, wrapping the sheets firmly about her.

She lay completely still awhile, then turned her face into the pillow and allowed herself the indulgence of a good cry. The tears seemed to help ease the weight over her chest, and by the by, she fell into an exhausted sleep.

9

The next morning, Aimee woke early and lay a good while staring dry-eyed at the ceiling. Her husband had not returned to her in the night. She had not really expected he would. It was no good lying huddled away here in her bedchamber, feeling bruised of spirit, she told herself sternly. Instead, she needed to start her day, for she had plenty to do.

She was already out of the bed when she heard Golda's tentative tap at the door. Aimee washed and chose a simply cut gown, for her day was to be one taken up with household affairs. As her servant was currently working as maid of all duty, Aimee dressed her own hair, piling it into a simple arrangement, first braiding it and then coiling it twice about her head before pinning it in place.

Adding a gauzy kerchief to the top of her head in acknowledgment of her wedded status, she told herself that would have to do. Her looking glass had not yet been unpacked, so she would have to hope for the best. Reaching for her gold chain, she fastened it about her neck, slid two of her jeweled hairpins into her dark hair, and decided she was ready to face the world.

Resisting the temptation to creep down the stairs as quietly as possible, she made her way down the steps with a firm, determined tread. She managed to reach the bottom without bumping into a single soul.

Wondering at what time the new servants would be joining the household, she opened the door to the left of the passageway which led into the dining chamber and entered the large room. From the crumb-laden plates upon the table, Aimee deduced someone in the house had already broken their fast.

"Milady," came a brisk voice from the doorway, and Aimee turned to see Golda bustling into the room carrying a platter of fresh bread.

"Who has already eaten this morn?" Aimee asked.

"His lordship," Golda admitted. "*And* gone out. Him and his manservant together." She pursed her lips.

Aimee swallowed her pride. "Did they say where they were going?" she asked.

"To practice," her maid responded. "For that royal tournament in four days' time."

"Oh, of course," Aimee responded, feeling a little foolish. She had forgotten all about the Summer Tournament in the run-up to her own nuptials.

"Where are you going, milady?" Golda called after her as Aimee exited the room.

"To fetch another chair," Aimee called back over her shoulder. She moved too quickly for Golda's objections to reach her. In any case, she wanted to have enough chairs for herself, Magnatrude, and Freda to sit together that morning. By the time she had returned carrying the chair, Unwin was setting down a platter of roasted fish.

Aimee gave him a quick smile and returned to the cluttered storerooms which currently housed all their furniture. She knelt down beside the first of her wedding trunks and slipped her hand inside to retrieve the two packages she had tied up with ribbon. Hurrying back to the dining chamber, she placed the gifts for her new in-laws next to the two empty place settings and only then sat in her own chair.

Golda reentered the room with butter and a jug of ale which she set down. "What's this?" she asked, eyeing the packages with disfavor.

"Gifts for my new sister-in-law and cousin."

Golda sniffed. "Thought it was customary for them to welcome *you* into their family."

"This is a custom of my mother's people," Aimee told her quietly.

"Oh," said Golda, looking chastened, for she knew that Aimee's mother hailed from lands east of Karadok. She likely would have said more, but at this point, the door pushed open and the servant Ingrid, who Aimee had met the night before, stood on the threshold.

Ingrid nodded her grizzled head. "Morning," she said in clipped tones.

"Morning, *milady*," Golda corrected her sharply. "It seems you have not yet been introduced to your new mistress."

"Good morning," Aimee said, forestalling Ingrid's need to answer this incorrect statement.

"Milady," Ingrid mumbled and bobbed an approximation of a curtsey done by someone with very stiff knees. Likely her knees *were* stiff at her advanced age, Aimee thought, darting a meaningful look at Golda. Her maidservant seemed remarkably inclined to snatch up cudgels on her behalf.

Ingrid cleared her throat. "They'll be wanting the butter dish once ye're done with it and the rest of the loaf."

"Who will?" Golda demanded, plunking her hands on her hips.

"The Mistresses Magnatrude and Freda," Ingrid replied impassively.

Golda spluttered indignantly. "There's only one mistress in this house!" she retorted darkly. "If they want to break their fast, they can haul their carcasses down here to take it like decent folk!" she burst forth angrily.

Aimee placed her hand gently on Golda's sleeve, silencing her. "It is their wish to take their meal above stairs?" she asked carefully.

Ingrid jerked her chin up in an aggressive nod. "They's set up camp in that oaken parlor on the first floor," she admitted before adding a belated, "milady."

"Bloody cheek!" Golda burst out. "That's your own retiring room, Miss Aimee. For you to do your needlework and such! Not for them to set up separate dining quarters."

"It is of no matter," Aimee said soothingly. "It is a large house and can accommodate all our needs, I am sure."

"What will I tell them, then?" Ingrid asked, squinting at Aimee.

"You may present them with the butter dish with my compliments," Aimee answered, slathering a piece of bread and sliding it over to Ingrid. "Now that I am now finished with it."

"Humph!" snorted Golda, hovering at the table like a tigress in defense of her cub. As she had been in the Ankatel's employ for only some two years, Aimee was a little surprised by her feudal attitude. Ingrid lingered a moment before taking up the bread and butter. She executed another approximation of a curtsey and scuttled sideways from the room, rather like a crab.

Golda muttered something under her breath that sounded venomous.

"What time will the new staff be arriving, Golda?" Aimee asked, thinking a change of subject was in order.

"The gods alone know!" Golda huffed and stalked out of the room.

Aimee took a bite of her bread and butter and hoped devoutly that they would be more even-tempered than the servants they currently possessed. She tarried awhile over her simple meal before moving across to the large window. The sky was blue and the sun already shining high in the sky. It felt pleasant to bask a moment in its warmth.

The street outside was quiet, though some folk were already out about their business. Aimee spent a few moments in contemplation before turning from the view with a sigh. Eyeing the brightly wrapped packages on the table, she pondered her next move. What would Ursula advise? She already knew her sweet, grave sister would tell her she had to give Magnatrude and Freda more time. There was still the chance it was mere awkwardness or an excess of formality that had led them to shun her this morning.

After all, they were northerners, and their habits and ways were as foreign to her as her own would be to them. Picking up the packages, she took a deep breath, went out into the hallway, and mounted the stairs. When she reached the first floor, she paused briefly outside the parlor room and knocked. The flow of conversation abruptly halted as she pushed open the door.

"Good morning," she greeted them politely.

"Oh! Good morning," Freda twittered. "I—that is—we hope you are well this morning, Aimee?" She faltered, her eyes darting nervously to Magnatrude.

"I am, thank you. I hope you spent a pleasant night's sleep?" Aimee enquired.

"Oh, I did! Most pleasant!" Freda enthused, but her anxious gaze was still on her cousin and not Aimee. "Such a comfortable house, I have never slept under the eaves of one so newly built. Such large chambers," she exclaimed. "Konrad is to be congratulated."

"Did you see him this morn?" Aimee roused herself to ask when she realized that Freda's babble of conversation had dried up. "Before he went to practice for the tournament?"

"Oh no!" Freda looked shocked. "I am sure my cousin is far too busy for womenfolk before midday."

Aimee forced herself to walk into the room without waiting for an invitation which would not come. This was her house, she reminded herself. To feel like a trespasser in it would be foolish. "I have here a token for you both," she said with a smile, setting a package down first by Freda's plate and then one next to Magnatrude's. "My mother hailed from Samare," she explained. "Among her people, it is a custom for the bride to give gifts to the womenfolk in her new family. I hope you like them."

Freda's mouth formed an unspoken *oh*, but she did not speak it, merely sat with a look of frozen embarrassment. Aimee wondered if that lady started every sentence with the same exclamation. It certainly seemed that way. She glanced at Magnatrude, realizing that the proud lady had not uttered so much as a word to her so far.

Magnatrude roused herself at this point, seeming to realize some conversation was required of her. "You are quite the bountiful lady, are you not?" she said in her deep, low voice,

105

and Aimee felt herself coloring. The way Magnatrude uttered the words seemed vaguely accusatory.

Freda coughed. "Your mother's people hailed from Samare, you say?" she said nervously. "That would explain your black hair, my dear."

"Yes," Aimee agreed.

"And Ursula is your full-blood sister?" Freda continued, rattling on. "Only she does not seem so dark in her coloring as you."

"She is, yes," Aimee answered, though she suspected Freda's chatter stemmed more from a desire to fill any awkward silences than a real interest in her family. "She takes after my father whereas I favor my mother's side."

Freda nodded. "So interesting!" she said, nodding her head. Aimee lingered hopefully, but as nothing more was forthcoming, she set her hand on the door.

"I will bid you good morning, then," she said. "I believe I will spend a good deal of today unpacking, but you should be able to find me easy enough if you should desire my company."

"Oh yes, my dear!" Freda said in a rush. "I'm sure we wish you a most pleasant day!"

Aimee made her way downstairs feeling a little baffled. It seemed the ladies of the household were not keen to merge into one party. She wondered for a moment what they intended to do with themselves all day and then banished the matter from her mind. After all, she had made it plain she would welcome their company, and it was now up to them to take her up on her invitation, or not, as the case might be.

As she approached the foot of the stairs, she heard voices in the hallway she did not recognize. Quickening her step, she glanced down to see Golda having a spirited conversation with a burly-looking man in a yellow tunic.

"Milady," Golda called. "This is the new servant your father employed on your behalf. His name is Matthews." Matthews shuffled about to face her and performed a clumsy bow.

"Good day," Aimee greeted him. "We are glad you have come, there is much furniture to cart about the house. Has Golda showed you where it is all piled up?" Without waiting for his reply, she made her way to the first of the two doors and threw it open, showing the abundance of furniture within. "You see?"

Matthews cleared his throat. "I see, milady."

She opened the second door to show him, and he nodded again, rather mournfully.

"I've sent the new cook along to the kitchen to make a list of all his needs," Golda told her. "He won't be pleased to see it so poorly equipped, but he'll have to make do!"

"What was his name?" Aimee asked.

"Stirling, milady."

"Is that all of us, then?" Aimee asked with interest.

"The maid of all work did not show up," Golda answered, sounding chagrined. "We will just have to make do with Unwin for now."

Aimee nodded and firstly set Matthews to carry up her two wedding chests. "They are to go into the two largest bedchambers on the third floor. One for each room."

Golda bristled at this. "You will surely be wanting both of those in your room, milady!" she protested.

107

"One for each room," Aimee insisted. "One for my husband's room and one for my own."

"Do ye have a preference as to which one?" Matthews asked, scratching his head.

Aimee glanced from the lavish decoration of the bridal procession to the one of succulent fruits. "It is of no matter, for I like them both. Then I want these two matching chairs with the carved arms to go in his lordship's chamber along with this studded trunk." She moved from each group of stacked furniture directing where in the house they were going to go. The simple wooden benches were for the kitchen. The high-backed chairs with the rush inserted seats were for the dining chamber. The seats with the arched backs were for her own room. Matthews nodded and set about his work at once.

When Golda looked as though to leave them, Aimee forestalled her. "What about your own room, Golda, and the rest of the servants?" she asked. "Is there anything we need to send for?"

"There was a bunch of new pallet beds in the attics, milady," Golda said, shaking her head. "We're adequately provided for."

"You and Unwin have everything you need? Have you allocated rooms for the rest of the servants?"

Golda nodded. "Ingrid has the small room between her mistresses. Jakeman is up in the attics though he has his own separate room. Stirling and Matthews will have to share."

"Jakeman?" repeated Aimee. Had she heard that name before?

"That is his lordship's manservant."

"Oh, I see. And you are happy with the room you have?"

"Oh yes, Miss Aimee," Golda said, relapsing to her former title. "Most happy. I'm tucked in the furthest corner of the third floor. A little room facing the back of the house."

Aimee nodded. "And Unwin? He will not be nervous up in the attic with all these newcomers?"

Golda hesitated. "Unwin is in with me at the moment," she said after a slight pause. "He's a nervous lad and needs his—" She broke off. "My support," she stressed carefully. "Soon as he's ready he can go up and join the menfolk, but not before then."

Aimee was a little surprised that brusque Golda, who had been so fierce to defend the boundaries of her duties as lady's maid in her father's house, should now be willing to share her quarters with a former stable lad. She nodded. "I'm sure you know what is best," she murmured.

Aimee returned to the Great Hall and drank a cup of ale before she climbed the stairs again to the third floor. As she reached the top step, Matthews came out of Lord Kentigern's room and nodded to her. "I'll fetch the other trunk now, milady," he said and started down the stairs. Aimee took a deep breath and walked into her husband's bedchamber.

Matthews had set the handsome wedding chest under the window, and glancing about the room, Aimee saw the bed had been straightened and the wash basin emptied out of the window. She wondered if that was the handiwork of the elusive Jakeman, for somehow, she could not imagine her husband tarrying to tidy his bedclothes after he had arisen.

Thoughtfully, she made her way over to the chest and unfastened it to start unpacking all of the purchases she had made for her married life. She spent a good hour unpacking only the first of the trunks. At the very bottom, she found the particolored gown she'd had commissioned using the colors of Lord Kentigern's crest.

The robe was formed of sections of alternate blue and yellow satin with the portcullis motif emblazoned right across the chest. Aimee admired the garment prodigiously, though when she had declared she would wear it to watch her husband compete, her sister had looked at her a little askance.

"It's just that—the daughter of an earl can wear something that will not draw even a murmur whereas the daughter of a merchant…" Ursula had let her words trail off, and Aimee had shrugged off the comment. Very likely the gesture did lack subtlety, but Ursula was so reserved and Aimee, quite frankly, was not. Aimee added the gown to the pile of things designated for her own room.

The very last item in the trunk was a gift for her groom, a doublet of burgundy brocade studded and decorated with velvet-covered buttons. She laid this on the large scarlet bed for him to see and then closed the trunk and made her way to her own room, carrying her pile of things. On arrival, she found the second trunk had been placed at the foot of her bed and set about unpacking it at once.

A knock on the door heralded the arrival of Matthews and another man with the first of the large carved cabinets she requested for her chamber. This must be the cook, Stirling, she realized. She directed them to the spot she wanted it set down in, and they shuffled off to fetch the second one. Aimee found the small velvet pouch she had been looking for which she had rolled up in the toe of one of her stockings.

She did not open the drawstring bag, but instead went on her tiptoes and secreted it into a small hidden recess in the top of the wooden cabinet. A master craftsman had made the piece of wood that fitted into place so well that the join was scarcely discernible to the eye. Indeed, even the grain of the wood seemed a perfect match.

She had no sooner sealed up the hidey-hole than she heard a soft scratching on the door. "Come in," she called out, and Unwin's head peered around the door. "Good morning, Unwin." She smiled at the boy. "What have you there?" He came carefully into the room, balancing a tray against his hip. "Is that for me?"

When he stood mute in the doorway, she gestured toward a small table, and he set the small jug of ale and dish of fresh figs and nuts down there. "Thank you, that looks delicious." Unwin gave a hurried bow and scurried from the room under Aimee's rueful gaze. She would just have to trust that Golda was right and give the boy time, she supposed. The same way that she needed to with her husband.

10

The sun had long set by the time Konrad left the practice field. He ran a damp cloth over his face and neck before pulling his jerkin on over his shirt. He glanced over at Jakeman, who had already started packing up his discarded armor.

"A good day's practice, my lord!" Sir Douglas Farleigh called out, and Kentigern raised a hand to him in a farewell gesture. He was damned if he knew why, but some of the youngsters, like Farleigh, seemed to be going out of their way to persecute him with their friendship these days.

"Let's get out of here," he rumbled at Jakeman, who was strapping his breastplate to the back of his horse. His manservant nodded, hastening to fetch the discarded pile of lances.

"Do we return to the house on Lime Street?" Jakeman asked.

"Where else?" Kentigern asked irritably. His servant had brought the last of their things from The Jennet Tree that very morning.

"I heard that several more knights arrived in the capital this day," Jakeman replied calmly. "The King is holding a banquet tonight at the palace welcoming all knights to this summer's tournament."

Kentigern scowled. "I received no invitation."

"It's open to all competitors," Jakeman responded, unruffled. "There were notices posted on all the city gates this morn."

Kentigern considered the prospect. "Who's arrived?" he asked abruptly. "Vawdrey? Orde?"

"Sir Roland and Sir Garman have both arrived today, my lord," Jakeman responded promptly.

"Good," Konrad grunted. It would be the first tournament this year where all the major players were present, he thought sourly. "What about that arrogant bastard, de Crecy?" If he was going to beat the best, they may as well all be present.

Jakeman looked thoughtful. "I have not heard tell of Sir Jeffree," he admitted, then seemed to hesitate.

"What?" Konrad barked suspiciously.

"It's naught, only there is some rumor doing the rounds that Sir Jeffree is recently married."

"What does that have to do with anything?" Konrad demanded, swinging himself up into his saddle. "I am lately married. I fail to see why that should influence my tournament attendance."

Jakeman shrugged his shoulders slightly. "As to that, my lord, I am sure I couldn't say."

Konrad glared at him. Jakeman's tact could sometimes be damnably annoying. "What of de Bussell?" he growled, thinking of the impudent dog who had lately taken the northern princess to wife.

Jakeman shook his head. "He is not expected, my lord."

A pity, Konrad thought bitterly. He would have enjoyed rubbing Armand de Bussell's face in the dirt for his damned impertinence in laying his filthy hands on the princess. He was a fair competitor too, Konrad acknowledged grudgingly, when he kept his focus on the competition field. You never knew with de Bussell whether he would pose a threat or not.

Dismissing all thought of his rivals, Konrad let his thoughts wander back to the same subject that had been plaguing his mind all morning. The black-haired beauty he had left in the early hours of the morning. For some reason, he could not quite banish the vision of her that rose in his mind's eye or the disquieting memory of washing her maiden's blood off his cock.

For some reason, he recalled particularly vividly the expression in her eyes when he had left her lying on the bed. It was not just her rounded, lush body that was soft and yielding, but her feelings too. She had expected him to tarry and give her gentle words after her deflowering, he supposed with scorn and a hint of something else. Discomfort.

Why he felt this way he knew not, for he had not led her to suppose he would be a considerate husband. He had not misled her at all. Beddings were never enjoyable for virgins, he reflected with an irritable shrug of his shoulders. If she had been told aught else, then *they* were the ones to blame for her expectations, not him.

For some reason, Renlow flashed into his mind and the conviction that Renlow would not have given sweet Aimee such a wedding night. His jaw tightened. She must have bitterly repented the impulse that had seen her swap places with her mewling sister. Renlow would not have strode from the bedchamber, leaving her a pale, trembling wreck in his wake, that was for damned sure. He cursed beneath his breath.

"My lord?" Jakeman looked across at him.

"It's nothing," he muttered. "Let's get out of here."

It did not take long to make their way through the city, reaching the impressive-looking townhouse Gerold Ankatel had bought for his daughter in the prosperous quarter of town. Konrad looked up now at the looming black and white monstrosity and dismounted, passing the reins to his manservant so Jakeman could lead Actaeon to the ostler he had employed in the next street.

Steeling himself, he walked into the house and found the entrance passageway quiet and unobstructed. The door to the buttery was wide open, showing evidence of some industry. The mounds of furniture had been removed, and all the room contained now were two large ale casks and some sacks of grain. Konrad pulled the door shut and carried on to the door that opened into the largest room, the dining chamber.

He checked on the threshold thinking it was empty, before perceiving his wife was sat very quiet and still before the unlit fireplace. In her lap were two unopened packages which she seemed to be regarding with some blankness. When he cleared his throat, she looked up quickly, shoving both packages behind a cushion.

"Good evening, my lord," she said with studied brightness. "You have had a good day?"

"Tolerable," he answered, coming into the room. He wanted to ask what she had hidden behind the cushion. Unwelcome bride gifts? He felt strangely curious. Instead, he looked about. "Where is everyone?"

"Golda is in the kitchen supervising the new staff," she answered after a moment's pause. "Our cook, Stirling, joined us today, and a manservant named Matthews who seems a very capable fellow."

He collapsed into a large chair opposite her and regarded her broodingly a moment. "I thought you didn't approve of letting old servants take over new households," he found himself pointing out rather bluntly.

Aimee frowned over his words. "I don't think I quite—?"

"When it came to your sister, at least," he interrupted her.

Her expression cleared. "Oh, I see. Well, it is a *little* different in this case. I have not been sat here all day while Golda takes the lead, if that is what you're thinking." She gave him a rueful smile.

"What have you been doing, then?" he asked brusquely. Strange to say, he was actually interested in her answer.

"Overseeing the unpacking and the furnishing of the house," she answered promptly. "A carpenter came out this afternoon to see to a few things that needed doing. Then I made an inventory of the items we still need." She shrugged her shoulders. "I have been very busy, for all I now seem at leisure."

He grunted. "And how would it have been different if you had ended up with Hilda instead of Golda?" he heard himself ask.

Aimee looked just as surprised by his question as he felt voicing it. "Well," she said slowly. "Hilda would have done her utmost to get under my feet, tutting at every decision I made and imploring me to remain in my bedchamber, while she imagined a hundred slights against me which she would then pour in my ears, whilst assuring me that she was my only ally," she finished dryly.

Kentigern's eyebrows rose as he turned this over. "Why would your father keep some tiresome woman in his household?" he asked.

"She was my mother's servant before his," she answered simply. "He will never turn her out for that reason alone."

"No, just palm her off on one of his daughters," he pointed out.

"I'm sure he thought he was doing Ursula a kindness," she said mildly.

116

"She sounds more of a hindrance than anything."

"Yes," Aimee agreed. "Though in truth, she does not irk Ursula as much as she does me."

He thought there was probably a reason for that but managed to hold his tongue. No doubt her sister would encourage such mawkish thinking. Once again, he congratulated himself on having avoided taking the elder Miss Ankatel to wife.

"Supper will be served in here in half an hour," his wife said with a studied casualness that made him immediately wary. "Perhaps you could send word to your sister and cousin informing them of the fact?"

He regarded her in silence a moment and saw her color rise before she turned her face away. He was just supposing there must have been some ruffled feathers when he heard a footfall he recognized in the passage outside. "Jakeman!" he hailed his servant loudly.

The sandy-colored head peered into the doorway. "My lord?"

"Run up a message to Mistress Magnatrude and Freda, would you? Tell them they are expected in the dining chamber in half an hour."

"Yes, my lord."

He glanced across at Aimee, but she was avoiding his gaze. "My sister is obstinate," he found himself explaining gruffly. "She…has not had the easiest life." Aimee's expression was polite, but she did not press him for any more detail. For some reason, this spurred him on more than if she had actually shown interest. "Before the war, she was betrothed," he let slip. This did capture her attention.

"It was called off?" she asked, then her expression fell. "He did not die?" she squeaked, lifting her hand to her mouth in dismay.

Konrad smiled grimly. "He wed another, on the eve of the Battle of Demoyne. Can't say I blame him, as things looked bleak. Likely, Kimarne did not think to spend another night in a woman's arms." Aimee's lips formed an unspoken *oh*. "But Magnatrude did not see it that way. She took it hard."

"Yes," Aimee answered sympathetically. "I can see she might have."

"His wife was lowborn, an alewife from his own household," he found himself continuing. "Magnatrude saw that as added insult to injury."

For some reason, that made his pretty wife's color bloom forth again. "I see," she said quietly. "And he did not try to cry off from his hasty marriage when he lived to see another day?"

Konrad shook his head. "His wife never gave him cause to regret it. Nine months later she was delivered of his son and heir."

Aimee regarded him steadily. "I suppose that secured her position," she observed frankly. "Should you like a son?" she asked with a directness that almost floored him.

"Of course," he heard himself answer, though in truth it was not something he had considered in years. Not since he had lost his birthright. Of course, their marriage had returned that to him.

She nodded thoughtfully, and Konrad noticed a servant had entered the room bearing a tray with a pitcher and goblets. He sat forward in his seat as she plunked it down on the table and poured their wine. This must be Golda, he guessed, noting her steely-eyed gaze and firmly compressed lips. And though

Aimee might not realize it, this woman was just as staunchly partisan as Hilda would have been.

"I should wash and change before eating," Konrad muttered, hauling himself out of his chair. Aimee came politely to her feet. He frowned at her. "You don't need to do that now." She sat back down again, and he left the room.

By the time Konrad returned, Aimee was sat at one end of the dining table which was covered in dishes. He heard footsteps in the corridor outside. Sure enough, his sister came around the corner in a sober gown of dark red that he was sure she used to wear back in her court days. Freda followed on close behind her.

"Well, is not this nice," Freda said, fluttering her hands about to incorporate the whole room. "A vastly handsome chamber."

Magnatrude slid into the chair to his left, and Freda hesitated a moment before sitting next to her.

He glanced pointedly at his sister.

"Good eve, brother," she said colorlessly, and he guessed she must still be sulking about her prolonged sojourn to the southern capital.

"Well," he said. "And what have you been about all day? Moping about the place or making yourself useful?"

The heavy silence that greeted his words told him all he needed to know. Freda had the grace to turn very red, but his sister was rigid with anger.

"As you know, brother," she said in a furious undertone, "I am only here under protest!"

"What protest? I sent for you to celebrate my nuptials as any good brother would. You came soon enough." He was tactful

119

enough not to mention the purse he had sent to facilitate her journey.

"I did not think you would actually detain me at this accursed place!" she hissed.

Konrad rolled his eyes. "Stop being so dramatic, Trude, for the love of the gods," he said. "You're no girl."

"Then don't use that childish version of my name, then," she snapped. "For neither are you in your infancy, brother."

He glanced down the length of the table at Aimee, but she was selecting a bread roll with careful deliberation. It crossed his mind to summon her to the vacant seat at his right, but he might as well have something good to look at if he was forced to suffer his sister's carping.

"H-how was your day, cousin?" Freda asked in failing accents. "Were you practicing your sword skills?"

He opened his mouth to give her a stinging set-down only to notice Aimee look up with interest. "Quintain," he corrected her briefly.

"Practicing your quintain?" Freda quavered doubtfully. "You will have to forgive my ignorance, cousin. Is that the name of some other weapon in your arsenal?"

Feeling Aimee's eyes still on him, he cleared his throat. "'Tis a device for training with the lance," he corrected her grudgingly.

"I see." Freda nodded, looking gratified. Sensing another equally foolish question hovering on her lips, he turned instead to his wife.

"The royal tournament is in three days," he said abruptly. "Will you attend?"

Aimee's face brightened. "I would love to." Her dimple flashed out, distracting him.

"Will any prominent northern houses be in attendance?" Magnatrude asked, looking up quickly.

"Aye, very likely," he answered without taking his eyes off Aimee.

"Then I, too, should like to attend," his sister said in a confrontational tone.

His glance flickered toward her momentarily. "I'm not stopping you."

"How do we go about securing seats?" Aimee asked before Trude could harangue him further. "When Ursula and I attended Kellingford, our hosts, the Wycliffes, arranged it."

"Kellingford?" Konrad repeated. "You attended when?"

"Last October," she replied, looking strangely self-conscious about the fact.

Konrad cast his mind back and remembered his uncharacteristic loss to Renlow last year and frowned. Typical that would have been the tournament she attended. He was still glowering about this as the first course was served, which was a tasty broth served with strips of preserved meats and flatbreads.

Freda cleared her throat. "These seeds," she said, turning over her flatbread. "Are most curious. Flavorsome too," she added hurriedly.

"They are anise and caraway," Aimee explained. "Both are beneficial to the digestion. My father imports and sells many such herbs and spices."

Freda's face fell, and she lapsed into an awkward silence. Really, did she expect his new bride to try to conceal her origins? He shot a sardonic look at his cousin, but she was careful to avoid his gaze.

"I will make sure to let them know you will attend," he said gruffly. "The tournament, I mean."

Aimee looked gratified. He did not look to his sister or cousin. "Perhaps you could suggest a tailor for my sister's use," he said, ignoring the way Trude bridled. "She needs some new gowns made up. My cousin also."

"Oh," twittered Freda. "I am sure my own needs are amply met by my existing wardrobe." He ignored this, as her cuffs were plainly fraying for all to see.

"Of course," Aimee responded. "Mr. Fulcher in Kiln Street is sure to give satisfaction. He is patronized by a good many court folk."

"I am sure—" Magnatrude started stiffly, but he cut her off.

"Have him come to the house as soon as ever he may to attend on whoever has need of him. If Trude has no use for a new gown, then have him see to Freda or your own wants." Both his cousin and sister turned quite crimson at his words, though for different reasons.

"Aye, husband," Aimee said after a moment's pause. "I will send for him directly."

He gave a swift nod, and the second course was set down on the table by a solidly built male and a nervous-looking boy. It was roasted steak in a red wine sauce accompanied by a mushroom plate-pie.

Konrad applied himself to this with such absorption that the lack of table conversation did not unduly bother him. Freda made a few desultory comments to the table at large to which he thought either his sister or wife made murmured reply. He abstained from the final course, a tart of preserved apricots, cherries, and hazelnuts, and quit the table, making his way up to his bedchamber.

Konrad checked on the threshold, thinking for a moment that he had mistaken the room. In addition to the huge platformed bed hung about with its curtains, the room now contained several large and handsome pieces of furniture including a huge cabinet with decorated doors and a spectacularly decorated trunk. He eyed these a moment in silence and then turned to look at the fancy doublet laid across the bottom of the bed. Had Aimee Ankatel presented him with yet another gift?

As if on cue, he heard the tap on the door. Immediately, he knew it was not Jakeman and spun around. "Come in!"

His wife appeared in the doorway, smiling brightly. "My lord, I trust your new furnishings are to your liking?" she enquired politely.

Konrad paused before he made reply. He wondered if now was the moment for some plain speech between them. "Come in," he said slowly. It was a large room, and he gestured vaguely toward the seating area by the window. She surprised him by coming in quite readily and closing the door behind her.

He had expected some trepidation on her behalf, but she showed no unwillingness to be alone with him in a room with a bed. In view of the uneasy memories of last night that had plagued him all day, that did relieve him somewhat. She walked to the center of the room and turned about to face him, tipping her head to one side. "Yes?"

"Be seated," he said and watched her sit in a chair by the window. After a moment, he joined here there, lowering himself into the chair facing hers. "I think we should set some things straight." Instead of looking nervous, she gave him an encouraging smile. Konrad took a deep breath. "I think of this house as your domain," he said flatly. "Just as Bartree Castle will always be mine."

She nodded her head, though he was not sure she took his meaning at all. "You can put whatever you want in this room," he stressed. "I will not object because I do not consider myself to hold any sway here."

She frowned over his words. "My father gave us this house as a wedding gift," she pointed out.

He huffed out a breath. Clearly, she had not taken his meaning. For a man who habitually spoke with brutal frankness, he was finding it damned hard going for some reason. He placed his hands on the arms of the chair. "Look, Aimee, your father was quite open about what he wanted from our union." She blinked but did not speak, so he pressed on. "To speak plain, he wanted a stud for you and a title for his grandchildren."

Instead of turning pale at his blunt speech, as he had imagined she would, she turned instead a little pink. "My father has always liked children," she murmured. This confounded him for a minute, as he had expected her to protest his words.

"Well," he said gruffly. "Be that as it may. I can understand that you might need time to accustom yourself to the position you now find yourself in."

"Find myself in?" she interrupted him. "You misunderstand, my lord. The choice was all mine." She took a deep breath. "My father wanted a good marriage for me, it is true, but it was I who picked you out for my bridegroom."

Konrad stared at her uncomprehendingly. *What?* "But Renlow?" he floundered blankly. "Your sister—I thought—?"

Aimee gazed back at him with a puzzled expression. "What about them?"

"Was Renlow not your intended groom?" he demanded.

Aimee's mouth dropped open. "Sir Renlow?" She shook her head. "No, of course not!" She sounded quite indignant at the notion. "I told my father after Kellingford that it was you I wanted."

Her answer had Konrad reeling. He gazed at her in stupefaction.

"Sir Renlow was *always* intended for Ursula," she stressed carefully, then frowned. "Was that not plain from the outset?"

He cast his mind back to the meal at her father's house. "I do not think your father ever explicitly stated which of you was my intended bride," he admitted slowly.

Aimee blinked. "And you did not think to ask?"

"It didn't really matter," he answered with a shrug and saw the hurt expression that leaped to her eyes before she could disguise it.

"Oh," she said faintly, then swallowed. "So, you assumed Ursula was for you, then?" She twisted her hands in her lap.

"Yes. She was the elder of you two after all." When she said nothing, he added, "As I am older than Renlow." Why did she look suddenly so anxious? he wondered.

"Wh-when did you realize?" she asked in a high, unnatural voice.

Some inner prompting warned him against answering this. He certainly wasn't going to tell her it was in front of the priest, not when she was gazing at him with such an expression of dismay on her pretty face.

"Why?" he asked instead. "Why me?" It hadn't been what he was going to say. He had no idea why he was even asking it.

I told my father it was you I wanted.

The discreet tap at the door almost made him jump out of his skin. "Come in," he barked without thinking, for he recognized the knock as Jakeman's. The door opened, and his servant entered the room. He paused just inside the door, halting with surprise when he found his master was not alone.

"Forgive me, my lord, I did not mean to interrupt."

"My wife was just leaving," Konrad snapped back. Her shoulders slumped, and she stood, directed a brave smile in Jakeman's direction, and exited the room. He stood and turned to watch her leave, unable to stop himself. Jakeman's quietly spoken words did not even register with him. She had set her sights on him after Kellingford.

Kellingford? Where he had lost! He could not quite comprehend it.

"My lord?" Jakeman asked hesitantly.

Konrad waved an impatient hand. "What was it you wanted?" he asked irritably. "Speak up, man! I can barely hear you!"

Inexplicably, for the next hour or so, Konrad found himself unable to settle to anything, even oiling his blade. He flung it away from him in disgust and found himself considering striding down the corridor in search of his wife. What the hells had she meant by telling him that?

Why in the name of the gods would anyone think him a matrimonial prize after watching his defeat at Kellingford? If anything, that was the one time that idealistic young fool Renlow had appeared in a positive light. Did lovely Aimee Ankatel think consoling losers a more amusing role than rewarding victors? Gazing about the bedchamber at the lavish bed hangings and luxurious furniture did not make him one whit more reconciled to his role as her stud.

Maybe she did see herself in the role of the benevolent benefactress, righting all his wrongs and earning his undying gratitude. And if so, what of it? Women often got foolish ideas into their heads, or so he had heard said, by other men at least. Even if she had thought to act the role of benevolent wife, a voice whispered in his head, did she deserve the punishment of a rude and neglectful bridegroom? She was young and overindulged, but she was not spoiled or arrogant. On the contrary…she was… Words failed him at this point. He didn't know what she was precisely, but she hadn't deserved him for a bridegroom, that was for damned sure.

To escape his growing unease, he found himself, half an hour later, setting out for the knights' banquet at the palace. He reasoned to himself that he would at least glean some useful information about his competitors there. Once among his peers, he would shake off the discomfort of his new wedded status and forget the disquiet his temporary luxurious lodgings inspired in him.

However, once stood in the feasting hall, he found himself immediately regretting the impulse to attend. He was far from gregarious by nature, and functions such as this one left him cold. He performed his duty by making his bow to the southern king and retreated to a dark corner to fester as he usually did when surrounded by revelry. A passing servant offered him a

127

drinking vessel, and he took it, more for appearance's sake than anything else.

As he stood among the shadows, Konrad's eye traveled over the familiar banners hanging from the rafters, proclaiming the participants in the upcoming Summer Tournament. His own hung as usual with the top five, denoting his anticipated performance, but to his surprise, he saw Sir Roland Vawdrey's shield now included a coronet. When had that bastard succeeded to a title?

As his eye wandered, he realized Vawdrey's was not the only banner to have altered. Orde's remained the same colors of black and white, but his heraldic device had changed altogether. He was just pondering the meaning of this when a voice hailed him boisterously.

"Kentigern!" Turning, he found Roland Vawdrey heading in his direction. In his muscular arms he held a swaddled bundle which he thrust toward Konrad with a proud smile. "My daughter."

Konrad gazed down at the pink face of the infant. It was scrunched up in an expression of irritable discomfort. Above its face was a shock of black hair. When her eyes did force their way open, they looked murky and seemed unable to focus on either of them, before closing again.

She looked rather like a baby field mouse to Konrad's mind, all blobby and indistinct. He groped about for some comment that her sire would find acceptable, but his mind was a perfect blank. It wasn't even a son and heir. He marveled at Vawdrey's expression of awed gratification as he gazed down at his firstborn.

"Her name is Agnes," Vawdrey told him in hushed tones.

"A fine name," Konrad managed after a moment's silence. "Named for her mother's sake?"

Roland shot him a look of annoyance. "My wife's name is Eden," he pointed out.

"Oh." Konrad shifted onto his other foot, but still Vawdrey hovered. "Why has your banner changed?" he asked abruptly.

Vawdrey looked at him blankly. "Oh, that," he said in the manner of one recalling something wholly insignificant. "Been made a viscount. Want a hold of her?" he offered in the manner of one bestowing some grand favor. It took Konrad a moment to catch his meaning.

"Gods, no!" When the new father looked instantly incensed, Konrad added uncomfortably, "I know nothing of babies, I might grip her too tight or drop her."

Vawdrey's shoulders relaxed at once. "You'll soon learn when you've one of your own," he commented with a worldly wise air.

Kentigern was so flabbergasted by this notion that he just stared first at Vawdrey and then at the baby. "How old is it?" he asked grudgingly.

"Two months. A good size, you'll agree," Vawdrey boasted. Was it? Konrad gazed at it doubtfully.

"None of Mason's hellspawn were half so impressive," Roland continued, gazing foolishly at his daughter. "As for Oswald's, his twins were tiny for *ages*."

"How many has Cadwallader got now?" Konrad asked, thinking with dislike of Mason Vawdrey, who been a large reason why the north had fallen. Fucking bastard had been an inspired general.

"Four," Roland answered absently. "Lily, Meg, Archie, and Ben."

"Two sons?" Kentigern observed with disfavor. Stood to reason. Lucky bastard had always fallen on his feet.

"Not as pretty as Agnes," Vawdrey replied, dipping his head closer to the baby and using a doting voice that Konrad could only suppose he reserved for speaking to it with.

Konrad made a revolted face. *Who on earth wanted pretty sons?* Vawdrey was losing the fucking plot. He glanced at the child again. "How long before it walks?"

"Eh? Oh years, I expect," Roland replied airily. When the baby's mouth started working and she gave a whimper, he straightened up. "Looking to feed," he said hurriedly. "I'll take her back to her mother."

Konrad nodded with relief, and Vawdrey scurried off.

"Did he try to get you to hold it?" asked a voice from his left, which was his blind side. He wheeled about to find Garman Orde regarding him wryly.

"What?"

"The baby," Orde spelled out.

Konrad grunted. Why the fuck was Orde now wanting to talk about babies? "What's with the new banner?" he asked, redirecting the conversation by nodding toward the pennants at the far end of the hall.

"New title," Orde explained briefly. "My grandfather died."

"Your grandfather? Who was he?"

"Earl of Twyford."

130

"Your grandfather was the Earl of Twyford?" Konrad was honestly surprised he had not heard tell of it before. Twyford was an old and venerated northern title. Unlike Vawdrey, Orde was a countryman of his and a fellow northerner. They had served in King Magnur's army together, but he had certainly known nothing of his noble lineage.

Orde grunted in affirmation but showed no interest in pursuing the topic. "You hear about de Bussell and the princess?" he asked.

Kentigern stiffened. "I did."

"You hear he took her with him last month to compete at Areley Kings?"

Konrad squinted at him. "*What?*"

Orde nodded. "He won too. Made her tournament queen."

"The fuck he did."

A brief smile touched Orde's lips. "Saw it with my own eyes."

"He beat you?"

Orde shook his head. "I went out early. Injury. He beat de Crecy in the final round."

Kentigern absorbed this a moment in stunned silence. "De Crecy was having an off day, I suppose. It happens."

Orde shook his head. "De Crecy was *not* having an off day. De Bussell fought like a demon. Lenora has this theory that old Armand has never really had his heart in the game before now."

His heart? Kentigern lowered his goblet. He squinted at Orde. Was this bastard quoting his wife to him now, like she was some kind of expert on jousting? Surprisingly, he knew full well who Orde's wife was. Everyone knew who Lenora Montmayne was—or had been. The fairest maid in all Karadok.

She had lost that title when the red pox had swept through the capital the summer before, her famous face falling victim to its ravages. Or so popular opinion held forth. Kentigern had regarded the pock marks and reddened skin on her face with skepticism. They were not scars as he knew them.

Still, he held a certain grudging admiration for Lenora Orde, as she was now known. Or rather, the Countess of Twyford. He might go so far as to admit, only to himself, of course, that he even felt *some* measure of fellow feeling toward her. One of his fondest memories was awarding her the winner's garland at Roget's Ford early that year, just to piss off her husband, who had been first runner-up.

He recalled the look of murderous rage in Orde's eye now and had to stifle a smirk into his wine goblet. In truth, the awarding of the tournament wreath was a mere afterthought to Konrad. He usually bestowed it wherever it would cause the most irritation. He had given it to Vawdrey's wife in the past too, much to her husband's ire.

"Heard you'd got married," Orde commented.

"What of it?"

An uncharacteristic smile tugged at Orde's lips. "No need to spring to your defense," he muttered. "It happens to the best of us."

"What does it have to do with you anyway?" Konrad demanded belligerently.

"Naught." Orde shrugged, with as close an expression of affability that Konrad had ever seen on that surly bastard's face. "You're not the only newlywed here tonight, as it happens."

Guessing he was referring to Renlow, Konrad glanced about for his brother-in-law.

"You seen de Crecy?" Orde continued.

Konrad turned back to Orde in surprise. "De Crecy? I'd heard he wasn't attending."

"He showed up today with his new bride in tow," Orde said, lowering his voice. He cocked his brow and nodded in the opposite direction to the one Konrad had been looking in.

Jeffree de Crecy was sat glowering across at a female in a drab gown of brown wool with a matching brown veil. Even Konrad knew that only veils of crisp white linen were worn at court. She looked like a nun, a plain-faced nun moreover, and a total mismatch for de Crecy, who he loathed but had to admit was a handsome bastard, with his short blond beard and piercing blue eyes.

"*That's* his wife?" Konrad asked blankly. He couldn't even make out her hair color, it was scraped back so severely behind the dark veil.

"No one can make it out," Orde continued in a low voice. "He looks as though he'd like to strangle her, and you should hear the way he speaks to her."

Catching sight of the angry glance DeCrecy flung at her across the table, Konrad felt a strange stirring of pity for the wretched wench. She looked poor as a church mouse. Magnatrude's gowns were shabby, but you could see that at one time they had been grand enough. De Crecy's wife looked like she would be more at home on a farm than at a king's court.

The least that arrogant bastard could have done was buy her a new gown for the occasion, Konrad thought dispassionately. He watched as she lifted her head and met her husband's furious

133

gaze full on. She lifted her glass to toast her new husband with an expression which Konrad could not quite place. De Crecy turned crimson and rose unsteadily from his seat to fling away, leaving her sat quite alone. For an instant, Konrad could have sworn he saw the woman smile to herself, then she obscured his view by sipping at her wine. Mayhap this time he would award the crown to de Crecy's bride? That would have the bastard choking on his own spleen.

"Where is she, then?" Orde asked, snapping him out of his observations.

"Who?"

"*Your* new bride," he elaborated. "Everyone's dying for a glimpse of her."

"Not here," Konrad responded briefly. It occurred to him that it would make perfect sense to everyone if de Crecy's bride was Aimee, while his own was that rather homely creature sat by herself.

"You did not bring her to the feast?" For some reason, Orde looked surprised by this.

"It is not obligatory to bring one's spouse, that I'm aware."

Orde directed a pitying look at him. "'Tis plain to see you are but newly wed," he murmured.

As Konrad could think of no reply to this, he merely scowled before glancing around. "I do not see your own wife," he pointed out. *For once.*

"She's seven months along now," Orde replied promptly. "And long tired by this hour. She should probably have stayed at home, but..." He shrugged as though he had little say in the matter.

Something about his indulgent expression made Konrad uncomfortable. Orde had gone soft. "Seems to me *you* should be the one carting Vawdrey's infant about," he pointed out snidely. "To grow accustomed to it!"

"Oh, I have," Orde responded comfortably. "You forget, my wife is first cousin to Vawdrey's."

It would be hard to forget something he had not been aware of in the first place, Konrad thought, but did not voice.

Orde drained his cup. "Lenora will be waiting for me to join her in our chamber." He clapped a hand to Konrad's shoulder, startling him. "I'd best be joining her, or she'll be sound asleep."

With this startling announcement, Orde turned on his heel and made his way out of the hall. Konrad gazed after him blankly. The whole world was going mad, he thought. Then he noticed Douglas Farleigh making a beeline for him and helped himself to another flagon of mead. The feast had not turned out to be the distraction he had hoped for.

11

Aimee woke the next morning and turned her head to look at the empty space beside her in the large bed. Lord Kentigern had not joined her the previous night. She had not really expected him to, but even so, it was a disappointment. While the loss of her virginity had not been exactly pleasurable, Old Janet had told her that such things improved with practice. But how were they supposed to practice when her husband now shunned her bed?

She washed and dressed slowly, admiring her new canopy which the carpenter had set up the previous day. Her green and gold bed curtains were now hung, giving the room a cheerful and feminine air. She would buy some matching cushions and place them in her window seat, she told herself in an attempt to lift her spirits.

Such thoughts did not distract her for long. Again, the uncomfortable reflections that had kept her awake into the early hours flooded back to haunt her. Lord Kentigern had thought he was marrying her sister and not her. It had been the offer of Ursula's hand that he had accepted, not Aimee's.

The realization was a blow. After all, Ursula was quiet and discreet, attributes much admired in a wife. Aimee was neither of these things. Would he have turned down the offer of her hand had he known he was being wed to the younger and not the elder sister? she found herself wondering with a sick feeling in her stomach.

Golda's head peered around the door. "Tailor's here, milady," she announced. "I've shown him into that small chamber at the end of the passage."

"The tailor?" Aimee repeated blankly, lowering her hair comb. Then she remembered she had sent a message around to Mr. Fulcher the previous evening. "Oh, of course." He had responded awfully quickly, she thought with surprise. Although she and Ursula had been good patrons these past two years, she certainly did not remember him responding the very next day to a summons. Then she remembered her new status of Baroness Kentigern.

"Golda, could you please inform Mistresses Magnatrude and Freda that the tailor awaits them?"

A martial gleam entered Golda's eye. "I'd be happy to, milady," she said with relish and disappeared.

Aimee finished arranging her hair and made her way below stairs to break her fast. Five minutes later, a harassed-looking Freda came tripping into the dining chamber.

"Oh dear, has the tailor indeed arrived?" she asked, practically wringing her hands at this news.

Aimee looked up from where she was sat. "Does my sister-in-law not wish to engage his services?" she asked calmly. "If so, then my husband's wishes were made quite plain. You must consult with him instead, Freda."

Freda bit her lip. "Oh, but I am sure she is merely in need of some persuasion," she said, looking anxious.

"Not from me," Aimee pointed out wryly. "I doubt there is anything I could say that would induce Magnatrude's cooperation."

Such straightforward speech was plainly too much for Freda, who looked quite appalled by her words. "Oh, but she would never mean to give offence to Konrad's wife," she said vehemently, two spots of color appearing in her gaunt cheeks.

"If that were the case," Aimee found herself retorting smartly, "then she would not have rejected my gift out of hand. Neither of you would have." Aimee pressed her lips together resolutely. She knew one thing for certain and that was that she would be making no more overtures of friendship toward haughty Magnatrude.

Freda looked to be on the verge of tears. "I never—that is, it was not my intent to cause offence, I do assure you, Aimee!"

"What else did you think it would do? To return both gifts unopened?" Aimee asked, genuinely flummoxed.

Freda sniffled. "It was only that—well, it is the bride who should receive gifts from the family she goes into, not the other way around."

The answer to this was so obvious, Aimee did not feel the need to point it out. Aimee had received no such gifts. She lowered her cup of ale, directing a very level gaze at the nervous woman. "Be that as it may, another such opportunity lies in front of you now, Freda," she said gravely. "You are free, of course, to similarly reject Lord Kentigern's gift of new gowns—" An involuntary sound of distress burst from Freda's lips, interrupting her.

"Oh no! I could not possibly do that!"

"Then your way forward must be clear to you," Aimee told her. "You must walk into the chamber at the end of the passage and consult with the tailor forthwith."

The color on Freda's face ebbed and flowed as she considered this. "Yes," she muttered after an agonized minute or two. "Yes, you are right." She flung back her head and straightened her narrow shoulders to make for the doorway. Once there, she halted and turned back with an agonized expression. "'Tis only that I should not have the smallest notion what to ask for," she confessed. "It has been so long since I have had anything new, and I never did have the smallest notion of taste."

Aimee looked at her with surprise. She had not thought that noble families worried overmuch about such things. After all, no fabrics or trimming were barred to their exalted status, save perhaps for ermine. "Should you wish me to accompany you?" she asked, hesitant to make the offer only to be rejected again.

"Oh yes!" Freda said, turning toward her gratefully. "Oh, would you, Aimee?"

Rather than speak an affirmative, Aimee rose at once from her seat, pushing away the remains of her toasted bread, and accompanied Freda out into the corridor.

They then spent the next two hours with Mr. Fulcher and his two assistants, looking at sample fabrics and discussing the most flattering silhouette for Freda's tall, rather stooping frame. Mr. Fulcher had been keen to urge a particularly beautifully patterned sleeve, but Aimee had deduced these would only be woven after Freda's measurements were taken.

"The first gown will need to be made from fabrics you already have woven on your premises, Mr. Fulcher. For Freda has need of it in three days' time." As expected, this reduced the tailor to impassioned denials that such a thing was even possible. As Freda held her breath, Aimee alternately soothed him with promises of renumeration and reminders of the many gowns she and Ursula had purchased from him over the last two years.

Mr. Fulcher climbed down off his high horse and grudgingly gave a promise that one finished gown decorated at the neck and cuffs with finger-woven braid would be delivered on the eve of the first day of the tournament. Freda was ecstatic and even shed a tear or two over the news.

They finally settled on an underdress of red silk with a decorated surcoat to be worn over this of a gold and brown pattern. The surcoat had open sides to show the long trumpet sleeves of the gown underneath.

Freda had drifted back upstairs after her measurements were taken, as though she were in a complete dream, leaving Aimee to sort out the details of a second gown to follow at a later date. Remembering the well-worn dress Freda had worn to her wedding, she selected a dark green fabric decorated with silver thread. Aimee had just returned to the main room to take a seat before the fireplace when she was surprised by Freda's sudden reappearance.

"Mr. Fulcher has just taken his leave, but we can always send Unwin with a message if there was some detail you forgot to mention," she said, looking up.

"Oh no, no," Freda said distractedly. "I am sure you thought of everything." She stood hesitating a moment before coming forward with faltering steps. When she reached Aimee, she thrust out one bony clenched fist. "This is for you," she said awkwardly.

Aimee blinked at her before opening her palm below Freda's. The older woman released her fingers, and an object fell into Aimee's outstretched hand. It was a large silver brooch in the shape of a heart with a hand closed about it. A scroll around it proclaimed "Heart Be Trewe," and there were three silver circles at the base of the brooch from which further adornment must have once hung down.

"It used to be a good deal more impressive," Freda admitted anxiously. "Apparently, there used to be small silver chains that hung down from the bottom with three precious jewels, but the chains were very delicate, and the jewels were lost long before it was given to me." When Aimee remained silent, Freda

140

pressed on. "I assure you it is mine to give. My grandmother received it on the occasion of her marriage."

Aimee looked up. "Are you sure you wish to give it now to me if it is a family heirloom?" she asked.

"Of course! Nothing could be more appropriate!" Freda assured her. "My grandmother was bride to a Bartree, the same as you now are. Unless," she hesitated, "you do not find it congenial to accept my gift, in light of, well—" She broke off her words in embarrassment.

Aimee closed her fingers about the brooch. "I am very happy to receive your gift, cousin," she said. "But you must now accept one from me also as is the custom of my mother's people."

Freda swallowed and nodded, and Aimee made for the oaken cabinet that stood in the far corner of the room. She brought both parcels she had placed there and presented them to Freda. "Which one would you like?"

Freda's eyes darted to her. "It does not matter? One is for Magnatrude, is it not?"

"It does not signify," Aimee replied firmly. "Take your pick."

Lightly, Freda touched the parcel done up with yellow ribbon, and Aimee passed it to her. "Shall I open it now?" the older woman asked self-consciously.

"It is up to you. You can open it in the privacy of your own room if you wish."

Freda hesitated and then carried the parcel over to the table where she carefully undid the knot of ribbons and revealed a fine long strand of gleaming amber beads. "Oh!" she breathed, lifting them out of the paper. "These are beautiful!" She turned

141

to look back at Aimee over her shoulder. "Are you quite sure that it is alright for me to accept so expensive a gift?"

"Yes, of course." Secretly, Aimee was pleased that Freda had taken the amber beads which she thought were far nicer than the red coral ones in the second package. "Try them on."

With hands that shook slightly, Freda slipped the rope of beads over her head. So long was the strand that it extended down to her narrow waist. With careful hands, Freda twisted the beads and looped them once again about her neck until they hung in a double strand. "How does that look?" she asked, turning to show Aimee with a faintly self-conscious air.

"They look lovely."

With an expression of wonder on her face, Freda examined the round polished beads. "Each one is so perfectly matched in size," she marveled.

Aimee nodded. "Do you happen to recall the lapis lazuli necklace I wore on the occasion of my wedding?"

"Oh yes," Freda agreed, nodding. "I remember admiring it excessively. Such rich blue beads."

"They were from the same merchant. Ursula and I became connoisseurs of beads when Father made his money. As the daughters of a merchant, we were not permitted to wear jewels and furs, but fine beads were not objectionable."

Freda looked a little disconcerted by Aimee's frankness. "Oh— er, yes, I see," she mumbled. "And now, of course, you may wear whatever jewels you so desire. What a pity that the family jewels were plundered during the war."

Aimee, who, prior to this moment, had heard no mention of any family jewels, made no reply. Freda closed the distance

142

between them with three impetuous steps. "Thank you, Aimee," she said, placing her hands lightly on Aimee's upper arms. She kissed Aimee's cheek, then looked a little startled when Aimee impulsively returned the gesture.

Clearly, her new kinswoman was not used to physical affection. "Oh dear," Freda said, pressing a thin hand to the slight swell of her chest. "I fear I must lie down awhile before supper. I am almost overcome with all the happenings of this afternoon."

"Why do you not lie awhile on that settle over there?" Aimee suggested, gesturing to a long wooden bench with a high back and sides which had a long cushion almost like a mattress along it. "I can sit nearby and make sure you are not disturbed."

Freda looked extremely touched by this solicitous offer, and after a moment's dithering, allowed herself to be shepherded in that direction and arranged onto the bench with her feet up and her head propped against another cushion. Freda closed her eyes with a faint sigh and lay as still as the dead while Aimee stabbed at her embroidery.

Much like her playing of the symphonia, embroidery was a recent pastime that Aimee had adopted since her stay last year at the Wycliffes'. As such, it was not something that came at all easily to her. She squinted at it now and wondered if the horse she was attempting did not look rather more like a hound.

Lowering her needle, Aimee glanced over at her new cousin-in-law. Freda did not seem robust, she thought, for she could not be much above forty years or thereabouts. Her untidy hair was an indeterminate shade, but there were no gray hairs present, and Aimee wondered if her husband's cousin had not suffered from poor health in her youth leaving her rather delicate.

She picked up once more the heavy silver brooch Freda had given her, examining it. It was clearly well-made by a master

143

craftsman, with many fine details. It was a shame that it should show so many signs of ill use, Aimee thought, turning it over. The heart showed many dents and dings, and the pretty embellishment that ran along the edges was bent and twisted in several places. She wondered if the jewels Freda had said used to hang from the empty holes had been roughly wrenched from the brooch. After all, the Bartrees had suffered many losses during the late war. Had Freda's brooch also been a casualty of violence?

A soft tap at the door had her sharply turning her head, but it was only Golda.

"It's the master, Miss Aimee," she said and moved aside to make way.

Aimee's heart lurched, but it was her father who came into the room. She instantly felt annoyed with herself at the instant stab of disappointment she felt.

"Father!" she said, jumping out of her seat and running to meet him with an embrace to make up for her unfilial thoughts.

"My Aimee!" he greeted her jovially before looking about. "Why have you not had a fire lit in here?"

"Father, Freda is sleeping," Aimee cautioned, lifting her finger to her lips, but Freda was already sitting up, bleary-eyed.

"Oh!" Freda exclaimed, swinging her legs over the side of the bench. "Oh, do forgive me, Mr. Ankatel." She rose to her feet, looking rather flustered as she touched a hand to her untidy hair.

"Nothing to forgive," Gerold assured her heartily. "I like to take a rest myself of an afternoon. How are you, Mistress Freda?"

"So very kind," Freda murmured distractedly, straightening her skirts. "Yes, I am very well, I thank you."

"Well, well, I am glad to see you keeping my Aimee company," he said genially as Aimee directed him to a seat. "You ladies are keeping yourselves occupied this afternoon?"

Golda appeared as Freda gave a somewhat incoherent reply and set down a plate of spiced biscuits before them.

"But what is this?" Aimee's father asked, leaning forward to pick up the silver brooch from the table.

"'Tis a gift from Freda to welcome me into the Bartree family," Aimee explained when Freda looked rather tongue-tied by the question. Her father regarded Freda with warmth.

"A vastly handsome piece," Gerold said, weighing it in his hand. "Substantial too, it's really quite heavy. It looks to be incomplete somehow?" He looked across at Freda after examining the holes carefully.

"Oh, er, sadly, yes," she stammered. "There used to be three matching gemstones suspended from the little holes, but the— er, the passage of years was such…" She trailed off into an embarrassed silence.

"Well, the fixings are intact, and the brooch could be restored easily enough."

"Oh, but, Father, it is still a fine brooch as it stands," Aimee said hastily, not wishing to cause Freda offence.

He pocketed the brooch and tipped her a wink. "You leave it to me," he said. "We'll soon have it good as new, and mayhap you can wear it to that tournament you're so looking forward to. In two days' time, is it not?"

"Oh, but—" Aimee bit off her words as her father patted her shoulder. She did not know how to explain that an old and venerated family such as the Bartrees did not seem to prize newness as a virtue.

"How very kind your father is, to be sure," Freda whispered when Gerold took his leave of them an hour later. "I am quite astounded at the thought of his restoring the brooch for you. Never did I think that one day it might be restored to its former glory."

"You shall not mind, Freda?" Aimee asked.

"Oh no, of course not!" Freda looked quite shocked. "It is a very great honor your father does my gift." Freda sighed. "I suppose I had better go and check on Magnatrude." She sounded rather guilty. "I have left her alone for a good deal of the day."

"It will not be long now until supper," Aimee consoled her, and Freda's expression lightened.

"Yes, that is true." Freda fingered her amber beads distractedly, and Aimee wondered if she would remove them before joining Magnatrude in the oaken parlor. After all, such a necklace was sure to be noticed.

However, when both ladies descended to supper an hour later, Freda was still wearing her new string of beads. She had made a valiant attempt to tidy her hair too, which surprised Aimee, for she had found at least six of Freda's hairpins strewn across the settle after she had left. A much-abused set of pins they were too, sadly twisted and bent out of shape. It was small wonder they could not hold their mistress's tresses in place.

Aimee wondered if Freda would accept the gift of some new ones or if that would be too much too soon. She realized by now that Freda's role was that of poor relation and companion. Freda greeted her shyly as both ladies slid into the same seats they had occupied the previous evening.

"We await Lord Kentigern," Aimee explained, even as she heard his approaching footsteps in the passageway outside. Turning her head, she instructed Unwin to run through to the kitchens and inform the servants they were ready for their meal. The boy nodded and ran out through the door at the opposite end of the room.

12

Konrad was quietly watchful at supper. It did not go unnoticed by him that Magnatrude was directing her conversation toward only him these days, while Aimee and Freda conversed quietly with one another. His wife's manner toward him was polite but more subdued than usual. She did not brighten like before whenever her eye happened to fall on him. He hadn't even realized she did that until she stopped doing it. For some reason, the change irked him.

Why the fuck had his loss at Kellingford made him a prospective bridegroom as far as she was concerned?

He felt an absurd impulse to bellow the question out loud to her now in front of everyone. What would she say? She liked losers? He threw down his bread and glared ferociously down the table in a manner that made Freda, happening to glance up at that moment, gasp and drop her spoon.

"Whatever is the matter, Konrad?" Magnatrude asked, catching sight of his expression.

"I was thinking of something else," he muttered ill-naturedly.

"Well, kindly direct your murderous glances elsewhere," his sister requested with a shudder. "We poor females are not used to such a terrifying sight across the supper table."

Aimee glanced up at this with a spark in her eye and looked, for a moment, as though she would join the fray. He felt a sharp stab of disappointment assail him when she did not. Had she been going to defend his right to scowl at his own supper table?

Absurdly, he found himself wondering if they might not be afforded the privacy of dining alone once in a while. He could ask her anything he damned well liked if his plaguey female relatives weren't cluttering up the place.

When he announced he was retiring for the evening, his wife bade him a good night and made no attempt to delay him with conversation or any other tactic as she had before. He frowned over this as he left the room.

Something was not quite right about how things were running; he felt it deep in his bones. As he mounted the staircase to his room, he spied one of the servants coming down. "Send Ingrid to me," he rapped out, sending the lad scurrying.

He was dragging a shaving blade down his unscarred cheek when Ingrid appeared in the doorway with her sleeves rolled up and a disagreeable expression on her face. This was nothing out of the ordinary for Ingrid. She opened her mouth but got no further than "I'm in the midst of—" before he interrupted her.

"Never mind that now!" he replied smartly, half turning toward her but keeping his eye on the mirrored glass. For some reason, he was attempting to keep his beard in some sort of order since his marriage. He didn't want to examine his motives for this too closely. "I want to know what's going on in this household."

Ingrid plunked her hands on her hips. "How do ye mean?" she stalled, looking suspicious.

"You know full well what I mean."

She shot him a wary look. "Among the womenfolk, ye mean?" she asked cautiously.

At her words, he briefly closed his eyes. He had known a houseful of fool women would be a damned nuisance. "Aye," he growled. "The womenfolk." *Godsdamn it.* He turned back to the glass.

Ingrid shrugged. "They ain't fightin' it out like what they'm s'posed to, that's all."

He frowned at her in the mirror. "I don't take your meaning."

She rolled her eyes. "A'course you don't, milord. Ain't got the first idea, have you, on account of your being a *man*." She pursed her lips, and he wasn't sure she wouldn't have spat after the word *man* if she hadn't been in his presence.

He lowered his blade and glowered at her in their reflection. "They aren't fighting it out," he repeated bitingly. "Explain to me what you mean by that."

"Well, there's a natural order and there's a pecking order in any fine house, ain't there?" When he continued to look blank, she sighed. "First ways, you've got the established order. Man at the head and mistress after him and such like." Ingrid started to warm to her theme. "But behind that, you got the pecking order, which is assumed by nature, so to speak."

Konrad picked up a cloth and dabbed at his cheek but kept his eyes on Ingrid. "Go on."

"Like sows," she said. "They'll go as far as to draw blood when it comes to showing dominance." *Sows?* When he continued to look unconvinced, she tried again. "Let me put it this way, consider the old place." He grunted. She meant Bartree Castle, of course. "Your stepmother, the Lady Adela, was official mistress of the house for a seven year, but everyone knew as she never had the running of the place. Mistress Magnatrude always kept the keys on her chatelaine, and she guarded them close by her. That's why she never married. Why should she? When she already had a home of her own where her word was law."

"Are you trying to tell me that Trude is trying to wrest the reins from my wife?" he asked, starting the tricky business of shaving the carved-up side of his face. He should just let Jakeman see to this, he thought as he navigated the scars. He made a far better job of it than he ever did. But he was always leery of letting people get up close to the left side of his face. It made him feel vulnerable.

Ingrid hesitated. "No," she said after a moment's consideration and scratched her head. "No, I wouldn't say as Mistress Magnatrude's done that." She frowned. "Truthfully, she ain't shown a morsel of interest in how this place is run."

Konrad considered Ingrid shrewdly in the looking glass. "Thinks a townhouse is beneath her interest, does she?" he grunted, thinking of Trude's grand manner. He pulled a face. "Of course she does." He dabbed a cloth at his cheek, deciding that would have to do, and turned to fully face her. "So, if she's not trying to lord it over Aimee, then wherein lies the problem?"

Ingrid rubbed her nose. "Like I said, they ain't fighting it out." At his expression, she plunked her hands on her hips. "It's like this. Your sister ain't letting the new baroness take her rightful place in rank above her. But the new mistress, she ain't the sort to be ridden roughshod over. She's got plenty about her, alright." She gave a chuckle. "I seed that alright when you sent me to tend her after your wedding night. 'I bleeds more on me courses, Ingrid,' that's what she said. 'Let him have his sheets changed, if he wants, you let me alone. I sat in a bath all afternoon, and I ain't a'takin of one now! A washcloth will do very well for naught but a spot of blood.'"

Konrad felt his color rise. "That's enough, Ingrid!" he snapped. The old woman snorted. For a moment, he considered dismissing the impudent old witch. "Just how would Trude

151

deny my wife's rightful place?" he demanded instead impatiently. Without preamble, she told him. "So Trude spends her day skulking above stairs?" he clarified.

Ingrid nodded comfortably. "Taken that little oaken parlor for her own domain, she has." Ingrid paused heavily as though debating telling him something. "And she's been sending out messages and greetings and such like today and all."

"Messages?"

Ingrid nodded. "She heard as how the Strethneals are in Caer-Lyoness."

Konrad's eyebrows rose. "My sister would surely not be so brazen as to invite callers to another woman's house without performing the correct introductions," he said heavily.

"Happen she don't think of it as Lady Kentigern's house," Ingrid sniffed. "Happen, she thinks of it as yours." Konrad bristled, but the servant rattled on before he could correct this misconception. "But as it happens, Mistress Magnatrude had a reply from the countess the self-same day, inviting her to call on them on the morrow."

"The Strethneals have lodgings in town?"

"They's taken quarters at the palace," Ingrid replied with some malicious satisfaction.

"What?" He did not even try to conceal his astonishment at this development. The Strethneals had always been staunch supporters of the Blechmarsh claim. For them to take up positions as courtiers now at the southern court surprised him.

"They're not the only northern nobles here, neither!" Ingrid carried on. "The Martindales is here too, at the palace."

Konrad grunted. Everyone knew Guy Randall was enamored of his southern wife. Consequently, their presence at court was no surprise. The Strethneals though… Times were changing, he reflected. Presumably, they were here for the tournament. He wondered if Princess Una would be in attendance and felt the familiar cold prickle of shame that washed over him when he thought of the fate of their northern princess. He had done nothing to save her from her unworthy marriage.

He had lost half his sight and endured horrific wounds in battle to defend the northern standard, but when it came to the fate of that ill-starred damsel, he had turned his back on the last of the Blechmarshes. The monarchs he had pledged his life to defend.

Was his sister in the right of it? Should he have competed to win Una's hand? There was no actual bar to northern entrants to the fray, though common opinion had been that Wymer would ne'er have allowed a former follower to win her hand. The fact of the matter was that Konrad had shrunk from the notion of spending the rest of his life with a constant reminder of all that he had lost.

He was ashamed of his behavior—that was the stark truth. He had made damn sure he was on the wrong side of the country when that fateful May Day tournament had taken place. He had spent a full week roaring drunk, holed up in a secluded hunting lodge.

What would he have done with the princess if he *had* won her anyway? Neither carting her from one tournament to another seemed right, nor leaving her to rot at Bartree Lodge with his increasingly embittered sister.

He dried off his face. It was a moot point now in any case. Both his and the princess's fate were sealed. He peered at the mirror and wondered how his bride could look him so squarely in the eye without flinching. So lost in thought was he that only

Ingrid's wheezing cough roused him from his ponderings. "Send my sister up to me," he said shortly.

Magnatrude took her sweet time making her way up from the floor below. By the time she knocked on his door, he had long finished his ablutions and was glancing into the cavernous cabinet that Jakeman had stored his clothes in. All his garments fitted neatly into one corner of the thing.

"Come in," he called back over his shoulder, and his sister came into the room, closing the door smartly behind her.

"My, what a grand bedchamber," she commented. "You must have the best in the house. Goodness," she commented wryly, looking down at the fancy doublet he had found laid on his bed that evening. "Your taste in clothing has grown a good deal grander than I recall."

"And yours a good deal shabbier," he responded, fastening the cupboard door shut and turning to survey her.

She bridled at his words. "I am not ashamed of the clothes on my back," she said, lifting her chin. "They have done me sterling service this past decade."

"Should you like to join a nunnery, Trude?" he asked forthrightly, making his sister gasp. "It could be easily arranged, and shabby black gowns won't raise an eyebrow there." He paused a moment before adding conversationally, "Was it your intention to make a show of me before the Strethneals with your mean apparel?"

She turned a dull red at that. "Someone has been talking," she muttered. "Ingrid, of course. Her first loyalty was always to you." He made no reply, as the matter of Ingrid's loyalty was obvious. It would belong, of course, to her liege lord. "You do not wish me to meet with the Strethneals?"

154

"I simply fail to see the need for all the secrecy. Why are you shutting yourself away all day in one room until my return of an evening?"

"I don't know what you mean!" she flung back at him. "I live very quietly at the lodge and am not used to the society of other women!"

Konrad snorted. "Yet you crave the society of the Countess of Strethneal." When she did not speak, he added, "Freda, too, shares your circumstances, yet she does not scorn my wife's company."

Trude's mouth twisted. "I always forget how confrontational you are," she mused. "It's a shame, brother, that you could not have brought this same fighting spirit to the May Day tournament last year." So, there it was. Evidently, she had still not forgiven him for that.

"A strange wish considering your avowed aversion to female company. Should you have liked a fellow inmate at Bartree Lodge, sister?" Konrad growled. "Another spectator to the slow degradation of our former home? Knowing how terrible you believe your own fate, you think Princess Una has not yet suffered enough that she should share in it?"

Trude flushed. "It would be better than the fate that has overtaken her," she flung at him.

Konrad shrugged. "De Bussell is an amiable enough fellow. I daresay his company is far preferable to my own."

His sister's breath hissed through her teeth. "That southerner is not fit to clean her shoes let alone to warm her bed!"

Konrad snorted. "What do you know of bed-warmings? If you had not been so capricious, you would have been wed years ago."

"You say to me?" she seethed. "You? Who was jilted just as I was! I would have thought your own experience would ensure some fellow feeling, but you are as cruel in this as everything else!"

"Spare me the histrionics, sister. Even without the intercession of the war, I doubt you would have wed Kimarne. You bickered more than you were ever in accord."

"How dare you speak his name in front of me!"

"And as for my own experience," Konrad continued dryly. "I consider the fact I never married to be a blessing. Grace Fultree would have been miserable indeed these last six years, rattling around Bartree Lodge with you!"

"Any wife of yours would be miserable!" Trude raged. "For you have a flinty heart and a cold, intractable nature!"

Konrad laughed. "Yet my wife seems content enough," he pointed out with a shrug.

"Oh yes," agreed Magnatrude. "She is vastly pleased with herself! But mark you, 'tis only because she does not know any better!"

The humor fell from his face. "Watch your words," he warned in a low voice, and to do her justice, his sister looked instantly contrite.

"I did not mean—" She broke off, before adding in a low voice, "You know I did not mean her lack of breeding, brother."

"Her breeding is none of your concern. It is thanks to her that the home of our ancestors is to be fully restored."

"Thanks to her father, the rich merchant, you mean!"

"No," Konrad corrected her swiftly. "For it was she that picked me out, not him." His sister was struck speechless for once. He had surprised himself by sharing that fact with her. Was he bragging?

It suddenly occurred to him with uncomfortable clarity that Aimee might have a thing for tragic figures. He stroked unconsciously at his mangled cheek. Could that be why pretty Aimee had picked out the ugliest knight in Karadok for her groom? The notion displeased him. Dimly, he realized his sister was speaking once more. Some rubbish about the company of her fellow countrymen being a balm to her soul.

"Karadok is one unified country now," he pointed out shortly. It was something he had never actually said aloud before. "You meet with these so-called countrymen in the palace of our former enemy, to whom they now bend the knee. Can you even hear yourself?" When Magnatrude opened her mouth to speak again, he threw up his hand. "Enough! You will show my wife due deference, Trude. Whether you like it or not. I will not have her insulted in her own home. Do you understand?"

His sister's expression turned mutinous. "I have never—" she started, but jumped violently when he repeated the last two sentences in a thunderous roar. "I understand!" she gasped, clapping her hands to her ears.

"There will be no more hogging of that withdrawing chamber. It is not for your exclusive use. From tomorrow, you will act as a civil guest in her house. Leave now."

Magnatrude hurried to the door, her face aflame. Once there, she hesitated with her hand on the latch. "What of my visit tomorrow to the palace?" she asked in a sullen voice. "Am I to go or not?"

"It's a little late in the day to ask me that, isn't it?"

"May I go?"

"If you wish it, but, Trude…"

"Yes?"

"At the tournament the following day, you will make the necessary introductions to my wife, do I make myself clear?"

An expression of anger entered her eyes, which she swiftly masked by lowering her gaze. "Yes, brother."

"You may go."

The door closed after her, and Konrad stared at it a moment with a heavy frown. He should have bundled Trude off to a convent years ago. She had fasted two days a week since girlhood and clearly thought herself some kind of martyr. Kimarne had doubtless known what he was about when he had thrown her over. Last he had heard, the bastard now had three fine sons to bear his name.

On impulse, he walked out of his room and up the corridor, pausing outside his wife's room. Before he could change his mind, he rapped twice and then pushed at the unlatched door. Aimee was stood by the window holding up a gown to the light.

He cleared his throat. "Can I come in?"

"Of course!" She lowered the gown at once, threw it on top of the trunk, and turned to face him. "Did you like your new tunic?" she asked with a faintly anxious look in her eyes.

New tunic? He nodded. For some reason, he couldn't remember what it was he had been going to say. "It looks different in here," he observed instead, looking about him.

"Oh yes." She looked pleased by his comment and pointed at once up at the ceiling. He followed her finger uncomprehendingly. "The carpenter fixed it up for me so I could hang my bed curtains. And there's more furniture, of course. Did you see I put one of our wedding chests in your room?"

He grunted. What the fuck was a wedding chest? She had put a whole bunch of clutter in his room, he knew that much.

"Would you like a seat?" she asked politely, gesturing toward two chairs she had set before the large fireplace. "Or…are you staying?" Her eyes darted to the bed, and her cheeks turned a little pinker, but she did not drop her gaze from his, and to his amazement, her expression looked more hopeful than otherwise.

She wanted that? He cleared his throat again and made his way over to a chair which he dropped down into. At once, she seemed to brighten right up and bustled over to a side table to pour some wine. When she fetched it to him and sank into the chair opposite, she was practically beaming.

"How was your training today? Is all looking well for the royal tournament?" She took a sip of wine, and Konrad found himself casting about for something agreeable to say.

"I don't plan on crashing out in the first round this time, if that's what you mean," he heard himself reply heavily. Not quite the tone he was aiming for, but she flashed her dimples at him in any case.

"I thought it was wonderful how you took your loss at Kellingford. That's what made me—" Her breath caught a moment, and her color heightened. "Like you so much."

Konrad was thunderstruck. How he had taken his loss? He cast his mind back. At the time, he had been so bloody surprised and pleased for Renlow that he had congratulated the lad. *Shit*. Did she think he was some kind of parfait knight who espoused fair play? If so, she was in for a rude awakening! "Was Kellingford the only tournament you've seen me fight in?" he asked slowly.

"No," she admitted. "I also saw you before once at the palace, but we were far from the nobles' boxes and did not have the greatest view." He made no reply to this, surmising she must have been among the crowds in the commoners' stands. She rattled on. "I wonder if my sister will attend with Sir Renlow? I must send a message to enquire."

He forced his thoughts back to the matter at hand. "You think they will have left your father's house by now?" He had his doubts.

"Of course!" Aimee responded at once. "Ursula was not really poorly, you know. The celebrations were all just a bit too much for her."

He shrugged. "She lacks backbone."

"No, that is not fair," Aimee objected. "She has a very sweet nature in truth…" Her words trailed off, and she traced a finger on the arm of her chair. "Were you disappointed?" she blurted suddenly, taking him by surprise. "When you found out?"

He lowered his goblet. "Disappointed? About what?"

"That it was me, I mean. That I was the one…"

The door flung open, and Golda came sailing in with a pitcher of water. "Oh!" She halted so abruptly when she saw them seated together that the water sloshed from the jug. "I had not realized, milady," she said, backing up.

"It is of no matter, Golda," Aimee assured her. "If you just set it down over there, it will suffice."

"And have someone light the fire," Konrad added.

160

Golda pursed her lips and set down the pitcher of hot water. "Yes, milord," she muttered and beat a hasty retreat. An awkward silence fell over the room in her wake.

"Should I have asked for Golda to send up some refreshment? Dates maybe or some pickled walnuts?"

Konrad ignored this as nervous chatter. "I was not disappointed," he said heavily.

Her eyes went wide. "Truly?" He gave an affirmative nod, though how she could think otherwise was beyond him. She lowered her voice. "Do you suppose Sir Renlow might also have been in the dark about which of us was his intended?" She looked concerned.

Konrad shrugged. "If he was, he likely kept his surprise to himself." It stood to reason that Renlow would have more discretion than a blunt bastard like himself.

"I hope so." Aimee bit her lip. "Ursula is quite sensitive, and I should not like her to have been upset by any misunderstanding." When he made no reply, he could almost see her casting about for some other topic. "My father came to the house today," she said brightly. "He spent above an hour with Freda and myself."

"Freda has been keeping you company?"

"Oh yes, for most of today."

"She won't tomorrow."

She looked startled. "She won't?"

He shook his head. "Trude will need her company when she goes visiting."

"Your sister has acquaintances in the capital?"

"Apparently," he admitted grudgingly. "Some visiting northern dignitaries."

"Oh."

"Doubtless she will introduce you to them at the tournament."

Aimee's expression wavered somewhere in between gratification and nervousness. "Last year, Ursula and I spent some months with the Wycliffe family. Do you know them at all?"

He frowned. "No. They are southern?"

"Oh yes. Their manor is only a day's ride from Caer-Lyoness." She hesitated before adding, "I did not like them very much."

He could not help himself from asking: "Why?"

"They were…stuffy and rather condescending. Sir Maurice apparently has debts which is why he agreed to my father's scheme in the first place." Konrad could think of no reply to make to this. After all, his own situation was not so very different. "I do not think Lady Wycliffe much appreciated having to squire about a pair of merchant's daughters to meet all her acquaintances."

He wondered if that had been a bone of contention. Was that why Aimee Ankatel had wanted to wed him? To secure a title to rival this Lady Wycliffe's own? The notion made him frown. "Do they attend the royal tournaments?" he asked abruptly.

"I should not think so," she answered at once. "They go to various royal functions, but they are a scholarly family and more interested in things such as astronomy and natural philosophy."

Konrad snorted disparagingly. "I'm not surprised you disliked them. They sound a dull bunch."

"They were," Aimee agreed fervently, her dimple flashing out at him again. "For a while, I was quite worried their son James might offer for one of us, but when it came down to it, he could not quite make the sacrifice. He is a great lover of music, you see, and our untutored playing made him wince. Then he took great offence to a song I sang one night after dinner."

Konrad frowned. First Willard Hemmings and now this James Wycliffe. It was a miracle Aimee Ankatel had remained unwed this long, especially considering her father's fortune. "Was there ever anyone you ever *did* want to marry?" he asked.

Her gaze flew to meet his before dropping. "Well, yes," she admitted simply. "There was you."

A knock on the door interrupted them, sparing him from making any answer. Golda reentered the room carrying a second jug of steaming water. A large manservant on her heels carried an armful of logs. Konrad was not sure if this water was for him to wash or to replace that she had spilled. Golda set it down and departed with a curtsey.

Meanwhile, the fire in the hearth was kindled and set alight. The burly servant stacked some logs at the side of the fireplace and bowed clumsily before hurrying after Golda. Neither of them uttered a word as these services were performed.

"That was Matthews, the new manservant I mentioned previously," Aimee said after the door shut behind him.

Konrad grunted. "He looks capable enough."

"Yes," Aimee agreed and turned toward him. "Will you spend the night in here with me tonight, my lord?"

He lowered his goblet. "Yes," he said shortly and knew it was the right answer when her face lit up.

163

She then surprised him by immediately rising from her seat and hurrying about her ablutions. If he didn't know any better, he would think she was almost afraid he would change his mind. She had no sooner washed and pulled the pins from her hair than she was tugging and loosening the laces of her gown at her neck and wrists. "Would you mind?" she asked, twisting about to glance over her shoulder at the laces she could not reach. "Or shall I call back Golda?"

He gestured for her to approach and then obliged with clumsy fingers at the small of her back. Her long hair was hanging loose now, and he had to push it out of the way to reach the fastenings. She must use some fancy soap, he thought, for he had never thought of hair as fragrant before, but Aimee Ankatel's hair smelled like roses and some other elusive scent that escaped him.

He passed his hand through it a final time, just to enjoy the sensation of the silken length slipping through his fingers. "Done," he said gruffly, and Aimee moved away with a murmured thanks. He cleared his throat and turned his back as she wriggled out of her gown. The least he could do was give her some privacy to undress, he told himself, as much as he wanted to stand and stare.

Reaching for the fastenings of his tunic, he shucked it over his shoulders and flung it on the chair behind him. The rustling stilled, and for a moment, he could have sworn he felt her eyes on him. Resisting the impulse to turn and check if she was watching him undress, he started unlacing his braies instead.

"Should I leave my shift on?" a voice enquired politely.

As he had stripped her of it last time with scant consideration, he really ought to let her keep it on this time. "No," he heard himself answer shortly.

There was another rustle and then the sound of bedcovers being drawn back. The bedframe creaked and then there was nothing but the crackle of the logs in the fireplace. He shed his chausses with quick economic movements and then blew out the candles on the table before moving toward the bed.

Aimee was sat up, showing her bare shoulders above the covers but keeping everything else demurely hidden from his devouring gaze. She *was* watching him, he realized with a start as he pulled back the covers and joined her in the bed. "You have a very impressive physique," she told him admiringly. "Your whole family is tall, is it not? Even Freda, though her frame is a lot narrower than that of you and your sister."

Konrad thought of his stringy cousin and was not flattered by the comparison. He settled back against the pillow bearer and squinted down at his wife. "We Bartrees are all tall," he agreed as she scooted closer to him, surprising him with her eagerness for proximity. She hesitated for just an instant before settling her soft, cushiony body against his side, and Konrad heard his breath hiss through his teeth.

"You are not injured?" she asked with alarm and would have drawn back if he had not taken that opportunity to slip his arm about her waist, urging her closer still.

"Injured?" he repeated blankly as his mind briefly stalled, pleasure flooding his body. Strangely, he felt himself relax against her; all save one part of him at least. He lifted his knees to prevent the blankets from showing the outline of his stiffening cock.

Aimee shifted closer again, and it was at that point he felt the hair of her mound brush against the outside of his thigh.

"From your practice?" she elaborated. "I thought perhaps you might have strained a muscle."

165

"No," he replied shortly. He wanted her to straddle his leg. He wanted to feel that springy triangle of hair pressed hard against thigh, while she rubbed her pretty slit against him and told him she wanted him. Of course, such things were hardly reasonable requests from a near-virginal wife.

"Put your leg over mine," he heard himself rumble at her. He had almost forgotten he was *not* a reasonable man. She had wanted him, and she had gotten him. Whether she would be happy with her purchase over the next gods alone knew how many years was another matter.

No, that wasn't right, he thought with a frown. They would be largely apart, he reminded himself. He would go north more often than not while she remained mostly here in Caer-Lyoness.

"Like this?" Aimee asked uncertainly as she swung her leg over his, and there was no hiding his body's reaction to her soft, sweet flesh pressed against the hard muscle of his thigh. He could not bite back his harsh groan, and she reared back a little in alarm.

"Like that," he told her raspily. "Exactly like that."

She nodded and resettled back against him, her face now aflame. "We did not—that is, last time—"

"Last time was for duty," he puffed out. "It was never going to be good for you." *Or me*, he thought grimly, not after all that time. It had to have been nearly six years.

"I knew that much," she admitted on an outward breath. "Old Janet told me."

Who? Maybe if he kept her talking, she would not get so nervous this time. "Who is Old Janet?" he asked huskily as he slid his hand down her short, smooth back to her ample rear.

166

Gods. He squeezed his eyes shut a moment to appreciate the feel of her soft backside.

"Oh, um—an old servant of my father's," she muttered breathlessly.

"Another servant?" he managed to utter, cracking his eye open.

Her lips twisted wryly. "He has a houseful, my lord," she whispered. He focused on those pretty lips, and the direction of his thoughts surprised him. It occurred to him that he would not mind a taste of them. "Up," he urged her. "Come up over me," he rasped, urging her off the mattress to sit on top of his thigh instead.

She moved obligingly enough, though she made a strangled noise in her throat as she straddled his leg. Without the sheet covering her, her breasts jostled for his attention, scattering all thoughts of kisses completely. Her nipples were dark, like ripe little berries, her breasts high and full. He wanted to feel the weight of them in his hands, against his chest.

"Where shall I put my hands?" she asked, sounding flustered. He hardly knew where he wanted to put his own, he was so spoiled for choice.

Instead of answering her, he caught her wrists and drew them down to his chest. "Here," he practically growled at her. He felt her fingers dig into his chest hair and groaned again.

"I am not too heavy?" she asked in alarm.

He ignored this question as it was patently ridiculous. He was about twice the size of her. "Bear down," he growled. "I want you to ride my leg. I want to feel it." Aimee gazed down at him, looking perplexed. "Here," he said, his voice so gravelly he was practically growling at her. He ran his thumb through the woman's hair between her legs. "I want to feel your silky pelt rub against me."

For a moment, she just stared at him with an almost comical expression of confusion. "My—I?" Words seemed to fail her.

"You heard me, Aimee. That's what I want."

Her gaze flew to meet his, and for a moment, he did not understand the expression in her eyes. Then he realized that must have been the first time he had used her given name. *Something* passed between them, he hardly knew what, and then she gave a little sob and rocked forward on his thigh.

It felt so good he had to stop himself from thrusting up. "Again," he bit out. She dropped her gaze and bit her lip, concentrating on moving on him the way he liked. "Eyes on me," he insisted tersely as she did her best to comply with his demands.

"Like this?" she asked breathily. He nodded, narrowing his eyes as he watched her curvy body undulate as she strove to please him. "This feels nice?" she asked.

"Yes," he rasped, but it wasn't enough though. Not by a long shot. He closed his eyes to savor the feel of her and that was when he felt it. "Stop," he said hoarsely. It wasn't just him feeling good. Aimee was growing wet. For him.

Aimee lifted her head. Her breathing was ragged and her eyes dark. "Stop?" She faltered.

He nodded. "Move back." She blinked but shuffled down his leg obligingly. He reached down and swiped his fingers along his thigh before bringing them to his mouth. When his gaze snared hers, she caught her breath.

"What are you doing?" she asked in a strangled tone.

"Tasting you."

Aimee's mouth fell open, but she didn't utter a single word, just stared at him with her beautiful dark eyes, her breath coming fast. What he really wanted to do was haul her over his cock and thrust right into the heart of her. He wasn't quite that selfish though. She was by no means ready for that kind of treatment.

Instead, he took a deep breath in and out and locked eyes with her. "How about you lie on your back?" he suggested. When she nodded, he rolled her carefully onto her back and loomed over her. It occurred to him that one hint of trepidation or fear from her at this point would be like being doused by a bucket of ice-cold water.

Lucky for him, his sweet little bride was inexplicably eager for his attentions, her hands reaching for him before she suddenly froze. "Is this…permitted?" she asked. He stared at her a moment. "For me to touch you, I mean. Last time, I gained the impression—" She broke off her words.

"You can touch me if you want," he replied and braced himself. Her touch was curious and caressing. She slid her hands along the muscles in his arms and made a murmur of appreciation.

"You're so strong," she whispered. "Your body is magnificent." *Magnificent?* He didn't know how to respond to that, so he just held still and let her run her hands up and over the bunched muscle, then up and over his shoulders. "Could we—that is—" She licked her lips.

"Tell me." Whatever it was, he was pretty sure he would be happy to oblige.

"Kiss?"

Oh. *That.* He really didn't like people coming in close to his face. In general, it wasn't a problem as he towered over most people. Kissing, though, tended to bring your face up close and personal. He squinted at her dubiously. She wanted to see his ruined face at close quarters? Her hopeful gaze didn't even waver.

Ah, what the hells. She really wasn't asking for much. Bracing himself, Konrad leaned down to press his lips to hers. He wasn't expecting her to fling her arms about his neck or come at him with such clumsy enthusiasm. Drawing back wasn't really an option when she had his neck in such a tight grip. If he was honest, though, the feel of her breasts pressed up against his chest made the experience a lot more tolerable.

He made no attempt to deepen the kiss, just waited patiently for it to be over, but Aimee seemed in no hurry to draw back. He frowned. He was pretty sure she was holding her breath. She would pass out at this rate. He jerked his head back, and sure enough, she dragged in a shuddering breath, gazing up at him with glazed, unfocussed eyes. Really? She'd liked it that much?

Well, they had done something she liked, so now they could do something for him. "Can I touch you, Aimee?" She nodded but tipped her face up again, clearly under the impression he had asked for another kiss. He'd better disabuse of her that notion. "I don't want to kiss your mouth."

"Oh." For a moment, there was a flash of disappointment in her eyes.

"I'll kiss you somewhere else though," he said quickly to make up for it.

"My hand?" she suggested with a distinct lack of enthusiasm.

His lips crooked into an involuntary smile. "Not your hand, no."

She waited politely, and he slid his hand between her legs, finding her so wet and warm that he could not hold back his deep groan of appreciation. Slipping his fingers between her folds made her tense, but she soon relaxed again when he took his time, swirling his thumb against the fleshy pink pearl hidden between them.

"I thought you were going to kiss me," she said shakily, and he frowned. He had touched her here the other night to ready her, so she knew what came next. Clearly, she did not relish the thought and wanted more kisses and *talking*.

"I will," he said tersely, breathing out. Aimee was clearly a talker. He was not. By habit, he was as stoic in the bedchamber as he was everywhere else. "I'm going to kiss your breasts," he said and shifted down her body, transferring his hands to her waist.

She seemed surprised by this but voiced no objection. On his wedding night, he had wanted to spare her any indignity and had got the consummation over with as quickly as possible. He licked his lips now in anticipation and tried not to feel conscious of his wife's intent gaze on his face. Should he pay her some compliment? He cast a quick look up at her face. "Ready?" he asked instead when words failed him.

She nodded and he lowered his face to trail kisses down the valley between her soft, full breasts. Her tender skin quivered beneath his mouth, and her breathing sharpened. He was just deciding if that reaction was good or bad when he felt her hand at the back of his head, lightly clasping him to her. *Good*, he thought. *She likes it.*

He continued his journey of closed-mouth kisses underneath and around one breast, then the other. Her breathing grew ragged, and the clasp on his head grew firmer. He opened his mouth over her nipple and greedily sucked it into his mouth. Aimee made a strange noise in her throat, half sob, half moan, which went straight through him like a bolt of lust. He wanted her to make that noise when he gave her his dick.

He swirled his tongue over her nipple and then released it to lavish the same attention on her other breast. Gods, but she had lovely breasts. Aimee was panting now, her breathing ragged. He rested the palm of his hand against the soft swell of her stomach. She was as pleasingly rounded here as everywhere else on her delectable body.

It occurred to him that perhaps, in the absence of any polished compliments, that he could speak some of these thoughts aloud. *Would that please her?* Even before the catastrophic battle scars, he had been far from a ladies' man. He had been betrothed, it was true, but his father had arranged that match. No wooing had been required of him. The only company of women he had sought out had required hard coin rather than soft words.

He lifted his head to look at his wife's flushed face. "How about giving me another taste, Aimee?" he suggested thickly. "From the fount this time." He saw her attempt to make sense of his words, before giving up and nodding anyway. *Obliging,* he thought. "Open your legs." He shifted down again, his hands on her thighs, urging them to part. "Bend your knees."

Aimee followed his instructions, though he heard a sharp indrawn breath, as though she would speak. He lowered his head, cutting off whatever words she had been about to utter as he pressed a lingering kiss to her sweet mound. She gave a startled squawk. He certainly had not done this on the previous occasion. "My lord?" she asked in a quavering voice as the trail of his kisses led downward.

He supposed he really should give her permission to speak his name, only his mouth was rather busy right now with other things. He paused a moment to breathe heavily against her as

172

her nether hair tickled his face. His chest was heaving as though in the midst of battle. Unable to hold back any longer, he dragged his tongue slowly and deliberately through her slick cleft.

"Ohhhhhh, Lord Kentigern," she moaned breathily, and his cock jerked hard. On the other hand, he kind of liked how she said his title. By the time he'd lavished his attentions there for a few minutes, he no longer minded the fact she was so vocal either. The words and broken phrases falling from her lips might not make a whole lot of sense, but they were stimulating as hell to hear.

He sucked her pearl into his mouth and felt her come apart around him with a satisfying series of whimpers and moans. She was still quaking in the aftermath when he slid back up her body, positioning his hips between her splayed thighs.

"Ready?" he rumbled. She gave him a dazed nod, and he reached down to align himself with her before starting to push inside. This time was a lot less of a struggle, but Aimee held very still and fell disappointingly silent. He suspected she was once more holding her breath. Once he was fully seated, he stilled himself and looked down at her red face. "Are you…comfortable?" he asked, unsure of his word choice.

She puffed out her breath and pulled a face. "Yes?" she answered but did not look at all convinced.

"Would you tell me if you weren't?" he asked shrewdly. He was holding his weight off her with his forearms, but the difference in their size was considerable. He was aware how intimidating it must be to have him in her bed and that wasn't even taking his mangled face into account.

"Of course," she answered in a strangled voice.

He still wasn't convinced, but the promptings of his own body were fast overtaking his scruples. He rocked his hips, and when she didn't protest, he set a pace brisk enough for him to reach release. It didn't take long, but he couldn't resist from lowering his face into her neck at the end and pressing his mouth to her smooth skin. He stayed there a moment, breathing raggedly, and it was only when he felt her hand softly stroking his side that he mustered the energy to withdraw and roll onto his back beside her.

He lay waiting for his breath to even out before hauling himself up into a seated position and turning his head to look at her. She reached for the sheet to cover herself. "It will get better for you, or so I believe," he said harshly.

She turned her head and sent him a reassuring smile. "I know."

She did? Then he remembered. "Old Janet told you so?"

Her smile widened. "Yes, Old Janet."

He grunted. *That pleased her?* "I'll send someone in to attend you."

She glanced at the second pitcher of water. "Why? There's still water warm enough for me to wash. I don't need anyone."

He wanted to ask why she was still lying there. Didn't she want to wash all traces of him off her body? "It's been a long time," he heard himself admit instead, "since I've been with a woman." Gods, was he making excuses now? "Not since—" Instead of vocalizing it, he gestured to the left side of his face and braced himself to bear her sympathetic reaction.

"Good," said Aimee Ankatel simply.

He turned his head sharply to look at her in surprise. *Good?* He huffed out a breath in something damned near a laugh. Probably the closest he had come to it in years.

When he walked back to his room moments later, entirely naked, he was still fighting the upturn of his lips. *Good,* he thought. His little wife thought it was good he had not lain with a woman in six years. He made for the washstand and briskly washed himself down before dropping into his own bed and scooting into the middle of it.

He stared up at the canopy. He doubted she would think it so good if he had declared an intention of staying in her bed until he was good and ready for another round in the sheets with her, as for an instant he had felt strongly inclined to do. *Or would she?*

He hesitated, considering the matter. For the first time, he noticed his own crest on the pillow bearer beside him. He turned his head and stared at it. Then, slowly he cast his eyes around the room, taking in all the costly furnishings and gifts his wife had showered him with.

His crest was fucking everywhere. He turned over the top of the sheet covering his stomach and saw a whole line of portcullises embroidered in gold thread. Why hadn't he noticed them before? He puffed out his breath. Had Aimee sewn the devices with her own fingers? He ran a blunt fingertip over the tiny stitches. And if she had, why did that suddenly make his chest feel so tight?

175

13

Aimee woke late the next morning, and by the time she had descended downstairs, the table in the dining chamber was empty, though it bore signs of more than one person having broken their fast. "Good morning," she greeted Golda, who was sweeping up crumbs from the table. "It seems I am last one down this morning."

Golda pursed her lips, straightening up. "Both ladies graced us with their presence this morn," she commented dryly. "Before they set forth a-visiting."

Aimee nodded, sitting herself down. "Lord Kentigern told me they would be visiting acquaintances at the palace this day."

Golda sniffed. "I doubt they will set the place alight. Pair of old crows!"

"Golda!" Aimee reproached her mildly. "Mistress Freda and I actually spent a very pleasant day together yesterday."

"Good of her!" Golda huffed. "She ought to be waiting on you, not that sour bag of goods as is her cousin!"

"Well," Aimee said soothingly, "she *is* my sister-in-law's companion. It is small wonder her loyalties are divided."

"Huh!" Golda slammed a plate of baked fish before her. "You should tell his high and mightiness how his own sister thinks herself too good for your company!"

Aimee helped herself to a piece of bread. "I think he knows," she admitted ruefully, remembering their conversation from the night before.

Golda's mouth fell open. "Who told him, do you suppose, milady?" she wondered aloud. After a moment, she shrugged. "I daresay he has eyes in his 'ead, for all one of them's blind."

Aimee shot her an admonishing glance, but as her mouth was full of bread and butter, she could utter no reproach. It wasn't really Lord Kentigern's conversation that had occupied her thoughts thus far this morning, she acknowledged to herself as her cheeks warmed. But rather, his *actions*.

She felt tender between her legs, reminding her of what had transpired between them, but she was nowhere near as sore as she had been before. She had certainly enjoyed it a good deal more this time. Last time, she had been unable to lie easy when he had toyed with her body. He hadn't really spoken much, and she had been tense and nervous. She had also harbored a horrible suspicion that he did not enjoy touching her.

Last night had been different somehow. *It's been a long time*, he had told her. *Since I've been with a woman*. Aimee could not help the wayward smile that curved her lips, so she pressed her ale cup to her mouth to hide it from Golda's sharp gaze. Lord Kentigern had not lain with any woman but her, not since he had been so brutally injured in the war. That had to be six years at least, she marveled.

She felt highly gratified by his admission. She was his wife, and it was right that he should tell her such things. She was unspeakably proud that he could let his guard down around her. She wanted to receive all his confidences and guard them jealously. She would say all the right things and soothe his savage brow. She would be the companion and helpmeet of his bosom.

Her spirits, which had plummeted to an all-time low in the wake of their marriage, were soaring giddily once more. All would be well, Aimee thought. She just had to be patient and give him time to accept her in his life. It was bound to be strange and even jarring to him to suddenly have a wife by his side to make room for. She just had to be patient and slowly prove herself invaluable to him and all would fall into its proper place.

At midday, her father called in. "I cannot tarry long, daughter," he told her, clasping her hand in welcome. "For I am speaking at the guild this afternoon. I just wanted to drop this by for you." He handed over a wrapped package.

"What is it, Father?"

"I had that brooch of yours straightened out," he said genially.

Aimee unwrapped the silver heart and found it polished and gleaming with all dents disappeared and the decorative edging, which had been bent and twisted, standing proud. The lettering which spelled out "Heart Be Trewe" was now inlaid with gleaming gold. "Oh, Father!" she exclaimed. "Why, it looks almost a different brooch! How lovely it now looks!" Carefully, she lifted it out of its wrappings and found that a short silver chain was now hanging from the central eyelet at the bottom. From this chain was suspended a large and lustrous pearl. "Oh!" she exclaimed. "Oh, how beautiful! A pearl!"

Her father shrugged. "It's a shame the brooch is not gold," he said. "But it's a pretty enough trifle."

"I could not possibly like it more than I already do," Aimee said stoutly. "I shall wear it to the tournament tomorrow with pride! How pleased Freda will be to see it looking so well."

Her father patted her shoulder. "Well, well. It was a nice gesture of hers to give it to you." He looked around. "Mistress Freda does not keep you company today?" He sounded a little disappointed.

"No, alas," Aimee answered quickly. "She had a visit to make with Magnatrude, so I will not see her until this evening."

Her father accepted this without comment. "I must eat my supper alone tonight, I find," he sighed. "For your sister is moving out today into her new house."

Aimee frowned. "I thought she would have moved out quite two days ago!"

Gerold shook his head. "Hilda did not think Ursula was feeling strong enough for such exertions."

"Hilda!" Aimee exclaimed with displeasure, thinking of the overprotective old servant.

"Well, well, you know she can be a bit of a mother hen where Ursa is concerned."

Aimee pulled a face. "Ursula is now a married woman, Father!"

"Now, now, Aimee, you must not take on so," he counseled, patting her shoulder. "You know your sister is not so stout of heart as you."

Aimee tutted. "At this rate, Sir Renlow will think she is frail as an old woman!" She bit her lip. "Of course, I will see her at the royal tournament tomorrow. I can speak to her then." Her father avoided her eye. "Why do you look like that? Ursula surely means to attend the royal tournament, Father?" she asked with some misgiving.

Gerold looked evasive. "As to that, she was undecided last time it was mentioned."

"I daresay Hilda thinks it would be too much for her!" Aimee could not help but retort. "Why, I have half a mind to come back with you now and give her a piece of my mind!"

"You must not do that, Aimee!" her father said hastily. "She will be far too busy overseeing her packing. Besides, I am not going back to the house. I told you, I am attending the merchants' guild this afternoon."

Aimee huffed with displeasure. "I had thought to see my sister on the morrow!" she muttered. "I thought for certain that she would wish to cheer her husband on."

"Well, you may still see her there," her father said without conviction.

Somehow, Aimee doubted it very much. With an effort, she pulled herself together. "I am sorry, Father. I should not be complaining to you of it. Not after you have just given me such a handsome present."

"Nay, it was not I who gave you the brooch, but Mistress Freda."

"The pearl was from you," she pointed out, taking his hand. "And I dearly love it." He beamed at her. "If you have no desire for your own company at supper this evening, then you could always take your meal here with us."

He waved away her offer at once. "Nay, certainly not, child! I spoke in jest," he said hurriedly. "In truth, I do not lack for company. I daresay I shall sup with Master Crawley," he said, mentioning another senior at the merchant's guild. "It has been an age since we exchanged our news, and I have much to apprise him of with two daughters lately married."

She smiled perfunctorily at that, and he kissed her cheek and hurried off about his business. The rest of the day passed quietly. The first of Freda's new gowns was delivered, and Aimee set this carefully on her new relative's bed herself so that it would not crease or wrinkle before the next day. Then she set about selecting her own outfit for the big day. She would, of course, be wearing the particolored gown in the Kentigern colors of blue and yellow. With it she would wear her gold chain, her blue beads, a gold thread hairnet, and her silver brooch with the pearl.

She ate her supper alone as none of the Bartrees returned in time to take it with her, a fact that made Golda's expression grow tight with disapproval. After that, she took a long, leisurely bath and retired early to bed, both nervous and excited for the morrow.

14

"Freda?" Aimee called quietly, knocking on her new kinswoman's door. "Are you awake?" She had risen ridiculously early and had washed and dressed over an hour ago but had not wanted to break her fast alone. Golda had scolded her as she dressed Aimee's hair in a heavy, gold-beaded hairnet, for she had risen at the crack of dawn. *And far too early, Miss Aimee!*

Aimee had not admitted it, but in truth, she had hoped for a glimpse of Lord Kentigern before he left the house that morn. To her disappointment, by the time she had dressed and adorned herself, he had already left, and since then, she had been racketing about the house quite by herself.

On impulse, she had gathered up a handful of her glass-topped hairpins to gift to Freda after she had seen the sad state of Freda's own a couple of days before. The door swung open, and Freda stood in her shift, her hair stood about her in an untidy cloud. "Oh, Aimee!" she said distractedly. "Oh, I scarcely know what I am about this morn. And you already dressed and looking so fine!"

Aimee took one look at Freda's nervous state and stepped into the room, resolutely closing the door after her. "You have plenty of time, Freda," she assured her. "I could not sleep and woke betimes. Allow me to assist you in getting ready."

"So very kind," Freda twittered, dropping her hair comb and glancing nervously toward the bed. Aimee followed her gaze and to her surprise found a large ginger cat curled up on the covers. "Oh dear," Freda said, twisting her hands together. "I— I do hope you do not mind my co-opting the kitchen cat. Such a comfort, I always think, and such very good company." She looked to be on the verge of tears as though anticipating a telling off.

"Of course not!" Aimee assured her smoothly. "I did not know we even possessed a kitchen cat, truth be told." One of the cat's eyes flickered open to glint at Aimee a moment before he decided she was not worth the effort and shut it again.

"Oh, most houses do," Freda answered fervently. She twisted about to retrieve a moth-eaten mantle which had fallen off one of her bony shoulders. "They always seem to find their way to me by hook or by crook. I'm afraid Trude always gets rather cross with me appearing with cat hairs all over me. I always think they are such *instinctive* animals though. As though they sense a creature who is in sympathy with them and seek them out."

As she spoke, Freda drifted across the room toward her wash basin, the shawl slipping off her other shoulder and trailing along behind her.

"You have warm water to wash?" Aimee asked, kneeling to retrieve the fallen hair comb and carrying it to the dresser where Freda's beads and veil lay in an untidy heap. She set the hairpins next to them and shook out the linen veil.

"Oh yes! Ingrid was good enough to bring me some when she woke me." Freda set about washing her hands vigorously. "She is attending Magnatrude, so I usually shift for myself. It will be quite the luxury," she twittered, "to have you help me dress, Aimee, dear." It was at this point she noticed Aimee frowning over the creased veil.

"Oh dear, I am afraid I have always been a very untidy and disorganized creature," she apologized. "I was so tired when we got back last night…"

183

"Well, it must have been rather late," Aimee answered sympathetically.

"Oh, it was!" Freda seized eagerly on the excuse. "I was quite ready to drop! The Countess of Strethneal was so very accommodating that we tarried for far too long, and I fancy the dear earl was heartily glad to be rid of us. But there, Magnatrude could not be dragged away by wild horses!" She bit off her words with a sigh. "Though in truth, I must confess, my dear," she added conscientiously. "I usually throw down my things any old how. It is a disgraceful habit, and my poor nurse used to scold me dreadfully."

Aimee smiled. "I am sure there are worse faults to possess. I have brought you some new hairpins, Freda, for I noticed the other day your own are looking in sad repair."

"Oh, Aimee! How kind!" Freda's pale eyes filled once more with tears. Aimee's heart went out to her. She was starting to suspect that Freda was so used to being overlooked by everyone except household cats that she was pathetically grateful even for a few copper hairpins.

"It is nothing," Aimee hurried to assure her. "I have dozens of them."

Freda was drying herself off now and started toward her before halting with a loud "Oh!" She covered her mouth with her hand and stared transfixed at Aimee.

"What is it?" Aimee asked, straightening up. "My gown?" She held out her arms so that Freda could get the full effect. Suddenly, she was filled with misgiving. "Do you think it is too much?"

But it was not the gown which held Freda's gaze but the brooch pinned beneath the insignia of the Kentigerns. "My brooch!"

184

she breathed, then seemed to catch herself and colored violently. "*Your* brooch, I mean!"

"Yes," said Aimee, touching a hand to the large silver heart. "Does it not look fine? All polished up and with the dents worked out?"

"Oh, it looks *magnificent*!" Freda sobbed with tears rolling down her cheeks.

"Freda!" Aimee said with dismay. "Why are you crying?"

Freda shook her head, flinging out a hand. "Do not pay it any attention!" she begged. "It is simply that I am a little overcome!"

"Come and sit on this chair," Aimee said, walking over to her and ushering her to sit before the looking glass. She rested her hands on Freda's shoulders and gave them a squeeze. "It is quite the nicest thing that I own."

Freda's mouth formed an unspoken *oh*, and she gazed at the brooch in their reflection. "I can scarce believe it," she muttered and colored again before dropping her gaze. "And for it to be your favorite adornment too, but perhaps you said that just to please me."

"No," answered Aimee, beginning to run the comb through Freda's hair. "I said it because it is true. What do you think of the pearl my father added? Would it originally have had a pearl embellishment?"

"It looks beautiful!" Freda opined. "But as to its originality, I'm afraid I could not say. By the time it was passed to me, it bore no jewels whatsoever." She scrunched up her face. "I think my mother mentioned it had a sapphire, but I could not say for certain, for it was many years ago, and I did not have the slightest expectation of being able to restore it."

Between the two of them, they managed to get Freda into her new gown of red satin.

"Oh," Freda said, turning this way and that as she tried to admire the effect in the looking glass. "I do think the sleeves are most cunningly cut," she said, holding up one skinny arm to show the trumpet shape. "Does it not almost make me look elegant?" Her enthusiasm had given her a pretty flush in her cheeks.

"It looks very well indeed," Aimee told her. "But I am determined to fetch Golda now to dress your hair, otherwise it will not match the effect of your handsome outfit. And you must borrow a veil from me as this one is so sadly crumpled."

Freda protested that it was far too much trouble to go to just for her but was overruled. Golda duly tamed her fine flyaway hair and fixed a veil with a wide gold border to the top of her head. "For it matches your surcoat very well indeed, Mistress Freda," Golda told her sternly.

"Oh, the surcoat," Freda murmured. "I had almost forgotten." She glanced at the over-robe of brown and gold. "And very nicely it will go with my amber beads too!"

Both she and Aimee were far too excited to eat much at table. Freda was just telling her that she had not been to a tournament in *why, it must be quite ten years* when Magnatrude came into the dining chamber. Aimee was so surprised to see her sister-in-law taking any meal bar supper below stairs that she almost dropped her slice of bread.

"Good morning," Magnatrude murmured and seated herself with scant ceremony. She was wearing the maroon velvet gown she had worn to Aimee's wedding. It was clearly a grand gown which had seen better days. This time, she had teamed it with a close-fitting velvet cap which concealed her hair almost completely and looked very severe. Over this was draped a very translucent silk veil without any structure underneath it. Aimee thought she looked more like she was going to her own execution than a royal tournament.

"Oh, er, good morning, dear," Freda replied. Clearly, she was just as distracted by Magnatrude's appearance as Aimee was. The two of them exchanged startled glances. Aimee wondered if her sister-in-law was making some sort of point about attending only under sufferance. She shrugged at Freda, and they both looked up as Matthews entered the room. He coughed and stood with his back to the wall, letting them know he was available to escort them when they were ready. They waited only while Magnatrude ate a plate of baked fish and then left for the palace.

*

"Aimee!" Aimee turned her head and smiled politely as Freda introduced her to yet another pair of nobles when she would much rather be concentrating on what was happening in the field. She looked up at the towering male and the diminutive female stood beaming at his side as she rose to her feet and performed an obligatory curtsey.

"This is the Marquis and Marchioness Martindale," Freda twittered excitedly. "Their estate in the north is not far from where the Bartree lands always stood."

There was an awkward silence as everyone was reminded of all that Lord Kentigern had once lost. It trembled on Aimee's lips to point out that the lands had now been restored to him, by dint of their marriage, but an inner voice pointed out this might appear rather crass.

"And this is our son and heir, Viscount March," the exquisite little marchioness announced, filling the gap with proud words.

She gestured toward an elder woman following in her wake who wore an enormous white wimple and carried an infant who could surely not be more than a year old.

Aimee froze, unsure what the form would be in this case. To be on the safe side, she performed another curtsey in the direction of the baby.

"This is the Lady Kentigern," Freda continued in her thin, high voice. "Who has lately married my cousin."

The marquis cleared his throat. "I was glad to hear," he said gruffly, "that Kentigern's fortunes have picked up." He looked as though he wanted to say more but seemed uncertain how to proceed. "It never sat easily with his neighbors that he should lose everything," he added in a low growl, and his wife placed a hand on his forearm. At that, he looked down at his marchioness, who sent him a reassuring smile. He visibly relaxed.

"You must forgive Guy," the marchioness said, leaning forward conspiratorially. Aimee's eyes widened at this lapse in formality. "He is always somewhat ill at ease here in the southern capital. He attends court for my sake alone," she added. "He is the very best of husbands."

"You are southern," Aimee blurted with surprise, and the marchioness burst out laughing.

"Oh yes, but he stopped holding that against me a long time ago!"

"Mathilde!" the marquis rumbled, a slight flush mounting his cheeks.

"I am only teasing," his wife hastened to assure him, but she rolled her eyes speakingly in Aimee's direction. "We must visit with one another when you are in residence at Bartree Castle," she said, her eyes twinkling. "I look forward to having a neighbor with whom I have so much in common."

"That was kind of her," Aimee murmured to Freda as the Martindales moved away. For she must surely know that as a merchant's daughter, Aimee did not have so very much in common with her after all. Unless, of course, she did *not* know. Somehow, though, considering the number of curious stares being shot in her direction, Aimee fancied that the marchioness must surely know.

"Such a pretty little thing, is she not?" Freda said aloud, echoing Aimee's own thoughts. "The marquis clearly dotes on her which, you know, was a great surprise to everyone. For you see, Martindale had a great many sanctions imposed on him after the north fell. His marriage was one of the conditions he was forced to meet before he was freed." Freda dropped her voice. "Remind me to tell you about the feast where I first clapped eyes on his marchioness. It was a very great scandal in our part of the world and a nine days' wonder, I assure you."

Aimee opened her eyes wide. *Now what did that mean?* she wondered, glancing after the Martindales. As she watched, the marchioness turned her laughing face up toward her husband, and as though unable to do otherwise, he stooped at once to kiss her mouth. "They seem a most devoted couple," she observed wonderingly.

"Oh, they are," Freda enthused. "It quite gives one hope that one day all of Karadok will be healed and unified."

Freda's comment startled Aimee a little. She had almost taken it for granted that the country was no longer torn asunder. Of course, her whole life, she had scarcely strayed from the southern capital. As a southerner, on the winning side as it were, it was easy enough to believe that all was now as it should be. Aimee shifted uncomfortably in her seat. For the first

189

time, it occurred to her that she might not receive the warmest welcome in the north.

"Ah, here comes Magnatrude," Freda observed, and they stood to give her wide skirts room enough to move into their box. "You have just missed the Martindales, cousin."

Magnatrude's face fell. "Freda," she tutted, berating her cousin as she dropped onto the bench. "You must know how particularly I wished to see our neighbors! Did you not tell them I would return directly?"

"No," Freda answered forthrightly, a hectic flush entering her sallow cheeks. "For their purpose in approaching was to request an introduction to Aimee, not to ask after you!" Magnatrude was clearly astonished by this tart response from the usually meek Freda. Her mouth fell open, and she made a faint spluttering noise, though words seemed to fail her.

Freda turned determinedly toward Aimee. "Are you enjoying the spectacle, cousin?" she asked with an exaggerated civility, clearly demonstrating the attention she felt Aimee was due from her sister-in-law. Magnatrude's color deepened as Aimee made some polite rejoinder.

"I wonder when we will see my lord take to the field," Aimee murmured, glancing once more to where the milling knights were taking position for the second stage of the melee.

"As to that, I am not certain," Freda responded. "But we are sure to spot him. Really, you cannot miss him."

Which was true enough, Aimee reflected, considering his size. A good many of the knights were tall and even broad, but few possessed her husband's impressive build. "Oh!" she uttered, sitting up in her seat. "Is that not Sir Renlow d'Avenant? My brother-in-law," she elaborated, leaning forward as she tried to make out his device.

Though really, she reflected, she was still not at all aware what the crest of the d'Avenants even was. Unlike her, Ursula had not seen fit to embellish all of her bridal trousseau with her new husband's emblem. She felt a pang of unease when she thought of Ursa. Not seeing her since made her worry that something must be amiss. Was it possible that she had been wrong to persuade her sister into marriage?

It was a new and uncomfortable notion that had assailed Aimee in the early hours of a sleepless night. If only she could snatch a moment's conversation with her sister, she thought, biting her thumbnail, she could be easier on that score. But though she had cast about most diligently on arriving at the teeming palace grounds, she had searched in vain. She could spot neither hide nor hair of her sister in the crowds and had long since concluded she could not be present.

"I believe it is Sir Renlow," Freda said consideringly. "For I can see some hair curling underneath his helm, and it is that precise shade of hair that he possesses. He wears it rather long, does he not?"

"He does," Aimee agreed automatically. "Let us support him in this round," she said impulsively, turning to Freda and touching her forearm. "It adds a certain enjoyment to being a spectator, or so Ursula and I thought at Kellingford."

"Of course, my dear," Freda responded at once. "I have not watched Konrad compete in an age," she confessed, wrinkling up her eyes. "Why, it must have been before the war that I last watched him," she observed with faint surprise.

"Really? It has been that long?" Aimee murmured as she watched the two separate sides forming into their mock battle

191

lines. In truth, she was not so very surprised to hear this. She had started to form the impression that the Bartrees were not the closest of families.

"Sir Renlow's side are wearing the red armbands, are they not?" Freda observed as Magnatrude leaned across her to address Aimee.

"The Strethneals are approaching," Magnatrude interrupted them. "They are an earl and countess, so you must be sure to observe the correct depth in your curtsey." When Aimee's expression did not show sufficient gratitude for this honor, she added stiffly, "Konrad particularly asked me to introduce you to them!"

Aimee sighed and came to her feet. The Strethneals were duly introduced, and Aimee was scrupulously polite. The earl was a man of middling height with a rather forgettable face. His countess stared at Aimee rather hard and addressed some remarks in an aside to Magnatrude in a manner which Aimee thought rather rude. It seemed ill breeding was not the only excuse for poor etiquette. "And now we must go in search of the Martindales," the countess said, turning back to Aimee. "Perhaps we could introduce you to them at some point," she added in a rather condescending manner.

"The Martindales have already introduced themselves to Aimee this morning," Freda replied promptly. "And the marchioness invited Aimee to visit with her at Acton March."

Lady Strethneal's smile froze. "Oh," she replied. "I see." Some inner struggle seemed to wage for a moment before she managed to force out, "When you journey north, you must come and visit with us too, Lady Kentigern, at our residence, Jennings Park."

192

Aimee performed her curtsey and turned back to the arena. To her disappointment, the participants of the melee seemed to have descended into a chaotic cloud of dust and flailing limbs. Around the edges lay various inert bodies. "Oh dear," she muttered. "Did you happen to see what became of Sir Renlow at all?"

"I'm afraid not," Freda replied apologetically.

Unable to make sense of the struggles below, Aimee let her attention wander to the royal balcony where the King sat next to his yawning Queen. For some reason, Aimee had thought the King would be taller. In all the ballads, he was the golden Argent lion, famed for his warlike prowess.

Somehow, he did not look at all like she had imagined he would. His arm rested on the ledge, showing a slashed and puffed sleeve and a large gold ring on one finger. He had a square face, a pugnacious expression, and his hair was more tow-colored than gold.

His Queen by contrast was dark, with olive skin and a regal bearing. Her glossy hair was caught up in a caul studded with pearls, showing off a long and graceful neck. At her throat she wore a heavy necklace of gold and green stones which Aimee imagined must be emeralds.

"The Queen is very beautiful, is she not?" she said aloud.

"Oh yes. That is, I suppose she is," Freda replied doubtfully. "Though for my part, I think she is one of those women who appears attractive due to her bearing, rather than possessing any true purity of feature."

Aimee turned to Freda with surprise. "How so?" she asked curiously.

"Well…" Freda flushed. "I only mean that her supreme confidence so impresses her audience that they all agree she must be worth looking at!"

Aimee regarded Freda with interest. Once she got over her shy awkwardness, Freda had plenty to say for herself, she realized. She was a good deal less reserved than Ursula, for instance, who would never dream of saying something like that about so lofty a personage.

Then again, she reflected, perhaps Freda only felt that way because she saw Queen Armenal as a southern usurper. "Was the northern queen a great beauty?" she asked, deciding to test her.

"I shouldn't think so," Freda replied absently. "I never saw her at close quarters, but King Magnur was as ugly as a squat toad." At Magnatrude's shocked gasp, Freda gave a guilty start. Aimee giggled, and after a moment, Freda joined her with a nervous titter.

"You two are behaving abominably!" Magnatrude hissed. "Have you been drinking strong wine to let your tongues wag so?"

"No," Aimee responded at once. "But that is a very good notion! I am feeling somewhat parched." She turned back to where Matthews stood in attendance. "Matthews, would you be able to procure us some cups of wine?" Discreetly, she passed him a purse of money. "And please procure some refreshment for yourself. The sun is becoming very warm at this point."

"Yes, milady." He took himself off and returned within minutes with a jug of wine, three cups, and a foaming tankard for himself. When Magnatrude refused her share with a stony shake of her head, Aimee shrugged and set it instead at her feet. She was just straightening up when Freda gave an excited gasp.

194

"It looks as though the next event must be about to start!" A flurry of squires had entered the ring bearing an array of banners which they paraded about the arena, displaying the colors of the various knights. "There! Our colors!" Freda squeaked as a yellow and blue pennant came into sight. She reached out and clutched Aimee's hand in her bony fingers in a gesture of solidarity that she found quite touching.

Aimee held her head up high, filled with pride to see the likeness of the portcullis she had stitched so lovingly being flourished now before this huge crowd of spectators. Hearing a murmuring in the stands around them, she realized that people must have noticed how closely Aimee's own gown echoed the Kentigern banner in every way.

She felt her cheeks grow hot as she saw people pointing and talking behind their hands. It suddenly occurred to Aimee that she might have gone rather too far with flaunting her husband's colors on her body. Had she committed some sort of chivalric faux pas?

Mercifully, the next banner, a red field bearing a panther of black in a walking stance, one claw raised, drew the crowd's attention away from her, and a mighty roar of approval went up from the masses.

"Dear me!" said Freda. "This one must be quite a southern favorite."

The wheels of Aimee's recollection turned. She cast her mind back to the very first tournament she had ever attended. Who had won that one? A famous southern champion, she seemed to remember, with curling dark hair and a handsome face. *Vawdrey*, she recalled with effort. *Sir Something Vawdrey.*

"Vawdrey," she said aloud. "That is his name, I believe. I have seen him compete before, and he is a great crowd pleaser." She glanced up at the royal box. "I believe they call him the King's Champion." Both Magnatrude and Freda looked strangely disconcerted by this information. "What is it?" she asked. "What have I said?"

Magnatrude looked away, but Freda reached out to touch her sleeve. "'Tis naught, Aimee. Only that—well, Konrad used to bear the same title. For the—er—" *For the northern king,* Aimee realized. *Oh.* "I mean, in different times," Freda finished with effort.

Aimee swallowed and nodded. How strange it must feel for northern nobles to attend these events, she realized, which must mirror in many ways the court at Menith, where they had previously served as courtiers. She took a sip of her wine in an effort to dispel such sober thoughts.

The squires were now lining the edge of the field with their banners, standing well back. Trumpets were raised and blasted, and some twenty or so horses entered the arena from the left and the same number from the right.

"It's Konrad! It seems this time there will be a mounted charge," Freda announced excitedly.

"Yes," Aimee agreed, striving to regulate her suddenly shallow breathing. How funny, she thought, to remember how differently she had viewed his emergence into the competitors' field previously. Then, he had seemed like some sort of terrifying monster about to lay waste to all around him. Whereas now, she could point and say, *Who, that? Oh, that is my husband, you know.*

What a pity, she reflected ruefully, that there was no one to hand who she could brag to. It was pointless saying it to Freda or Magnatrude, who knew him far better than she did. Glancing up at that moment, she met the eye of a lady in the next box who was gazing at her with a lively interest.

Aimee flushed with the uncomfortable thought that her face must have betrayed what she had been thinking. The lady looked most definitely amused. She lifted a hand in greeting, and Aimee returned the gesture, a little hesitantly, but with a smile. She jabbed Freda in the ribs with her elbow. "Who, pray, is that lady over there?" she hissed.

Freda glanced across. "I do not know any of these southern nobles," she answered apologetically. "We could enquire. Which do you mean?"

"The lady with the golden hair in the rose-colored gown."

Freda looked again. "Do you mean the—the—er…" Freda faltered, and Aimee realized she did not wish to refer to the fact the lady was heavily pregnant.

"The one who is *expecting*," Aimee supplied helpfully.

Magnatrude leaned forward and spoke in the discreet, low tone she clearly thought her kinswoman should display. "That is the Countess of Twyford," she murmured. "An old and venerable northern title," she added. "The current bearer only acceded to it in the past year. Dear Elizabeth was telling me of it only yesterday."

"She is very lovely," Aimee observed, surreptitiously stealing another look at the countess. While it was true, the skin on her face was far from unblemished, Aimee did not think this detracted in any way from a very charming profile. The countess was not wearing her spouse's colors of black and white, Aimee noted with unease. She glanced down and suddenly wished fervently that she was wearing any other of her own gowns.

"The rumor is, she used to be the greatest beauty in all the south," Magnatrude added, as though unable to stop herself from sharing a piece of salacious gossip. "Before she was struck down with the red pox, that is."

"Oh!" Freda lifted a hand to her mouth, and she and Aimee exchanged wide-eyed looks. "How tragic!"

"Well, she is still a fine-looking woman for all that," Aimee said, feeling her color rise. "After all, what are a few scars?" She stared steadfastly ahead at the arena as an awkward silence greeted her words. She focused on the horned helmet and the looming figure on the huge destrier. He was magnificent, she thought, her bosom swelling. And he was hers!

Magnatrude coughed. "Prevailing opinion places her husband, the earl, as the favorite to win this afternoon's joust," she continued loftily.

"The Earl of Twyford jousts?" Freda asked, sounding startled.

"Before he was the Earl of Twyford, he was one Garman Orde," Magnatrude imparted. "A very great northern champion."

Aimee turned her head at that. "Oh, I had not realized they were one and the same. He won the joust at Kellingford last year and is a very fierce competitor."

Of course! She remembered now, the heavily veiled lady who had accompanied him and so captured her own and Ursula's imagination. There had been that terrible stand collapse, and Aimee had watched, her heart in her throat, as Sir Garman had dug his wife out of the rubble with his bare hands. She had been enthralled by his eventual win and the victory lap he had taken with his wife sat up on his charger before him.

Unable to resist the temptation, Aimee glanced over again at where the countess sat, serene and round with child. Love must

198

have restored her looks to her, she thought, tears springing sentimentally to her eyes.

A cheer from the crowd had her quickly turning back. The King's flag must have been waved as the two sides were now riding toward each other with their swords drawn. They wore colored armbands, one side green and the other yellow. Lord Kentigern's arm displayed a green band.

"None of them are bearing spears," Aimee realized suddenly, turning to Freda. "At Kellingford, they had spears."

Freda looked bewildered. "Oh, do they not?"

Aimee wondered if there would be many more differences between the royal and the rural tournaments but did not have time for further speculation, for the two sides had met with a jarring clash of steel. Dry dust flew up from the ground and obscured everything as sword arms flailed and shields were raised to deflect the blows raining down on them.

"Oh dear!" Freda flinched. "I had forgotten the wanton savagery of it all!"

The trumpets blasted again, and the horses wheeled about, the two sides separating again and retreating to the opposite side. At least three men had been unhorsed in the hostilities. The squires ran forward to catch their horses by their reins and lead them out of the arena.

One knight sat upright, clutching his helmet, but the other two were lying insensible in the dust. Aimee noticed that instead of being claimed for ransom by the knights who had unseated them, the fallen were instead helped to their feet or dragged from the ring by attendants whose express purpose seemed to be retrieving these unfortunates. Two of those hobbling toward the exit wore green armbands. As they were helped out, the squires withdrew their flags from those displayed. Aimee leaned forward but did not recognize the crests of those being folded up and put aside.

"How do they determine the winning side?" Freda asked in faltering accents.

"Presumably by the side with most still seated after a certain number of charges," her cousin pointed out witheringly.

Aimee wondered if this was true. If so, it vastly differed to Kellingford, where there had been no prescribed number of charges. There, they had simply continued to scuffle until the final man stood. She supposed it made sense that things would be more organized at a royal tournament.

"Don't forget your wine," she prompted Freda, who was stood looking dazed as the royal standard of the golden lion was raised ready for the next charge.

"Oh yes," Freda murmured, sinking down onto the bench and raising her cup to her lips. "I think I'll just sit awhile if you don't mind, dear."

"Of course not," Aimee assured her over the thunder of hooves from the second charge.

The heat was growing almost oppressive in the stands by the time the number of knights had been whittled down to less than ten. The last two knights had fetched each other off and tumbled to the ground, still struggling with one another. When they attempted to continue sparring on foot, officials had interceded, and they were forced to break apart.

Aimee watched as they took the news with very bad grace. One flung out of the arena while the other dragged off his helm to argue the decision. "How strange," Aimee murmured, for she had certainly seen knights sparring toe-to-toe at Kellingford. It must not be allowed here, though. Aimee recognized the short blond beard and handsome features of the infuriated competitor, even though they were streaked now with dirt and sweat and contorted with anger.

"Who is that?" Freda wondered aloud. "He is exceedingly good-looking, is he not?"

"'Tis Sir Jeffree de Crecy," Aimee responded disapprovingly. "And in my opinion, handsome is as handsome does." To her eye, Sir Jeffree looked every inch as proud and disagreeable as he had when she had seen him compete before. She almost fancied she could see the arrogant curl of his lip as he shoved the unfortunate attendant backward, sending him sprawling to the ground.

At their exchange, a lady sat on the bench in front of their own turned around to glance at them. Aimee did not recognize the lady, though in truth, she looked rather out of place among all the silks and satins, for her gown was extremely plain and somewhat homespun in appearance. Aimee wondered how she had managed to secure a seat in such a prominent position unless she was a servant to some grand lady.

The crowd started to boo, though whether it was because of the argumentative knight's behavior or the fact he was not being permitted to fight on, Aimee was not certain. Sir Jeffree showed no sign of caring either way. He flung his helmet on the ground so hard it bounced and then turned on his heel and stormed out of the ring.

"Such conduct," Freda tutted, looking shocked.

"Most unbecoming in a knight," Aimee agreed as the remaining knights reformed their lines. She was distracted again by the lady in the homespun gown, who was summoning a page from the sidelines. Aimee watched as she gave him a coin and partook of a cup of wine with every sign of enjoyment.

Decidedly, she was not a servant of anyone here present, Aimee thought. For some reason, Sir Jeffree's ignoble exit seemed to have cheered the woman considerably. She looked quite invigorated as she sat up in her seat and looked around with renewed interest in proceedings.

Aimee was so absorbed in her observations that she quite missed the last charge. Only the blast of several horns recaptured her attention.

"Oh, is it over?" Freda exclaimed, sounding confused.

Aimee glanced down at the arena. "There is only one yellow band remaining on his horse," she observed. "So, then the green side must be the victors." Her eyes sought out her husband, but to her disappointment, he had not removed his helmet as the others were doing. She would like to have seen how his expression looked when celebrating a win.

After some bustling by the squires and the attendants, the remaining yellow knights left the ring and the greens lined up to salute the royal box. The King rose and lifted his hands to signify the watching crowds should cheer the victors.

"It is quite deafening, is it not?" Freda quavered. "I declare my ears will be ringing tonight."

Aimee nodded, but she was watching the victorious knights clapping each other on the back. A couple of them went so far as to grasp Lord Kentigern's shoulder, but she noticed he did not return the gesture. It seemed he was not at all physically demonstrative when it came to his emotions. Was he smiling behind his visor? Aimee doubted it. Somehow, he seemed isolated and quite alone down there, for all he was flanked by a knight on either side.

Did nothing bring a smile to his face? she wondered sadly. She wanted to ask Freda what he had been like as a boy but sat among this noisy crowd was not the time for such questions. Perhaps, she thought hopefully, Lord Kentigern would triumph this afternoon and would find winning the joust more an occasion for celebration?

It grew steadily hotter as the afternoon progressed, and soon, all three women in their party were feeling the effects. Halfway through the jousting, a red-faced Freda was forced to remove her surcoat, though she did it with much lamenting and embarrassment.

"The red satin gown is entirely suitable to wear without it," Aimee assured her as she folded the garment and set it on the bench beside them. "And you will feel a good deal cooler now."

The jousters had been steadily whittled down from the starting fifty to now only four men remaining. They comprised of Lord Kentigern, Sir Roland Vawdrey (or Viscount Vawdrey as he now seemed to be addressed by the announcers), the Duke of Twyford, and a popular knight called Sir Edward Bevan of Knollesley. From the buzz of speculation in the crowd, it seemed any one of them could win, though Sir Edward was clearly the underdog.

"This southern heat is so oppressive," Magnatrude huffed tetchily, flapping her veil. "I wonder that everyone can stand it!"

Neither Freda nor Aimee made reply to so obvious a statement, and so she turned instead to Matthews, requesting he bring her a cup of ale. To her visible annoyance, he turned at once to Aimee for confirmation of the order.

"Yes, Matthews," Aimee agreed smoothly. "That sounds a very good notion. Do fetch us a pitcher so we may all quench our thirst." She passed him her purse again, and he bowed and disappeared into the crowd.

Magnatrude's color rose. "How closely you guard your purse, sister," she said pointedly. "I suppose you must have learned that at your father the merchant's knee."

Freda drew in a sharp breath, but before she could check her cousin, Aimee responded.

"Not as closely as you, sister," she replied at once. "Did you expect Matthews to pay for your refreshment with his own coin?"

"Of course not!" Magnatrude snapped contemptuously. "My brother would have reimbursed him in due course."

Aimee narrowed her eyes. Her sister-in-law was sweating profusely and looked to be in extreme discomfort. Even so, she could not bring herself to let such a comment pass. "I wonder if you would even have remembered so paltry a sum," she said aloud. "Paltry to a baron's daughter, that is, though not to a servant." Her words were quietly spoken but held a sting. She doubted very much Magnatrude would have remembered to pay Matthews back. "My father, the merchant, taught me many things," she said gravely, rising from her seat. "Including the prompt payment of debts. If my manners offend you, doubtless it is the disparity in our upbringings which is at fault."

Magnatrude's face was scarlet by this point, though whether it was from the hot summer sun or Aimee's response, she neither knew nor cared by this point.

"Where are you going, Aimee?" she heard Freda cry as she walked to the end of the bench. "I think Konrad competes next."

"I am going to stretch my legs and find some shade," Aimee flung back over her shoulder and was glad to hear her voice sounded steady. She could feel the angry tremble in her fingers as she clenched and unclenched them. She'd had quite enough of Mistress Magnatrude, she seethed as she stalked down the steps with a rigid back. It was one thing to slight her, but she would not tolerate snide remarks about her father spoken to her face! Who did Magnatrude imagine she was anyway, to look down upon Gerold Ankatel, the wealthiest merchant in all Karadok?

Choking back angry words that made her throat burn, Aimee turned and paced the narrow walkway that separated their stand from the next. When she reached the next flight of stairs, she wheeled about and retraced her steps. She was fuming and still shaking with anger.

If there was some form she was supposed to follow, such as giving Matthews her monies to caretake, no one had troubled to inform *her* of it! She came to a halt and bit her lip. Was that what one was supposed to do? Ursula had taught her to keep a firm hold of her purse and to know where it was at all times.

She supposed it probably *was* different for nobles. She tapped her foot angrily as she contemplated the fact. Now she came to think of it, she had never seen Lady Wycliffe handling a coin in the entire month they had stayed with her. As she plunked her hands on her hips, it occurred to her perhaps they considered the handling of vulgar coin as beneath them somehow?

"Milady." The gruff voice made her turn in alarm, but it was only Matthews. "You can't be down here by yourself," he said

205

apologetically. "It ain't safe. Not for a fine lady like you to be unattended."

Aimee nodded, though for a moment the words *I am not a fine lady* had hovered perilously close to the tip of her tongue. It was no good taking out her anger on Matthews, who was simply being conscientious. "I will just tarry a moment longer, Matthews, if you would not mind waiting," she forced herself to say on an outward breath. "It is a good deal cooler down here, out of the sun."

He nodded and reclined against one of the low separating walls as she retrod the same path for one final time in a vain attempt to soothe her ruffled feathers. She did not like her sister-in-law, she finally admitted to herself. And Magnatrude did not like her. It was not the end of the world and certainly not the first instance of such discord among in-laws. Even those who were all on equal footing. She shut her eyes and lowered her shoulders, breathing deliberately in and then out again. Another clamor went up from the crowd, and Aimee reflected that she had probably missed the final two bouts. She turned back to Matthews and forced a smile. "Let us return to the box."

Hot tears pricked at the backs of her eyes as Aimee climbed back up the steps to their stand. She did not want to return to her seat, she realized dully. Which was *ridiculous*. To act as though this spat with Magnatrude had spoiled everything was indescribably foolish. This moment was what she had been daydreaming about since Kellingford. Why, then, was she letting it be spoiled by the opinions of someone she did not even respect?

She was not the sensitive one, she reminded herself. That was Ursula. It wasn't like her to take someone's criticisms to heart. Then something flashed into her mind with unpleasant clarity. They were her sister's words from before her marriage.

Anyone who marries outside the rank they were born into would need to be hardy of nature indeed.

Ursula, she thought, had been right all along. She had been naïve where Ursula had been shrewd, she thought, swallowing down a sudden lump in her throat. She *had* thought herself resilient enough, but Magnatrude's refusal to accept her kinship had been steadily chipping away at her confidence since her wedding day.

Perhaps if Lord Kentigern had proved himself an attentive bridegroom, she could have withstood it, but he had been far from that. She remembered how she had stood alone at the bottom of the stairs to hand out the wedding favors to their attendants. *Far, far from that.* When she emerged blindly into the sunlight at the top of the steps, the arena fell into a deathly hush.

As her dazzled eyes adjusted, Aimee realized that all eyes in the arena were fixed on their box. She cast about in bewilderment. What had happened? Why was everyone staring at them? Then she saw it. The extended lance and the flower garland crown which a lady was taking from the proffered tip. *That* was what everyone was looking at, Aimee realized with a rush of relief, and not at her after all.

Her eyes sought out Freda for reassurance, but when she picked her out from the crowd, she knew something was very wrong. Freda had a hand over her mouth, and her eyes were stricken. Aimee felt a pang of dread. What was wrong? Her heart lurched. Had Lord Kentigern been injured? Then the murmuring started, growing louder and louder until it seemed almost deafening.

Aimee's head spun. She looked back at the lady with the flower garland and found she, too, was staring at Aimee with a frozen look on her face. She had not placed the crown on her head, just held it in her hands as though she was uncertain what to do with it. To her surprise, Aimee realized the tourney queen was the humbly dressed woman in the drab gown who was sat on the bench in front of theirs.

A sudden presentiment of dread crept along her spine and up to her neck where the fine hairs stood on end, and Aimee shivered in spite of the heat. Slowly, her eyes traveled along the length of the lance, tracking it back to its master, the knight that held it, sat so proudly on his horse at the foot of their stand. Even if she had not known him by sight, the colors on his shield matched so precisely her heraldic gown that every man, woman, and child in the audience must know they were a matched pair.

A sudden burning sensation in her chest jerked her out of her stunned stupefaction. She glanced down stupidly at her chest as though expecting to see at least a dagger, if not a spear had pierced her to the quick. There was nothing there, save the emblazoned crest of the Kentigerns to mock her. As she turned dizzy, it dawned on Aimee that she had not drawn breath in the last few moments and that was what was causing her pain. She dragged in a gasp of fortifying air and teetered a moment where she stood.

Every impulse in her screamed to turn and flee back down the steps from whence she had come, away from the prying eyes and the scalding *humiliation* of the scene playing out in front of her. She was poised perfectly for flight, her rioting thoughts screamed at her. Flee, flee from everyone, back to what she knew. Back *home* to her father and sister who loved her.

But no, she could not do that, another voice counseled. That was what all these fine folks no doubt *expected* from the upstart, lowborn bride Lord Kentigern had been saddled with. Aimee's spine stiffened. Instead of pelting back down the steps, she curled her fingers into her palms and plastered a smile to

208

her face. No doubt it looked more like a grimace, but it was the best she could manage, when inside her heart was shattering into a hundred tiny pieces.

She slid one foot forward and then the other as she made her way toward the central aisle of the stand. At least she hoped she was, for she had the strangest feeling that her head was floating off her shoulders, while her body was falling, falling into the depths of hell. Only the grainy wooden floorboards beneath the soles of her feet reassured her that she was still grounded and moving forward. Fortunately, the soles of her best slippers were so thin, she fancied she could feel every bump and knot in the wood.

The speculation of the crowd felt deafening by this point. She barely knew what she was doing when a hand grasped her arm in a tight grasp.

"I have you," came a harsh voice. "It's this way." She did not recognize the voice at first. It was Magnatrude, she realized dully, who had pulled her arm through hers and held it in so firm a grip now as she led Aimee toward their bench. How strange. Her sister-in-law was speaking, she realized. Aimee looked at her lips and saw them moving, but she could make no sense of the steady stream of words. It didn't matter, she realized. The words didn't matter, only the actions.

One phrase muttered through gritted teeth suddenly did make sense to her stunned brain. "You're doing well. Don't stop now."

Aimee nodded and smiled, smiled and nodded, concentrating on putting one foot in front of the other. "Where is Matthews?" she managed to ask between numb lips.

"Behind us. Do not worry, just keep moving forward."

Between the two of them, they managed to reach the end of their bench. Aimee felt fit to drop, and if it were not for Freda's welcoming arms, helping her down onto the seat, she might well have sunk to the floor.

"Oh, my dear!" Freda said in a choked voice and was immediately blasted by Magnatrude's icy gaze.

"Do not undo all her good work now," her sister-in-law said fiercely. "Pass her that goblet."

Wine was pressed into her hand, and Aimee raised it to her lips with nerveless fingers. She managed a glance toward the arena and found Lord Kentigern had retreated to the center where he and a second knight were awaiting the King's commendation. Vawdrey, she realized, was the runner-up. They both knelt awaiting the command to rise.

Aimee moistened her lips with wine and tried to moderate her grip on the goblet stem. She could still feel curious, burning gazes directed at her, but strangely enough, she felt more clammy than hot. Her gaze fell on the lady in the brown dress who was sat in front of them with her back very straight. The garland lay neglected on the bench beside her, for it seemed she had no desire to wear it on her head. She had a small patch of sweat at her middle back where she had perspired through her woolen gown.

With an effort, Aimee dragged her gaze away. Not for the wide world would she want anyone to notice the direction of her stare. *He had given the tourney crown to another.* She felt raw, a figure of pity and ridicule. Holding her head high, Aimee wished she could sink through the floorboards.

This dress, too, she thought wretchedly, made things worse. If only she could rip it from her body. Devoutly, she wished she had been led more by her sister's advice. Ursula had known the dress was too much, and Aimee had not heeded her. How much she would have been spared if she had only listened to Ursa's wise counsel. Freda's hand lightly covered her own, and Aimee turned her head to give her a reassuring smile.

From the pained look on Freda's face, Aimee guessed her efforts were not convincing. Freda leaned forward and whispered, "She has gone."

Aimee blinked. "Who has?"

"*That woman*," Freda replied, nodding significantly.

Aimee ventured another glance in front and saw the empty spot on the bench. The beautiful garland of summer flowers lay forlornly in the spot she had vacated. Aimee felt another pang. How highly she would have prized such a gift, and yet the woman in the brown dress had rushed away and abandoned it!

It really did seem the final insult to the whole debacle. She sat and smarted, barely noticing the flurry of approaching footsteps until the royal pages were stood in front of her, bowing low. One of them was speaking in a clear, boyish voice. "Her Majesty, Queen Armenal, requests your presence in the royal box, milady."

Aimee blinked. A royal audience! At this, her lowest, most disgraced hour. She looked hopelessly, first at Freda and then at Magnatrude.

Her sister-in-law nodded grimly. "We shall accompany you, of course," she said, looking as though the prospect were something akin to mounting the executioner's block.

"Of course!" Freda agreed hurriedly, though she had turned very pale at the prospect.

Aimee tried to remind herself as they followed in the wake of the youthful pages that she had always dreamed of such an honor. In her dreams, of course, the moment was vastly different to this one. She did not feel sticky and wilted from hours sat packed in the stands on a hot summer's day. She had not been scorned by her own husband in favor of another woman. She did not look like a prize idiot.

The royal box was flanked with guards and attendants. Aimee was waved through, but Freda and Magnatrude were bade to sit and wait on the outer edges. Her Majesty was all benevolent smiles. Aimee gave her lowest curtsey and hoped she did not look the crumpled wreck she imagined she appeared.

"My dear Baroness Kentigern!" the Queen welcomed her as though she were quite an old friend. "Come, approach me."

She turned to frown at the ladies-in-waiting who flanked her. "Shoo! Away with you! How closely you do clamor! All of you shall retreat now," she commanded imperiously. "Apart from Jane." She turned back to Aimee, who was approaching with some trepidation. "Jane is wholly trustworthy and shall not betray our confidences."

Aimee's eyes widened. *Confidences?* She could see no sign of the King, who had absented his own seat and must have taken himself off. The ladies-in-waiting fluttered away from the Queen like a flock of pretty birds, leaving only one who stood very demurely and quietly to the Queen's right. With much dragging of feet and clear reluctance, the gaggle filed out to the outer benches of the stand casting a good many glances and pouts over their shoulders.

"Stupid creatures," the Queen complained bitterly. "If you only knew what it was like to be surrounded by fools all day. All the sensible ones have lives outside of court, and I am left with the dregs!"

Unsure what else to do, Aimee bobbed another curtsey by way of reply. The Queen patted the brocade footstool that matched her own chair. "Come and seat here beside me. You must not be shy, for I am quite delighted to make your acquaintance. You have enlivened an event that threatened to be most dull!"

Aimee approached and hitched her skirts carefully before sinking down onto the cushioned footstool. The Queen extended a graceful hand to her, and Aimee dutifully kissed it.

"I thought so," Queen Armenal exclaimed, capturing Aimee's chin and turning her head, first one way and then the other. "Why, you are quite a pretty creature! Certainly, far too pretty to be married to that brute Kentigern! They say your father is the richest merchant in all Karadok. Is that so?"

Aimee's head whirled at the Queen's rapid change of subject. "I believe so, Your Majesty."

"Certainly, he must be a very cruel man," the Queen commented thoughtfully, releasing Aimee's chin to cup her own. "Who cares only for his coffers!"

"Oh no, Your Majesty!" Aimee objected, quite horrified that the Queen should think such a thing. "My father is the most kind and considerate of men."

"Kind? Considerate?" The Queen seemed astonished. "But how can this be?"

"He has always been the best of fathers."

The Queen seemed much struck by this and nodded slowly. "Ah, now I see," she said, with dawning comprehension. "Your greatest desire in life, it was to be a great lady?"

"Oh no, Your Majesty!" Aimee gave a bitter smile. "I was a good deal more foolish than that."

213

The Queen tipped her head to one side. "But I do not think you look like a fool," she said. "And I am quite an expert on these matters, I assure you!"

"Oh, but I was," Aimee argued bitterly, quite forgetting one should not disagree with one's monarch. "The biggest fool in all Karadok!"

The Queen's eyes gleamed, and she seized Aimee's hands in her own. "You shall tell me now, all about it! Jane!" she said, turning her head sharply. "Fetch for us now the wine and the honey cakes!"

Aimee did not know quite how it was, but when she sat back a half an hour later, she had poured out all her woes into the Queen's interested ears. It had all tumbled out, her ridiculous infatuation, her desire to win Lord Kentigern's heart, her disappointed love. Her chest had heaved, her cheeks had turned a deep poppy red, and there had even been a few tears. The Queen, bored with reserve and discretion from her courtiers, was highly gratified.

"And now, to crown his folly, he makes another woman the Queen of the Tournament!" Armenal declared wrathfully. "It is too much! It is an outrage!" She rolled her *r*'s in a magnificent manner. "It is not to be borne!"

Aimee strove to get control of her wobbling bottom lip. She was not used to be indulged in her passions. Usually, Ursula's sensible attitude tipped a bucket of cold water all over them. Suddenly, it occurred to Aimee that her sister would not think it a good idea to air her grievances like this and certainly not in such exalted quarters. She regarded the Queen doubtfully. "Y-you do not think I have made a mountain out of a molehill?" he gulped.

214

"A mountain out of a molehill?" the Queen echoed, sounding mystified by the expression. Then its meaning seemed to occur to her. "What a droll saying! But no!" Queen Armenal assured her. "You were oh so dignified when all eyes they were riveted on you. Quite the grand lady, I assure you. For one moment, I held my breath; I wondered if you might not snatch the crown from your rival's head." The Queen flashed her an apologetic look. "I did not know then that you were so nice in your manners."

It occurred to Aimee that the Queen had expected her to act like some fishwife in a common market brawl. Then her words registered. "My rival?" she blurted in dismay. "I do not suppose"—Aimee hated herself for even asking, but she could not help herself—"that Your Majesty knows who—who that lady was that my husband crowned?"

"You may be sure I do!" Queen Armenal said with a benevolent air. "When I saw the drama unfolding in your box, you may be assured that I made the enquiries. I had, of course, heard all about Lord Kentigern having married a commoner," she continued smoothly, and for some reason, Aimee found it hard to take offence. "But I had not heard so much as a peep about Sir Jeffree de Crecy's tumble from grace!" She turned impetuously to Aimee. "Tell to me, are you acquainted at all with Sir Jeffree?"

"I have seen him joust before on two occasions," Aimee admitted, wondering why the Queen had strayed so far from the point. "He—he always seemed a most proud man." Aimee was hesitant in her description, not liking to use the real words she would have liked to have used, such as *arrogant* and *disagreeable.*

"But yes!" the Queen agreed delightedly. "Me, I would say that always he seems like he has a stick up his bottom." Aimee

215

choked on the tentative bite she had taken of her honey cake. The Queen waved a hand. "I am not a native of these parts and I do not have the natural reserve. We will dispense with it between us, for I can see your nature is also very easy and open like my own."

Aimee nodded though she cast an uneasy look at the lady-in-waiting. Her grave expression did not alter by so much as a twitch of her eyebrow, so Aimee turned her attention back to the Queen. "I do not quite understand what bearing Sir Jeffree has upon the matter," she admitted.

"Oh, do you not?" The Queen looked at her for a moment, a small smile playing about her lips. "Tell me, are you aware at all that Sir Jeffree has recently taken a wife?" She sat back and regarded Aimee with amusement.

"He has?" Slowly it dawned on Aimee that the Queen saw some connection between this fact and her own predicament. "You mean—? That lady is—? But surely not." Aimee faltered. *Surely, that lady in the plain woolen gown could not be the wife of one such as Sir Jeffree?*

"But yes." The Queen nodded. "That drab creature is the new Lady de Crecy."

15

Konrad threw down his knife and pushed back his chair. Supper had been an oppressive affair. He moodily surveyed the three other occupants of the room. He couldn't quite put his finger on it, but something was decidedly *off* this evening. He had never been one to be affected by the atmosphere of a room, but even he could tell a frosty air hung over the supper table.

He cleared his throat, and no one looked up, not even Freda. Now he came to think of it, his cousin had not made any of her usual empty small talk at dinner. Strange to say, her silence had not been the relief he had once thought it would be. "Is no one going to congratulate me on my victory?" he asked sardonically, throwing caution to the wind. His sister gave an incredulous huff, but his eyes were not on her, but his wife.

Aimee dragged her eyes from her plate and lifted her goblet. "Congratulations on your victory," she said flatly. He narrowed his eyes at her, but to his disappointment, she could not be goaded into any further speech. Neither Trude nor Freda echoed the toast, though his cousin did lift her cup and take a small sip of her wine.

"Will you go to the victory feast tonight at the palace?" Aimee asked in a cold, clipped voice he had not heard from her before.

He looked down speakingly at his empty plate. "I have already eaten my fill. Besides," he added, "I am not much of one for feasts or celebrations." Though why he was explaining himself to her now, he had not the smallest notion.

"A pity," Aimee replied with a decided edge to her voice. "Perhaps you could have celebrated your win further with Lady de Crecy."

Either Freda or Magnatrude uttered an exclamation that turned into a hasty cough, but Konrad did not have eyes for anyone apart from his wife just then. He cleared his throat. "And just why would I do that?"

"I am sure I could not say. Past form, perhaps?"

Konrad drummed his fingers on the table as he surveyed his wife. She had changed out of his colors before dinner and now wore a gown of palest yellow. It became her well, he thought, for the hue did not wash her out as it did pale women.

"The Queen has invited me to attend the palace tonight as her guest," Aimee continued, thumping her goblet back down on the table so hard that two drops of wine sloshed out and stained the tablecloth red.

"We are not attending," Konrad replied, finally adding up all the signs: the overbright eyes, the red cheeks, the slight tremble in the hand that held her drink. His wife was in a high temper, he realized incredulously. A temper with him.

"It is a pity you find yourself unable to attend," Aimee replied and, yes, there was a decided bite to her tone. "But I could not possibly disappoint Her Majesty."

Konrad snorted. "You both can and will disappoint the southern queen. *I* am the only one you need to worry about pleasing, wife, and me alone."

Aimee's expression tightened. "I do not care about that anymore, my lord!" she flung at him, abandoning all pretense of coolness. "*For I no longer love you!*"

You could have heard a pin drop. Then all hell broke loose. Konrad had dragged his chair back, and Magnatrude jumped up from her own seat. "No, Konrad!" she wailed as Freda burst into shocked tears. Konrad ignored them, hauling Aimee out of her chair and slinging her over his shoulder.

"What are you doing, my lord?" Aimee enquired in tones of outrage as he flung open the door and started up the stairs. "I have not finished my supper!"

He gave a short mirthless laugh, though why he should feel invigorated by her defiance he had no notion. He did though; his blood was positively coursing through his veins and pounding in his ears. He hadn't known he could feel like this anywhere other than the battlefield, he marveled as he sprinted up the steps to her bedchamber. "Well, if you have any appetite left when I'm finished with you, you can return to the table and eat your fill. How's that for a bargain?"

On the threshold of her bedchamber, he paused a moment in surprise, for on her bed lay his banner cut into ribbons. Nay, he realized incredulously, it was not his banner but her dress. The one she had worn that day in his honor. She had slashed the damned thing to pieces! He slammed the door shut behind them and shot the bolt across before setting her on her feet.

Aimee glared back at him, her chest heaving as her flashing eyes dared him to demand an explanation for the dishonor to his colors. "Take off your dress," he heard himself rumble. "Unless you want that one in pieces too," he added dryly, reaching for his belt.

"I will not," Aimee flung at him, her chin in the air. "I can simply raise my skirts for what you intend. I told you, I mean to attend the palace this night."

He stared at her a moment, then shrugged. "Your choice, but you won't be fit to be seen after I've finished with you," he growled, and Aimee's eyes widened when she saw him cast the belt onto a nearby chair, shortly followed by his tunic.

"What are you—?" She broke off. "Oh." Her cheeks flamed. "I thought you meant to beat me!"

He shot a heated look at her. "Did you?" he asked without much interest. "If you don't take it off, I'll rip it off you," he said, stalking toward her now. "Last warning, Aimee."

"Wait!" she blurted as he seized her about the waist and flung her onto the bed, right on top of his mutilated colors. She bounced, but before she'd managed to struggle upright, he was on top of her and dragging her skirts up to her waist.

"Let's try it your way," he said affably. "And afterward, if you can stand, I'll even let you stagger to the palace." He dragged her undergarments down. "With my seed trickling down your thighs," he said, running a fingertip down one inner leg by way of illustration. Aimee gasped at his shocking words. "Ticklish, wife?" he asked, cocking his head to one side. She stared up at him, open-mouthed.

"Speechless?" he asked. "An admirable quality in a wife." He had no idea why he was still talking. If he didn't know any better, he would almost think he was teasing her.

I no longer love you. That was what she had said.

The answer he should have made had been an obvious one. *I neither desired nor asked for your love.* He knew the exact tone he should have employed too. A scornful one. A curl of his lip, a cold look in his eyes, and any budding affection she harbored for him would have promptly withered and perished in the bud. It was a miracle such tender shoots had put forth in the first place.

Then he should have exited the room, the city, and her life for at least a twelvemonth. Let her see just how insignificant a place in his life she occupied. Aimee had enough pride to have met him thereafter with only the coolest formality. But he simply couldn't do it. Not for the life of him could he have dealt the death blow to her silly, girlish fancies. Somewhere, a small part of him wondered why the hells not, but he pushed that to one side for now. He would worry about that later.

For now, he had more pleasurable things uppermost on his mind. *Perhaps you could have celebrated your win further with Lady de Crecy*, she had sniped at him with her color high. She had been jealous. Over him. He did not know why, but that realization made his chest burn. Out of nowhere, the thought occurred to him that he should have given her the damned tourney crown.

He let her feel his full weight bearing down on her, just for a minute. "I will never raise a hand to you, Aimee," he said in a serious tone, and her eyes flew to meet his. "But every time you flout me, I will drag you upstairs and thoroughly demonstrate my ascendency. Do you understand?"

She considered this a moment breathlessly. "What if it's not at home?" she asked in a strangled voice.

He suppressed a crazy impulse to laugh at her retort. "I would not recommend defying me outside our home," he replied, catching her two wrists in one hand and pinning them above her head as he slid a muscular thigh between her own. *Our home? What was he even talking about?*

"But if I did?" The fact she was even persisting in this made him feel ridiculously heated.

His hot gaze ensnared her own as he slowly and deliberately lowered his head so their faces were very close together. "Well, then, I guess I'd have to improvise," he said huskily and felt her soft thighs squeeze around his own. She was holding her breath again, and her eyes were huge. Seeing the direction of her gaze, he realized it was a kiss she was wanting.

Strange to say, the thought was no longer a displeasing one to him. "If I kiss you, you have to keep breathing this time," he said. "Through your nose." Aimee sucked in a breath, and realizing he was about to get a piece of her mind, he closed the distance between them and pressed his lips to hers. For a minute, he thought she was resisting, then he remembered this was how she had kissed him last time. Her lips closed and fiercely mashed against his own. He barely remembered how to kiss himself, but closing his eyes, he dredged the distant memory to the surface and let his own turn soft and coaxing against hers.

It was a strange sensation to be exchanging sweet kisses like this, lying on top of a shredded dress. He felt more inflamed with lust than he could remember ever feeling, even back in the dim days before his grievous injuries. Somehow, though, the throb in his chest made him feel conscious of every hitched breath between them as he nibbled on her bottom lip and tipped her jaw to angle her mouth to his satisfaction. It overruled even the insistent throb of his cock which did not know what the hells he was playing at.

He had hurt her. His mind reeled at the realization. He had hurt her when he had given that ridiculous garland to another woman. The tourney queen was an empty convention, nothing more. He had barely given the matter a second thought. She had not been in the stands when he had glanced that way. De Crecy's wife had, and he had wanted to score off de Crecy. That was how he always did it, so it stuck in his competitor's craw. He never meant it as a compliment, but always as a blow.

He hadn't meant the blow to fall on Aimee though. He wanted to make it better. The thought almost staggered him. The fact that he even wielded any power to hurt her feelings was frankly ludicrous. He dragged the tip of his tongue over the seam of her lips and groaned when she did not take the hint. He lifted his lips away. "Let me in," he murmured.

"What?" Aimee's eyelids fluttered open. She had shut her eyes too. His gaze roamed over her dazed expression, the dark hair spilling out of its tidy arrangement. This wasn't going to cut it, he decided suddenly, her still being half-dressed in this yellow gown. He wanted her naked against the remains of the particolored gown, caught up in the ribbons of the slashed fabric. He caught his breath at the picture it conjured up in his mind's eye.

"I want you naked," he said roughly, voicing his thoughts aloud.

"Oh," she said, struggling to oblige. He helped her up and started immediately loosening the laces at her back and sleeves. As soon as there was room enough, he maneuvered the gown up and over her head, dropping it over the edge of the bed.

When she lay back down, he immediately crowded back around her, seeking her mouth with his, showing her what he wanted. The moan she gave around his tongue reassured him she was fully on board. *Thank the gods.*

He sank one hand into the hair at the nape of her head, tipping her head back for his consuming kiss. The other reached for her hand and pushed it over her head. Once there, he reached for the blue and yellow ribbons of one shredded sleeve and wrapped them about her wrist, entangling her there.

When she showed no sign of alarm, he grabbed her other hand and did the same, securing it over her head. Aimee watched him with a faint pucker between her brows as he reached behind her

223

and drew scraps of yellow and blue silk across her bared breasts.

"Wha—?" she started, but he cut her off.

"I don't know," he admitted gruffly. "I just want to see it."

Aimee's eyes were very round as he drew long slivers of what was left of the skirts around her body and trailed them across her stomach and between her legs. With a bolt of shock and something else, he realized that he would like to secure her legs too. To bind her pretty ankles up in blue and yellow and tie them to the bedposts. Fuck, where had that come from? He swallowed, his throat suddenly dry.

Abstinence did strange things to a man, or so it seemed. He'd never entertained such thoughts before. He gave his head a slight shake.

"What about you?" she asked boldly.

He shrugged, looking down. The only thing he hadn't shed were his braies and chausses. He shoved down his braies and kicked them on to the floor but didn't see that his leg coverings were either here or there. They certainly weren't an impediment. "I'm naked enough."

"Neither of us is entirely naked," she pointed out, biting her lip. She sounded breathless, and he noticed her nipples pointing through the scraps of silk were hard. He couldn't resist running a hand over her full breasts, giving them a savoring squeeze. She gave a whimper, followed by a full-body shiver.

"Open your legs, Aimee," he said thickly. *Gods.* She didn't even hesitate. He reached between her legs and grabbed a handful of the tattered silk, draping the strands first over one thigh and then the other. Aimee lifted her head to watch him, but she left her hands where they were above her head.

He had no idea why it was having the effect on him that it did, but seeing her tangled up in his colors was making him feel almost frantic. She had chosen him, a voice whispered in his head. She had chosen him, and he had given the crown to another. He tugged at one blue and yellow ribbon, and it slipped right up between her legs, lodging in her sweet cleft.

They both caught their breath, and Aimee's eyes flew wide. "My lord—?" she quavered uncertainly.

"I want you to get it nice and wet for me, Aimee," he replied, his voice pure gravel. "Can you do that?" She made a strangled noise in her throat. "Well, can you?" he persisted.

When she nodded, crimson-cheeked, he tugged it again and Aimee gasped. "Good," he replied, dragging the length of the fabric slowly through her nether lips. Then he pulled it back the other way, carefully repeating the lightly sawing motion before tugging the length of sopping ribbon back through her pussy lips. He stared at it a moment, at the telltale spotting, before raising it to his face, breathing in her musky, womanly scent.

Gods, she smelled incredible. His mouth watered, and feeling her eyes on him, he kissed the ribbon of fabric, slowly and deliberately. Aimee hadn't closed her legs, and he shifted over her, seeking relief for his throbbing cock as he pressed into her soft belly. He gave a harsh groan as his hard hips settled against the cradle of hers.

Gods, that felt good, but he realized with surprise that he wanted her mouth again. Which was inconvenient as their height disparity would mean him shifting down and breaking the contact he craved. Or he could just bend his neck and get her to lift hers. Clamping a hand to the back of her neck, he angled her head up and lowered his lips to hers.

Aimee's kiss was so enthusiastic it nearly blew the top off his head. She didn't kiss any different, he thought, now she didn't love him anymore. It was a shock to realize he had been scared she might. He was the one forgetting to breathe now as their tongues stroked and tangled together. He kind of missed her arms wrapped tight about his neck, though. He slid his other hand up to find hers still wrapped up in the tattered dress.

When her fingers returned the press of his own, the throb in his chest became an exquisite pain. He groaned against her mouth. The shredded silk dress and Aimee's hard nipples brushed against his chest. He wanted to be inside her. Deep inside. He took his hand from her neck and slid it over the dark hair of her mound, caressing her there before his fingers dipped inside her, finding her delightfully wet and slippery.

"Ohhh!" Aimee gave a broken moan as he slid a finger right up inside her. Konrad swallowed it and caught her bottom lip between his teeth as he lifted his mouth from hers. He simultaneously didn't want to stop kissing her yet wanted to hear any words she might let fall. It had been stimulating as hell last time.

Still, he remembered as he added another finger, last time had been with his mouth between her legs, not his cock. *Also*, a voice whispered in his head, *last time she had thought she was in love with you*. Should he bring her off with his fingers first? After all, it was only the third time he had bedded her and…

"My lord!" Aimee whined and twisted underneath him. *"Please!"*

"Please what?" he asked gruffly, though she probably wanted playful words, *teasing*. He didn't really do teasing, despite his strange behavior of late. "Do you need my fingers here or my mouth? Tell me."

226

"You," she said tightly. "Inside me."

Which could mean any of the three, he reflected, even as he shifted over her, shoving her legs apart, aligning the head of his cock at her wet slit. He was going to take it in the most literal sense and pretend she had begged for his cock. The muffled sob she gave when he started to push into her made him check, though it caused him actual physical pain at this point to halt his progress.

"Don't stop!" she protested, canting up her hips to encourage him. *Oh fuck.*

He all but roared as he surged into her tight heat, not stopping until he was deeply seated. Then he paused, his chest heaving, staring down at her. Usually, she would pass her hands around his back at this point, he realized, running them over his muscles, maybe telling him how nice they felt. And he godsdamned missed it.

He glanced up at her captured wrists and started trying to unravel them. He didn't have a knife handy. *Damn it.* Aimee made a muffled sound and moved beneath him, as though desperately seeking the friction she needed. Abandoning his attempt to untangle the silken strands, he grabbed a firm hold of her hips instead and thrust into her. "This what you wanted?" he rasped.

"Ohhh, oh, yes, yes!" Aimee sobbed. "Yes, keep doing that! *Please.*"

"I intend to," he assured her, jolting her against him with increasing firmness. "Wrap your legs around me." He grabbed her round thighs and hauled them up around his hips. "Feels good?" he asked sharply.

"Y-yes," she replied, but there was *something.*

227

"What is it? Tell me."

"I wish I could touch you, that's all." Her tone was strangely wistful as she glanced up at her hands.

He glanced up again. "I want that too," he admitted tersely. "But not enough to pull out and fetch a knife. You can touch me afterward."

"Oh. Really?" She looked so happy at this small concession that he almost lost his rhythm. He loosed one hip and reached down to pull the silk tight across her generous breasts, then leaned down to capture one nipple between his lips and suck it into his mouth. Aimee jerked and let out a suppressed moan.

The noises bursting from her lips told him he was on the right track. He gave the other breast the same treatment before lifting his head. "You going to reach it for me, Aimee?" Possibly that term meant nothing to her, for she did not answer, only gave another gasp. "Your peak?" he persisted, lowering his voice to a growl.

"I can tell you're climbing now, wife, and once you reach the top, I want you to fling yourself right off, you hear me?" She gave a whimper. "And I want to hear it, you understand? I want you to let me know you've gone over the edge."

Truth was, he was drawing pretty close to the summit himself. He shut his eyes fast against the enticing picture she made beneath him. The bounce of her full breasts may have disappeared from view, but he could still feel the jiggle of her soft flesh jostling back against him. The slide of the shredded silk, the tight, wet clasp of her wrapped around him, getting tighter and tighter still. He drew a sharp breath. It was too good. At this rate, he was going to power right past her.

He reached down between them, parting her petals and seeking out that fleshy pearl hiding between them. Aimee gave a muffled shriek. "There?" he demanded. "Like that?"

She arched right up into him and exploded. He just about held things together until she finally stopped writhing and lay panting beneath him. He would just wait a minute, he vowed, tensing his jaw, remaining where he was, planted deep. Then he would drive back into her in a steady pursuit of his own pleasure.

"Ohhh, Lord Kentigern," she moaned breathily against his ear, and just like that, he tipped right over the edge with a lusty curse word.

16

When Aimee woke the next morn, Lord Kentigern was gone
and so was all trace of her shredded gown. She checked under
the bed and behind the bed curtains, but there was no sign of it.
With dawning embarrassment, Aimee hoped that Golda had not
come across it and taken it for the rag bag or even worse, for
mending. It was quite beyond repair, she was sure, but the
thought of anyone else laying hands on it was mortifying,
especially when she thought about the places the garment had—
well—*been*.

When her maid brought her hot water half an hour later, no
mention was made of the ill-treated garment, and Aimee
decided against enquiring after it. Instead, she washed
thoroughly and dressed in a sage green gown. She arranged her
dark hair with great care, adding a small veil with pretty edging
to cover the pinned braids.

In her mind was the idea that if she took the time over her
appearance now, then she could appear below looking a picture
of decorum and dignity in direct contrast with how she had
behaved the previous day. Her cheeks flamed hot when she
thought of how she had conducted herself, and she clapped her
hands to them, gazing unseeingly into her looking glass. For a
moment, when her husband had flung back the bedchamber
door revealing the remains of that wretched gown, she had
thought she would *die* of mortification on the spot.

She let her hands drop from her face and frowned. Certainly,
Lord Kentigern had not reacted to her act of passionate
vandalism at all how she had expected. She relived the moment
now in her mind's eye and marveled at the strange culmination
to her day. She had been publicly disgraced, been shown great
royal favor, had committed an act of blatant destruction, and

been ravished by her own husband all in the space of one day! In the aftermath of their spent passion, he had even given her an explanation of sorts.

No sooner had he freed her from the shredded gown than he had rolled onto his back and drawn her down on top of him. Aimee had needed no prompting to run her hands over his magnificent chest, and he had lain passive while she had run her palms all over the mighty muscles in his upper arms and shoulders.

"I should probably explain about the tourney crown," he had said at last in a voice that cracked slightly.

Aimee had made no reply, just waited. She was too sated and exhausted to make any gesture of resistance by this point, so she remained slumped over his chest as he gave his justification.

"I always give it where it will cause the most strife," he had admitted bluntly.

She had lifted her head at that. "What do you mean?" she'd croaked.

He had looked irritated at having to spell it out, perhaps even guilty. "Such as awarding it to my competitor's spouse."

She regarded him doubtfully. "You mean…like a poisoned chalice?"

"I'm not the only one that does it," he had said defensively. When she had made no reply, he had asked "What?" in a testy manner.

"Oh, 'tis nothing," she had managed. "It's just… Well, I thought that it meant something else. When a knight awarded it to a lady, I mean." When he didn't speak, she had quickly added awkwardly, "I daresay you know much more about it than I."

He had made no rejoinder to this, though he had lifted a large and hesitant hand to press her head back into his chest. Not long after that, Aimee had fallen fast asleep. She told herself it did not matter how long he had tarried before leaving her bed.

Before, when she still foolishly thought herself in love with her husband, she would have cared about such things. Not now though. Now, she took an entirely practical approach to her marriage.

She drifted downstairs and found Magnatrude and Freda both stood before the fireplace in some low-voiced conversation. They turned and greeted her hastily. "Were you waiting for me?" she murmured, taking her seat at the table. "I apologize. I was dallying this morning."

For some reason, her words seemed to freeze the words on their tongues. They both gazed at her in seeming dismay. Aimee leaned forward to help herself to a piece of bread and could not help but wince in discomfort. Her muscles were stiff this morning, particularly her thigh muscles which burned. Her husband's lovemaking had been extremely vigorous, and in truth, she was not sure you could call it lovemaking at all. She wished her own reaction to it had not been so…enthusiastic.

"Oh dear," said Freda with a muffled sob. "Was he very brutal?"

Aimee nearly dropped her cup of ale.

"Freda!" Magnatrude upbraided her. "It is not our place to—"

"Oh, really, Trude?" Freda rounded on her. "It was not I who jumped out of my seat and begged dear Konrad not to beat his own wife!"

232

Belatedly, it occurred to Aimee that her in-laws had misinterpreted the nature of Lord Kentigern's punishment for his recalcitrant wife. "No, no," she said weakly. "Of course he did not. I am quite well this morn, I assure you."

Magnatrude bent her neck and fiddled with her napkin. "Aimee," she said, taking a deep breath before lifting her head. "I owe you an apology." Aimee was so surprised she didn't know what to say for a full minute. "I realize it will take time for you to determine my sincerity, but I hope that one day, in the not-too-distant future, you will give me another chance to be your sister."

"Of course," Aimee replied, and Magnatrude's shoulders relaxed.

"Thank you," she breathed, looking relieved. "I wish you would call me Trude, then, as my family do."

As Magnatrude had not seemed particularly reconciled to this informal shortening of her name, Aimee was again surprised. "I would be happy to, Trude," she said truthfully and remembered the string of coral beads still sat in the cabinet. She rose and fetched the package, setting them down by her sister-in-law's plate before returning to her own seat.

Magnatrude opened them and slipped the handsome string of beads immediately over her head. "Thank you, sister," she said politely. "I am afraid that, well, the family jewels were lost during the late war, and there are none left to bestow on you."

Aimee's hand flew to Freda's brooch which was pinned to her chest. "I have this one," she said, looking across at Freda, who looked highly gratified.

Magnatrude blinked. "Oh yes," she said. "Of course, that is a handsome piece, though it could not possibly compare to the

Bartree diadem which was exceedingly famous." She turned to her cousin. "Is that not so, Freda?"

"Oh yes, dear," Freda answered absently. "Though they say it is women with golden hair who desire opals, and Aimee is so very dark."

"Golden hair?" Magnatrude repeated, sounding irritated. "What *are* you talking about, cousin?"

"I am sure I am right," Freda said. "For a particular friend of my youth was mad for them." Freda's eyes glazed over with the effort of recollection. "She always said opals would prevent a golden head from fading or darkening."

Magnatrude looked taken aback by this information but soon rallied. "There were not only opals on the diadem but also emeralds," she pointed out sternly. "Emeralds would look very fine against the black of Aimee's hair."

Aimee's thoughts wandered as the cousins debated the properties of various jewels. If the diadem was gone, it was gone. She could see no point in debating it. Instead, she wondered what time Lord Kentigern had risen from her bed. She had slept so soundly; she had not stirred once. Had he only waited for her to close her eyes, or had he tarried longer? She cupped her chin in her hand and let her thoughts drift away. Directly after she had broken her fast, she would place the signet ring on his pillow, she decided. Then he would find it there when next he returned home.

A sharp rap on the door recalled her to her surroundings. All three of them turned as one to regard Golda coming through the door, her eyes wide and her breathing labored. "There's an invitation here, miss—I mean, milady. From the *palace!*"

Aimee stared in astonishment as a smartly dressed youth strode through the door in a royal blue tunic with scalloped sleeves. He bowed smartly and looked quizzically at the table occupants. "Lady Kentigern?" he enquired politely.

"That is me," Aimee replied, and he bowed and introduced himself as one Gordon Fairfax, emissary of Her Majesty, Queen Armenal.

"I am come to extend the Queen's royal invitation for you to join her this afternoon at the summer palace, my lady. The Queen has had a pavilion set up and has her temporary court of love and beauty set up along the south lawns."

"Love and beauty?" Aimee repeated with misgiving.

Gordon cleared his throat. "The ladies are mostly employed in embroidery," he admitted. "While a bard sings to them many famous tales of romance."

"Embroidery!" Aimee exclaimed with dismay. She was far from confident in the art. Recalling herself to the honor being done to her, she mustered up some hurried semblance of gratitude. "H-how very kind of Her Highness, to be sure. Am I to accompany you now?"

He bowed again with a flourish. "I will both escort and return you in good time," he promised, beaming at Freda and Magnatrude.

"Should we accompany you?" her sister-in-law asked, and to Aimee's mind she looked willing though not particularly enthusiastic. Wondering if Magnatrude had been intending to visit with northern nobles again today, she turned back to young Gordon with an enquiring look.

He spread his hands wide. "The invitation is ostensibly only addressed to you, my lady, but the Queen would not be surprised to find you accompanied and would not turn anyone away, I am sure." He smiled seraphically at Magnatrude, who obligingly rose from her seat.

"Oh dear," said Freda. "Would you mind terribly, dear Aimee, if I did not accompany you?" She bit her lip. "Only I am lamentably shortsighted these days, and my embroidery was never as good as Trude's."

"Of course not," Aimee assured her soothingly as she and Magnatrude made haste to depart. She squeezed Freda's bony shoulder in passing. "Only, make sure you bid Golda to light a fire if you remain in one room, for it can grow quite cold in the shade."

She hurried upstairs to fasten her gold chain about her neck and replace her thin slippers with a pair of smart ankle boots with cross lacings down the front. She tarried only to fetch the gold signet ring from the hidey-hole in her cupboard and carry it into her husband's bedchamber. This she placed in the middle of her husband's pillow bearer, still in its velvet pouch. After stepping back to survey the effect and check he could not miss this latest gift, she turned and flew down the staircase to join those waiting for her below.

17

Konrad arrived early at the palace jousting grounds and soon retrieved the last of his kit, strapping it to Actaeon's broad back. The tents, which had been set up to house the various bits of equipment, were mostly empty, though a few people were milling about, mostly servants and attendants. He expected the likes of Vawdrey and Orde were still lolling abed with their wives at this time.

He was just passing the last of the striped tents when he was hailed by Sir Douglas Farleigh, who came rushing after him. Kentigern halted and wondered for the thousandth time why it was that Farleigh was always so damned pleased to see him.

"Well met, my lord!" the younger knight enthused, hurrying to his side. "I was sorry you did not attend last night's feast."

Konrad eyed him askance. "I rarely attend such functions."

"True, but in light of your triumphant win…" The other trailed off.

Konrad shrugged. "I am sure there were revelers enough to fill the hall. I doubt my presence was missed."

Farleigh stared at him. "A good many looked for you there, my lord. I was one such."

Konrad blinked, taken aback by so plain a statement. He scratched his neck. "I am lately married," he heard himself say in the manner of one making some sort of lame excuse. What was he doing?

Farleigh's frown cleared in an instant, as though his words explained everything. "Congratulations, my lord! Your bride does not care for the clamor of boisterous knights, I take it, and

I am sure none could blame her." He looked suddenly wistful. "My own wooing, I confess, has been far from smooth. You have heard of Lady Constance Northcott?"

Konrad glanced about him, but there was no one in sight to stem Farleigh's flow. "Er…no?" he said in lieu of anything else occurring to him.

"She is the most beauteous maiden in all Karadok," Farleigh said fervently. "But she is very cultured and has many suitors." He pulled a face. "Alas, she does not care to watch the lists."

"Maybe you should find one that does."

"One what?"

"Woman."

"Oh." Farleigh looked flummoxed. "Well, as to that…" He scratched the back of his neck. "After all, Kentigern, you said your own wife—"

"Aimee is not like that," Konrad cut across his words. "She likes the lists. All this"—he waved a hand vaguely—"pageantry and so forth." After all, she had worn his banner as a dress for all to see. And he had repaid her for that display of loyalty by giving the crown to another woman.

Farleigh placed his hands on his hips and breathed out. "Where are you headed now, my lord?" he asked beseechingly. "Fain, would I have some speech with you."

"Oh, yes?" It was not that Konrad was flattered precisely. It was more that he did not know what to do with himself this morning. Which was why, precisely half an hour later, he found himself sat in an accommodating inn looking across a table at Farleigh as the younger knight poured out his woes.

238

Konrad lowered his tankard and wiped the back of his hand across his mouth. The ale was good. Several platters were plunked down on the tabletop before them. He pulled the nearest toward him and tucked in as Farleigh listed Lady Constance's virtues. He let the lad speak his fill, and there was plenty on his mind. Konrad had eaten most of the beef slathered in hot yellow mustard by the time Farleigh's words had petered out.

"It amounts to this," Konrad said heavily, pushing his trencher away. "What does she want from life? Have you asked her?"

"Oh, I know that alright," Farleigh answered frustratedly. "She wants music, enlightened conversation, and such like."

Konrad blanched. "You think you can give her that?"

Farleigh shrugged a moody shoulder. "I don't know," he mumbled into his ale cup.

Konrad found himself reminded of that godsawful family Aimee said she had spent time with. *What was their name? Highcliff? Wycliffe?* "You'd have to invite philosophers and poets to your table for after dinner speeches," he warned.

"Vawdrey seems to manage alright," Farleigh mumbled mutinously.

"What's that you say?"

"Vawdrey's wife is one of that set. Patroness of the arts and the like. He seems happy enough with her."

Konrad reflected on this. "Vawdrey has an affable nature," he said after a minute. "Besides," he added gruffly, "they—er— want the same thing. Vawdrey and his wife. To be together. That means they find a way to make it work." Farleigh's mouth

239

dropped open. "It's true," Konrad said with surprise, for he had never really thought about it before.

"So." Farleigh glared into his ale cup. "You mean I have to make sure the lady returns my affections?" That had *not* been what Konrad had meant at all, but when he opened his mouth to refute this, words failed him. "That way," Farleigh carried on, "she won't care about me being an uncultivated dog." His frown cleared. "Yes, I suppose that simplifies things."

"Does it?" Konrad gazed at him in surprise.

"If I secure her affections, then our differences won't truly matter." Farleigh nodded. He reached into his tunic. "Tell me, my lord, what think you of this?" He withdrew his hand and held out his palm to show something that Kentigern first took to be a coin suspended on a gold chain, but on closer inspection turned out to be a disc decorated in colored enamel.

"What is it?"

Farleigh blushed. "A token for my lady," he explained. "See, it shows a knight, depicted in armor. I thought it might make her look favorably on me." He directed a hopeful look in Konrad's direction. "Do you think it might soften her heart toward me?"

Konrad frowned and took another swig of ale. It seemed to him that if Lady Constance was not a fan of knightly pursuits, then such a present was unlikely to curry favor. He cleared his throat. "Maybe you ought to get her something she likes," he suggested uncomfortably.

"Such as?"

"A book?" he suggested feebly as Farleigh clapped a hand to his forehead.

"You mean commission a poet!" he yelled, drowning out Konrad's words. "Of course! Why did I not think of that?" He fingered his hairless chin. "I could get him to pen me a ballad that pleads my cause!"

Konrad eyed him doubtfully before inspiration struck. "Why don't you just ask Vawdrey how he won over *his* wife?" he suggested with what he thought to be an almost staggering logic.

Farleigh cast him a horrified glance before lowering his voice. "Everyone knows Vawdrey seduced the Lady Eden," he answered in hushed tones. "It was a huge scandal at the time. Do you not remember the Queen demanded an account of it at court?"

"No, did he?" Konrad asked with a certain grudging respect. He knew Vawdrey was brave, but not *that* brave. Even he could tell the Lady Eden was a formidable sort.

"I could *never* disrespect Constance so," Farleigh said virtuously.

"Hmmm." For his part, Konrad was starting to think Farleigh's cause was a hopeless one. "Where did you get the necklace?" he asked on impulse. He did not think Aimee possessed much by way of jewelry. In any case, she never seemed to wear much.

Farleigh brightened. "A goldsmith currently much in favor at court. He has premises in Bulwark Lane. Blyfield is his name."

"He ever do any work resetting jewels?" Konrad asked, thinking of the sorry state of what remained of the Bartree jewels. They had been wrenched from their gold settings which had been donated to the Blechmarsh cause. His father had kept the precious stones back, though he had gladly handed over every piece of plate, every coronet, ring, brooch, chain, or chalice about the place.

Farleigh shrugged. "As to that, I couldn't say," he admitted. "But it's likely, if they are good enough quality."

Konrad bristled, but realizing that Farleigh meant no offense, he let the implied insult pass.

He considered the matter as Farleigh wolfed down his share of the meal. He would pay a visit to this jeweler on Bulwark Lane. He should have thought of it before, of course. Women liked jewels and received them on betrothals and marriages. That Aimee had not had been an oversight on his behalf. Their meal finished, the two knights bade each other farewell, Farleigh thanking him fervently for his "advice." Konrad suspected his intention was to seek out a poet forthwith.

Konrad turned his feet impulsively toward the house on Lime Street. Jakeman had retrieved the last of his banners and practice spears, and he had returned Actaeon to the ostlers himself before his meal. Making your way through the twisting streets and alleys of Caer-Lyoness was far easier on foot. He would collect the pouch of jewels from his strongbox and take them to the goldsmith. After all, why should he not? he reasoned with himself. Aimee was their rightful owner now.

Letting himself into the house, he ran straight up the stairs to his own bedchamber. Throwing open the cabinet doors, he retrieved the key from around his neck and undid the big, studded strongbox he kept right at the bottom. It was a large, battered trunk, which had been with him for many years and contained all his most valuable treasures.

Ignoring the several bags of gold which Ankatel had bestowed on him and the shredded gown he had balled up in one corner, he reached instead for a leather pouch and tucked it into his

242

tunic. Then he took out the uppermost bag of coins, which constituted his winnings from the previous day. It felt right somehow that it should be his own money which paid for Aimee's finery. He relocked the trunk and closed the cabinet, turning around.

That was when his eye fell on the little velvet bag on his pillow bearer. He made his way toward it with some reluctance and tipped the contents of the drawstring bag into the center of his palm. Was she going to reward him every time he bedded her? he wondered impatiently. A gold signet rolled to its side, showing its oval cabochon of red carnelian. As suspected, it was carved with the Kentigern portcullis. Konrad rolled his eyes.

Did she not think he would have reached the grand age of thirty-one without possessing a signet ring? True, the one he had been given by his father on his twenty-first birthday had been stolen from his finger as he lay near death on a muddy battlefield. But he had inherited his late father's own ring two years later. The thing had never fitted him, and he had to wear it about his neck, but even so, it was functional still for pressing into sealing wax.

It was not half so fine as this one though, he acknowledged, sliding it onto his finger with ease and lifting it for further scrutiny. For the first time, he noticed the gold border that circled the emblem was intricately carved with a lettering he had to squint to make out. With a muffled exclamation, he read the familiar words. *Resilient Under Adversity.*

When had she found out his family motto? He lowered his hand, staring blindly ahead of him. Could it be, he pondered slowly, that Aimee Ankatel had noticed he wore no signet ring upon his finger? Not at Kellingford, no, but later mayhap, when he had taken that meal at her father's house? The idea that, even

243

then, she had been looking for ways to please him gave him the oddest sensation of tightness in his chest.

The thought of buying her gifts or betrothal tokens had not even occurred to him. In truth, he had not thought of her at all. But she had thought of him, he realized with uncomfortable clarity. Maybe constantly since he had caught her fancy. The thought was a strangely disquieting one.

He remembered the encouraging smiles, the frequent way she had touched his hand at their wedding feast, the hopeful look in her eyes. She had not been so free and easy with him since, he did not think. That struck him now as all wrong. If the stark reality of the wedding bed had not been enough to kill Aimee Ankatel's idealistic fancies, then his behavior at the palace had likely dealt the death blow.

His steps slowed as he recalled other things he would as soon not remember. Leaving her at the foot of the stairs to deal with the dismissal of the wedding attendants. He should not have done that. He had been irritated, harried by the heat and his responsibilities toward his own kinswomen. Not just that though, he acknowledged. He had blamed Aimee for the ostentation of their wedding celebrations.

It had been an embarrassing rigmarole for him to get through, but she had been a young and hopeful bride who had thought herself...what? In love with him? The startling notion caused him to stand stock-still in the act of shutting his bedchamber door behind him. He swallowed, his throat suddenly dry. In truth, nothing else really made sense when it came to her selecting him for a bridegroom.

Why else would she have picked him over the many younger and handsomer knights paraded before her? Renlow for one, Farleigh was another. Both were far better suited for Ankatel's beauteous daughter than he. They might not have a title, but what did that matter when you had as much wealth as Ankatel?

I do not love you anymore. He had no notion why Aimee's words kept drifting back into his head.

He started down the passageway, squaring his shoulders to face the fact head on. She had seen him suffer a crashing defeat to Renlow. She had thought his subsequent actions demonstrated some nobility of character he did not possess. She had fancied herself in love with some chivalric figure and then, gods help her, she had woken to the reality she was wedded to an inconsiderate brute without a noble bone in his body.

Even then, he reflected, she had not despaired but tried to make things work and win his favor. She had welcomed his return to her bed. She had worn his colors to the Summer Tournament. *And she had suffered for it.* Not only that, he thought, she had demonstrated the value the Bartrees had always prized most highly. Aimee had shown resilience under adversity.

He dared not dwell on the pleasure he had drawn from her body the previous night. He should have been down on his knees apologizing, not slinging her over his shoulder like that. *Gods!* So lost in thought was he that he did not even register at first the voices drifting along the corridor. Then he heard masculine laughter and bristled all over. Who the hells was that in his house?

He advanced to the end of the passage and threw open the door to the oaken parlor. Freda, who was sat before the fire facing Gerold Ankatel, let out a startled shriek. Seeing who it was framed in the doorway, she sank back in her seat and pressed a thin hand to her meagre bosom. "Oh, Konrad!" she whimpered. "How you did startle me!"

"Kentigern," Gerold Ankatel greeted him, rising to his feet. He eyed his son-in-law cautiously. "Is all well?"

Konrad recovered himself in an instant. "Your pardon, Ankatel," he said, coming at once into the room. "I—er—did not realize this room was in use."

"I am keeping Mistress Freda company this afternoon," the other man responded easily. "As I find my daughter away from home."

"Away from home?" Konrad repeated sharply. He shot a quizzical look at Freda.

"Oh—er—that is, Aimee received a personal invitation from the Queen this morning," Freda stammered. "A most gracious attention from Her Majesty."

Konrad stared at his cousin a moment. "Oh?" he said testily. What the hells was the southern queen playing at, he wondered, taking such a particular interest in his wife.

"Indeed, she seemed very taken with Aimee yesterday," Freda observed. "Really, she was speaking to her for an age. Nothing would do for Her Highness except to send everyone else away and have Aimee sit at her feet and tell her all about herself."

Konrad felt a twinge of misgiving. *All about herself?* It seemed unlikely to him somehow that Queen Armenal would find the life of a merchant's daughter so very fascinating.

"Well, well." Ankatel's chest puffed out. "The Queen of Karadok taking a fancy to my little Aimee! Mind, she's a taking little thing, even if I do say so myself," her fond father commented with pride. "Takes after her mother in that respect."

246

"Mistress Ankatel must have been a very charming creature indeed," Freda twittered and earned a beaming smile from the amiable merchant.

"Well, she wasn't a lady, strictly speaking," he conceded. "Her father owned some very fine vineyards in the east. But I have never found anyone to rival her. Not in my estimation."

"Oh!" said Freda, who seemed almost brought to the brink of tears by these words. "Such sentiments do you credit, good Master Ankatel."

"Sit down, my boy! Sit down!" Ankatel urged. "For your cousin was telling me you were victorious yesterday, both in the melee and the jousting."

Konrad lowered himself gingerly onto a seat. "Yes," he agreed tersely. Seeing two pairs of enquiring eyes directed his way, he reached into his tunic for the leather pouch. "I just came back to fetch these," he admitted and loosed the strings to show the jewels within.

Gerold whistled. "A pretty haul! They must have cost a small fortune, my lord!"

Konrad shook his head. "These have been in my family for centuries."

Freda gasped. "Are they truly the Bartree jewels, Konrad?"

He nodded. "My father kept hold of them and nothing else."

Freda's face fell. "The diadem, it's truly gone, then? And my aunt's collection?"

"Long gone," he confirmed. "Donated to the Blechmarsh cause. It would have been melted down." He spilled the gems into his hand and pointed to three large green stones. "These are the emeralds from the diadem though."

"Oh," Freda sighed. "At least they remain."

"I thought to get them reset," he admitted cautiously.

Freda clapped her hands. "For Aimee?" she said excitedly. When he nodded, she breathed, "What a wonderful idea, Konrad! She will be thrilled! Once I understood how things stood, I thought it such a shame that there was no family jewelry."

"What do you mean?" Konrad frowned. "How things stood?"

"Well, er…" Freda flapped her hands around and turned very pink. "I mean, that Aimee has never owned any jewels, due to, um…her status."

"Her former status," Ankatel corrected her mildly.

"Yes, of course!" Freda said quickly. "And she owns that remarkably fine gold chain and such beautiful beads. The strings she gifted to me and Trude are very fine indeed."

Konrad opened his mouth to demand a clearer explanation, but seeing the meaningful frown his father-in-law was directing at him, he shut it again. What was he missing here?

"Are you heading in that direction now?" Ankatel enquired politely. "I could perhaps accompany you part of the way."

Konrad agreed cautiously, and after the older man had taken a punctilious leave of a clearly flustered Freda, they started down the staircase together. It wasn't until they were out on the street below that it occurred to him that his cousin might have been telling tales of yesterday's marital strife. He shot a wary glance at his father-in-law, for the other still looked gravely thoughtful.

Side by side they started off down the cobbled street toward the city center. Konrad was just casting about for some opener to conversation when the other cleared his throat.

248

"Your cousin is a kindly soul," Gerold observed. "It must be hard for her to navigate life among a family such as yours. She is your sister's companion, is she not?"

Konrad stared at him. "Yes," he managed after a moment's heavy pause. What the hells did Ankatel mean by that? *A family such as yours?* "I might remind you that you married your daughter into my family," he pointed out with an edge to his words.

Ankatel waved this aside. "As to that, Aimee will have no problem with plain dealing. She does not shrink from brutal fact. Mistress Freda, however, is of an altogether different nature."

Konrad grunted. He could not disagree with a plain statement of fact. "She's always been like that," he conceded. "For as long as I can remember."

"A gentle creature." Ankatel nodded. "You have never considered marrying her off? She has a…a sweetness a certain type of man might find agreeable in a wife."

Konrad nearly missed his footing. "No," he admitted, wondering what type of man would appreciate taking his meals with watery eyes blinking at him across his table, constantly on the verge of tears.

As though aware of his skepticism, Ankatel added, "Perhaps a man in the later stages of his life who no longer has an appetite for fire and fury but still has much to offer? A widower, for instance."

Konrad was quite frankly flummoxed by the turn their conversation had taken. "No one has ever approached me about Freda's hand," he answered frankly.

"Curious." Gerold shrugged. "But then, the war... So many things were put on hold."

Konrad made a noise of agreement, though as far as he was aware, the war had not put a stop to weddings, far from it.

"Jewels are used to denote a highborn status," Ankatel said suddenly. "That was what your cousin was struggling to express. I could have bought my daughters many jewels, several times over, but if they could not wear them in public, what would have been the point?"

Konrad turned his head sharply. *Oh.* "Well," he said, rallying. "I will see to it that she will have plenty hereafter."

Ankatel nodded approvingly. "Quite right." He beamed. "And if you are looking for suggestions, might I propose that you add two of the smaller gems to Aimee's brooch?"

"Her brooch?"

"The one your cousin gifted to her." It was news to Konrad that Aimee had received any such gift. As he hesitated to admit this, Ankatel took pity on him. "It was handed down from her grandmother. A betrothal gift, I understand. Is Freda your first cousin? If so, then it would have been your own grandfather's gift to your grandmother, on the occasion of their betrothal."

Konrad cleared his throat. "Freda is my first cousin," he confirmed. He had not thought to give Aimee a betrothal token, but clearly Freda had. Probably the only piece of jewelry she owned. "It has jewels missing?" he asked gruffly.

"Yes," Ankatel responded. "There are three eyelets along the base of the brooch. I already donated a pearl, but two vacant spots remain."

250

"Perhaps you should come along with me," Konrad suggested, feeling suddenly ill equipped for his mission. "I know nothing of…women's trinkets." Perhaps, it suddenly occurred to him, he ought to have brought Freda along with him. He glanced back over his shoulder to see the house was still in view.

"An excellent notion," said Ankatel, clearly guessing the direction of his thoughts and clapping a hand to his shoulder. "I am sure Mistress Freda remembers exactly what shape the Bartree jewels used to take."

18

It had been a strange afternoon, Konrad reflected on their way home, the culmination of a strange day. Freda had been almost incoherent with gratification at her inclusion on their expedition. She had made a good many exclamations and ramblings off subject on their way, which had almost made Konrad regret the impulse to invite her. Her nervous chatter had always annoyed him, and her timid manner around him somehow made it ten times more irritating.

Once sat in the goldsmith's workshop, however, she had proved invaluable. Freda remembered, in what Konrad considered to be astonishing detail, the various pieces that had made up the Bartree collection. She painstakingly sorted little piles of gems for the different pieces. One pile of emeralds and opals was designated for the diadem, or coronet as the goldsmith referred to it, another for a necklace of rubies and pearls.

Freda conferred with the goldsmith, a short man with intelligent eyes and a long white beard, as he sketched out small designs from her various descriptions. However, even after she had set aside several stones for remembered rings and brooches, there was still a pile of random jewels remaining. Freda had eyed them anxiously. "Oh dear!" she had exclaimed, turning to him. "So useless of me, but I really don't remember any more, try as I might. I have an idea there was a sapphire brooch that my aunt owned, in a sort of bar design with a pearl on either side, but…" She bit her lip. "I cannot recall it precisely to mind just now." She pressed her fingers to her temples. "It is most vexing, for I feel as though my memory of it is enshrouded in a sort of fog."

"You have done very well," Konrad assured her. "Far better than I expected. And in any case, he has enough to be going on with for now."

Blyfield looked up from where he was poring over his sketches to nod vigorously. "Quite so, my lord."

"Perhaps you could confer with Mistress Magnatrude this evening?" Ankatel suggested helpfully. "It may be that, between the two of you, you could shed some light on the matter."

"Oh yes!" Freda said, turning to him with enthusiasm. "What a very good notion! For Trude is sure to recall with greater accuracy than I her own mother's brooch."

Konrad wondered if that was true. Freda almost looked like a magpie, presiding bright-eyed over the shiny piles of stones. He could not see his sister taking such delight in the task as she had. Then again, maybe all women liked jewels.

His father-in-law coughed. "Perhaps a brooch or ring could be fashioned for your kinswomen, Kentigern?" he suggested.

"Oh no!" Freda had sounded quite shocked. "The collection must be kept together, not broken up. They are for the Baroness Kentigern alone. I know Trude will feel the same."

Ankatel frowned. "Yet you inherited your grandmother's brooch," he reminded her.

"Well, yes, but that…" She fidgeted. "It was a minor piece and not made of gold."

For a moment, the older man looked as though he would say more but then checked himself. "Which reminds me," he said, turning to Konrad. "Two are for the silver heart brooch, are they not?"

"Silver heart?"

"The brooch Mistress Freda gave unto Aimee."

"Oh yes." Konrad gazed down at the pile. "Which would you...er...suggest, Freda?" he asked his cousin. "You will be most familiar with the brooch after all."

Freda turned quite crimson. "Two of the jewels for Aimee's brooch?" she said breathlessly. "Oh, how...how very touching." She frowned fiercely down a moment before selecting two sapphires of matching size. "I always think that blue and silver looks well together. On either side of Master Ankatel's perfect pearl, I think these would look exceptional." Her face fell. "Unless, of course, they should be designated elsewhere. Do you think we ought to wait until Magnatrude has had a chance to have her say?"

"No," replied Konrad succinctly. At Freda's slightly scandalized gaze, he added, "We were never going to be able to entirely replicate the past, and I don't think we should try." He glanced down at the pile. "Which stones are Trude's favorite?" he asked impulsively.

"Rubies," Freda said.

"And yours?"

"Mine?" Freda was startled. "Why, I...that is, I scarcely know. I have never really considered the matter."

"Sapphires?" Konrad guessed shrewdly, going from her previous choice.

"Yes, I suppose they probably are," she admitted, looking dazed.

Konrad reached across and slid two rubies and two sapphires toward the jeweler. "A matching brooch and ring. One in rubies, one in sapphires," he said.

254

Freda almost fell off her wooden stool. "Konrad!" she yelped. "You must not think that I—"

"Now, Mistress Freda, you must allow him his head in this," Ankatel soothed her. "There is nothing remiss in Lord Kentigern making such a gift to you and his sister."

"He ought really to have conferred with Aimee first," Freda protested, dabbing the corner of her eyes with her long, draping sleeves. Though why she should be reduced to tears, Konrad really did not know. "They really all belong to her and—"

"Aimee would be the first to agree," Ankatel said firmly.

"Aimee can present them to you," Konrad said. "They will be her gift to you."

"An excellent gesture," the other man agreed, flashing him a look of approval.

Freda made a good many exclamatory phrases, none of which made any sense, but his father-in-law helped her down off her stool and tutted and murmured soothingly in reply, and soon he had shepherded her down the rickety stairs and into the street below. Konrad left his purse of coins with the jeweler and followed them out.

Konrad glanced up at the sky and realized suppertime must be fast approaching. Gerold Ankatel allowed himself to be persuaded to join them, and it occurred to Konrad that the old man might be feeling rather lonely in his empty house. Maybe that had been the reason for his strange comments earlier?

Konrad spared a glance for the picture Ankatel and Freda made walking down the street together arm in arm. Freda was at least a head taller than Gerold Ankatel, yet he cut a neat and spritely figure beside her in his orange and brown robes. His gray beard and whiskers were neatly trimmed, and he wore a tall, soft hat upon his head which almost made up for the height disparity between them.

Would Freda be receptive to the addresses of a merchant? Konrad wondered. He had not the faintest notion. It was one thing for him to wed Aimee, for a wife assumed the social status of her spouse. If Freda were to marry a merchant, then her standing would plummet rather than rise. Then again, he reflected wryly, she had spent the last eight years living with his frequently ill-tempered sister in a falling-down lodge with a roof that leaked in a downpour.

Ankatel's wife would have every comfort money could buy, a fleet of servants to wait upon her every whim, and be mistress of her own household. Not just that though, Konrad found himself reflecting as he watched Gerold Ankatel pat Freda's hand. She would have congenial company and the fellowship of someone who *actually* wanted to hear what she had to say. Neither he nor Magnatrude had ever taken the smallest pleasure in Freda's society.

Then again, would Freda really have anything in common with a room full of merchants and guildsmen? He doubted it somehow. Still, he thought, remembering her chattering away at his wedding, without anyone to keep her ruthlessly in check, Freda would likely twitter on regardless, whether it be to a duchess or a market stall holder.

He had been in an oddly thoughtful mood by the time they reached the house on Lime Street. Thoughtful had swiftly become wrathful when he found his wife and sister had not yet returned from the palace.

"Ingrid?" he roared, heading back into the passage after the other two were seated. Then he recalled the name of Aimee's servant. "Golda?" Golda appeared, wiping her hands on her

256

skirts and looking startled. "The fire needs lighting in the main chamber. Also bring some ale."

She nodded and disappeared, and Konrad returned to the dining chamber. "It's getting late," he muttered and was only appeased when the boy scurried into the room carrying an armful of logs. Golda followed on his heels with a pitcher of ale and cups which she set down before them. "You have heard no word from your mistress?"

"No, my lord." Golda shook her head and knelt down by the fireplace, taking over for the boy.

"It will have been a long day for them and no mistake," Ankatel commented. "Needlework, did you say?" He turned to Freda. "In an outdoor setting? It goes off very cold in the evenings, very cold indeed. I hope Aimee thought to take her mantle."

Konrad doubted it somehow, remembering the blazing sun from earlier. A small tug on his tunic had him looking down. The boy pointed toward the window, and he glanced in that direction. "They're back," he said and strode out into the hall.

19

Aimee sat down to supper feeling somewhat baffled. For some reason, her father had accepted her husband's offer to remain and sup with them, though he had spurned her own invitation the previous day. Throughout the first course, the men had exchanged low murmured conversation, and Aimee had craned her ears in vain to catch what on earth they could be speaking about.

Sadly, she was able to catch barely any of it as Magnatrude seemed determined to talk Freda's ear off about every last detail of their visit to the palace. Her sister-in-law's eyes gleamed as she told her cousin of the many embroidered scenes the ladies had been working so diligently on.

"Indeed?" Freda said politely, and Aimee harbored the sudden suspicion that Freda was no more gifted with a needle than she was. It was a comforting thought, for Aimee had been riddled with a crippling sense of inadequacy all day. Some of the Queen's ladies had been so *very* talented. Aimee vowed she must practice as Lady Wycliffe had adjured her and not neglect the art so shamefully as she had been doing.

"The scenes are religious in nature?" Freda hazarded as she lowered her spoon. "Or perhaps depict King Wymer's sporting victories?"

"Not at all," Magnatrude corrected her with a superior air. "The scenes depicted are ones that the Queen believes should be commemorated. They have absolutely nothing to do with the masculine pursuits *or* her husband."

Freda looked taken aback. "What sort of things?" she asked, looking genuinely interested for the first time in the subject at hand.

"Courtly happenings within the feminine sphere," Magnatrude said loftily.

"Such as marriages and births? That sort of thing?" Freda guessed uncertainly.

"Nothing of the sort," Magnatrude responded, tutting with scorn and returning to her food.

Freda turned her enquiring gaze on Aimee, who cleared her throat.

"I confess," Aimee admitted with reluctance, "that my ignorance of courtly affairs meant that I could make scarcely head or tail of most of them. The ladies in the group nearest to us were working on a scene of a lady having her long hair cut short with a pair of shears. She was depicted wearing…" She cleared her throat. "Men's clothes. I think they said it was something to do with the Martindales, although I scarcely liked to ask for a clearer explanation."

Freda's eyes widened. "What else?" she asked with interest.

"Another had a man stood before a pair of scales, and on the one side was a woman with red hair and on the other a pile of gold. He was pointing to the woman."

"An allegorical tale no doubt," Magnatrude interrupted in a know-it-all voice, though Aimee suspected her sister-in-law was as ignorant of the intrigues of the southern court as herself. "Of a good woman being worth more than gold."

"Actually," Aimee corrected her, "the Queen told me it represented the history of the Duke and Duchess of Cadwallader."

Freda made a startled noise in her throat. "Perhaps it is the custom here in the south for noble grooms to demand a dowry equal to their wives' weight in gold?" she suggested.

An awkward silence fell over them, and Magnatrude turned rather red. "Freda!" she said freezingly. "Try and have a little tact, for heaven's sake! The way you let yourself rattle on really is most unfortunate!"

"Oh, but I…!" Freda turned crimson. "I—I did not mean—" Her eyes filled with tears, and her spoon clattered into her bowl. "Oh!" she sobbed, pressing fingers to her mouth and turning to Aimee. "Aimee…"

"I'm sure no offense was taken by me," Aimee assured her. She frowned at Magnatrude. For her part, she thought her sister-in-law was the tactless one, to make so much of something said without malice. "If that *was* the custom, then I am sure the feminine ideal at court would not be for slender, elegant women!" She did not think her jest a poor one under the circumstances, but neither of the two women met it with so much as the flicker of a smile.

"If what was the custom?" rumbled a voice from the other end of the table. An awkward silence greeted her husband's question. *Oh bother!*

"We were just discussing the Queen's unusual taste in needlework," Aimee answered brightly. "She means to capture scenes with subjects outside of the usual fare. Subjects pertaining to women at court."

"Usual fare?" her father repeated, looking puzzled.

"Hunting scenes," she elaborated. "Battle scenes, on land and by sea. That sort of thing."

"Ah!" He nodded his gray head and returned to his meal, but to Aimee's discomfiture, she found her husband still regarding her narrowly. She dropped her gaze back to her plate of stew and tried to ignore the rising tide of panic she felt on remembering the Queen's vow that she would have a panel made up to represent the Kentigerns too.

The gods alone knew what Queen Armenal believed would be a fitting tribute to their union, Aimee thought queasily. Perhaps her sat forlorn as Konrad presented the garland to Lady de Crecy? She pushed away her trencher as her stomach roiled at the thought. *Gods. Would that not just be the crowning indignity!*

Pushing all such disquieting thoughts from her head, she turned to Freda and set about lifting her spirits. She soon had the other woman smiling again, then her sister-in-law started holding forth on what stitch *she* would have used instead when representing oak leaves.

"'Tis a pity," Magnatrude concluded, "that we did not see the Marchioness of Martindale in the Queen's tent. She has a fine way with a needle, and I was quite shocked she had not been recruited for the task."

"Perhaps because she has such a small baby," Freda ventured timidly.

Her cousin sent her a scathing look. "I'm sure the child has a nurse," she retorted, clearly of the opinion that a Queen's demands were of higher importance than those of a mere infant.

"I think the Queen finds herself less able to rely on ladies who have family lives outside of serving her," Aimee commented, remembering Queen Armenal's pointed remarks on the subject.

Magnatrude looked much struck by this and was quiet for a full minute, frowning into her goblet of wine. "I think you should offer your services, Aimee, in completing the Queen's task," she said at last. Aimee almost choked on her mouthful of sweet cheese tart. "She has shown you great favor," her sister-in-law persisted. "And it is only right and fitting that you should do so."

"I am afraid," Aimee wheezed once her eyes had stopped watering, "that I am not at all proficient in the art."

Magnatrude looked shocked. "Surely you know how to embroider and weave?"

"Not well," Aimee answered with perfect truth.

When her sister-in-law opened her mouth as though to respond, Freda interrupted breathlessly. "I myself wield very little skill, despite instruction from an early age. You are by far the most talented needlewoman I know, Trude. You should volunteer your needle to the service of the southern queen! I am sure she would consider herself fortunate to number you among her ranks."

Magnatrude's color deepened. "I?"

Aimee had just steeled herself to argue the point when they were interrupted by her husband.

"Aimee cannot volunteer for the Queen's task right now," he said pointedly. "I am taking her to Beres Caple with me in two days' time."

Aimee's head came up sharply. "Beres Caple?" she repeated. He was taking her with him? Her heart lurched. "What, pray, is at Beres Caple?"

He frowned. "It is a rural tournament, a half a day's ride from here."

"Some obscure tournament hardly sounds a pressing obligation for your wife," Magnatrude said coldly. "Certainly not as pressing as waiting on a Queen." She leveled a look at him and paused a moment. "This Queen has taken a liking to Aimee," she said stiffly. "She could even make her a lady-in-waiting."

Lord Kentigern shrugged his massive shoulders. "If I had wanted a courtier for a wife, I'd have married one," he replied dismissively.

Aimee's breath caught in her throat. He had not married a courtier; he had married *her*. Then she noticed it, the signet ring on his finger. He was wearing it. She felt herself turn quite pink with pleasure before caution reasserted itself. She was not the naïve bride of a week ago. Since then, she had learned some harsh lessons indeed. It would not do to let her reckless heart run away with her.

Instead of letting her head crowd full of wishful dreams, she turned resolutely to her father. "How is Ursula faring in her new house, Father? You must tell me what street it lies in so that I may visit with her."

Her father cleared his throat. "I do not think she will have much time for visits at present, daughter," he said. "I was just telling Kentigern. Your sister is nursing her husband, for he broke a limb at the royal tournament."

"No!" burst forth Aimee. "That is a good deal too bad!" She cast her mind back to her brief glimpse of her brother-in-law. "Was it during the melee that his injury occurred?"

"It is of no use asking me." Her father shrugged. "It was in some skirmish, is all that I know. He got stamped on by a horse which broke his arm."

"It *was* the melee apparently," her husband clarified.

"Poor Sir Renlow!" Aimee's sympathies were firmly engaged.

"How wretched for the unfortunate young man!" Freda concurred.

"Certainly, a most unlucky start to wedded life," her father agreed heavily.

Aimee only hoped it would prove a bonding experience for the new husband and wife and that Hilda had not been permitted to take over the nursing in Ursa's stead. "What a pity that they will not be able to attend the tourney at Beres Caple."

She, Trude, and Freda withdrew to the oak parlor after supper, while the menfolk had remained in the large chamber below stairs. Magnatrude talked a good deal about their visit that day, and if Aimee had not known better, she would almost have thought she was bragging about her visit to the southern court.

After an hour or so, Aimee made her excuses and retreated to her bedchamber. She had requested a bath be taken up to her room after supper, and she found it had been set up for her with a canopy suspended from a hook in the ceiling. Herbs were strewn into the water, giving it a fresh and pleasant smell. Aimee lowered herself into the warm water with a delighted sigh.

"Can I get you anything else, milady?" Golda asked, fetching her soap scented with musk and cloves.

"No, you have thought of everything, Golda."

"Here's drying sheets for you," she said, gesturing toward a chair. "Shall I return in a half hour?"

"That would be perfect, thank you."

No sooner had the door closed than it seemed to open again. Aimee craned her neck around. "Golda?"

"It's me," a gruff voice rumbled.

Aimee's eyes widened, and she withdrew behind her curtain. "I am just taking a bath," she said needlessly.

She heard a huffed breath, then a dry: "So I see." Something scraped along the ground which she realized after a moment was a chair by the fire.

Quietly, Aimee rearranged her curtain so she could peek through it at him as he threw himself down into the chair, staring moodily into the fire. She cleared her throat. "All is well with you, my lord?" she ventured.

"I want you to buy another gown," he said heavily. "In my colors."

The breath stuck in Aimee's throat, and she clutched at the canopy. Like hells she would! When she made no verbal reply, his head swung around, and she realized she was on his blind side.

"For Beres Caple," he elaborated.

"It would be quite impossible on such short notice," Aimee forced herself to reply. "No tailor would accept such a commission." She had aimed for a light tone, but even to her own ear her voice sounded strained.

His eyes narrowed. "For enough coin, I think you will find they would oblige."

Aimee shook her head. "Not Mr. Fulcher," she said resolutely. "He hates being hurried."

"So then, find a different tailor." Aimee's fingers tightened on the edge of the wooden tub, but she kept her mouth closed. "Aimee?"

She gave a tiny nod. She would tell him she had failed in the task! There was no way on this earth that she was wearing his colors again. Grabbing her washcloth, she started enthusiastically splashing around in an attempt to put the conversation to an end.

Aimee scrubbed her neck and then thoroughly soaped and washed out her hair, all the while avoiding looking in his direction. As she squeezed the water from her locks, she ventured a sneaky glance his way and found him stretching his legs out in front of him and scratching the side of his face. *Was he going to just remain here, then?*

Why was he still sat there? Why didn't he just go? She could feel hot color creeping up her neck even at the thought of lying to him. She had a horrible suspicion he would be able to tell. "Was there something else you wanted to ask of me?" she heard herself ask with a slight edge to her voice. His head turned sharply, and the soap slipped through Aimee's fingers. It made a thud as it hit the bottom of the tub.

"It so happens," he answered slowly, "that there is."

266

She waited but he seemed to be debating what he was going to say next. "What is it?" she asked at last, unable to bear the suspense.

"Outside of the bedchamber," his harsh voice grated over the words. "Call me Konrad."

Aimee stared at him. "*Outside* of the bedchamber?" she repeated in surprise.

He gazed steadily back at her. "Yes."

"Surely, my lord," she could not stop herself from protesting, "you mean the other way around?"

His lips thinned. "That's the way I want it."

"Oh." Aimee regarded him doubtfully. In the most intimate setting, he wanted her to use his most formal title. It made no sense to her. Unless… Unless he merely wished there to be a public show of informality between them that did not exist in private.

Her poor heart throbbed, and Aimee lifted a hand to it almost to comfort herself. Then she remembered she was not in love with him anymore and lowered her hand. She no longer cared.

Lord Kentigern cleared his throat. "Freda gave you a brooch, I hear." Aimee blinked, but before she could answer, he growled, "Can I see it?"

"It's on that table over there." She lifted her arm out of the water to point at a side table. "Next to my beads."

He stood up and walked to the table. To her surprise, she watched him lift her gold chain first, examine it, and then finger the lapis beads before he picked up the brooch. He half turned toward her. "Is this the one?"

"Yes."

He grunted, turning it over as he began to speak. "The family jewelry was broken apart during the war and donated to further the northern cause."

Aimee nodded, drawing up her knees and hugging them. "Your sister said as much."

"There are some stones my father put by. With your leave, I will get two of them added to this brooch."

Aimee flushed. "That would be lovely," she said simply. "I think Freda would like that."

He frowned. "And what of you, wife? Should you like that?"

"O-of course!" Aimee stammered, wondering at his expression.

His gaze fell. "I should have had it done before," he murmured. "I am not good at such…attentions. Not like you." He lifted his hand, and she saw he was showing her the signet ring upon his finger.

Aimee felt her heart lurch. "It fits?" she asked breathlessly. He nodded. "I'm glad."

He dropped his hand and glanced about. "Should I leave you to your bath now?" he asked, his tone gruff.

"Stay if you wish it," she answered uncertainly, though if that was the case, she had no clue what she was supposed to do with him. He gave a brief nod and dropped back into the chair next to the fire. He did wish to stay! Aimee gazed at him in something like astonishment. He had not shown much partiality for her company thus far.

A rap on the door made them both jump, and Golda sailed in carrying a small bottle of milky-looking fluid. "Your father's warehouse sent over a new one, milady," she said, pulling out the stopper and sniffing it. "Smells like roses." Then she caught sight of Lord Kentigern and gave a violent start. "Oh, you did make me jump, milord!" she berated him before something occurred to her and she gave him a swiftly assessing look. "Happen you'll find this more of a treat than me." She thrust the bottle toward him. "Here."

"Golda!" Aimee protested.

"What is it for?" Lord Kentigern asked, taking the bottle from her and sniffing it.

"For applying to her ladyship's skin after bathing," Golda answered swiftly. "It keeps it supple and sweet-smelling." She snatched up one of the large drying cloths from the chair and approached Aimee with it, shaking it out.

Seeing as her servant had stepped between her husband and the bath, Aimee made haste to rise out of the water and was enveloped in the large sheet and wrapped about with it. Golda fetched the second sheet from the chair and wrapped it about Aimee's long hair before leading her in front of the fire and swiftly departing.

Aimee looked after the rapidly disappearing servant with an open mouth. "Gol—" The door shut firmly behind her. "Oh."

"It seems Mistress Golda expects me to attend on you this evening," her husband said with a quirk of his lips. If she didn't know any better, she would almost think he was amused by the notion.

"You don't have to…"

"Never let it be said that I shirk my duties."

Aimee stared at him. The lurking gleam in his eye indicated he was jesting. "Well, but—" she started to protest, but he was already pouring a drop of the scented liquid into his hand and rubbing his palms together.

"Come here." He widened his legs so Aimee could stand between them, and she shuffled closer, still clutching at her sheet. He reached for one of her hands and placed it on his shoulder. At the feel of that solid muscle under her fingers, Aimee's heart gave a squeeze. "Lift your foot."

It took her an instant to register his words, but when she did so, she found it immediately engulfed in his large hands. "How's that?"

Aimee gave an approving murmur as he stroked his thumb over the arch of her foot. "Nice," she admitted cautiously.

"Your father sells this stuff?" he asked. She nodded. "I thought he was a spice merchant."

"That was how he started out," she agreed. "But he soon expanded. Now he imports all sorts of wares, including scented oils, balms, and lotions."

"Mmmm. Have you ever traveled with him?"

"Not since I was small. We visited the lands of my mother, but I do not remember it as well as Ursula." Her voice wobbled as he stroked his fingers up over her ankle and calf, tickling the backs of her knees. His touch was light though his fingers were rough and calloused. "My father has not traveled the routes for many years. Not since he established them and hired dependable delegates."

"Other foot." He poured more from the bottle, and she stood on her other foot as he repeated the firm, light strokes.

270

"Will you let me do this for you at some point?" Aimee asked impulsively. His hands paused.

"I don't know," he admitted cautiously.

"Why not?" Aimee prodded. "You don't like to be touched?"

"It's not the same thing."

"What isn't?"

He hesitated. "Your body is…small and neat. It's pleasurable for me to touch it."

Aimee considered this. "Well, your body is large and magnificent. It would be pleasurable for me to touch it also."

He made a choking sound in his throat. "Aimee." The groaned word sounded almost like a warning. "Be careful what you ask for. You may get more than you can handle." He released her foot. What did that mean? she wondered. "What does Golda do next?"

"Hands and arms," she replied promptly. "But I need to untangle my hair and let it dry before the fire first."

He gave a rumble of assent, and Aimee sank down onto the hearth rug and unwrapped her hair from the drying cloth. "Can you pass me that comb?" she asked, spreading the sheet to dry over the second chair by the fire. He reached out an arm and grabbed the comb, handing it to her.

Efficiently, Aimee saw to the snarls and knots until her hair lay tamed and damp and curling at the ends. Setting aside the comb, she turned back to her husband to find him steadily watching her.

"Ready?" he asked. Aimee extended her hand by way of an answer, and he took it and started rubbing the fluid into her palm. "What is this?"

"'Tis an almond milk lotion infused with scented oil. This one smells like attar of roses." She hesitated and directed a look at him through her lashes.

"What?" he prompted, lifting his brows.

"I could get a different scent for you if you did not wish to smell of flowers."

He snorted and laced his fingers through hers, spreading the lotion over her fingers. "Like what?" he asked after a pause.

Aimee swallowed, her throat feeling rather dry. "Musk," she suggested. "Or mayhap sandalwood." His hands were stroking up her arm. It was odd how conscious she felt of every pass of his fingers.

"You have no dry patches," he commented. "Not even here." He tapped her elbow and then circled it with his fingertips.

"Well, no," she responded virtuously. "I always apply unguent after every bath. It prevents your skin from drying out. You should try it."

He gave a reluctant smile as though her persistence was starting to amuse him. "Maybe I will," he said absently and repeated the process on her other arm. "Where else?" he asked when he reached her shoulder. There was a decided rasp in his voice.

"I beg your pardon?"

"Where else do you spread your lotion?" He was kneading her shoulder now, and when he spread his hand, his fingers reached the edge of her collarbone.

"Golda only does those areas," she squeaked back truthfully. Even she could hear the wistful note in her voice.

"What about you?"

"Me?"

"Don't you have any areas that you see to yourself?"

Aimee gave a strangled cough. "Well…yes," she admitted.

"Where? Tell me." His fingers were tracing lightly along her collarbone now, making her shiver.

"Well…" She gave another cough. "The, er, parts that are kept out of sight," she admitted, glancing at him and turning bright red.

"Yes?" he said huskily, and she saw his eyes dip to where she had knotted the sheet. "Would you permit me to do them?"

"You would want to?" she asked, faintly incredulous.

"Very much so," he replied steadily.

Aimee huffed out her breath. The thought of standing there stripped naked while he rubbed lotion on her made her knees quake. "I would feel nervous of you seeing me like that. All over, I mean." She pulled a face. "My form is…not ideal."

He gave a dissenting growl. "I've seen you all over already, Aimee," he reminded her. "And let me assure you, I took great pleasure in the sight."

"Yes, but…not stood prone before you, letting your eye dwell overlong on me," she burst out. "I'm not slender," she muttered, dropping her gaze. "You may not have noticed so much before as you were in something of a hurry."

He paused as though measuring his next words. "It seems I have been remiss," he rumbled. "If I rushed before, then this time you must permit me to linger."

"That's not what I—"

"What if I promised to return the favor?"

Aimee gasped. "Really? You would allow me do the same for you?" He gave a brief but decisive nod, and she caught her breath. "Then, yes," she vowed at once. "A thousand times, yes."

Her turn would have to wait until another day, she realized moments later after his hands had slid under her drying sheet. For she would not have the strength to devote to the task after he had finished with her. The way he was spreading the lotion over her thighs, hips, and belly was making her feel weak. It was almost…worshipful. She blinked down at his bent head, feeling the unhurried way his big hands moved over her skin.

"Next time, you will let me do this without the sheet obstructing my view," he said throatily. *Next time?* "Why don't you straddle my thigh?" he suggested, glancing up, and she wondered if he had felt the trembling in her legs. Aimee gulped and he patted his leg. It seemed he liked her sat astride him, she recalled dimly as she swung her leg over his and seated herself. Which was curious as he seemed to steel himself as she settled over him. Was it because his seated position meant her face was now perilously close to his own? she wondered.

Carefully, she averted her eyes from the ruined side of his face. He breathed out. "That's it, take your ease," he murmured as his hands started moving again, swooping over her hips to squeeze her buttocks. Aimee felt her face grow hot. Clearly, her body remembered the feel of him between her thighs, and she grew

274

short of breath at the sensation of his hard muscle pressed against her.

Oh gods, she thought, biting her lip. She hoped she did not grow wet as she had before. He still wore his chausses, and likely they would show a wet patch. She bit her lip and suppressed the impulse to groan. You would almost think he was *savoring* her extra flesh, she thought in confusion. Certainly, he seemed to enjoy handling it, if his kneading fingers were anything to go by.

"Why do you say your form is not ideal?" he asked thickly as his fingers relaxed and tightened over her backside. When she could make no reply, his hands slid up from her bottom to her lower back, his thumbs caressing the slight dip of her waist. "Aimee? Answer me." He sounded genuinely mystified.

Aimee's answer stuck in her throat. She hardly wanted to point out her defects to him. Then again, he must already be well acquainted with them by now. "I'm not slight," she said awkwardly. "I wish I were more delicately made."

"Delicate?" he repeated with a derisive snort. "If you were, I would be scared to trust myself with you. A delicate woman would not be up to my weight." *Up to his weight?* Aimee glanced at him dubiously. "It is true," he insisted. "I would be scared of crushing you. Besides…" His words trailed off.

"Besides?" Aimee prompted him breathlessly, though it felt rather indecent talking to him while his hands roamed over her so freely.

"I like the feel of you," he said with a shrug. "I always appreciated a voluptuous woman. Your body is perfect to my taste."

Aimee wasn't sure her mouth didn't fall open. She was to his taste? She hesitated. "You are not just saying that?" she croaked. "To reassure me?"

"As you know," he answered wryly, "I am far from considerate when it comes to my actions and my words. I just say what I think."

Aimee took the opportunity to stare at his face as he was otherwise occupied with the lotion. As usual, she felt giddy being in such close proximity to the object of her affection. Would that slightly breathless feeling wear off eventually? When she got used to being around him? Would he even allow her to become accustomed to his presence in her life? Apparently, he truly liked her body. He thought she was perfect according to his tastes. *Perfect.*

His eyes fell to where her hands clutched the top of her sheet. "I need to do your front now," he said pointedly.

She nodded, her throat dry. "You want me to remove the sheet?"

He lifted his gaze so it locked on hers. "Would you, Aimee?" he asked richly.

Oh gods, when he looked at her like that, she did not feel in the position to deny him *anything*. She nodded and started tugging at the knot. The sheet slid to the floor.

Lord Kentigern caught his breath. "*Gods*," he groaned, his eyes on her breasts. "How can you not know you embody every womanly ideal?"

Aimee gazed at him, dumbfounded, still perched on his leg. "Are you in earnest?" she managed to choke out as he poured more of the lotion into his palms.

His reply was to gently cup her breasts with something approaching reverence. "Deadly earnest," he said in a gravelly voice. "Does this feel good?"

"Yes," she admitted with a whimper as his slick thumbs passed over her nipples. "But it's getting harder to sit up straight. I feel like I'm melting."

His lips quirked up at the one corner. "Do you want to lie down, Aimee?" She nodded, and he scooped her up with the greatest of ease, carrying her over to the bed and laying her back down on her mattress.

She sighed. "I think you've covered all areas of my body now." There was a slight hitch in her voice, betraying her disappointment that his attentions were completed.

"Should I leave you now to sleep?" he asked.

Aimee slanted her gaze to meet his. She shook her head. "Stay," she said softly, and after the briefest of hesitations, "I want you to."

She thought he looked pleased by her boldness as he swiftly undressed and washed in the cooling tub. If she did not feel so limp with pleasure from his hands, she would have liked to have sat up and watched him perform his ablutions and maybe even offer her services.

Sadly, it was as much as she could do to stop her eyelids from drooping down and drifting off into a contented sleep. When he climbed into the bed beside her, he reached for her at once. Aimee went willingly and found him strangely tender in his ministrations. She almost reminded him she was up to his weight, but though he was careful, he still stole all her breath away.

"I confess I am curious as to how you will reward my performance from tonight," he mused in a satisfied voice as they lay side by side in the aftermath.

"Reward?" she murmured.

"Yes, for you've given me costly raiment and jewelry already."

"Oh? And what, pray, do you think would be due recompense?"

"More importantly, wife, what do you?"

She considered this a moment. "A new pair of hose?" she suggested tartly.

He snorted, crossing his ankles. "I was thinking at least a ship."

Aimee tapped her chin thoughtfully. "I could buy you a piglet from the market?" she suggested in the spirit of one generously upping the ante. "And mayhap a tub of liniment for your aching bones."

He gave a short laugh. "I suppose I'll find out later," he said, sitting up. Aimee's heart sank. He was leaving? It seemed, even though she no longer loved him, that still stung. "Can I take the brooch with me?" he asked as he picked his clothes up from the floor.

Aimee nodded, then realized he was not looking at her. "Yes, of course. 'Tis on that table…" she started to explain but saw him cross to it before she had even finished her words. Of course he knew where it was, he had seen it earlier. He moved to the door.

"I will see you on the morrow. Don't forget to contact that tailor," he said and slipped out the door.

Aimee flopped back down on the bed. She *still* wasn't going to order that damned dress.

20

Konrad dropped off Aimee's brooch first thing on Bulwark Lane and extracted a promise that it would be ready on the next morn. Then, having gleaned the address from his father-in-law, he had called at another large townhouse situated at a five-minute walk from his own. Here, he had been admitted and led to a handsome sitting room to await Lady d'Avenant. As his sole purpose had been to visit with Renlow, Konrad had chafed rather at this, but the maid would not be browbeaten. The master was convalescing, she told him pertly, and was not to receive any visitors without his wife's say-so.

Konrad had given an exasperated sigh and walked over to the window to stare out onto the street. It was a fine view, though quieter than the one they enjoyed in Lime Street. The door opened and closed very quietly, and he turned to find Aimee's sister stood in the doorway performing a neat curtsey.

"My lord, I am happy to see you. I trust my sister is well?" she greeted him politely.

"That she is," he responded with a nod. "How is d'Avenant?"

"He is recovering apace," she answered with a relieved smile. "Should you like to see him? It is good of you to visit with us."

He nodded again, and she gestured for him to follow her up the wooden staircase. Ursula Ankatel looked well, he thought with surprise. She was dressed a good deal less fussily than when he had last seen her, and she looked all the better for it. Her hair, too, was simply arranged, without ornamentation, but that did not wholly account, he thought, for the subtle change that had taken place in her.

No, it was something in her manner, he thought. She had a sort of luminous calm and assurance about her that he did not remember her possessing previously. He could have sworn she was an anxious, highly strung type like Freda, but it seemed he had not done her justice. When Ursula reached a door at the end of the passage, she gave a firm knock and then walked in.

"Ah, there you are, Ursa," Konrad heard a familiar voice greet her boisterously. "Where have you been this age? I vow you have been shamefully neglecting me all morning."

Konrad stood at the doorway as Ursula swiftly crossed to the bed where Renlow lay in the midst of a pile of cushions. His face looked flushed, and his hair was tousled. One of his arms was bound up with a splint, and he had a good deal of nasty bruising on view up his neck and shoulder.

"Nonsense, husband!" she chided him affectionately and reached across the bed to take the hand that was not bound up with a splint. When Renlow tugged on her hand as though to draw her down to him, she said quickly, "Such good fortune, my dear. I have brought you a friend to visit and sit with you awhile."

Renlow glanced toward the door in surprise, though Konrad noticed he did not release his wife's hand. His expression immediately brightened. "Kentigern! Come in, it is good to see you!" He struggled to sit upright, and Ursula immediately bustled about, placing pillows behind his back, helping him into a comfortable position.

When Renlow held an uninjured hand out to him, Kentigern found himself grasping it warmly.

"What have you been doing with yourself, you young fool?" he rumbled, shaking his head.

Renlow grinned. "Came unseated in the melee, like the biggest dullard in all Karadok."

"This seat should be comfortable, my lord," Ursula murmured, gesturing to a bedside chair. "I will leave you to exchange your greetings while I fetch some refreshment." She sent a beaming smile their way and swiftly left the room.

Kentigern lowered himself into a chair, noticing the way Renlow's eyes followed his wife as she exited the room. He turned back to Konrad with a rueful smile. "I couldn't have laid myself up at a worse time," he groaned.

"Not true," Konrad corrected him. "For there are no tournaments of note held from now until September. You have a good two months for your bones to knit."

Renlow scratched his nose. "Aye, true enough," he agreed absently. "Though I was not thinking of the tournaments precisely."

Coming from someone who lived and breathed solely to compete, as Renlow did, his statement was an astonishing one. Konrad beheld him speechlessly. As though what he had said had only just dawned on him, Renlow coughed and reddened. "You are going to Beres Caple, my lord?"

"I am."

Renlow looked a little wistful. "I hope you find sport worthy of you there."

Konrad shrugged. Beres Caple was a minor tournament, ill attended by the more celebrated knights. "Wherever I go, there seems to be a target marked on my chest plate and someone thirsting for my blood."

Renlow laughed. "Everyone wants to beat you, my lord. You should not take it as an insult, but as a compliment."

Konrad grunted. It was true, he never took it personally, and even some unknown local knight could put up a good fight if you caught them on a good day in front of a home crowd.

"Who else goes?" Renlow enquired.

"Probably a lot of obscure yokels. You know the sort."

"Like me?" Renlow said without rancor.

"You may have started out that way," Konrad acknowledged. "But you're well established as part of the tournament crowd now. Even the King knows your name." A slight frown marred Renlow's brow. "What?"

Renlow shot him a curious look. "You did not say 'southern.'"

"Pardon?"

"You did not say 'even the southern king knows your name.' All you northern knights do that."

Konrad paused to consider this. No, he realized with surprise. No, he had not. "Magnur is dead." He shrugged. "We all need to move on with our lives."

Renlow eyed him thoughtfully. "You are finding married life to your taste, then, my friend?" he said simply. "I'm glad."

Konrad bit back a splutter. He had no idea where Renlow had drawn that conclusion from. He gazed back at him in bemusement. "What of you?" he barked to hide his discomfiture.

"How could it be otherwise?" Renlow asked simply. "Ursula is an angel. I am the most fortunate of men." His clear blue eyes were without guile, and Konrad guessed he would simply have to take his words entirely at face value.

"Did you know you were getting the elder sister?" he asked on impulse.

Faint color stole into Renlow's cheeks. "No," he admitted. "But it made sense, I thought, on reflection."

"It did?"

Renlow smiled faintly. "Your wife has a strong personality. I think she has ruled the roost in her father's house for a long time, while mine went overlooked."

Konrad found himself bristling. "What do you mean by that?"

Renlow's smile grew. "I meant no offence," he said. "But have you not heard, my lord? How Aimee decided last year that they should both be married? It took her a mere four months to wear her sister down. There is a reason, I think, that Ankatel did not buy us neighboring homes on the same street."

Konrad shot him a shrewd look. "You think Ankatel is that discerning?"

"He would not be such a good man of business if he were not."

It was on the tip of Konrad's tongue to point out that if Aimee could be thought overwhelming, then her sister could be considered distinctly underwhelming. However, it was at this point that Ursula entered the room, followed by a plump woman carrying a tray of refreshments.

"Hilda and I have brought you wine and cakes, though you must mix water with yours, my love," Ursula informed Renlow in an indulgent tone. Konrad observed Hilda with interest, remembering Aimee's disapproval of the servant accompanying her sister into her new household.

The woman looked to be in her mid-fifties, with a mild, benevolent face and neat appearance. She set the tray down carefully onto a side table. Certainly, she made no overt attempt to usurp her mistress's authority that he could see. Indeed, she consulted Ursula most scrupulously as to how much water she should add to Renlow's cup.

"Yes, that will be excellent, Hilda," Ursula murmured approvingly as she moved to smooth Renlow's pillow bearer. "I hope you have had a pleasant catch-up." She looked from her husband's face to their guest's with a faint question in her eyes.

"Very," Konrad responded promptly. He knew for a fact that he would find Ursula's conscientious solicitude irksome, but Renlow seemed entirely at ease with it as she passed him his watered wine. Yes, he thought, things certainly had worked out for the best. Though, how much of that was down to Ankatel's astuteness, he was not so sure.

He passed another hour or so in their company. Ursula seemed pleased to hear that Aimee was accompanying him to Beres Caple. "She will enjoy that exceedingly," she had replied with an approving smile.

He had the strangest impulse to shatter her newfound serenity with the news that Aimee had not enjoyed the one tournament she had attended since her marriage one bit. That, in fact, she had suffered a scalding humiliation, thanks to her thoughtless husband.

He squashed the notion as ignoble and absurd. He was the one who needed to atone for that mishap, not Ursula. The fault was his and so should the remedy be. Besides, he was not at all sure why he felt so unaccountably annoyed with his sister-in-law's tepid attitude toward his wife's well-being. It stood to reason that Ursula d'Avenant was wrapped up in coddling her new husband.

284

Maybe he should be flattered that she was so confident in his abilities to keep her sister happy? She could not know that Aimee would have to contend with disagreeable in-laws on top of a difficult husband in her new household.

It only occurred to Konrad as he walked out of their house at midday that he did not know if Aimee owned her own horse. If not, he would have to purchase her one, for it was half a day's ride to Beres Caple. Turning about, he made for the house in Lime Street instead of the practice ground and was just striding down the passageway in search of his wife when he heard a strident voice from the dining chamber that he did not recognize.

"Well, you girls certainly got your money's worth out of your father," said the person disagreeably. "I only hope you do not rue the day that you got ideas above your station. If one of you had seen fit to accept my Willard's proposal…but there! Clearly, you imagined yourselves a deal too good for an honest man…"

Konrad flung the door open, and Aimee, Freda, and the unpleasant widow from the wedding feast all spun in their seats to look at him. "Is someone casting aspersions on my honesty?" he asked dryly and watched the woman turn rather pink. *What was her name? Stimson? Leeming?*

"I'm sure his lordship must realize that was not my intent," she answered with two spots of high color in her cheeks as she rose to perform her curtsey.

He glowered a moment before turning resolutely in his wife's direction. "Have you a horse of your own, wife?" he demanded. "Or do I need to buy you one?"

285

"I already have one," Aimee replied hastily. "The Widow Hemmings was just paying us her compliments." She made a vague flapping gesture with her hand toward the old hag.

Hemmings, that was it. Konrad ignored the empty social pleasantries. The woman had come to vent her spleen and for no other reason. He wasn't about to squander any more words on her, and he certainly had better things to look at. He scanned Aimee's face. "You have sent word to that tailor yet?" he asked.

Aimee's chest heaved, and he saw a spark of indignation flash in her eyes. "I have been rather busy this morning, my l—" She bit off the word. "Konrad," she corrected herself with a slightly self-conscious air.

He felt a surprising lurch in his chest when she spoke his given name and darted a quick glance at his cousin. Freda's head was tipped to one side, and she was watching them rather like an inquisitive bird. Konrad cleared his throat. "Aye, well, make sure you do," he said brusquely, then glanced about the room. "Where is my sister?" He directed the question at Freda, and she gave a guilty start.

"Oh," she responded breathlessly. "It is the most fortuitous thing. The Queen sent a messenger again this morning and, well, Trude answered the summons from the palace."

Her words startled him. "Trude went to wait on the Queen?"

"She did," Freda agreed, looking faintly furtive. "She is most intrigued by the Queen's avowed task." She paused and plucked at her skirts. "I only did not accompany her because well—er— needlework is not something I really excel at."

"And I had too many arrangements to make for our upcoming tournament," Aimee put in hurriedly in the manner of one also making an excuse.

Both of them were avoiding his eye, and he realized that neither of them had wanted to go to the palace. He gave a short laugh. "Well, if Queen Armenal will be content with Trude's presence, then so be it."

Aimee's shoulders relaxed, and she and Freda exchanged a conspiratorial look.

"I must take my leave of you, Baroness," their visitor cut in, sounding annoyed at the fact she no longer had Aimee's undivided attention.

"Please give my compliments to Willard," Aimee murmured as the older woman stood, gave a shallow curtsey, and stalked to the door.

"Why are you sending your compliments to Willard Hemmings?" Konrad asked testily before the door had even shut after her. "Is he ill?"

"No," Aimee responded mildly. "But I *have* known him all my life."

Konrad snorted.

"Will you take some refreshment now, cousin?" Freda asked quickly with a gesture toward the table. "Stirling has baked fresh loaves this morning."

"No," he answered curtly. "I need to get back to the practice field." He hesitated. "Freda, while we are at Beres Caple, you should invite Ankatel to take supper with you here of an evening."

Freda blinked. "I should?"

He nodded. "He—er—sits to an empty table these days."

"Oh, the poor dear man!" Freda exclaimed. "Of course, if you think I should, Konrad."

"I do. You could send word when Aimee arranges for her horse to be sent around." He shot a glance at Aimee, whose eyes were very round. He wondered if it had never occurred to her that she could end up with the ghastly widow for a stepmother. "Do not forget the tailor," he warned his wife direly and was heading for the door when he paused and turned back again.

"While he is here, he could fashion Freda another gown. Magnatrude also, if she intends swanning off to the palace on a daily basis." Seeing they were both lost for words, he nodded again and made his exit.

Konrad was feeling pleased with himself as he set back off for the practice ground, and it was only when he had reached it that it occurred to him to wonder what preparations Aimee had needed to make for Beres Caple. The only thing he could think of was requesting her horse be brought around, which he had sorted, and the ordering of a new gown in his colors, which she plainly had not yet done. He frowned as he dismounted and was so distracted as he fastened Actaeon to a tethering post that he scarcely noticed the irate figure advancing on him.

"So, you're here, are you?" Sir Jeffree de Crecy said with deep loathing, coming to a halt before him.

Konrad glanced about the mostly empty field. A few knights were drifting toward them, but for the most part, the more serious contenders had departed directly after the royal tournament.

"As you see," Konrad grunted. "What do you want, de Crecy?" He turned to face the other man.

De Crecy's blue eyes narrowed. "You intend on competing at Beres Caple?" he asked tersely.

Konrad nodded warily. "You?" He was pleasantly surprised to hear there would be some decent competition at least. You were unlikely to find a Roland Vawdrey or a Garman Orde present, especially not since those bastards had married. De Crecy was a stiff-necked, pompous ass, but there was no doubting his caliber as a competitor.

"I will," de Crecy said stiffly. "And I trust you are taking your good lady wife with you," he practically spat the words.

Konrad glared at him. "What's it to you?" he demanded.

"Oh, naught," de Crecy replied through gritted teeth. "Except I look forward to presenting her with the tourney crown, that's all."

Konrad opened his mouth on a sharp retort but felt a hand clapped to his shoulder.

"Kentigern, well met," Douglas Farleigh hailed him heartily. "You are headed for Beres Caple—us too!" He gestured to another couple of knights close by. Konrad had seen them around but did not remember their names. They were southerners like Farleigh but returned his nod in a cautiously friendly manner. "Have you been introduced to Sir Leonard Symes and Sir Fulke Lowell?"

"Excuse me, Farleigh!" De Crecy seethed. "Kentigern and I were in the midst of some conversation before you charged in with your cronies!"

Farleigh glanced back blankly at the irate knight. "Oh, I did not realize. I thought you had finished your conversation." He shrugged. "I can wait until your business is concluded." He placed his hands on his hips and looked enquiringly from one to the other.

De Crecy ground his teeth. "I have said everything I intended," he said stiffly and swung around to stalk away, still muttering under his breath.

"He's been spoiling for a fight all morning," Farleigh muttered under his breath. "Do not let him incite you."

Konrad glanced at him in surprise. Had Farleigh been attempting to prevent an altercation? He was grimly amused. "Whatever else he may be, de Crecy is a professional," he muttered. "He leaves all disputes for the field."

Farleigh snorted. "'Tis plain you have not heard how he conducted himself at the celebration feast the other night."

Konrad blinked. "He got in a fight?"

"A fight, you ask?" Farleigh answered, his lips twitching. He turned to his friends. "Fulke, Leo, Kentigern here asks if de Crecy got into a fight at the feast."

They laughed. "It was a full-scale brawl," the shorter of the two replied. "The King had to send in his guard to pull them apart at the point of a sword."

When Konrad looked incredulous, Farleigh took over the tale. "De Crecy was trying to wring Throckmorten's neck with his bare hands. Astleigh and Faversham were trying their damnedest to prevent him, but they couldn't tear the bastard away."

"De Crecy?" Konrad repeated in dazed accents. De Crecy, who was always so stiff-rumped about his own consequence? De Crecy had disgraced himself in the King's hall? "Why in the name of the gods?" he persisted.

290

"Throckmorten asked de Crecy's wife how she enjoyed being tourney queen," the third lanky knight replied, scratching the back of his neck.

Oh. That.

So taken aback by the tale was Konrad that not much later he allowed himself to be steered toward the same inn that he and Farleigh had frequented the previous day.

"Don't you ever visit The Jennet Tree on Panyer Street?" he asked with disfavor, glancing about the general murk of the low-beamed room. The place didn't seem to possess any windows that he could see.

"Never," Fulke replied, for he now knew that Fulke was the shorter and stockier of Farleigh's friends and Sir Leonard the taller, leaner one. "Would you recommend it?"

"The ale is far superior to this establishment."

"You don't say?" Fulke looked intrigued. "This place is popular in our circles due to the name." He nodded toward the fireplace where a battered-looking chest plate and shield hung. The device meant nothing to Konrad, but he guessed it was some patron saint of combat here in the south.

Farleigh flushed. "Don't be a fool, Fulke!" he begged. "It stands to reason Kentigern knows more of knightly circles than the likes of us, who have only been competing some two years or thereabouts."

"Nay," Konrad protested mildly. "For I have not moved around much in the company of knights outside of the arena."

"Your pardon, Kentigern, if I gave offence," Fulke said, ducking his head by way of apology.

"None was taken," Konrad replied truthfully.

In truth, the ale here was not so bad. "So then, finish the tale of the other eve," he said, seeing some awkwardness had fallen over the table. "Does de Crecy face consequences for fighting in the King's palace?"

Farleigh grinned. "That he does. Fifty gold ducats and he must perform a forfeit for Her Majesty the Queen when she so desires it." Kentigern grimaced.

"I'd lay a wager he would rather pay a hundred and be done with it," Sir Leonard chimed in. "The Queen is an ingenious woman." He shuddered. "I should not wish to lie under such an obligation. You may be sure she will extract her due with the maximum discomfort on Sir Jeffree's part."

Konrad thought of Wymer's dark-eyed Queen and realized Sir Leonard had a point. He eyed him with a good deal more appreciation than he had before.

"Come, Leo, you are unchivalrous," Sir Douglas chided his friend. "The Queen does not deserve such a harsh summing of her character."

Sir Leonard shook his head and shot a speaking look first at Kentigern and then Sir Fulke. Clearly, it communicated at a glance, *Douglas knows nothing of women.* Konrad agreed silently and took a swig of his ale.

"How goes your wooing with Lady Constance?" Fulke asked so forthrightly that Douglas winced.

"Slowly," he answered in a hollow tone and shot a conspiratorial look at Konrad. "I have lately taken some good advice and hope it will speed my wooing."

Konrad doubted it, if his young friend was referring to their conversation the previous day. He glanced across the table at Sir Leonard. "You are married, Symes?" he asked curiously.

Leonard shook his head. "Sisters," he explained succinctly. "A whole brace of them."

Sir Fulke snorted, sending the foam off his ale flying. "I keep telling you I would take one of them off your hands, right willingly!"

"I wish you would," his friend retorted. "But you would not be so keen if you knew the size of their portion." He glanced across at Konrad. "They are undowered and give me many headaches."

"I can well imagine. I have one who never wed," Konrad admitted, thinking of Magnatrude.

"So, she must needs reside forever at your table," Leonard said sympathetically. "There's only one of my sisters I could tolerate in that capacity, but alas, she's the only one anyone would willingly take to wife!"

"Your sister Helen?" Fulke said, nodding his head sagely.

"Helen!" Leonard exploded. "Gods blood! I did not mean Helen, for that wench is the worst of the lot!"

Fulke bristled, but before he could argue, Douglas interrupted. "Miranda," he guessed, looking supremely confident.

If anything, the color in Leonard's cheeks climbed higher. "Miranda!" he echoed with disgust. "She's not far behind Helen! No," he said resolutely. "Sybil is the only one of the pack that I would entertain providing for the rest of my life."

"Sybil!" both his friends cried in astonishment.

"Why," Fulke burst out hotly, "she's not even your full-blood sister!"

"She ain't blood of his in any way," Douglas pointed out with disgust. "Her mother was barely married to Leonard's sire before he keeled over."

Sir Leonard hunched a shoulder and scowled. "I still maintain her company is far superior to that of any of the others."

"Strictly speaking, she's not your actual sister though!" Fulke grumbled.

"No, she is not," Leonard said with such vehemence that Konrad paused in the act of lifting his tankard to his mouth. He was filled suddenly with the strangest suspicions about the nature of feelings Sir Leonard harbored for this Sybil. He eyed the man askance and saw the guilty flush mounting his neck before he pushed back his chair.

"I'm off to the privy," the younger knight growled and sloped off.

"Leonard can be a trifle morose sometimes, though he is the best of good fellows," Fulke confided. "He has a lot to contend with at home, his father having died two years ago and left him with a lot of debt to cover. I'll order us another pitcher, shall I?"

Konrad nodded as he watched Sir Leonard cross the room. He supposed, on reflection, that his own problems could be a good deal worse. The afternoon passed with surprising swiftness, and after leaving the other knights at the town square, Konrad swung by Bulwark Lane to check on the jeweler's progress.

A blue sapphire now hung either side of the teardrop pearl, lending the silver brooch a far grander air. Blyfield had only a few more touches to add before it would be ready for collection. The jeweler showed him some new sketches he had made for other pieces. He had lately received a note which Magnatrude had sent around with her own recollections of her mother's collection. These had proved a considerable help to him in his work.

Konrad approved the sketches and arranged to collect the brooch before they left for Beres Caple when a sudden thought occurred to him. "By the way, can you recommend somewhere I can buy a strand of pearls?" he asked the goldsmith.

Blyfield considered the matter, pursing his lips. "Of what quality?" he asked.

"The finest."

The jeweler nodded and named an establishment three streets over.

21

Aimee did end up sending word to Master Fulcher, though she had no intention of requesting a new particolored gown. Still, her husband had raised a good point about both Freda's and Magnatrude's wardrobes needing refurbishment. When she received an answer that the tailor would call at her house the following week on Wednesday, she relayed this news to Freda with perfect calm.

"Oh, but—er, will that be acceptable?" Freda started awkwardly. "That is—my cousin seemed to think 'twas you that stood in need of some particular garment."

Aimee lifted her chin. "Freda, do you honestly think anything could induce me to wear another gown in his colors?" she asked hotly. "When you know how—how *humiliated* I felt that day?"

Freda's eyes widened. "Is that the gown he wants made up?" she asked, sounding bewildered. "Whatever happened to the one you already owned?" Aimee's heightened color seemed to dissuade her from pursuing the subject. "I am sure none could blame you," Freda quavered. "But Konrad can be so very difficult to dissuade when he gets an idea in his head."

"Well, I, too, have a stubborn streak," Aimee said with resolve, and she wasn't sure she didn't toss her head. Poor Freda looked very alarmed. To distract her, Aimee suggested they walk to the Thursday market with Matthews for an escort. Freda brightened at this suggestion, and they ambled along the stalls arm in arm and had a very jolly time picking over the wares.

As Freda had no money of her own and refused to accept any, Aimee was forced to take Matthews to one side while Freda was distracted talking to a woman with two chubby babes. She pressed a purse into the burly manservant's hand.

"Can you make sure you spend this on anything my cousin shows a particular interest in?" she murmured. "Discreetly?" He nodded and Aimee returned to Freda's side, agreeing the children looked healthy and bonnie and did the woman credit. As they moved away, Aimee was pleased to see Matthews hand the proud mother a coin to treat the children in Freda's name.

"The gods bless you, ma'am!" the woman called after an oblivious Freda.

"What lovely people you meet hereabouts," Freda commented, nodding and smiling. "Do you know, Aimee, I blush to say this, but when we were traveling here, I had the most foolish misgivings about the south. It just goes to show, doesn't it? I daresay I could be just as happy if I ne'er set foot in Vettel again." She glanced about nervously as she said this, as though someone might spring out and denounce her for lack of loyalty to the north.

Aimee laughed. "We will make a southerner of you yet, cousin."

Freda gave a nervous titter and promptly got lost in rhapsodies over some embellished head coverings. Aimee turned to give Matthews a significant look but found him already watching to see which ones Freda favored.

It wasn't until the final row of stalls that Aimee was tempted to make a purchase for herself. She had been drifting along, wondering if the items she had requested from her father's warehouse might yet have arrived, when her eye caught sight of the cheap-looking trinkets scattered over a dark blanket and glittering in the sun.

"Let me just take a look at these, Freda," she murmured as an unholy idea started forming in her head. Her husband had told her he looked forward to seeing how she would reward him for his continued presence in her bed, she remembered, stepping forward to look at the shiny tin and lead alloy tokens. Why not reward him each time with one of these?

They were fashioned in all sorts of fancy shapes: hearts, flowers, shields. She picked up one, which looked to be a pair of kissing cupid heads, and wondered what her husband would make of it.

"Oh!" muttered Freda. "I suppose they are rather pretty, though." She coughed delicately. "I believe such things tarnish very quickly or get bent out of shape, for they are fashioned so thin."

"How many designs do you have?" Aimee asked the stallholder, who was picking his teeth with a twig.

"An 'undred," he answered, casting a desultory look over them. Clearly, he had decided these ladies were unlikely to buy and wasting his time.

"I'll take one of each," Aimee said, reaching for the purse attached to her belt.

As soon as they reached home again, Aimee ran up the stairs gleefully with her two bags of lover's tokens. Freda had been both horrified and astonished by her purchase. "Whatever will you do with them all, Aimee?" she had asked in hushed tones as the stallholder had sorted her selection. "Give them to servants, I suppose, but you don't even have that many!"

Aimee had tried to imagine giving Golda or Ingrid such a token as thanks and failed. Both, she thought, would give her short shrift, infinitely preferring a ha'penny. Rather than explain her intent, she had distracted Freda by congratulating her on her own purchases, explaining what Matthews had been up to.

Freda had spent the entire walk home exclaiming tearfully that Aimee should not have done something so wildly extravagant. "You did not buy that beaded cap?" she demanded in failing accents of Matthews. He gave a nod, and Freda squeaked in dismay, covering her mouth with her thin hands. "Oh gracious! Whatever will I do with it? I am far too old to wear anything so pretty!"

"Nonsense!" Aimee disagreed. "You may wear whatever you like. There is no one to stop you. And besides, you are not old."

"What about that carved wooden spoon?" Freda asked with misgiving. Matthews thought a moment, then gave another nod. Freda's face fell. "Oh, but I had no purpose for it!" she gasped. "I was simply admiring the craftmanship."

Aimee shrugged. "You could always give it to someone for a gift," she suggested. "Ingrid maybe?"

Freda blinked. "You think she would like it?"

"She might."

"Oh dear," Freda fretted. "Aimee, I have no way of repaying your generosity."

"And neither should you, for we are family now."

By the time they had reached home, Freda's dismay had turned to excitement, and she had been almost giddy as a girl when Matthews had handed over the sack of her wares to her. Aimee ran upstairs, reached into the first of the two bags, and pulled out a shiny badge which seemed to depict a hedgehog.

After stashing the rest of the tokens in her wedding chest, she slipped into Konrad's room and placed it carefully on his pillow bearer. She almost hugged herself with glee, imagining his bewilderment on receiving it. Hurriedly, she sped back out of the room and rejoined Freda in the oaken parlor where they sat and went through the bag of Freda's unwitting purchases.

They were still laughing over a pair of bright orange stockings when Magnatrude burst into the room and stood there shaking, her back to the door and her eyes full of tears.

"What is it, Trude?" Aimee asked with alarm, while Freda sat frozen and speechless. "Has something happened?"

Her sister-in-law stumbled into the room, wild-eyed. "I—that is—Queen Armenal has done me *great* honor," she blurted and then burst into tears. Aimee sprang from her seat and drew Trude down onto a seat by the hearth.

"There, there," Aimee murmured, chafing Magnatrude's cold hands. "Freda," she said calmly. "Could you call for someone to bring us some apple logs for the fire, for 'tis going off cold already. And if we could be fetched some wine and spiced biscuits."

Freda ran from the room, sending a grateful glance over her shoulder. Aimee had realized by now that poor Freda tended to bring out the worst in Trude in moments of raised emotion.

"I don't know why I'm acting like this," Magnatrude sobbed. "It's the single most wonderful thing that has ever happened to me." She covered her face with her hands, and Aimee made soothing noises as her sister-in-law dissolved into a fit of uncontrolled weeping.

When Freda returned, she brought Ingrid and a threadbare mantle for Trude's shoulders. At Aimee's nod, she resumed her seat, and the three of them sat in silence as Ingrid kindled the fire. When Unwin soundlessly slipped into the room carrying three goblets and a flask of wine, Aimee bade him pour for them, and he did so quietly and efficiently, handing the cups around.

Magnatrude accepted her cup of wine with thanks and took a sip. She sighed and rested her head along the back of her seat. "The Queen has asked me to become a formal part of her retinue," she said with a gulp. "I am to be a Lady of the Bedchamber and to have my own room at the palace and an allowance made to me." She moistened her lips. "I am to travel with her between the summer and winter palace, and it makes not one whit of difference to her that I am unwed. In fact," she continued in awed tones, "it almost seems as though she prefers that I am not."

She reached out a hand blindly, and Aimee grasped it. "But this is wonderful news, Trude," she said warmly. "I am sure you are fully aware of the compliment she pays you."

Trude nodded vigorously. "She is too good—too generous," she said brokenly. "I do not deserve her condescension." She pressed a hand to her brimming eyes, and Aimee found herself exchanging raised brows with Freda.

Ingrid gave a suppressed snort and straightened up from the fireplace, her creaky knees protesting. "Will that be all, milady?" she asked Aimee loudly.

"Thank you, Ingrid, yes." The old servant stumped out of the room.

"You are happy to serve the southern queen, Trude?" Freda asked timorously.

"She is Queen of all Karadok, Freda!" Magnatrude corrected her cousin with all the energy of a newly converted zealot. She took another sip of wine and let out a shuddering breath. "My only concern," she said heavily, "is that you are not put out by this, Aimee."

"Me?" Aimee exclaimed with surprise.

"After all," Trude said heavily. "It is you that is Baroness Kentigern, not I."

Aimee made haste to assure her that she could bear the disappointment as Golda entered with a plate of marzipan cakes. "We've no spiced biscuits at present," she said briskly, setting them down on a side table. "These will have to do. Mr. Stirling said he would make another batch directly."

"Those are much more appropriate for a celebration in any case," Aimee said. "Have you heard the felicitous news, Golda?"

"No," Golda said, looking quizzically from Aimee to Trude's tearstained countenance. "Old Ingrid never said owt."

Privately, Aimee suspected it was because Ingrid was not impressed by the honor. Aloud, she said, "Mistress Magnatrude is to join the royal household as one of the Queen's ladies-in-waiting, no less."

Golda gasped. A native of Caer-Lyoness, she was a good deal more impressed. "You'll need a page, Mistress Magnatrude, to take care of your errands and see your rooms is taken care of. Those palace maids are naught but slatterns," she said scornfully, turning and motioning to Unwin, who trotted dutifully forward to stand beside Trude's chair. "Might I suggest you take this boy of mine with you. He's a quick learner and—er—very discreet."

Aimee was so surprised by Golda's claiming ownership of Unwin that it took her a moment to notice how hopefully the boy's gaze was fixed on Trude's face. Magnatrude passed the boy a marzipan cake and nodded absently. "Yes, of course," she murmured dazedly. "You make a good point, Golda. I will certainly have need of an attendant."

"You would be happy to go to the palace, Unwin?" Aimee asked incredulously.

He nodded and lowered his marzipan cake. "Yuss, milady," he whispered through a mouthful of crumbs.

Aimee gaped at him. She did not think she had even heard the lad speak before.

"You will need a haircut however," Magnatrude said critically. "And a new suit."

"Fulcher the tailor is coming to the house on Wednesday," Aimee remembered. "He can measure Unwin then. You will also have need of new gowns, Trude. Indeed, you cannot join the Queen's retinue without them."

Magnatrude accepted this as meekly as a lamb, and Golda bustled from the room, vowing the cook must be made aware that tonight's meal was a celebratory affair. By the time Konrad joined them in the dining chamber a couple of hours later, everything seemed more or less settled. Aimee thought her husband was more surprised by his sister's willingness to join the royal household than anything else.

"You've refused to leave the lodge for the last five years," he pointed out critically. "Yet now you propose a permanent move down south?"

Magnatrude gazed back at him steadfastly. "Yes," she said finally. "I do."

"Well, if that is your will, sister, then so be it." He lifted his goblet and toasted her silently.

Aimee thought her sister-in-law breathed a sigh of relief; certainly the atmosphere at the table seemed to lighten. "Freda," she said, turning to the lady. "You must take charge of the house next week in my absence. Trude will have far too many things to prepare for her move. You will have Matthews and Golda—" She broke off, a sudden thought occurring to her. "That is, do we take Golda with us to Beres Caple to wait on me?" she asked doubtfully of her husband, who was carving up the meat. "How do these things work?"

"No," he answered briefly. "We will take Jakeman, who will be sufficient for both our needs."

Aimee nodded and turned back to Freda. "You will have Golda, Matthews, Stirling, and Ingrid to instruct."

"Yes, of course," Freda answered, looking nervous. "Oh dear, I do hope I will not let you down."

"Of course you will not," Aimee replied bracingly.

"Did you invite Ankatel to dine with you yet?" Konrad asked, passing a plate of meat to his cousin.

Freda turned bright red.

"I'm afraid she has not yet had time," Aimee interjected smoothly. "For we went to the marketplace this afternoon, did we not, Freda?"

Fortunately, Trude interrupted at this point to tell her brother that she was the first prominent northerner to become a woman of the bedchamber, for though the Marchioness of Martindale was officially one of the Queen's circle, she was rarely in the south. Aimee and Freda covertly exchanged a look of relief that they were off the hook so easily.

Aimee's gaze wandered to where Unwin stood behind Trude's chair having already started his training as her sister-in-law's page. She noticed with amusement that he was wearing the bright orange hose that Freda had purchased in the marketplace. It seemed his transformation into a smart page was already beginning. Everyone seemed to be falling into their new roles with such ease, she thought with a sudden pang. Yet she still did not really feel a true baroness in any way.

No one had given her an update on Bartree Castle since the renovations had begun, not even her father. Certainly, her husband had not mentioned when they might be traveling north to visit his birthplace. In fact, she thought forlornly, the only reference he had made to it in her presence had been to tell her he considered himself master there, and her mistress here at the townhouse. She ran over the conversation in her memory and wondered if she had not attached the significance to this conversation at the time that she should have.

She was quiet for the rest of supper, not that she thought this would be remarked on, for Magnatrude was full of praise for the wit and vision of Queen Armenal. According to her sister-in-law, the Queen was a woman ahead of her time. Trude was fulsome in her praise of a tapestry that had been completed that day to show the Countess of Twyford falling out of a balcony only to be caught in her husband's arms below.

"Falling out of a balcony?" Freda repeated uncertainly. "That sounds an extremely dangerous manner of eloping. It is fortunate the countess was not hurt."

"It was not her means of escape," Trude corrected her impatiently. "But an incident that happened sometime later and demonstrated the sincere attachment of their union."

Aimee frowned, wondering if the scene was a retelling of the stand collapse at Kellingford. If so, certain liberties had been taken with the facts. The earl had not, in fact, caught his wife or spared her from injury, but she did not voice this, seeing that it would be an unwelcome interruption in Trude's narrative. Privately, she wondered if the rest of the Queen's depictions played as fast and loose with the truth as this one.

After supper, Aimee visited the garderobe and was just walking along the passage back to the oaken parlor when Ingrid waylaid her. The old servant was brandishing the large carved spoon in one hand which Freda must have wasted no time in making her a present of.

"Us Oakdens have served the barons of Kentigern for near five generations," she started belligerently, thrusting out her chin.

Aimee gazed back at her, feeling mystified. "I see," she lied after a moment. "Do you have children, Ingrid?"

"Two sons," Ingrid replied grudgingly. "They's had to take on other work since Bartree Castle fell."

"What are they doing now?" Aimee asked with interest. She had often wondered what became of the staff and retainers who must have lost their positions.

"Wylie works as a farm laborer, and Elton's working for a cooper in Vettel."

"Do they like their new roles? Or will they want to return once Bartree Castle is restored?"

Hope flared for a moment in Ingrid's eyes. "The elder would be back like a shot," she said quickly. "My younger son's different. Settled into town life, he has. He likes delivering the cooper's wares and he's courting some maid, but Elton follows his father, the gods rest his soul. Farming ain't in his blood."

Aimee nodded. "Well, the gods willing, you will have six generations of Oakdens serving at Bartree," she said, stepping around the old woman. "When the castle reopens, I am sure the previous servants will be reinstated there, if they wish it."

"What about me?" Ingrid demanded, whirling around. "And that worrisome old maid, Mistress Freda. What's to become of us now? That's what I want to know!"

Aimee looked back at her in exasperation. "I am very fond of Freda, and she will always have a home in my household. If you wish to remain serving Mistress Magnatrude, then you can accompany her to court, but should you wish to—"

"It's the Baroness Kentigern I's always served!" Ingrid burst out hotly.

"Very well, then," Aimee responded calmly. "Long may you continue to."

Ingrid opened and closed her mouth, then gave a brusque nod. "Milady," she muttered and stomped off down the corridor. Aimee watched her a moment before swinging open the door to the oaken parlor. Freda was stood beside the fire, wringing her hands.

"Did you mean it, Aimee?" she asked tearfully as she entered the room, and Aimee realized she must have heard every word of the exchange, including the part where Ingrid had referred to her as an old maid. "About my always having a home with you, I mean?"

"Of course, Freda," Aimee assured her, joining her before the fire and taking her hand. "You must not worry about that."

Freda's narrow shoulders drooped, and she touched a scarf to her reddened eyes. "Well, you see, my only usefulness was in attending Trude, and with her gone…"

307

"Nonsense!" Aimee said bracingly. "You are very useful to me, Freda. Did I not just tell you that you are to oversee the running of this house next week?"

"Yes," Freda quavered, brightening. "You did, did you not?"

"And you are to make sure my father does not become too lonely in the meantime. Perhaps you could send word to my sister's house, inviting her and Sir Renlow to supper one evening? He must be sufficiently recovered from his injury by now to welcome a change of scenery."

Freda's expression wavered between uncertainty and alarm. "Oh, I should not wish to do anything presumptuous!" she exclaimed. "The first time your sister visits your house should be under your direction, Aimee, not mine!"

Aimee brushed this aside, steering Freda into a chair. "There will be plenty of time for me to entertain Ursula when I return from Beres Caple. Now, let us sit together quietly this evening and—"

A loud knock at the door interrupted them before it was smartly flung open by Unwin, who announced in a high, boyish voice, "Mistress Magnatrude Bartree!" then stood to one side.

Trude sailed into the room. "Very good, Unwin," she approved and then swept back out again. Unwin hurried after her, swinging the door shut behind him.

Aimee turned to look at Freda, whose jaw had dropped open. They were still laughing when Konrad joined them moments later.

"I am glad to see you so merry," he said, dropping onto a seat. "When you were both so quiet at supper."

Aimee saw the glint in his eye and had a sudden misgiving that he must have found the hedgehog token she had left in his room. She cleared her throat. "Well," she said lightly. "I think we were just letting the momentous news sink in. Is that not so, Freda?"

"Yes, indeed," Freda answered, backing her up at once. "Such a very great honor for the family," she murmured vaguely.

Konrad shot his cousin a sardonic look. "You do not aspire to join the Queen's retinue, Freda? I'm sure Trude could put in a good word for you."

Poor Freda blanched.

"I am sure we could not be expected to spare two members of our household," Aimee put in quickly. "The Queen would not expect us to make such a sacrifice."

Konrad snorted and crossed his ankles. Aimee saw Freda glance longingly toward the door before suppressing a sigh and drawing a gray garment of indeterminate age and purpose from her work bag. With her tongue stuck out of the side of her mouth, Freda started attempting to thread her needle.

Aimee shot another glance at her husband, but he seemed in no hurry to leave. Reluctantly, Aimee retrieved her long-neglected embroidery from behind a cushion. It looked no better now than it had the last time she had seen it.

The door opened behind them. "Mistress Magnatrude Bartree!" Unwin announced smartly, and Aimee swiveled in her seat to see her sister-in-law bend an approving nod on her new page.

"Ah," Trude said, stepping forward. "I am pleased to see you two are plying your needles." She leaned over the back of the settle to inspect Aimee's handiwork.

Instinctively, Aimee stiffened, and she felt herself grow hot and uneasy. Her sister-in-law's needlework was exquisite whereas Aimee's was abysmal. The fact that Magnatrude arched a brow but made no comment only served to make her feel worse.

Freda cleared her throat. "Could you light me a candle, Unwin?" she requested. "I am afraid I cannot see to thread this needle."

Unwin rushed to oblige her, and seeing Magnatrude drift to the window, Aimee rose from her seat with as much dignity as she could muster and swiftly exited the room. She had no sooner closed the door behind her than it opened again. Instead of glancing back, Aimee quickened her steps and rushed along the corridor to her bedchamber.

This time, she did not even attempt to close it behind her, for a bulky figure was following her to the doorway. Konrad shut the door behind them and then walked over to the bed, sitting on the edge of it.

"I hope you are packed for the morrow, wife," he commented.

"I am!" Aimee replied tartly. "Are you?"

He snorted. "It does not take me long to throw my things into a pack. Besides, I am used to it."

He held out a hand to her, and Aimee looked at it blankly. He nodded toward her own, and it was only at this point that she realized she was still clutching the embroidery in her hand. "Let me see."

Swallowing her instinctive refusal, Aimee passed it to him. "I am a very poor needlewoman," she said, bristling all over as he glanced over it. "And wield nothing like the skill your sister would deem necessary in a lady."

310

A smile lurked at the corner of his mouth. "She did not actually comment on your work."

"No," Aimee acknowledged, firing up. "But she *looked* at it and lifted her brows in the most infuriating manner! Even *my* sister, who has the patience of a saint, would have been goaded into a passionate fury by the sight of it! I am convinced!"

Konrad laughed. "It's rather an unusual-looking hound to be sure—"

"It's a horse!" Aimee burst forth wrathfully. "*Your* horse!"

He squinted at it again. "Well, the colors are somewhere near," he conceded. "But Actaeon's neck is definitely longer than this beast's…"

Aimee rushed toward him, snatching it out of his hand. "Oh, never mind!" she burst out hotly.

He caught her about the waist as she whirled around to make her retreat, hauling her back against him so she was pulled down into his lap. "Don't be a little shrew," he breathed into her ear. "If it makes you any happier, I don't give a damn about your proficiency with the needle."

"It doesn't!" Aimee huffed.

"And why not?" he demanded. "Is it not my good opinion you should seek above all others?" When she did not answer, he squeezed her waist. "Well?"

Because I don't love you anymore, she thought mutinously, but did not dare voice. "You are easily pleased in a wife," Aimee said in a brittle manner. "Ladies are more discerning and less easily appeased."

"Not true," he growled in her ear. "I am very *hard* to please. As you shall soon discover, wife." He squeezed her again, and

311

Aimee grew slightly breathless. Then he sighed, loosening his grip. "Though not tonight, as we leave early on the morrow and have a five-hour ride ahead of us."

"Oh," she responded, and even to her own ear, the faint disappointment was apparent. He gave a snort of laughter and reached into his tunic, drawing forth a long rope of pearls.

"These are for you."

Aimee stared. "For me?"

He nodded and dropped them into her lap. "Betrothal gift," he said shortly.

Betrothal gift? "Oh," Aimee breathed in astonishment, only just catching them before they spilled onto the floor. "They—they are beautiful, my lord." She lifted the strand to look at the magnificent, lustrous pearls. "Were they part of the Bartree collection?" she asked in awed tones.

He shook his head. "No, I bought those for you from my winnings at the royal tournament." He cleared his throat. "Mayhap they will make up for the wrong I did you there."

Aimee felt the color drain from her face before it surged back, hot and shaming. It seemed Lord Kentigern had finally realized how much his actions had hurt her. Jumping up from his lap, she hurried to the looking glass and held the pearls up to her neck, though in truth she could see nothing through the sudden tears obscuring her vision. "What a shame I cannot take them with me to Beres Caple," she heard herself say aloud.

"Why can you not?"

"Well, only think if they were to be stolen—" she began.

"You think anyone would dare to steal the pearls from my wife's neck?" He sounded offended, annoyed even.

"I should wear them, then?" Aimee asked uncertainly, glancing back over her shoulder.

"Do what you like," he said gruffly. He picked up the embroidery she had abandoned on the bed. "Will you finish this?" he asked, holding it up.

"It *is* finished," Aimee replied stiffly. "Whenever I try to improve it, I only succeed in making matters worse."

He muttered something, which sounded remarkably like "I know how you feel," though she was sure she must have misheard him.

"I shall leave you to your packing, then, wife," he said, getting to his feet.

Aimee turned from the mirror and gave him an awkward curtsey. "I thank you for your generous gift, Lord Kentigern."

He looked startled a moment before clearing his throat. "When I said 'bedchamber,' I really just meant...in bed," he said, and if it had been anyone else, she would have thought the slash of hot color along his unscarred cheek denoted blushing.

"Oh, I see," she replied blankly, though of course, she really did not. At all.

The funny thing was that, after he had gone, she could not find her embroidery of Actaeon anywhere.

22

Konrad rose early the next morning and collected Aimee's
brooch from Bulwark Lane. He swung by the ostler's on the
way back and collected Actaeon. By the time he had returned to
Lime Street, Jakeman was in the courtyard loading up his own
brown mare and the skewbald packhorse with saddlebags. A
fine white mare was stood tethered to another post close by.
Once Actaeon was added to the mix, the small courtyard
seemed to be teeming with horses.

"They sent around my wife's horse, I see."

"Aye, my lord."

"Where's the boy?" Konrad asked, looking round. "Didn't I
hear tell he used to work in Ankatel's stable?"

Jakeman shook his head. "The lad is clearly nervous around
horses, my lord, and better off where he is."

Konrad shrugged and made his way inside, where he found his
sister sat at table breaking her fast. She looked up at his
entrance. "Ah, Konrad," she greeted him, almost affably for
Magnatrude. "I was hoping I would see you before you
departed."

He dropped into a chair opposite her. "Were you? Are you
going somewhere?"

"The palace," she replied, and he steeled himself for another
account of Queen Armenal's beneficence. "But 'twas not that I
was hoping to converse with you about." She lowered her
voice. "It is my hope you will take this opportunity to shore up
and fortify the foundations of your marriage. They were badly
shaken by your actions at the royal tournament. It is my sincere

wish that you will not subject your wife to such an indignity again."

Konrad stiffened. "I am well aware that I made a misstep there," he replied brusquely. "And do not require your counsel on the matter."

"Is that so?" Trude responded with raised brows. "I am still your elder sister, Konrad. You will allow that, if nothing else."

"You are my elder sister," he agreed. "But in truth, you know even less of marital accord than I."

She considered this before inclining her head. "I will own you may have something there. We neither of us had much of an example held up before us." They fell silent as the specter of their long-dead parents rose and fell between them. "Perhaps you should take her north to Bartree Castle after your tournament?" she suggested.

"It will take months before the place is habitable," he pointed out.

"It might be an adventure," she said brightly. "To one such as Aimee."

"Even an adventurous woman would be daunted by camping out in a soot-blackened shell," he pointed out damningly. "She is used to every comfort."

"Perhaps so," she agreed. "But she has a good deal of spirit, and besides…"

"Besides what?"

"That girl believes herself to be in love with you, Konrad," she said heavily. "So long as she is by your side, I believe there are few experiences she would not relish."

Her words struck him dumb for a moment. "Perhaps in the beginning that was so," he said harshly. "But you heard what she said that day." To both their surprise, he broke off, his words half-choked. He could not quite bring himself to repeat Aimee's claim she no longer loved him.

Magnatrude snorted. "She has some pride. What did you expect the poor girl to do? How do you imagine she must have felt in such exalted quarters? She must have been quite sick with nerves, without having to sit by and watch you favor another." Konrad threw up a hand to stem the flow. He did not wish to hear the words aloud. His sister sucked in her cheeks and paused before proceeding. "Lord knows, the difference in your stations in life is insurmountable enough without you flouting it in front of everyone!"

"You know nothing about it, Trude. That is not what I was doing!"

"Very well," she retorted. "I will admit my knowledge of tournament etiquette is slim. However—"

Konrad drew back his chair. "You have delivered your lecture, sister," he said. "I can assure you that I have no intention of repeating the offense."

She eyed him doubtfully. "I did not mean to lecture you, Konrad," she sighed. "I am well aware that my own conduct toward Aimee has not been beyond reproach."

They sat a moment together in awkward silence. "You really want to become a courtier?" he asked gruffly. "It seems an odd choice for you to make at this time."

"You mean with the estate being restored to you?" she asked. "Your wife will be mistress there, Konrad," she said almost gently. "Not I."

316

"I know," he answered, though he vaguely remembered a time when he had not thought this would be the case. He had thought it would be in name only. "I could dower you now," he pointed out. "Handsomely."

Magnatrude's smile was wry. "I do not want you to buy me a husband, Konrad, though I thank you for the offer. I have been given an opportunity to make my own way in life. On my own merit."

Konrad grunted. He wasn't so sure that bowing and scraping and constantly flattering a monarch would be an easy existence. "You wouldn't rather be set up in your own household?" he suggested. "Able to call your soul your own?"

"At the constant beck and call of a husband?" Magnatrude asked dryly. He blinked, having never really considered it in that light. "No," she said, shaking her head. "That is not the life for me. You were right about Kimarne," she said, taking him by surprise. "We would have dealt very poorly together. Things worked out for the best there."

"You could always remain at Bartree," he suggested.

She shook her head. "No," she said resolutely. "Already, Ingrid has started checking my orders with Aimee. It is only natural that she should do so. Your wife is not the sort to be ridden roughshod over. She will be mistress in her own home and rightly so."

They both lapsed into silence. "If you are sure this is what you want," Konrad said after a moment. "Then I will support you in it."

"Thank you."

A footfall in the hallway alerted them to Aimee's approach. She appeared in the doorway wearing a plum-colored gown with her new pearls worn in a double strand and pinned to her bodice by a small brooch in the shape of a portcullis.

"Good morning to you both," she greeted them brightly before turning to Konrad. "Husband, I am ready to depart when you are."

"You have not yet eaten," he pointed out with a frown.

"Oh yes, I have," she assured him. "I took mine earlier with Freda when you were from the house." She turned to Trude, and they exchanged some small talk as Konrad reached into his tunic to extract the newly restored brooch.

"Here," he said, placing it on the table and sliding it toward her. "I'll go and check on the horses. Join me outside when you are ready." He left the room before she had the chance to do anything other than reach for the wrapped package. Twenty minutes later they had set out and were on the road for Beres Caple.

To his surprise, Konrad found that he experienced none of his customary emotions when exiting the walled city of Caer-Lyoness. Usually, riding out of the armed gates felt like shrugging a heavy cape from his shoulders. Today, he felt none of the usual relief and cast an uneasy glance back over his shoulder as the city retreated further into the distance.

Was it possible, he pondered, that his feelings toward the place had undergone some sort of miraculous change? The notion that the southern capital could ever be anything other than detested by him was a startling one. He glanced uneasily across at his wife, but Aimee's concentration was focused solely on staying in her saddle.

His wife was not a natural horsewoman, which perhaps he should have expected in a city girl born and bred. She clung grimly to her reins and stared doggedly ahead as they trotted along. In truth, she would be far happier on an older, placid mare, but Ankatel had purchased her a showy mount with plenty of spirit. Each time the horse tossed its head or kicked out, poor Aimee braced herself and held her breath.

"Your horse could do with a gallop," he commented, lifting his voice so she could hear him above the horse's hooves.

Aimee frowned. "She will be tired enough after a five-hour ride without galloping."

"Aye," he agreed. "But it might take the fidgets out of her legs."

Aimee shrugged. "Maybe so," she agreed, straightening her shoulders as though steeling herself to an unpleasant task. He was pleased she did not argue, however little the idea appealed to her. "Why don't you swap seats with Jakeman for a while?" he heard himself suggesting. "He could ride on ahead and let her stretch her legs."

"Really?" She looked so relieved by the proposal that he almost laughed. They effected the switch with little bother, and Aimee looked a lot happier on his manservant's well-behaved mount. "What a sweet horse," she commented, patting the chestnut's neck. "What is her name?"

"'Tis Ivy, milady," Jakeman told her cheerfully as he swung up into her own horse's saddle. "This one's a beauty."

"Yes." Aimee winced. "Deirdre is very headstrong, though I can see she is in expert hands."

Jakeman grinned and touched his cap to her. At the dig of his heels into her sides, the white horse took off, and they watched as they disappeared into the distance.

"How long has Jakeman been in your employ?" Aimee asked curiously.

"It must be some five years all told."

"That long?"

"Why do you look so surprised?"

"It is just that…" She glanced down at her hands. "Well, he's a southerner. When you employed him, the war must not have been long over." She shrugged. "I suppose it surprised me that you would have taken someone into your service who had been so recently your enemy."

Konrad considered his answer. "Jakeman was a soldier on Wymer's forces, it is true," he acknowledged. Aimee's eyes grew wider. "But I did not hold that against him. A man fights for his king and country as he is honor bound to do."

"Did you have no manservant from home that served you?"

"I did," he acknowledged. "But he was killed in battle. Strictly speaking, I ought to have taken another from the estate, but…" He shrugged.

"You did not wish to uproot anyone from their home?" Aimee suggested.

Konrad dismissed this notion with a wave of his hand. "Most of the servants were scattered to the four winds when the estate was razed. Very few were retained by the Crown to oversee a ruin."

"Why, then, did you not employ one of them?"

He was quiet a moment. "It seemed easier to just take on a new man. One who had not known me before."

"Before the war, you mean?"

He nodded and Aimee was silent a moment, likely in deference to his dour tone. When she spoke, her tone was thoughtful. "Ingrid said that one of her sons is happier in his new place than in his old, though the other misses the castle life."

"Ingrid told you that?"

"She did."

"She likes you," he growled. "Has done from the start."

"Ingrid?" Aimee sounded startled. "Did she say so?"

"As good as. She said if you and Trude were sows fighting for dominance, you would come out the victor."

Aimee's mouth fell open, and Konrad felt the absurd impulse to laugh. This time he did not stifle it.

"Did she really say that?" Aimee sounded incredulous.

"She did."

"What an odd thing to say!"

"She's an old countrywoman," he pointed out. "The comparison would be a natural one to her."

"Yes, but to voice such a thing aloud to her master!"

"That's the thing with old family servants. They get away with a good deal. Ingrid's gnarled old hands boxed my ears when I was a lad. She will never forget the fact."

Now Aimee laughed. "She is fortunate you do not bear a grudge now you are grown."

"I'm sure I was deserving."

"What were you like?" Aimee asked impulsively, turning toward him.

"Before the war?" he asked with an edge to his voice he had not intended.

"I meant as a boy, but I confess, that would interest me also," she answered wistfully.

The sound of approaching horse hooves cut off their conversation. "Jakeman is back," he said needlessly, and Aimee nodded as though she understood the time for exchanging confidences had passed.

The rest of the morning passed without event. Aimee returned to her own mount's back, now Deirdre was less inclined to act out. He suspected she would have been happy to remain on the brown mare, for her own horse would never be docile, but she seemed resigned to her fate.

After that, he kept a close eye on her progress, steering Actaeon to her side when they passed carts or wagons in the road and Deirdre shied or caviled. His destrier was steady as a rock, and his example seemed a calming presence. Then, too, Actaeon was so large that when beside him, the mare could not see anything to alarm her around his solid bulk.

They stopped at the halfway point to give the horses water and to briefly stretch their legs. Aimee leaned stiffly against a wooden fence and rubbed her backside beneath her cloak when she thought he and Jakeman weren't looking. He guessed she would be stiff and uncomfortable by the time they reached their destination, though there was little he could do to spare her that fate.

The idea occurred to him that if she had brought her lotion, mayhap he could rub her limbs for her later. He adjusted his stance and tried to think of something less stimulating. He ought to by rights ask the Lady Howard, who ran things these days, for a room at Caple Hall for his wife to sleep in, for Aimee would be unaccustomed to sleeping out of doors in a pavilion. However, it was unlikely she would suffer any ill effects from a couple of nights in such accommodation, especially with him wrapped around her to guard her from the cold.

His aspect brightened considerably at the prospect, and he plucked apples from low-hanging branches to feed to the four horses. He gave the pack horse two apples, for the beast was loaded up with the cumbersome pavilion. Actaeon, who was huge, carried his weapons and armor, which left Jakeman's horse to carry the rest of their things. Only Aimee's pretty white mare was not burdened with anything additional but for her rider and a set of blue and silver tack.

The rest of the journey passed without event, and they reached the village of Beres Caple by three o'clock. Caple Hall stood on the outskirts of the village, a large manor house, of half-wood and half-stone construction with a handsome, prosperous appearance. They had no sooner turned up the driveway than they spotted people teeming about the grounds and setting up for the tournament. Their appearance seemed to cause something of a flurry, for there was a series of shouts and hurried footsteps at their approach.

"Do they know you?" Aimee asked with interest. "You seem to have caused quite a stir."

"It's the sight of a charger," he said with a shrug, patting Actaeon's neck. "They do not get many knights traveling in from out of the county. This tournament is not a well-established one. I am not displaying my banner," he elaborated when Aimee continued to look unconvinced.

323

His words were then dashed, rather, when he was hailed loudly by a stocky young man approaching from their left. It was the eldest of the Howard sons, he realized, though he could not recall if this was Chaucey or Darby, for there were two of them and both very similar in age and appearance.

"Lord Kentigern! You honor us with your presence!" he called out, beaming. "We hoped you might, but we weren't sure you would manage to fit us in after your recent victory in the capital."

Konrad nodded to him. He had only just growled out a "Well met" when his brother hurried over from the opposite direction. "You might have waited, Chaucey!" he puffed. "So we could greet his lordship together!"

They exchanged some words in a furious undertone before both swung back around again, once more wreathed in smiles. "We have saved you the best spot, my lord," Darby assured him. "Mother said we ought to have given it to Sir Jeffree, but we stood firm. After all, de Crecy hath only attended once before, whereas you have attended four years out of five."

"Everyone from hereabouts knows you are a local crowd favorite," Chaucey added, clearly not wanting to be outdone by his brother.

Feeling Aimee's eye on him, Konrad cleared his throat. "This is my wife, Baroness Kentigern. Aimee, this is Sir Chaucey and Sir Darby Howard, who are our hosts here at Beres Caple."

The Howard brothers' eyes nearly fell out of their heads. "You have brought your wife along?" Darby stammered before giving a nervous chuckle. "That seems to be the new custom!"

"Mother will be relieved at all events," Chaucey said, nudging his brother in the ribs.

Relieved seemed an odd choice of word, but as they were performing their bows with frowning concentration, Konrad let this pass.

"I am pleased to meet you," Aimee responded amiably. To Konrad's discomfort, she seemed to be deriving great entertainment from the way the brothers vied for his attention as they were led to a meadow lying to the west of the house.

A few tents were already set up, and Chaucey pointed out one that was for equipment and one for servants' use. "This spot is the one we had marked out for your use," he said with satisfaction. "As you can see, it has the best views all round and is at a clear vantage point if it should rain."

Konrad nodded, glancing at Jakeman, who was already driving a stake into the ground to tether the horses.

"We can send a couple of servants to help you set up," Chaucey offered generously.

"You will dine with the family, of course, in the Great Hall," Darby interrupted. "As our guests."

"Lord Kentigern knows how we run things, Darby," his older brother chided him. "He is not new to our ways here at Caple Hall."

"Aye, but I wanted to make sure he would join us at supper tonight," Darby persisted. "For only recollect, sometimes he shuns the company of the Great Hall and has his food brought to his tent."

His brother looked much struck by this, and two pairs of brown eyes were suddenly trained on him in appeal. Why were they so anxious for him to join them at table? he wondered. One of the things he most enjoyed about the smaller tournaments was the usual lack of attendant ceremony.

"I, for one, would like very much to make Lady Howard's acquaintance," Aimee said as Jakeman helped her to dismount.

"Excellent," Chaucey said, relaxing. Clearly, he thought Konrad would adhere to his lady's wishes. "In truth, you will be doing us something of a favor. Poor Mother has been thrown into a serious quandary by the seating arrangements, but with a baron and baroness here, you will clearly take precedence."

"Take precedence over who?" Konrad demanded, feeling totally at sea by this point. He reached into his saddlebag for a flask to fortify himself.

The Howard brothers exchanged glances. "Oh, didn't we say?" Darby asked, looking embarrassed. "You'll have to excuse us, my lord. With so much going on, our wits have clearly gone a-begging."

"You see," Chaucey said, lowering his voice and casting an excited look about. "It's not just you and de Crecy who have graced us with your presence this year. We have another knight of considerable fame. He won the cup at Areley Kings in June."

Areley Kings? Orde's words flashed back into his mind. But that would mean…

"De Bussell's here," Darby broke in in a hushed voice. "And he's brought *her* with him. You know." He nudged Jakeman in the ribs. "*The northern princess!*"

The flask that Konrad had been raising to his lips slipped through his fingers and fell at his feet, spilling water into the grass.

23

Aimee sat perched atop the low wooden stool which had been set to one side for her to take her ease as they set up the pavilion. She felt far too uncomfortable to sit observing them with any contentment as frankly her backside was aching like the devil from five hours in a saddle.

Aimee shifted onto her other buttock and winced, clasping the edges of her seat. It felt like she would never get comfortable again! A bee buzzed loudly in her ear and she gasped, waving a hand about to dislodge it from wherever it had landed.

Really, it felt particularly disobliging that, in a positive *sea* of meadow flowers, this bee had decided she was the landing spot it most desired. She regarded the pretty summer's view with a jaundiced eye. It *was* a very picturesque spot, she acknowledged. The green grass was scattered liberally with harebells and daisies and even the odd poppy. The afternoon sun was low in the sky, but it was still warm, and she had long since abandoned her cloak and hat into the long grass.

Another loud buzz had her sharply turning her head as something winged skimmed past her nose. She wondered if a night sleeping outdoors would mean being crawled all over by insect life and shuddered.

Aimee had not much appreciated her only other previous stay in the countryside last year with the Wycliffes, then again, they had not spent much of it out of doors. She remembered the pastures surrounding their ancient home had smelled extremely strongly of dung at the time, as the land was being prepared for planting.

Of course, cities could smell pretty objectionable too, Aimee reflected fairly, but she was used to the smell of Caer-Lyoness and knew whereabouts she needed to hold her breath or press a scarf to her nose and walk quickly. The countryside was unfamiliar to her and seemed to assail her senses with fresh outrages at every turn.

She shifted again on her seat in a vain attempt to get comfortable. The pavilion was taking shape now, and though the shape and size was impressive, she was a little disappointed by the drab brown color of the Kentigern tent. It ought to be blue and yellow by rights, she decided. Maybe if his tournament abode were decked out in his colors, then he would stop hankering for his wife to parade them on her person!

Biting her lip, Aimee wondered if he was going to be really put out when she was forced to confess she had not brought along a new heraldic gown. She would not feel guilty about it, she told herself. She was entirely justified in wanting to avoid repeating that whole debacle. No reasonable man would expect such a thing from his wife!

Then again, she was not entirely sure Lord Kentigern *was* a reasonable man. She sighed, plucking on the large silver brooch which she had pinned to the center of her bodice. Freda's gift was barely recognizable these days, she thought, glancing down at it and the double rope of pearls that swathed her upper body. She was decorated like a noble these days, if nothing else.

She would have to wear her grandest gown to dinner, she thought with determination. If she was expected to take precedence over a genuine princess of the blood! Aimee knew precious little about the last of the royal house of Blechmarsh, but she had seen the ill-done renditions showing the popular image of Una wearing full armor astride a horse. What would it be like being sat down to supper with such a warlike creature? she wondered.

She had not missed her husband's thunderstruck response to the fact that the northern princess was present at Beres Caple, and she had felt a nasty jolt of something she was worried might be jealousy. He had gone to war for the Blechmarsh cause, she thought with a cold feeling in her stomach. He had lost everything and nearly died for it. If he *were* to win the joust here, she already knew who he would award the crown to, and it would not be his wife.

"Aimee!" She looked up to find Lord Kentigern—Konrad, as she should think of him by now—regarding her critically as he stood at the entrance to the tent. "What ails you, woman?" he asked with a frown. "You look sour as curdled milk."

She stood up, bristling all over. "I assure you I am quite well," Aimee answered huffily, sticking her nose in the air. "It is only that I am a little stiff and sore from the journey."

He grunted and held out his hand to her. "Come and see if there is enough here for your comfort."

She made her way gingerly through the long grass toward him. "Well, it all looks very nice," she said uncertainly as she stepped into the interior. In truth, she was not sure what she had expected, but the low bed stacked up with blankets and furs and the pile of saddlebags and armor was not it. "Are there not any chairs to be had?" she asked.

Konrad turned to the two servants hovering to one side. "Two chairs," he said succinctly before turning back to Aimee. "Anything else?"

His tone was rather dry, but she considered the matter seriously a moment before making her reply. "A small table," she said resolutely.

"You heard my lady," he said, turning back to the servants again. They bowed and hurried away, and Aimee wondered where she was supposed to put herself as Konrad moved to his pack and started untying the strings.

"Where is Jakeman?"

"He's seeing to the horses. The Howards have offered us the use of their own stables."

"That was nice of them." He grunted. "They seem very much in awe of you," Aimee added.

Konrad snorted. "Like I say, they don't get many knights from other parts traveling here."

"Well, this year it seems they have. You said their mother presides over the feast?"

"Aye, for her late husband, Sir Bortram Howard, had no sooner set up the tournament here than he died of the ague. His widow continues it now in his memory."

Aimee watched as he started removing several things from his pack. Most of the objects were wholly unknown to her, and she guessed they were for treating his weapons. He looked up as though aware of her scrutiny. "Why don't you sit down?"

"Where?" she asked pointedly, glancing around the bare interior.

"On the bed."

"Oh."

The corner of his mouth on the uninjured side of his face tilted up in that lopsided smirk he seemed to favor. "You seem a little disappointed by the pavilion."

Aimee sank down onto the bed with a grimace. Her rump really was painful, and the mattress was very low to the ground. Once she made contact with it, she was relieved to find it was reasonably soft. Her expression must have registered this, for he gave a short laugh.

"It is stuffed with grasses, so it should be comfortable."

"Yes," she hastened to assure him. "It is."

"If you dislike it out here, I am sure Lady Howard would offer you a bedchamber within," he answered, picking up his sword and examining the hilt.

"What about you?" she asked.

He looked up. "What about me?"

"Where would you sleep if I go within?"

"Out here," he answered with a trace of impatience. "Where else?"

Aimee swallowed down the bitter taste in her mouth. Obviously, her presence or no would make little difference to him. "Of course," she said blankly and rose from the bed. "How silly of me."

"Where are you going?" he asked sharply when she took a step toward the tent entrance.

"I thought I would just take a step around the meadow," Aimee said, brushing aside the flap to the entrance and exiting before he could voice any objection. Not that he *would* object, Aimee thought furiously, dashing her forearm across her eyes as she stalked away, when he did not care remotely about her whereabouts!

The ground was uneven in the meadow, and Aimee winced over every bump which she felt in her sadly jolted spine and sore behind. She was just picking her way over a particularly lumpy patch which must surely have been churned up by horses' hooves after rain when she felt herself seized and whirled about so fast, she nearly lost her footing altogether.

"Don't be a little fool," her husband growled down at her, a thunderous frown at his brow. "You can't wander about the place wearing a king's ransom in jewelry! This may not be Caer-Lyoness, but people are still robbed in the country and wind up dead in a ditch!"

Aimee glared up at him. "Very well," she said, reaching for the pearls and starting to draw them up over her head. She had lifted them no further than her ears before she was roughly seized and slung over a large and burly shoulder. "Konrad!" she shrieked. "Put me down!" She might have even added *you brute* at this point, but her necklace was swinging about her face and a mouthful of pearls prevented her.

He made no reply, just swung about to return to his own tent, when a cleared throat in the vicinity made them both freeze in their place.

"Kentigern," said a deep, pleasant voice. "Well met."

Aimee found herself rotated again as her husband turned to face the speaker. Shoving her palm between Konrad's shoulder blades, Aimee levered herself up to squint over his shoulder at a tall, good-looking couple who were stood arm in arm and regarding them with varying degrees of curiosity. While the male's gaze was curious and amused, the female's expression was full of lively horror.

332

"De Bussell," her husband answered through clenched teeth, his grip on her buttock tightening momentarily and making Aimee yelp.

"I believe you know my wife," de Bussell continued with a lift of his eyebrows.

Konrad cleared his throat, clearly at a loss how to address the former princess now her station in life had quite altered.

"Indeed, we are old friends," Princess Una said hurriedly in an attractively full-bodied voice, which sent another pang through Aimee's being. *Of course the princess would be a tall and majestic auburn beauty*, Aimee seethed. *And look absolutely nothing like those slanderous likenesses that flooded the marketplaces of Caer-Lyoness, lambasting her for an ugly fright!* "How are you, my lord?" Una continued warmly. "Well, I trust?"

A horrible realization flooded Aimee's being that they were going to ignore her embarrassing presence. Likely, they thought her some buxom serving wench that Lord Kentigern was dallying with! An awkward silence fell over the group.

"This is my wife, Aimee," Konrad said as though the words were dragged from his lips by wild horses. Aimee closed her eyes in mortification, and suddenly Armand de Bussell gave a hearty laugh.

"Armand!" the princess murmured to her husband in reproach. He sobered at once. "Perhaps if you put her down, Lord Kentigern?" she suggested, sounding flustered. "And perform our introduction?"

Aimee felt Konrad's shoulder stiffen beneath her. Her face turned as red as an apple as she prepared herself for the inevitable and humiliating descent from his shoulder. She just hoped her legs would be able to hold her up.

"We have some business to see to back at our tent," her husband replied shortly. "I am afraid the introductions must wait until supper." With that, he turned around and started back up the bank toward their tent.

Aimee gasped, inhaling her necklace, which she hadn't realized was still in her mouth. She spat the pearls out. "What are you doing?" she choked out in a furious undertone, venturing one glance back at the couple watching them with open mouths. "You can't just—"

"Actually, I can," he responded. "And I just did." He ducked into the entrance and then turned, releasing some strings so the material swung shut. Then he carried her to the bed and lowered her down onto the mattress, so they were face-to-face. "Not another word," he warned, and rolled her over onto her stomach.

Aimee felt her gown lifted up over her legs and settled at her waist, followed by her shift. He made short work of the strings tying her fine linen under-clouts and dispensed with them altogether. "In case you're confused, I'm not about to spank you," he rumbled.

"Then what are—?"

"Not good at following orders, are you?" His tone was strangely relaxed now. Aimee turned her head to look at him, but at that moment, his big, warm hands settled over her bare buttocks and started to rub her so firmly, he startled a surprised exclamation out of her.

"Too hard?" he asked.

"N-no…ow!"

334

"There?" His hand paused a moment before concentrating on the spot that had caused her to cry out, circling the pads of his fingertips against the sore area. "This is where it hurts the most?"

"Yes," Aimee admitted, tears starting to her eyes, but his carefully rotating fingers felt good. Her breath came raggedly as he continued his ministrations, switching to his strong thumbs and then back to the palms of his hands. He took his sweet time about it, and it felt so nice Aimee was tempted to admit she had brought her lotion with her should he wish to use it. By the time he had finished, Aimee was lying there like a limp rag, her face pressed into the blanket. It was the first time she'd felt comfortable all day.

"I will do it again before bed," he promised.

"I cannot believe I have to ride all that way home again," Aimee groaned. "Riding is torture."

He gave a short laugh and drew her shift and then her skirts down, resting his hand on her rump over her clothes. "My poor, spoiled little wife. I suppose you will require a carriage to convey you north to Bartree," he said thoughtfully. "When it's finally habitable, that is."

Aimee felt the warmth from his hand through her clothes and strangely did not even feel embarrassed. "Did your sister ride all that way?" Aimee croaked. Oh, gods, she could not even imagine a weeklong continuous ride. Did not want to imagine it!

"She and Freda were raised in the country. Both were taught to ride in their infancy."

Aimee pulled a face. Yet another thing she would have to improve on. She filed it away next to music and embroidery.

335

She had so many shortcomings as a baroness that it was becoming alarming. "I expect Princess Una is a good horsewoman," she heard herself say, and to her shame, she sounded a little sulky about it.

"She attended a good many battles," he answered, swatting her backside and rising from the mattress. "If she had not been able to ride well, her life would have been in grave peril. Well, more in peril," he added wryly.

Aimee turned her head to watch as he peered out of the tent. "Who are you looking for?"

"Jakeman."

A horrible thought occurred to Aimee. "He—he would not have looked in just now when you were—" She broke off, her face flooding with color.

Konrad shook his head. "He will not come in if the entrance is unfurled."

She rolled onto her side. "Is that some sort of signal between the two of you?" she asked with sudden suspicion.

He glanced back over his shoulder at her. "What are you implying?" His tone was sarcastic. "That I drag lots of women back to my pavilion?"

Aimee plucked at the blanket, not quite meeting his eyes. "No, of course not," she huffed, though that *had* been what she was thinking. Was she turning into a jealous harpy now? On top of all her other shortcomings. She groaned, rolling onto her back and covering her face with her hands.

He turned from the tent entrance and regarded her. "What now?"

"You made me look like such a fool in front of the princess!"

He snorted. "Pretty sure you should not refer to her as such anymore."

Aimee lowered her hands. "What is her new title again?"

"Lady de Bussell." He scowled.

Aimee regarded him a moment, her heart in her mouth. "You do not care for her husband?" she asked, striving to keep her tone light. Gods, she hoped it was that and not anything else.

"He's wholly beneath her notice," he growled. "Or should be."

Aimee remembered de Bussell's laughing countenance and undeniable good looks and held her tongue. To her eye, the princess had looked well matched. "She doesn't look a thing like they depict her," she complained. "She isn't at all masculine, and her hair is quite different."

Konrad shrugged. "She used to wear a wig" was all he would say on that score. "Here's Jakeman now," he said.

Aimee sat up, tidying herself, for she was sure her hair must have come loose in the exertions of the past hour. Jakeman carried in a basin of steaming water with cloths over his arm. "There's a table and two chairs outside the tent, my lord," he said. "I will fetch them in—" But whatever he was going to say he left unsaid as his master went out to fetch them himself.

Jakeman hovered while Konrad found the most even ground for the table's four legs, then set the basin on top of it.

"You wash first," her husband said as Jakeman retreated, and Aimee made haste to make the necessary reparations to her disordered appearance. She washed, redressed her hair, and changed into a gown of royal blue which she thought showed off her brooch and its new sapphires to perfection. When she added her pearls and two little copper portcullis badges to

337

secure them at either side of her neckline, she gave a nod of satisfaction. A short, gauzy veil with a gold embroidered border was the final touch, and she pinned this to her coiled braids with pins topped with blue glass.

It was only when Lady Howard exclaimed over her appearance as they were welcomed into the manor house that it occurred to Aimee she might be rather overdressed.

"Baroness," the older lady commented, her hawklike gaze raking over her. "You put us all to shame with your finery!"

Aimee glanced about with sudden misgiving and realized the only other ladies at the table were dressed a good deal more plainly. She gulped and sent a vaguely accusatory gaze up at her husband. He might have told her!

"Oh, to be a cosseted bride again!" Lady Howard continued as she led Aimee to a prominent seat at the table. "You must sit here to my left, Lady Kentigern, and then Lady de Bussell and Lady de Crecy can take their seats further down from us."

Aimee looked up sharply at the mention of Lady de Crecy. Had Sir Jeffree brought his wife here too? It seemed strange how he was dragging her about the tournaments considering his open contempt for her. Sure enough, the lady stepped forward, emerging from the shadows in a dress just as shabby as the one she had worn at the last event. It was not brown this time, but a faded green which suited her just as ill.

"Is everyone acquainted?" Lady Howard asked, her gaze sweeping over the company that had been shepherded toward the dais. In addition to the guests, Lady Howard's two sons joined them at the top table. They were unaccompanied by ladies, so Aimee assumed they were unwed. As their mother received no immediate answer, she went ahead and introduced Aimee first to Sir Jeffree, who looked as mutinous and arrogant

338

as ever. He gave her a rather hard look at their introduction as though committing her face to memory before he gave his short bow.

Aimee, whose confidence had dipped considerably, thought he must have been glaring at her over-ostentatious appearance. Perhaps the pearls *and* the brooch combined together were too much? Lady de Crecy acknowledged the introduction with a curtsey but otherwise avoided Aimee's eye. To her discomfort, Aimee found herself wondering if that lady was recalling the business of the tourney crown and felt herself turn rather pink.

Sabina de Crecy's features were regular enough, but she was clearly no outstanding beauty. Aimee thought she would look better with her hair worn in a more becoming style rather than scraped back under the stiffened torque that she wore to secure her opaque veil flat to her brow. She wore no ornamentation and seemed to give little if any thought to her appearance. Certainly, she made no effort to match her handsome husband in his doublet of orange and black.

The princess, or Lady de Bussell as she should think of her, bestowed a warm smile on Aimee and greeted her as though their previous meeting had not been a source of embarrassment for them both. Aimee returned her welcome as best she could with a horrible suspicion that the princess must be heartily pitying her. Either that or judging her as gauche for the fact she was strewn about with jewels when she, through whose veins royal blood flowed, wore no necklace or brooches at all.

Una de Bussell wore only a simple bronze circlet at her brow which kept her white veil in place, and this was studded with garnets. A single diamond ring adorned one finger, and Aimee felt even more ridiculous in her excessive finery by way of contrast.

Sir Armand's eyes danced when their introduction was given, and Aimee found herself echoing his smile in spite of herself. He seemed eminently likeable, and as they took their seats, Aimee decided with a sinking heart that the only possible reason her husband could have to dislike him must be jealousy.

"Baroness Kentigern," Lady Howard began, leaning forward from her position at the head of the table. "You must tell us about this extravagant love token," she said, gesturing toward Aimee's brooch. "For surely it was a betrothal gift." She cast an arch look in Konrad's direction, but as he was looking elsewhere, he missed it. "You must prize it highly."

Aimee cleared her throat. "It was a betrothal token, yes, but for my husband's grandmother," she explained. "It is an heirloom and was gifted to me by Mistress Freda Bartree on the occasion of my marriage."

"But how generous," Lady Howard commented, gesturing for the goblets to be filled with wine. Servants hurried forward to comply, and Aimee glanced at her husband, but Konrad seemed to have abandoned her to her fate, for he was absorbed in gazing about at the knights present, possibly trying to gauge his competition from those gathered within.

There were several burly-looking fellows eating at the long tables that ranged throughout the hall. Aimee noticed that a good deal of them were gazing toward the high table with great interest. She guessed that Konrad, Sir Jeffree, and Sir Armand must be the persons to beat.

"Forgive me," Una de Bussell said, leaning forward to address her with a faint pucker between her brows. "I did not think Lord Kentigern's sister went by that name."

Aimee waited a moment to see if her husband would answer, but he made no attempt. "No, indeed," Aimee explained. "Freda

340

is my husband's first cousin. My sister-in-law's name is Magnatrude."

"Ah," Lady de Bussell replied, her frown clearing. "That was it, and how is Mistress Magnatrude? Did she journey south for your wedding?"

"She did," Aimee replied, making a concerted effort to be lively and engaging. All she really felt like doing was withdrawing into herself to lick her wounds. She almost envied Sabina de Crecy's severe wimple which swathed her head so thoroughly that only her face showed. Her neck, chin, forehead, and even the sides of her face were concealed from her fellow diners altogether. It might be unbecoming, but at least it provided protection against attack!

No, that was not fair, Aimee conceded as the meal continued. Una de Bussell and Lady Howard were doing their utmost to keep conversation flowing at the table despite the general awkwardness. Konrad was taciturn, Sir Jeffree aloof, and Lady de Crecy stubbornly mute. As for the sons of the house, Chaucey and Darby Howard seemed tongue-tied in their exalted company and addressed themselves to their trenchers more than their guests.

Aimee found that, despite her greatest efforts, she could only bring herself to join in fits and starts, and she wasn't sure she contributed much. Her growing awareness of being overdressed made her feel awkward and out of place. She fidgeted in her seat, wondering if the rest of the hall was whispering behind their hands about Lord Kentigern's lowborn bride.

Sir Armand gamely assisted his wife and their hostess, but conversation frequently fell flat, and to Aimee at least, it felt painfully obvious how mismatched the company was. She found herself heartily envying the less-favored guests, though

341

once upon a time she, too, would have gazed with envy at the dais. How times had changed!

By the time the final course was brought to table, Aimee had fretted herself into the beginnings of a headache.

"My dear Lady Kentigern," Lady Howard said, lowering her goblet. "I meant to say earlier that there is a spare bedchamber for you in the house if you should prefer it to sleeping out of doors. I know Lady de Bussell positively revels in the experience." She pulled a face, and the de Bussells both laughed. Aimee noticed the way Sir Armand reached for his wife's hand. "But not all of us relish such things," Lady Howard continued smoothly.

Aimee thought their hostess inclined her head slightly toward Sabina de Crecy as she spoke, and she wondered if that lady had accepted a room in the manor. "That is very generous of you, Lady Howard," she replied, hesitating, and shot a look at her husband. He paused in his conversation with Chaucey Howard to throw a glance her way.

"As I said earlier," he remarked coolly. "If you would prefer it, I am agreeable."

Aimee swallowed hard and turned back to her hostess. "In that case, Lady Howard, I would be very glad to accept your kind offer."

"Of course," Lady Howard cried, clapping her hands for silence in the hall. "But as a forfeit, my dear Lady Kentigern, and as the highest ranking of our lady guests, I must demand a song from you as payment of your board."

So sunk in misery was Aimee by this point that this did not even register as the source of terror to her that it would usually.

She smiled rather wanly and rose to her feet before the enormity of the request could catch up with her.

Aimee thought her husband made a movement as though to speak, but the noise of her dragging back her chair drowned out whatever he had started to say, and she followed Lady Howard to the front of the dais as a hush fell over the hall and all faces turned her way.

A short man with very red hair stepped forward offering Aimee his lute, but she waved this away. She had no intention of trying to pluck any tune with her own untutored fingers. "Do you know 'The Tree, the Moon, and the Lover's Promise'?" she asked him abruptly.

According to the Wycliffes, it was unsuited for decent company, but Aimee no longer cared. She knew the song suited her voice, and she could sing it in her sleep. She could sing it now, even though her head felt heavy and clouded and her heart ached as though it bore a fresh wound.

The little man scratched his head. "I think 'tis a tune we call 'The False Lover' in these parts, milady," he ventured. "At least the refrain to that one mentions a tree, the moon, and a broken promise." He strummed a few chords to illustrate, and Aimee nodded.

"That is the very one," she said. "I think my version may differ, but doubtless the tune is the same."

"Aye, milady," he said and started to play the lilting, haunting melody. Aimee lifted her head, drew in her breath, and let the song flow through and out of her. She sang the tale of sweetness, longing, and love as though the tale was in truth her own.

Her words rang out with the piercing conviction of one who had once believed in a love so strong that it swept away all other considerations, only to have her hopes and dreams dashed by a seemingly broken promise. Never before had Aimee's voice swelled with such haunting sweetness, even with her sister at her side, marrying her voice to hers.

Indeed, Aimee could almost believe that she could hear Ursula singing beside her now. Nay, not Ursula, she realized, but instead three Aimees singing side by side, as the words were echoed and bounced off the high vaulted ceiling, reverberating back to sound almost as though they were being chanted in a round. At the end of each verse, her own words were repeated back to her in a mournful echo before dying away so she could start the next.

Aimee had always enjoyed the bittersweet tale, but previously, when she had sung the words, she had not known what heartbreak truly felt like. She had sung the words as a maiden happy and secure with her lot. Now her voice throbbed with the emotion of a woman who knew both sorrow and disappointment.

When she sang of the tree bursting into blossom and the fullness of the moon and the babe she carried beneath her heart for her true love's sake, a single tear spilled down her cheek. It was only when she reached the final verse that her voice lacked conviction. Usually at this point, Aimee lifted her voice joyfully to tell of the lover's triumphant arrival to claim his bride.

This time, she sang it softly and sadly, her words taking on a dreamlike quality as though the happy ending was mere wish fulfilment on behalf of a broken woman who had lost everything including her grip on reality. She sang of the lover's return as though he were a ghost or a wraith who had come back too late to keep his word.

By the time her last word died away, a deathly hush had fallen over the hall. Aimee let her head drop and stared down at the scented rushes strewn underfoot. Someone sniffed. The musician turned toward her and bowed low. The applause started as one sole pair of hands and then raised to a thunderous clamor.

"My dear!" Lady Howard said, appearing at her side and clasping her hand. "I had no idea!" She pressed Aimee's fingers, and to her surprise, Aimee saw her hostess's face was wet with tears. "Sublime!"

The musician cleared his throat. "If you permit it, milady," he said humbly, "I would be honored to commit those words to parchment. I have ne'er heard that version before. It is far superior to the one I know."

Aimee cleared her throat. "Of course," she said huskily. "Though if I could confer with you on the morrow…for now I am a little tired." The pressure behind her eyes had not actually bloomed into pain but remained a lingering heaviness, weighing her thoughts and reactions down as though a heavy blanket had been dropped over her head.

"Of course," Lady Howard was quick to agree. "I will show you to your room myself—"

Here she was interrupted by the appearance of Lord Kentigern. "I've changed my mind," he said abruptly. "My wife is coming back to the tent with me."

Aimee nodded; in truth, she felt too exhausted to do anything else. She stumbled as she moved to his side, and once again, Aimee found herself swung up into his arms. As he carried her past the table, she heard Una de Bussell declining to perform next for the company.

345

"In truth, I do not think you will find anyone willing to follow that," she said apologetically to Lady Howard. "Lady Kentigern's turn is not one easily followed."

24

Konrad bore Aimee back to the tent in silence. Her head rested against his shoulder, and for once, she did not seem to have anything to say. Likely that performance had taken it out of her, he thought, glancing down at her dark head. *That performance...*

By rights, it should not have worked. Aimee Bartree was a spoiled little heiress decked out in jewels, the like of which most people in that hall would never possess. The precious pearls had glowed against her lustrous skin, the sapphires at her bodice had flashed in the candlelight, and *still* she had held every single last soul present in the palm of her hand.

There had been barely a dry eye in the house. Every woman there, from deposed princess to cynical widow to serving wench, had wept to hear Aimee's voice uplifted in that damned song. Part of it had been her untutored delivery, he supposed. Her unrestrained manner of singing it.

She sang her song with the simple straightforwardness of a country girl who had been seduced by words of love and had no defense against them. There had been no hint of performing to a crowd, no artifice to the way she had lifted her pretty face to the rafters and sung as though no one else were present, her tale of shining love that had turned to woe and misery and then swung back around again to snatch victory from the jaws of defeat.

That had been the only point at which she had not been convincing, he thought bitterly. The happy ending had convinced no one. The lover never had returned for her or her pretty babe. Everyone knew he had not kept his vows. In fact, he was pretty sure the name of the song reflected that fact.

Her voice had touched every man present, but he had felt pierced to his very bosom. He had heard her sing before, but she had not sounded like that. He had made her no false promises, he certainly had not seduced her with words of love, but all the same. It was *his* damned fault she sang like her heart was broken. Why did he keep fucking everything up with her?

As soon as he reached the tent, he set her down and started loosening the laces from her gown. Aimee stood as meek and still as a statue as he undressed her. She made no attempt to help, so he drew out her hairpins and set them on the table along with her veil and jewelry. Once she was down to her shift, he led her to the makeshift bed and set her under the covers. She had not moved an inch when he climbed in to join her and made no objection when he wrapped his arms about her and held her close.

He did not wake the next morning until he heard a footfall and an exclamation. Blinking, he found Jakeman gazing across the tent at him with a look of almost comical dismay on his face.

"Y-your pardon, my lord," he stammered, setting down the hot water he was carrying. "I did not realize you…" Words seemed to fail him. "Had—er—company," he ended lamely.

Konrad glanced down at Aimee, still fast asleep and tucked into his side. He did not think he had spent the whole night through in a woman's company in his life. Strange to say, his sleep had been entirely unbroken. "She's my wife," he pointed out acerbically, in case his manservant had somehow not recognized just who it was slumbering at his side.

Jakeman's Adam's apple bobbed up and down. "Yes, my lord," he agreed and averted his eyes. "Will your lordship require me to fetch bread to break your fast, or will you be going along to the Great Hall?"

Konrad considered the matter. In truth, he should have foreseen that both he and Aimee would require Jakeman's services, for he had never taken a squire. "Fetch me something, then you can accompany your mistress to the Great Hall to break her fast."

Jakeman nodded and beat a hasty retreat. Konrad carefully slid out of the bed and made his way to the wash basin clad only in his braies. He had washed and was drying himself off before he heard Aimee stir in the bed. She rolled onto her back and groaned.

"Still sore?" he asked, lowering his cloth and feeling his own body perk up with interest.

She sat up, looking adorably sleepy and confused. "Ouch!" she winced, answering his question.

"Roll onto your front," he instructed throatily, coming back to the bed and drawing down the covers.

"Konrad," she murmured in mild reproach, though he noticed she rolled onto her stomach obligingly enough.

He reached under her shift, his hands settling over her pleasingly plump behind. This time he knew exactly where her sore spots were and sought them out unerringly. Aimee whimpered and moaned in a very stimulating manner until he had finished his ministrations. Then she sighed, sounding so sated and relaxed while he felt anything but.

Swallowing deeply, he covered her back up with the blankets when his every impulse screamed at him to do the opposite. Considerate, that was what he was aiming for. A considerate husband did not make his wife cry herself to sleep at night. Nor did he lift her shift and swive her first thing in the morning in the middle of a field.

Half an hour later, he was striding over to the next field marked out for the competitors when he heard his name called. Swinging around, he saw Sir Douglas Farleigh and his two friends hurrying toward him.

"Kentigern!" Farleigh hailed him, clapping his shoulder. "We saw you at the feast last night."

"Don't think you saw us though," Leo Symes chimed in with a grin. "We were at the back of the hall."

"No," Konrad admitted. In truth, he had forgotten to look for them. "I was a bit preoccupied."

"Aye, well, small wonder as you've your wife with you," Lowell pointed out.

"Lady Kentigern enjoying it so far?" Farleigh asked as they fell in step beside him.

Konrad glanced at him suspiciously, but Farleigh's expression was guileless and open. Once again, he realized Farleigh was not the most observant when it came to women.

"Quite the songbird, isn't she?" Symes added wistfully.

Konrad cleared his throat. "Aye," he rumbled, hoping that answer would suffice for both questions.

"That hothead de Crecy didn't give you any grief, did he?" Lowell asked. "Only it doesn't take much to rile him up recently. Apparently, he blacked some fellow's eye yesterday for helping his wife down some steps."

"Did he now?" Konrad grunted with surprise. He would not have thought personally that de Crecy's wife had it in her to inspire jealousy.

350

"Helping his own wife or de Crecy's wife?" Farleigh asked critically.

"De Crecy's, of course," Lowell answered with exasperation. He rolled his eyes at Konrad, who found himself giving a reluctant snort of laughter. "Or the story hardly makes sense, does it, you dolt?"

Farleigh grinned good-naturedly and punched his friend in the shoulder. "How should I know! De Crecy's a damned odd fellow. He's been an icicle the entire two years I've known him, till this season."

"He didn't look much like an icicle when he was punching Stanyon in the face yesterday," Symes added. "Looked like the vein in his neck was about to explode."

They all lapsed into silent contemplation of de Crecy's unfathomable transformation of late.

"You don't suppose it's got anything to do with that his wife of his, do you?" Lowell speculated hesitantly.

"Shouldn't think so." Symes frowned. "I feel sorry for the poor wench."

"She's not much to look at," Farleigh agreed. "And that's stating a fact."

"Probably seething he was forced to wed such a plain specimen of womanhood," Lowell murmured. "She does not look as though she would have brought much money to the table neither."

The other two clicked their tongues and nodded dolefully at de Crecy's misfortune. Privately, Konrad agreed, but felt he ought to put in a word for the maligned damsel. "Well," he started, clearing his throat. "She obviously inspires some feeling in him, or he wouldn't keep getting into brawls over her. That's the reason he wants to crush my neck too," he added. When the others looked at him in surprise, he reminded them. "I gave her the tourney crown at the Summer Tournament."

"Oh, aye," Farleigh said, as though only just remembering. "So you did."

"That might have been a mistake," Symes said with an annoying air of wisdom.

"Think so, do you?" Konrad responded testily. "Well, at least she's not my sister!"

A stunned silence met his words before Farleigh and Lowell burst into loud guffaws of laughter. Poor Symes turned a dull shade of red, and Konrad felt a twinge of something he wasn't sure was not his conscience. Gods, what was going on with him lately? He was nearly as bad as de Crecy! He cleared his throat. "What events are the three of you signed up for?"

Farleigh immediately launched into a recital of events.

"Speaking of which," Lowell said, turning about. "We had better go and see if they've determined the teams for the melee. See what side we're all on." He pointed to a large white tent nearby. "That's the one where they're drawing the names."

The four of them proceeded in that direction, and Kentigern took his place in the tent beside them. Once inside, they appeared to assume he would remain in their company, so it seemed the easiest thing to go along with them. In truth, he felt less conspicuous surrounded by their boisterous company than he did standing solitary and apart from the crowd. Lowell snagged a passing servant's tray and pressed an ale cup into his hand as Symes leaned across, lowering his voice. "Don't look now, Kentigern, but de Crecy's glaring daggers at you!"

Disregarding his warning, Konrad turned his head to view the company, but when he scanned the knights assembled, all he saw was a sea of faces turned in his direction, expressions of mingled apprehension and curiosity.

"Do not pay them any heed," Farleigh recommended. "You are the biggest draw here, my lord. That's the only reason they stare."

"I know," he responded. "I am not offended." He lifted a hand to absently touch the scarring to the side of his face. With surprise, he realized he had not actually thought of it once all morning.

Beres Caple was old-fashioned in that the melee was fought on foot with no mounted charges. The entire company of knights had been divided into four, and over the day, three mock battles would be waged before one team emerged the overall victor.

Sir Chaucey Howard stood at the front and picked names, allotting them by turn to either the blue, orange, red, or green team. Konrad and Symes were assigned to the same orange team, Lowell to the blue, and Farleigh to the green.

Symes was jubilant about the fact he and Konrad were on the same team, crowing over it and rubbing it in his friends' faces. Konrad guessed he must have forgiven him that remark he made earlier about his sister. He found he was strangely relieved about that, though he was not sure why.

Jakeman found him shortly after and helped him don his armor. The others soon returned with their own gear, and preparations for battle took up the next half hour.

Farleigh scowled as he helped tie Konrad's orange armband to his upper arm. "Trust you to fall on your feet, Leo," he sniped at his friend. "By rights, Kentigern should be on my team, he was my friend before he was yours."

Symes chortled, not troubling to dispute this. Konrad was a little startled, for he had not precisely realized his standing among them. Apparently, they were friends of his. *Friends.*

"I don't know what you're carping about, Douglas," Lowell complained. "You have Sir Jeffree on your team. All I have on team blue are a lot of bumpkins who have scarce held a sword above twice in their lives!"

"Oh, I don't know, is not de Bussell on your team?" Farleigh asked. "On a good day, he's pretty formidable."

Lowell snorted. "Didn't he lose to *you* last month, one-on-one?" he pointed out scathingly.

"That was in May," Farleigh corrected him. "And since then, he's lifted the victor's cup at Areley Kings."

"Aye, well, I believe I'll hold off on praising Sir Armand till I see what kind of day he's having," his friend retorted with a curl of his lip. "On a bad day, any fool can beat him."

Konrad roused himself at this. "We all have bad days," he rumbled. When three pairs of eyes swung toward him, he cleared his throat. "Renlow beat me at the joust last year at Kellingford."

"Did he, by gods?" Symes demanded with a low whistle.

"I had heard that tale," Lowell admitted cautiously. "But some days we walk perforce under an unlucky star."

"He beat me that day fair and square," Konrad said frankly. "He was the better man on the field." When Farleigh opened his mouth as if to argue, he cut him off. "There is no dishonor in losing when that is the case, and I felt no shame in my loss."

Funnily enough, as he spoke the words aloud, he realized he was speaking nothing but the truth. Of course, knowing as he did now that Aimee had been sat in the audience that day ensured he felt little sting in his defeat. For it had been that very moment… He felt his chest swell before the depressing memory she no longer loved him slammed into his thoughts, cutting off all pleasure in the recollection.

"Where is Renlow anyway?" Lowell broke in with a frown. "I don't believe I saw him all day yesterday."

"Not here," Symes replied. "Broke his arm competing in the Summer Tournament."

"Broke it, did he?" Farleigh asked with interest. "Poor devil. He will be sorry to miss a tournament."

Konrad let their chatter wash over him as he tucked his helmet under his arm, and they made their way toward the field designated for the skirmishes. He had instructed Jakeman to escort Aimee to the Howard family to watch proceedings, and he looked for her now in the crowd. There was no mingling of blue and yellow in anyone's garb that he could see, but in truth, he had scarcely expected her to wear his crest today.

He glanced down at his own shield and surcoat that blazed with its yellow portcullis on the azure field. He was starting to suspect Aimee would resist wearing her matching heraldic gown even to the jousting on the morrow. The prospect dragged down his sprits. Once, she had worn his colors with pride before he had ruined it. He cursed under his breath as he looked about for the Howard party.

He soon spotted Chaucey, who was capering about in long scalloped sleeves and sending servants scurrying in all directions. Lady Howard was stood beside him looking harried with her hands clapped to her temples. She seemed agitated for some reason, Konrad thought, and supposed it must be the strain of hosting a tournament getting to her. Of Sir Darby Howard, there was no sign that he could see.

Konrad's eye passed over the family to see Aimee sandwiched between two women. One was a short, fair woman, wholly unknown to him, who seemed to be juggling two small children on her knees. The other was a tall, well-built female he barely recognized these days. The former northern princess was indeed changed.

He relaxed slightly on locating his wife, though it seemed to him the three women were too busy conversing among themselves instead of looking for their husbands as you might think duty would dictate. Even as he watched, one chubby infant was passed into Aimee's welcoming arms, making his chest feel strangely tight. She bounced it in her lap and turned towards its mother. He did not think she had even noticed he stood in the arena below.

Farleigh interrupted his thoughts, clapping both him and Symes on the shoulder. "Good luck, Kentigern," he said before turning to Symes and pointing a finger. "Watch your back, you bastard," he warned direly, making them all laugh as he headed off to join the opposing team.

"I had better go and see if I can find a decent spot in the stands," Lowell said, giving them a nod and wandering off in that general direction. He held up his hand. "Fight well and do me proud!"

Symes turned to him. "Isn't that your man over there?" he asked, pointing.

Konrad turned to see Jakeman waving from the sidelines, letting him know he was ready to count his hostages. "It is." He gave him a nod, letting him know he had seen him.

"Well, best we take up our positions," Sir Leo said cheerfully.

The first of the melee battles was something of a slog. Konrad believed for his part that he might as well have worn a target painted on his breastplate rather than his coat of arms. He had anticipated as much, but it did not make the constant deluge of opponents flinging themselves on him any easier to navigate.

These young, unseasoned knights were keen to prove themselves, but sadly not through strategy or playing the long game. They hoped for an opportunistic win, to catch him off guard or vastly outnumbered. A win against a knight of his renown would be a fine feather in their cap. They flung themselves at him with battle cries and fought with a desperation that showed they had given scant thought to pacing themselves for the end of the bout let alone the next round.

They thirsted for glory, even a brief taste of it would do. As he sent another one sprawling in the dirt with a well-aimed kick from his iron sabaton, he hoped that maybe a loss to the mighty Lord Kentigern would give them something to tell their wives and mothers at least, if nothing else. Grabbing his victim by the leg, he dragged him toward the edge of the field where Jakeman stood watch. He added him to the sizeable pile of "hostages," some of whom were now coming around and rubbing their groggy heads. Jakeman strode over and gave Konrad a nod, letting him know he had made a note of the latest coat of arms.

Many of these knights would never end up venturing to any of the bigger tournaments, so this would likely be the only test of their mettle they would ever get. So long as peace held over Karadok, he added, muttering a supplication that it would be so. Pausing to blink the sweat from his eyes before he rejoined the fray, Konrad noticed another knight who looked almost as beleaguered as himself.

Sir Jeffree de Crecy had no sooner dispatched three challengers than another four surrounded him in their place. Konrad surprised himself by the pang of fellow feeling that struck him as Sir Jeffree disappeared momentarily under a tide of his united foes. Part of it was de Crecy's own fault, of course, Konrad reflected, for none of these upstarts would face repercussions for their temerity in challenging him. De Crecy thought taking hostages beneath his dignity.

Konrad was pleased to see his young friend Sir Leo Symes was not among those vying for fame by taking down Sir Jeffree. Instead, Symes had cut his own way through their opponents and was engaged now in fighting off two knights wearing matching scarlet surcoats over their chain mail. Konrad headed in that direction, scattering all who stood in his way.

He found himself strangely tempted to glance up at the stands and check to see if his wife was watching him now or still occupied with other people's offspring. Mayhap it was about time he saw to giving her some of her own to worry her pretty head about.

For some reason, instead of picturing the required Bartree heir, a male vaguely in his image but without his scars, he imagined instead a little daughter who might reach for him and call him Father. His step faltered a moment. Such a short time ago he had thought Roland Vawdrey mad for simpering over a female child. Now Konrad realized he envied him.

He got his sword up just in time to fend off an attack from his left flank. Konrad found himself vaguely insulted, for his opponent clearly did not even know which was his blind side and which his seeing. He was followed in quick succession by two more overeager types who Konrad dispatched with the flat of his sword, bowling them over with his driving strength. Their armor was so ill fitting and dated, he thought it likely their

358

father's or even grandfather's. For this reason, he did not bother dragging these to the sidelines but left them to stagger to their feet and slink away.

The battle waged on for another hour or so, and it was no surprise that de Crecy was the last man standing on the green side. Farleigh lasted pretty well but went down in the last quarter of an hour. Konrad did not join the others who piled on de Crecy, though Symes ran over to get a view of him being forced to yield.

Horns sounded and the Howard banner was carried into the center of the ring. A flushed Sir Chaucey proclaimed the orange team victorious. Konrad reached up to pull off his helmet and made his way over to Jakeman, who was releasing Konrad's captors now they had pledged their word to pay. A few of them gave Konrad cautious nods which he returned.

"Help me take this off," he grunted, and his manservant sprang to unfasten his armor.

"Shall I leave on the chain mail, my lord?" Jakeman asked, stacking the smaller pieces atop the breastplate.

Konrad considered this. The next battle would last little under three hours by his estimation. "No, take it off. I'll go about in my gambeson between times."

"Aye, my lord." He passed a cloth to Konrad, who mopped his brow, glancing back toward the benches.

"I can tell you whereabouts my lady sits in, if that would be useful?" Jakeman murmured. Konrad waved the offer away.

"I already know," he said shortly. "Here." Jakeman took the proffered cloth, and Konrad narrowed his eyes. For a moment, he had definitely seen a glimmer of a smile. "Something to say?" Just as quickly it was gone.

"Nay, my lord." Jakeman's face bore only an expression of obliging helpfulness.

Konrad grunted suspiciously but left it at that, moving off toward where the Howard family were congregated.

Aimee looked up as he approached and came eagerly to her feet. "Well played, my lord," she said loudly, for all the world as though he had just completed a game of hammer throw. "I daresay you are far too tired now to take me for a turn about the field?"

Noting her anxious tone and the faint look of desperation in her eye, Konrad cast a quick glance about the company. Lady Howard was looking rather flinty-faced as she spoke to the comely mother of two, with the babes in a state of undress playing at their feet. The princess seemed to have disappeared, and Sir Chaucey was having a heated discussion with his steward about timings for the afternoon events.

"I could probably manage the exertion," he replied and offered his arm. She seized it at once and bestowed a relieved smile on him.

"You are sure you are not too tired?" she asked quietly as he nodded to the Howards and bore her away.

"I'd likely get stiff and sore if I sat about too long now," he admitted truthfully.

Her shoulders relaxed. "Oh, that makes me feel better about not letting you rest."

"You did not find your company congenial?" he asked with a frown.

"Oh, it was! The princess—I mean, Lady Una de Bussell is vastly pleasant company. So very down-to-earth and agreeable.

I quite see why—that is—I do not see how anyone could fail to be charmed by her." Her tone was strangely wistful.

Konrad hesitated before he spoke. He did not think *charming* was a word that had been used for any Blechmarsh in living memory.

"You do not agree?" she asked, giving him a sidelong look.

He shrugged his shoulders. "I never really gave much thought to her personality," he answered without thinking. "She was more a figurehead for the northern cause than a person," he admitted gruffly.

Aimee's brow cleared. "So then, you do not—? That is…" She corrected herself carefully. "Your admiration of her was not of a personal nature?"

Steering her around an arguing couple, he shook his head. "No," he said bluntly.

"Oh." Feeling her gaze on his face, he turned to look at her, but she looked quickly away.

"Are you going to tell me why you were so keen to part company with the Howards?" he asked pointedly, hoping this subject was an easier one.

"Oh that," she said, flashing him an apologetic smile. "Well, Sir Darby has thrown a cat among the pigeons this morning, and I am afraid that Lady Howard holds me at least partly responsible."

Konrad's steps halted abruptly. "She holds you responsible?" he echoed.

Aimee, still hanging off his arm, pulled up short. "Indirectly, yes."

"How?" he demanded, a heavy frown at his brow.

"I will tell you, if you will only stir your step." She tugged on his arm until he commenced walking again, albeit with some reluctance. He had half a mind to turn back and ask their hostess what the hells she was playing at!

"It seems my song at the banquet last night inspired Sir Darby to ride into Aldenbrook this morning at the crack of dawn and find a priest to bind him to the mother of his two children."

Konrad halted again. "Darby has children?"

Aimee nodded her head. "Apparently, the family knew all about it, but as she was the daughter of a mere farmer, they did not expect him to marry her."

"I see," he said, moving forward again. "Though I fail to see how you can be blamed for Darby's actions."

"I know!" Aimee agreed. "Especially as Darby is not even her eldest son, so what does it matter where he chooses to wed? Apparently, he has his own income from a property an unwed uncle left him, so he has promised Aileen he will set her and the children up there."

Konrad grunted. "It seems Aileen has fallen on her feet."

Aimee sent him a reproachful look. "She has had a hard time of it these past three years by all accounts. Her father was happy to accept Darby's money to keep her and the babes under his roof, but you may be sure he did not fail to call her some nasty names whenever she incurred his displeasure!"

Konrad grunted. "I expect he did."

"His own daughter!" Aimee said indignantly. "*And* he expected her to keep house for him as well as look after the children!"

362

Konrad eyed her curiously. "It sounds as though you have had the whole story from that lady."

Aimee nodded. "She told me and Una all about it. Lady de Bussell kindly said I could call her Una," she added a little self-consciously. "Aileen said you could have knocked her down with a feather when Darby banged on her door this morning and would not be dissuaded from marrying her. She even cried a little when she told the tale." Aimee lapsed into momentary silence. "I confess, it did make me think of Golda."

"Golda?" Konrad frowned. "Your servant Golda?"

"Yes," Aimee said sadly. "For it turns out that Unwin is her own son, who I never even knew existed. She was never married to his father, you see. When she came to work for us, she paid another woman to raise him with her brood, but he was not happy there. Golda took the opportunity of our setting up house to bring him close again. She told me Unwin was a stableboy at my father's house, but that was not true, and I should have realized that had I not been so distracted."

Konrad recalled Jakeman saying the boy was afraid of horses. "You think he will be suited to working as a pageboy to my sister?" he asked skeptically.

"Golda seems to think so. She came to speak with me before we set forth yesterday and told me the truth of it all. She seemed ecstatic at how things were working out. Indeed," Aimee confessed in a rush, "your sister has succeeded where I failed miserably. I could not get one word out of Unwin, but since she promised to make him her page, he happily announces her entrance into every chamber."

Konrad winced. "I hope we do not have to put up with that practice overlong."

363

Aimee laughed. "Anyway, it would be nice to think that things have worked out for the best for Golda and Unwin." She lifted her chin. "I am happy for Aileen too. She had me teach her that song this morning so she can sing it to her own children."

"You will have to sing the last verse like you mean it next time," he heard himself say sourly.

"What do you mean?" Aimee's tone was startled.

"You were not convincing when you sang of the happy ending."

"Oh." She sounded uncertain. "Well, Aileen has her own example to add conviction to her words," she said defensively.

He had just opened his mouth with a rejoinder when they were hailed enthusiastically by Symes and Lowell and glumly by Farleigh.

"Aimee," Konrad said, turning to her. "This is Sir Leonard Symes, Sir Fulke Lowell, and Sir Douglas Farleigh." He coughed and added, "Friends of mine," feeling rusty and out of practice with the phrase. "This is my wife, Lady Aimee Bartree, Baroness Kentigern."

Aimee made her curtsey and regarded the three knights with open curiosity. "You are friends of my husband's?" she asked with interest. Konrad could almost *see* the question trembling on her lips. *Why did you not invite them to our wedding?*

He supposed he would have to explain the friendships were only recently struck up. At least with Symes and Lowell, he reflected. Looking back now, he supposed Farleigh had been trying to make friends with him for months.

All three were answering Aimee's query with an enthusiasm Konrad felt a little embarrassed about. There was something puppyish about their attitudes. As Farleigh bent over Aimee's hand, it struck him forcibly that she would be much better suited to one of their number than she ever would him.

He cleared his throat. "You fought well, Farleigh," he said, distracting the young pup from his wife. Sir Douglas was immediately ensnared.

"You thought so? I was worried I made a damned poor showing in truth," he confessed, scratching the back of his neck.

Konrad shook his head. "Very creditable," he assured him. "You need have no worries on that score."

Farleigh brightened at once as Lowell regaled them with a spectator's view of de Crecy's sufferings.

"Serves him right," Symes chimed in. "The fellow is well-nigh insufferable. Always has been. His uncle's estate borders a second cousin of mine. The whole family is stiff-necked, but Sir Jeffree's the worst of the bunch. He's been raised his uncle's heir, you know, and is used to looking down on all his neighbors."

"Who is his uncle?" asked Lowell with interest.

"The Duke of Bethencourt."

Farleigh whistled. "That would explain it," he murmured. "Bethencourt is rolling in coin. Does he not own half of Ganfordshire?"

Symes grunted. "Aye, but here's the rub of it." He glanced around before continuing. "The uncle, a confirmed bachelor, has recently married some young bride and put Sir Jeffree's dukedom in jeopardy. That's one of the reasons de Crecy is in so foul a mood. If this new wife of his uncle's should catch for a child, he will be disinherited from a title he has always considered as good as his."

Kentigern looked toward Aimee, whose eyes were wide with lively interest.

"Well, that's one in the eye for Sir Jeffree," Lowell chortled. "No wonder he's been in such a passion of late."

"He is lately married himself, of course," Aimee pointed out. "That might also have affected his equanimity."

Konrad surprised himself with yet another pang of sympathy for de Crecy.

"What is she like, if you don't mind me asking, Lady Kentigern?" Lowell asked. All eyes swerved back to Aimee. "De Crecy's bride, I mean."

"She is…unusual," Aimee said after a moment's pause. "Not what you would expect Sir Jeffree to choose in a wife. And yet…" She tipped her head to one side. "I think she enjoys keeping him on his toes."

Konrad narrowed his gaze. Where the hells had she gotten that impression? The others made various noises of interest in this point of view. "Aye, well," he said. "One of us had best be strapping on his armor." He looked pointedly at Lowell, who gave a start.

"Good point," Lowell said, peering over his shoulder. "Have they assembled? I had better be on my way. Will you stay and watch, my lord?" he asked hopefully.

Konrad looked to Aimee before answering. She nodded encouragingly. "Aye, right willingly," he rumbled, and Lowell beamed before hurrying off.

"Shall we find a good place to sit?" Farleigh suggested, glancing toward the benches.

"Oh yes," said Aimee hurriedly and pressed on Konrad's arm.

366

He picked up on her unspoken message that she did not wish to return to the Howards' spot. "How about over to the left?" he suggested obligingly and was rewarded with a relieved smile.

"An excellent notion," she agreed. "That looks perfect." Some of the crowds had dispersed after the first battle had ended, and they soon found an empty bench.

"I will go in search of some refreshment," Symes said, heading off toward one of the more functional-looking tents.

Konrad allowed his eyes to wander over the crowd as Farleigh told Aimee enthusiastically of the tournaments he had attended thus far this year. He saw Una de Bussell had returned to the Howards and was looking about her with a frown on her face. He lowered his head to speak in his wife's ear. "I think the princess is looking for you," he said in a low voice.

Aimee glanced across. "Do you think so?" She sounded gratified. "In truth, I think she will find Lady Howard a good deal easier without me there while I am *persona non grata*."

"Why would Lady Howard think that?" Farleigh asked, his ears pricking up. Aimee explained about the aftereffects of her song, and he seemed to derive a good deal of amusement from the tale. When Symes returned with a pitcher of ale and four cups, Farleigh insisted on her repeating the story to his friend.

"It is hardly your fault that Darby's conscience smote him," Symes agreed. "I heard he was betrothed to some rich woman in Aldenbrook. A glover's widow. Likely, Lady Howard was not looking forward to imparting the news the contract was broken."

"Was he really betrothed to another?" Aimee looked stricken. "Aileen did not tell us that part of the tale."

"Apparently so," Symes told her. "But these things happen."

367

"I suppose they do," Aimee murmured guiltily. "But even so, I should not like to think of any lady planning for a wedding that will ne'er take place."

"I think Mistress Aileen might have the prior claim," Konrad heard himself point out dryly. "As she has twice born his seed." He thought Farleigh winced slightly at his blunt manner of speech, but Aimee did not seem to mind it.

"That is true," she agreed, looking relieved.

"Likely, Darby only pledged himself to the widow for her fat purse," Farleigh added in what the young fool probably thought a consoling manner.

Aimee's face filled with color. "Yes, you are probably right," she agreed in a subdued voice.

Inwardly, Konrad cursed the tactless young idiot.

"Look, they are taking now to the field," Symes announced. "There's Fulke," he said, nodding to Lowell.

"And is that not Sir Armand de Bussell?" Aimee asked, pointing to another knight who stood head and shoulders above the others.

"Aye, that's him," Konrad agreed.

"Let us see if today is a fair day or a foul one for Sir Armand," Farleigh suggested with a wink. "I do not know if you are aware of his reputation, my lady," he said, turning to Aimee and then proceeding to give her an account of Sir Armand's wild discrepancy in the field.

He might not have troubled himself, for from the moment the flag was waved, it was obvious Sir Armand was a man driven with resolve this day. As the knight of most repute in the field, opponents swarmed around him as much as they had Konrad or

368

de Crecy. However, de Bussell seemed to welcome the opportunity it afforded him to pile up his foes.

Watching him from an impartial distance, Konrad was suddenly struck by how cunning de Bussell was in battle. He feinted, he shammed, he wrong-footed his opponents and seemed to derive almost an unholy glee from the effectiveness of his sly approach.

Konrad frowned, for such a thought had never crossed his mind before and that struck him as odd. He had always thought Sir Armand an impulsive and frivolous sort, controlled by his impulses which led to either a good day or a bad when it came to combat. Now he realized that was not the case. De Bussell had been playing them for fools. But why?

A small hand pressed on his forearm. "Why do you glare so?" Aimee whispered. "Do you dislike Sir Armand so very much?"

"What? No," he answered distractedly, covering her hand with his own and holding it there. "I have never disliked de Bussell," he admitted. In truth, it was hard to dislike the merry Sir Armand.

"He's having the devil's own luck today," Symes said, leaning forward on his bench. "At least Fulke will likely make it to the final battle if naught else. De Bussell looks well-nigh unbeatable!"

Konrad turned to look at where Princess Una stood watching from the crowd, her hands clasped together and a smile playing about her mouth. Could it be that *she* had wrought this change in her husband? The idea was a ludicrous one, yet he found himself contemplating it all the same.

Farleigh groaned. "You spoke too soon, for Fulke's luck has turned," he commented, for circumstances had now driven

369

Lowell directly into a skirmish with three red knights cornering him like a rat. They watched their friend's defeat with a gloomy inevitability.

"There will be no consoling him this afternoon," Symes warned as they saw Lowell stoop to retrieve the sword that had been knocked from his hand. "He will be wholly lost to melancholy."

Farleigh made a noise of agreement in his throat. "He's not entered in the lists either, so this is his only event."

A dispirited Lowell dragged himself to the sideline and lowered himself to sit on the grass beside his fallen teammates with blue armbands. He looked crushed.

Belatedly, Konrad realized both Symes and Farleigh were looking toward him expectantly.

"It just was not his day." Konrad shrugged. "It happens."

They murmured agreement. "He might take that better from you, Kentigern," Farleigh suggested.

"After all, he will still make it to the final battle," Konrad pointed out. He was not so sure why they all thought Lowell would be so devastated by crashing out of this round.

"He wanted to impress you," Symes imparted, momentarily robbing him of speech. Aimee squeezed his arm. He turned toward her, lowering his head.

"Perhaps," she whispered in his ear, "you could call him by his given name when you extend your sympathies." When Aimee sat back, she gave him an encouraging smile.

Konrad blinked. *What was Lowell's name again?* He found it hard to concentrate when he could still feel where Aimee's breath had tickled his neck. Noticing Symes's and Farleigh's eyes were upon them, he cleared his throat again, giving his wife a brief nod to say he would consider it.

The rest of the battle held little by way of upset expectations. Sir Armand dominated, and the rest scrambled to keep up. It was no surprise when the blue team emerged the eventual winners. Farleigh sat up, rubbing his hands. "The final battle will be orange versus blue," he pronounced.

"And you will have to sit on the sidelines to watch it," Symes pointed out with a malicious grin. Farleigh punched him on the shoulder.

"You will have to keep my wife company," Konrad said and Farleigh brightened.

"I would be honored," he answered with a bow in Aimee's direction.

"But first there will be a break to allow the blue team to regain their strength, is that not so?" Aimee asked.

"It is," Konrad agreed.

Farleigh went off in search of pastries and ale, and Lowell joined them presently, his nose encrusted with dried blood.

"Well fought, Fulke," Konrad growled. "There's few who could stand against de Bussell today. His sword is guided by the spirit of battle." The saying was a northern one, and he had no idea if Lowell was even familiar with the term.

Lowell flushed. "Thanks, though I hope to put in a better showing this afternoon." He gave a faint smile.

Konrad shrugged and glanced at Aimee, who sent him a glowing look. It seemed he was back in her good graces again, though the gods alone knew how long that would last before he messed things up again.

Farleigh duly returned with ale and a maid carrying a platter of pastries. The next hour passed swiftly before he, Symes, and Lowell were required to go and don their armor once more for the afternoon's final deciding battle.

25

"I do not think I have seen Sir Armand compete before," Aimee said thoughtfully as another knight fell victim to his gauntleted fist. "Is he always this…formidable?"

Poor Sir Fulke had again gone crashing out of the battle early in the clash, but they had not had much time to mourn this, for both Konrad and Sir Armand were cutting swathes through the opposition.

Sir Douglas shook his head without taking his eyes off the field. "I have never seen de Bussell fight quite like this before. I had heard he was impressive at Areley Kings," he conceded after a faint pause. "But I thought that must have been a fluke or exaggeration. He will surely win the Autumn Tournament if he retains his zeal."

Sir Douglas pondered. "I can't even see the likes of Vawdrey or Orde vanquishing him." Then he seemed to remember his present company. "Though mayhap Lord Kentigern would give him a good fight," he added hurriedly.

Aimee's eye had already traveled to the opposite end of the field where her husband was dragging two fallen knights by their feet toward the waiting Jakeman. "Tell me, how are ransoms collected from those you defeat in battle?" she asked curiously.

"The correct form is to present the sum at the celebratory feast that evening. Of course, some knights do not attend the feasts, so in reality, you can just send along your squire with the fee to spare your blushes," Sir Douglas explained.

"Does my husband not attend the feasts?" Aimee guessed shrewdly. Her companion nodded his head, looking pleased she was so quick to catch his meaning. "But how does one ensure that all fees are paid?" she persisted.

"Some knights have tokens printed with their crests to give as pledges," he explained. "They hand those over as a marker to redeem at a later point."

"I see," Aimee mused. It still seemed an exercise of trust to her. She supposed it was a question of honor and principle, but she knew her father would have required a more secure means to ensure his debtors paid their dues.

"I think de Bussell will get today's trophy for most impressive in the field," Sir Douglas pronounced with confidence.

"You cannot yet be certain of that," Aimee objected. "For it seems to me that both my husband and even Sir Jeffree in the first bout fought just as many opponents this day."

Sir Douglas made a sound of cautious agreement. "That may be so," he conceded. "But it is Sir Armand's performance that draws the eye."

"I disagree," Aimee said, lifting her chin, though in truth, she herself had been staring in astonishment as Sir Armand outfoxed his opponents. Konrad was grim and steady in his progress. He methodically lay waste to all who stood against him, while Sir Armand seemed to be lit up from within.

Her heart sinking, Aimee was forced to admit, to herself at least, that Sir Douglas spoke nothing but the truth. Watching Konrad fight was not a joyful, but a jarring sight. His delivery looked bone-crunching, though undoubtedly there was skill involved and technique.

"What was it Kentigern called it?" Sir Douglas asked in an awed-sounding voice.

"Guided by the spirit of battle," she replied absently.

The two of them watched as the inevitable moment grew closer. The moment when Lord Kentigern and Sir Armand would be the last men left standing on the field. Already, Aimee could feel her stomach tensing into knots of nervous anticipation.

"He *is* going to triumph, is he not?" Aimee asked hollowly. Sir Douglas did not answer, but she felt comforted by his presence all the same. Clearly, his bond to her husband was a considerable one, though a good deal of it consisted of hero worship.

Still, Konrad seemed…benign in his attitude toward his young friends. Almost kindly, she decided, and for some reason, Aimee found herself suddenly wondering if that was the kind of father he might make to any sons they might have.

All such pleasant reflections were brought to an end when Sir Leonard was first defeated by the combined efforts of two blue sashes. He fought hard but could not withstand their coordinated attack, crumpling into the dust and rolling painfully onto his side before staggering to the sideline where he collapsed into a heap.

"Oh no!" Aimee breathed, covering her mouth. "I hope he is not too badly injured."

"Probably more his pride than anything," Sir Douglas answered gloomily. "At least he made final five by the skin of his teeth," he pointed out, and Aimee saw that was just about true. Both Sir Armand and her husband stood over insensible foes they had already dragged to the edge of the field. "That should console him in any case."

Sir Armand turned his head and seemed to be weighing up his opposition on the field. Apart from Lord Kentigern, there was only one other orange armband remaining. He started toward him with a disconcerting spring in his step. As for Konrad, he immediately made for the two other red sashes who had just defeated Sir Leonard.

Aimee watched him swing his sword with such ferocity that the first of the knights fell to his knees from the force and the second knight's sword went flying from his hand in a spinning arc. A ripple of excitement went up from the crowd as Sir Armand similarly made short work of dispatching the other orange knight.

When the two red knights held up their hands in acknowledgment of defeat, her husband pointed meaningfully toward Jakeman, and they trailed their own way toward the manservant with slumped shoulders.

"Here it comes," Sir Douglas said, leaning forward in his seat.

The two knights started walking toward each other, and the crowd sat up, a wave of excitement breaking over the benches.

Twenty minutes later, Aimee had wrung her scarf into a limp rag, and Sir Douglas had leaped twice to his feet in excited anticipation. The combatants seemed evenly matched, but even Aimee's untutored eye could see that the longer the fight continued, the greater Sir Armand's advantage grew.

Konrad was surely breathing hard now beneath his helmet. Aimee could only imagine how exhausted he must be under the combined weight of his armor and his mighty broadsword. When he wielded it, swinging high and wide, Sir Armand was one of the few present who was both tall and strong enough to withstand the onslaught.

The minute Konrad's attack was done, that was when her husband appeared at his most vulnerable, for Sir Armand was devious and seemed always to be prodding for an opening in his defense, setting Konrad onto his back foot and rocking him with a counterattack which managed to be both subtle and unanticipated.

Sir Armand seemed always to be looking as though he were doing one thing and then switching to another. Even Aimee could see his footwork was clever and light for his size, where Konrad's tended to be more heavy and lumbering.

Sir Douglas swore under his breath. "At least Kentigern's strong as an ox," he said. "He has the strength to keep going where a normal man will grow exhausted."

Aimee bit her lip. Her own inclination told her that Sir Armand was *not* an ordinary opponent. She suspected that the longer the fight continued, the tighter the traps Sir Armand was weaving would grow about Konrad's limbs.

Even as the thought occurred to her, she saw the trap sprung and muffled her cry with her hand as Sir Armand saw his opening and pressed his advantage. She closed her eyes and heard the mingled gasps and cries from the watching audience.

"Is it over?" she asked, even as she opened one eye to watch her husband drop his sword and yield.

"It is over," Sir Douglas answered with a groan.

Konrad reached up to wrench off his helmet, showing his hair drenched with sweat and a face quite red with exertion. He dragged his breath in and out before extending his arm to Sir Armand.

A grinning Sir Armand clasped wrists with him, and Aimee saw their lips move as they exchanged some words. Aimee saw Sir Armand laugh, and both stood catching their breath and conversing until Sir Chaucey approached to officially proclaim the winner.

Aimee felt herself slump with relief in her seat. Sir Douglas began a spirited theory on the change in Sir Armand's combative style as Aimee watched her husband's relaxed face and attitude. He truly displayed at his best, she thought dreamily, when you saw this side of him. He clapped Sir Armand once more between his shoulder blades and then, pausing only to retrieve his sword, stalked from the ring.

"Where will he go now?" Aimee asked, interrupting her companion's excited chatter.

"To wash and scrub up, I should not wonder," Sir Douglas hazarded. "He will be soaked through with sweat."

Aimee glanced back toward the sidelines where she saw Jakeman had already dismissed the hostages and was scurrying off, likely to heat water for his master. "Could you kindly escort me back to my tent, Sir Douglas?" Aimee asked.

"Right gladly," he responded at once, offering his arm.

"Thank you." Aimee felt keen to return, though she was not sure Konrad would be much in the mood for the celebrations after his defeat.

By the time they had navigated the crowds at the sedate pace Sir Douglas seemed to think fitted to a lady and made their way to the first meadow where the Kentigern tent stood, Aimee could hear her husband's voice from within.

As they approached, Jakeman came out carrying two large empty pitchers. "My lady," he greeted her. "His lordship is taking his wash. Should I bring out two chairs?" Aimee guessed this was the discreet servant's way of warning her his master was naked.

378

She turned to Sir Douglas. "You will want to return to your own pavilion to wash, I expect, Sir Douglas." She thought he looked a little crestfallen. "Perhaps you would like to return here directly after and bring Sir Fulke and Sir Leonard with you once they have cleaned up? I have brought some wineskins with me and some sundry foods I thought would travel. Perhaps Jakeman could fetch us three more chairs and another table, and we could take our ease this afternoon in one another's company?"

Sir Douglas brightened at once, rubbing his hands together. "I can answer for all three of us that we would be delighted, Lady Kentigern, if you truly think his lordship would be agreeable."

"Yes, of course," Aimee replied blithely. After all, if he was not, then he could always loll on the bed within while the boisterous younger knights sat outside. She could move between the two where her presence would be most welcomed.

Jakeman nodded and went haring off in search of the additional furnishings.

"I will see you presently, then," Aimee said, and with a final wave to Sir Douglas, she ducked inside the pavilion.

Konrad was stood facing away from her, vigorously soaping his chest. Aimee caught her breath. As always, she felt completely awed by his powerful physique. Clearing her throat, she let him know she was present, tearing her devouring eyes away from the view. Even the size of his calves and thighs was a source of wonder to her. She had never really seen his rear before, and she found the sight strangely enticing. She could stand and stare at him all day if only he would give her permission!

"Do you need any help?" she offered croakily.

He glanced over his shoulder. "No, keep your distance. I'm filthy," he said shortly.

Aimee heaved a sigh of disappointment. "When you are clean, I have some salve for sore muscles," she offered. "I could minister it, if that would be agreeable to you?" She held her breath for his answer.

When he gave a throaty rumble, she decided optimistically to take this for assent and made for her saddlebag. She soon found the bottle of green gelatinous fluid which her father imported from Samare. It was extracted from the fleshy leaf of a plant that grew there in abundance and was purported to contain soothing qualities.

"I have invited your friends to join us presently," she said in a conversational tone. "I thought I could serve the wines and the flatbreads and cheeses I brought with us, and we could sit outside in the sun."

He nodded, but made no other rejoinder, and Aimee carried the lotion over to the bed and sat down as Konrad stood in a large basin and emptied two jugs of water over his head to rinse away the soap. Grabbing a large drying cloth that Jakeman must have set aside for him, he wrapped it about himself and made his way toward the bed.

Aimee could see he winced with every step. "You are footsore?" she asked sympathetically.

"My whole body is sore," he corrected her as he gingerly lowered himself onto the mattress.

"This should help," she told him brightly, showing him the bottle. He turned his head toward her, looking at her face rather than the bottle. "What is it?" she asked, lowering it. "Konrad?" She pulled a face. "Or should I call you my lord?" She glanced about the interior. "For I suppose this counts as a bedchamber, strictly speaking."

He looked uncomprehending before his face turned a little red and he cleared his throat. "How about you forget I ever said that?" he suggested. "I only meant—well, I like how you talk to me in general. When you're unguarded in speech, I mean. But I especially like it when we're naked in bed together." He shrugged his bare shoulders. "I'm pretty sure you could call me anything there and I would like it."

Aimee regarded him in surprise. He reached slowly across the bed and touched the backs of his fingers to her cheek. Aimee leaned into his touch a moment before raising her hand to lightly clasp his own. "You were very impressive today," she said hesitantly, not knowing how to respond.

"Not as impressive as de Bussell." He grimaced, letting his hand drop.

"I thought you were. It was just luck that he won out in the end," Aimee insisted. "Either one of you would have been a worthy winner."

He gave a short laugh. "You are biased in my favor."

"Always," she agreed, and again his eyes sought hers.

"I just think you like me best when I lose," he said in an odd tone.

"Win or lose, you are the one my gaze is drawn to," Aimee admitted, drawing the stopper from the bottle. She did not dare look at his face as she admitted the fact. The scent was fresh and smelled of the leaves from which the balm was made. "Shall I do your hands or your feet first?" she asked cheerfully.

"Both ache," he admitted with a groan.

"I'm not surprised after jolting and jarring your bones the way you do." Aimee reached across and drew one of his hands into her lap. She spread the balm over his chafed knuckles first, working it into the dry skin by circling her thumbs. "Will you let me do all of your limbs?" she asked when he closed his eyes and relaxed against the bed with a sigh.

"All of them?" he asked drowsily.

Aimee decided to take that a yes. Turning his hand over, she smoothed the thick liquid over his calloused palm and along his fingers before rubbing vigorously. When that drew a groan from him, she reflected that gripping the hilt of his sword had likely left his palm aching and sore. She redoubled her efforts, circling her thumbs with increasing pressure as she moved over the area of his large hand, working the joints of each finger.

Interestingly, he never voiced any objection, however hard she pressed and pummeled, so Aimee decided brisk and firm was the method to employ. She did both hands and feet and then the fronts of his arms and legs, his chest and stomach, bunching the drying sheet about his hips as she worked so she could reach those thick thighs and then his muscular stomach.

"Konrad?" she murmured breathlessly, leaning over him. "Can I do your face?"

His eyes sprang open at once. "My face?" he asked, looking as though he had been disagreeably startled out of slumber.

Seeing the tension entering his frame again, she said quickly, "It does not matter, if you would rather I did not."

He lifted a hand from the mattress before letting it fall again. "No, you can do it," he said, looking as though he meant to say more but could not form the words.

"Would you rather I stayed away from the scarring?" Aimee asked carefully.

He did not speak for a moment, and when he did, his voice was low. "If you want to touch it, you can," he said gruffly.

Aimee nodded and tipped the bottle into her palm. "Tell me if anything does not feel nice," she said, setting her hands against each side of his face.

"You won't hurt me," he grunted. "There is very little feeling in that side of my face."

Aimee smoothed the lotion against his cheekbones and then massaged it into his cheeks, her fingers light yet firm. The scarred side of his face felt tight and tough under her fingers. Aimee wondered regretfully if it had been fresher, would she have been able to manipulate it back into supple skin.

"I wish I could have been there when you were recovering," she said, pressing her lips together. "I do not think they can have taken good care of you as I should have."

He let out a huff of laughter. "Very likely not. It was the not the place for a lady though," he said grimly, and she guessed he must have been a prisoner at the time.

"I would not have been a lady," she pointed out. "But the daughter of a spice and herb merchant."

He looked amused but did not pursue this line of conversation. Instead, she felt him slowly relax as she ran her fingers along the line of his jaw and chin, up and over his brow, and down the sides of his face until he was breathing deep and easy again. Likely, she could get some special oil for the dark beard which he had kept tidily trimmed since their marriage.

"I need you to turn over," Aimee murmured as his eyes drifted shut again.

"Mmmm, wha—?" he said with a start.

"I need you to roll over onto your stomach so I can do your back." She wiggled the bottle of lotion in his face, and comprehension dawned in his eyes. Aimee braced herself for objection, but when he rolled obligingly onto his front, Aimee breathed a sigh of relief. Her fingers were tingling and would likely ache later from overuse, but she was vastly enjoying herself.

Getting to run her hands all over the planes and bunched muscles of his back was a treat indeed, and Aimee reveled in the opportunity to enjoy his wondrous body in a manner she would never have dared to dream of a mere twelve months ago.

She thought of the Aimee who had sat enraptured at Kellingford and imagined telling her that one day she would have free rein and dominion over Lord Kentigern's magnificent body. She would scarce have been able to comprehend such a thing. She let her hands roam more greedily than worshipfully over his shoulder blades, curving them forward over the muscles in the base of his neck, and heard him give a muffled groan.

"There?" Aimee asked gently. "That is where my sister always gets her aches and pains," she said, working her fingers into the knotted muscle. "Though her neck and shoulders are a good deal more delicate than yours."

"That is where you learned this? On your sister?" he asked, his voice thick and husky, though whether it was with sleep or pleasure, Aimee was not sure. Perhaps both. For some reason, it made her pulse race and her own breathing quicken. Unable to resist, she leaned forward and brushed a kiss against the base of his neck. "Yes. She said I have healing hands."

384

When he groaned again, she concentrated on the area that wrung it from him until he relaxed again under her fingers, and she drifted down over the backs of his arms and then down his spine until she reached the curve of his backside. Here she halted, adjusted the sheet which was a little twisted, and then moved down the bed to see to his tense calves and the backs of his thighs.

He was sore in his thighs and flinched at the cooling lotion, so she tarried on them awhile, listening carefully for the telling hitch in his breathing. When she reached his buttocks again, she hesitated.

"Can I touch you here?" she asked curiously. When he did not answer, she realized he had drifted off into sleep. She hesitated. Was it proper? But after all, he had touched her there, had he not? Chewing the side of her mouth, she peeled down the sheet, exposing his backside. *How strange*, she thought*, but I find that beautiful too!*

She poured the lotion into her palms to warm it a moment before she smoothed it over his firm buttocks, kneading and spreading her fingers over the supple skin. It was smooth and soft here instead of rough and abused. This skin had not been exposed to the elements or chafed beneath chain mail.

"You had better stop," he said regretfully. "I am enjoying it a bit too much."

Aimee's hands halted even as she frowned over his words. "Why should you not enjoy it?" she puzzled.

He gave a huff of laughter and rolled lazily onto his back. "See?" He gestured toward his groin where the drying sheet was showing a good deal of disturbance. Aimee blinked. *Oh.* "If you are expecting visitors shortly," he continued dryly, "then I need to enjoy myself a little less or I will be embarrassing myself."

"Will it just go back down by itself?" Aimee asked curiously.

"It will," he answered. "If I shut my eyes and think of something disagreeable for a while."

Aimee thought about this. "Perhaps I ought not to have invited your friends to return," she said with some regret.

"That is not helpful," he replied. "Now I am thinking about what we would be doing if you were not such a keen hostess."

"So am I," Aimee agreed without thinking, and Konrad groaned.

"Stop talking, Aimee," he growled, so she stood up and made for their packs again to start unpacking the wine and wrapped cheeses, leaving him in peace to get control of himself.

When she heard someone moving outside the tent, she moved to the entrance and saw it was Jakeman, who had set down three chairs and a blanket.

"This is excellent, Jakeman. I wonder if you could find us a loaf of bread and three more wine goblets?"

"Right willingly, milady," he said and set off again across the meadow. Aimee watched him with approval for a moment before ducking back inside the pavilion.

The bed rustled, and Aimee allowed herself the briefest of glimpses in that direction. Konrad was running a hand over his face. With a resigned sigh, he sat up, swinging his legs over the side of the mattress. He flexed first one arm and then the other, a look of surprise spreading across his face.

Aimee hid her smile and carried the first of her packages outside to set on the table ready for their guests. She busied herself, laying out the cheeses, pickles, and nuts as Jakeman went back and forth emptying the basin of washing water and fetching more for her to wash.

She had just poured the first of the wineskins into a ceramic wine jug when Jakeman informed her that her water was readied, and Konrad came sauntering out looking refreshed and wearing a dark green tunic. "You look well," she exclaimed in surprise.

"I feel well," he admitted and dropped into a chair. "Quite revived, in fact. Thanks to you."

"Mayhap you should bring me to all your tournaments, then, my lord," she suggested boldly, before disappearing into the tent to complete her own hurried wash. By the time she emerged, Konrad had already been joined by Sir Fulke, Sir Douglas, and Sir Leonard. They greeted her enthusiastically, starting to scramble to their feet, until she bade them to take their ease.

Joining them, Aimee slipped into the seat next to her husband. She took a piece of buttered bread and cheese and accepted the goblet of wine that was pressed on her. "Have you all been regaling one another with tales of valor?" she asked, curious as to what they had been discussing. They glanced around at each other before her husband cleared his throat.

"We were just discussing de Crecy's pavilion," he admitted grudgingly.

"Sir Jeffree's pavilion?" Aimee echoed, lowering her cup. "I do not think I have seen it."

"No, you won't have," Sir Douglas agreed. "For it is not in this meadow but the next one."

"Pray, what about Sir Jeffree's pavilion makes it worthy of note?" Aimee asked.

"It is in his colors," Sir Fulke admitted with more than just a hint of scorn. "And emblazoned with his crest." Sir Leonard guffawed.

Aimee shrugged. "I do not see why you laugh," she said critically. "For my part, I should dearly love a pavilion decked out in the Kentigern colors of blue and yellow."

Sir Douglas cleared his throat. "You would not think that a trifle...ostentatious?" he ventured cautiously.

"No, I would not," she replied stoutly, before remembering her disastrous heraldic gown. *Oh.* "This one is a good deal too plain," she said hurriedly to cover up her embarrassment. Perhaps she was showing her upstart origins again!

Sir Fulke glanced over his shoulder. "Most will simply attach their own banner," he explained. "I see you have not, though, my lord."

Konrad shrugged. "Jakeman took the only one I had down to the arena. I do not bring spares."

An awkward silence reigned over the group for a moment before Fulke spoke again. "If you don't mind me asking, milady, what was it you meant by that comment you made before about De Crecy's wife keeping him on his toes?"

"Yes," Sir Douglas said. "I also meant to ask about that. For she seems a most pitiable woman to my mind."

Aimee looked down at her interlaced fingers a moment. "I am not sure," she said slowly. "I spoke aloud my observation without reasoning it through. It is only that, whenever I have observed that lady, she is not what you would expect her to be." She hesitated, unsure of the word to select. "She is wholly uncowed by Sir Jeffree's antics. If anything, she almost seems to derive a sort of dark amusement from them."

They exclaimed at this, and she thought Konrad seemed displeased. "I did not realize she was his wife at the royal tournament," she continued simply. "And when he was ejected from the melee, she summoned for more wine and seemed to be vastly enjoying the spectacle."

"Aimee," her husband growled as his young friends seemed unduly diverted.

"We are among friends, are we not?" she asked hesitantly. "Must I guard my words so closely?"

"We may be among friends but…" Konrad bit off his words before starting again. "Relations between a man and his wife should not be bandied about as idle gossip."

Aimee turned red, and glancing sidelong, she thought Sir Douglas did too. "Your pardon, I had not realized," she apologized. Likely, she was being vulgar again. She would have felt free to say such things in front of Ursula or Freda, though Ursa would likely have reproached her, but male company was doubtless different.

Or perhaps it was a societal issue again? Her father discussed the marriages of his acquaintances, but perhaps the nobility did not do so. She tried to imagine the Wycliffes discussing the state of their acquaintances' marriages and failed. They would think such a thing highly improper, she realized with a sinking heart. Sir Leonard cleared his throat and offered a judgment on some knight's performance that day who Aimee had never heard of.

Instead of listening, she ate a handful of dates, a fig, and then two walnuts as she debated whether she should retreat inside the tent and leave them to their conversation of battle. Konrad's hand settling over hers startled her from her thoughts, and she looked up to find him looking at her with a faintly questioning look on his face.

"My lord?" She faltered. Had he directed a question her way that she had missed?

"You have fallen silent," he said.

Aimee was startled. "This displeases you?" She gave an awkward laugh. "I had thought to let you gentlemen converse without me adding a discordant note."

"I did not mean to reproach you," he said abruptly. "Or to stifle your speech. 'Tis only that…" He frowned a moment as though mustering his thoughts. "To me it seems the bond of matrimony is a sacrosanct one." Aimee's mouth fell open, and someone sat to her left gave a muffled cough.

Konrad's frown grew more pronounced. "I heartily pity de Crecy *and* his wife," he added heavily. "To be joined in life to someone without affection must be a terrible thing." He gave her a level look. "Not everyone can be as fortunate as we."

Aimee gazed at him, her breath coming thick and fast. "I—that is, when we married—" Suddenly, she became aware of three pairs of eyes avidly watching them and swallowed her words. It would surely not be appropriate to raise this now!

His thumb passed caressingly over her knuckles. "When we wed, you brought all the affection to the table," he acknowledged. "As well as everything else. However, I hope I have never been accused of being a slow learner."

Aimee swallowed, her head reeling with what he was saying. He had grown accustomed to her presence in his life? Perhaps even fond of her? She lifted her goblet and took another hurried sip to mask how shaken she felt.

Sir Douglas sighed. "You make us quite envious, my lord," he said.

"Not me!" Sir Fulke objected with a shudder. "No offense, my lady," he added quickly when his friends upbraided him as unchivalrous.

"Farleigh is unlucky in his wooing," Konrad said after a moment's pause, catching Aimee entirely by surprise.

Was he…attempting to introduce a topic she would have interest in? The possibility made her heart lurch. "He is?" she asked, lowering her cup.

"Aye," Sir Douglas agreed with a sigh. "The lady I most esteem does not look favorably on my suit."

Sir Leonard snorted. "I daresay she is not even aware you are wooing her!"

Sir Fulke sniggered, and soon the tale of the perfect Lady Constance tumbled out along with Sir Douglas's failure to engage her affections. Aimee found it most interesting, and the afternoon under the golden sun seemed to slip by after that. All three wineskins were drunk, the food consumed, and Jakeman dispatched to fetch more ale from the hall.

After Sir Douglas's ineffective wooing, they heard all about Sir Leonard's three grown sisters and how he must scheme and save to provide for them all, now he was the head of the family. "The misfortune of it is that the sole sister who possesses a dowry is the only one I do not want to be parted with."

"How is it that this one sister possesses a dowry when the other two do not?" Aimee puzzled.

"Aye, well, there you have it. She is not *actually* Leo's sister at all," Sir Fulke explained. "She was fully eighteen years old when he met her."

"Her mother was only married to my father for a sixmonth before he died," Sir Leonard agreed. "But in any case, I am in no hurry to part with Sybil. The other two, certainly," he said, pursing his lips. "But not Sybil."

After that, they heard all about Fulke's struggles to remain in his father's favor now he had a stepmother and two stepbrothers to supplant him. "Perfect paragons, the pair of them," Fulke said glumly. "Or so my stepmother would have you believe. And I can't put a foot right in her book!"

By the time suppertime rolled around, Aimee felt well acquainted with all the young knights' hopes and aspirations. They seemed a pleasant and straightforward bunch, and she was pleased Konrad could call them his friends. She took her husband's arm as they made their way to Caple Hall for the evening banquet. The sun was so low in the sky that all the fields about them seemed bathed in a golden glow, and Aimee felt such a surge of contentment that she was forced to give herself a stern talking-to.

She was *not* about to go and throw her heart at Lord Kentigern all over again. She had learned her lesson well and from now on would keep it well guarded. He did not want love from her, merely respect and affection. She would not permit herself to be disappointed by this, for in the first place, he had not even wanted that! They were learning to deal well with one another, that was all, she told herself firmly.

On arriving in the Great Hall, Aimee was pleased to see Aileen Howard was sat at the high table next to her new husband, Sir Darby. Lady Howard, too, seemed reconciled to the match, for she performed Konrad's introduction to her daughter-in-law with a serene calm. To Aimee's surprise, the de Bussells did not turn up to the celebratory banquet, despite Sir Armand's day of triumph. Maybe they were celebrating just the two of them, she pondered. After all, Sir Armand must surely be exhausted after his exertions.

Conversely, the arrival in the hall of the de Crecys arm in arm caused quite a stir, as no one expected them to show. She fancied Sir Jeffree's eyes strayed rather often to his wife's profile with a faintly baffled look lurking in his gaze. Something had clearly happened between them, and Aimee felt most curious as to what it might have been. Whatever it was, Lady de Crecy seemed to have the upper hand to her mind. She looked composed and cool, where Sir Jeffree looked decidedly sheepish.

Tonight, Aimee did not feel self-conscious about the fact she was the most elaborately adorned in the room. She had debated removing her pearls or her brooch beforehand, but after all, she could scarcely leave them unattended in the pavilion, so instead, she had kept them on. Perhaps the several cups of wine she had drunk over the course of the afternoon had helped blunt any feelings of doubt.

Throughout the course of the meal, various figures kept materializing at her husband's shoulder, hovering nervously. Aimee, catching sight of them, would tip her head to make Konrad aware of their presence, for half the time they stood at his left shoulder where he had something of a blind spot. Whenever he turned frowningly to see who it was, he found a stammering knight attempting to present their ransom to him from the melee.

Konrad would enquire their name, nod, accept their coin, and they would drift away stammering their thanks. "I'm blessed if I know why they keep giving it to me here," her husband commented. "For they would find it far easier just to pass it to Jakeman on the morrow."

Aimee, recognizing one knight in a rather threadbare-looking tunic as someone her husband had declined to take for a hostage, guessed that they just wanted this moment of exchange with him. She could not say as she blamed them. If she were a young knight, she was convinced she would hang on his every word also. She wasn't sure she would needlessly pay money for the privilege though, she thought, watching the knight return to his friends looking flushed and triumphant. "He asked my name!" she heard him exclaim excitedly before he reclaimed his seat among them. She wondered if it was because he was so popular at Beres Caple that they dared approach him now, or if it was simply because he so rarely attended the evening banquets.

A sudden thought occurred to Aimee. "Do contestants never—" She broke off her words and frowned.

"What?"

"Try to—take advantage of the lack of vision in your left eye?"

Konrad shrugged. "It depends. Gallant fools like Vawdrey would never stoop so low."

"Is Sir Roland gallant, then?" Her belief in knights had taken rather a battering since marriage to one.

"He'd be furious at anyone who suggested such a thing," Kentigern acknowledged dryly. "But, aye, the King's Champion is an honorable fighter." He gave her a level look. "Vawdrey is young. In the war, he served briefly as a squire, nothing more." He hesitated. "He wasn't taught his craft on the battlefield."

Aimee dimly realized there was some distinction being pointed out to her here. "I see," she said slowly. "Sir Roland still believes in ideals, then? Like Sir Renlow."

Kentigern laughed. "No one is quite as pure-hearted as Renlow. Before your sister came along, I thought him a likely candidate for the cloister."

Aimee frowned. "Is there such a thing as monk-knights?" she asked.

Kentigern tipped his head to one side. "I came across a holy order of fighters once during the war, and they were some of the most ruthless I ever encountered. No, Renlow is something quite apart from their like."

Aimee regarded him intently. Something was niggling away at the edge of her thoughts. "What of less gallant knights than Sir Roland?" she persisted. "Would they attempt to use your blind side against you?"

Kentigern huffed out a breath. "Some," he admitted. "You must watch all your vulnerabilities around the likes of Orde. He would not let such a thing as chivalry get in the way of a win."

Aimee lifted her chin. "I like Sir Roland," she said defiantly.

"Everyone likes Vawdrey," he replied scathingly.

"Even you?"

Her reply seemed to flummox him. His eye skewed away from hers a moment. "Even me," he rumbled reluctantly. "Damn him!"

Aimee felt a flicker of triumph at this admission. "I did not take any instant liking to Sir Garman Orde," she ventured experimentally.

"No one likes Orde."

"Not even his wife?"

Kentigern shifted in his seat. "How should I know that?" he prevaricated, looking slightly hunted.

"I think you do know," she persisted.

"Very well, his wife is biased in his favor."

"Biased? Some might say she was in love with him," Aimee argued. "'Tis plain evident for anyone with eyes to see!"

Kentigern snorted. "Likely, she feels indebted to him."

"What do you mean by that? Oh, you mean because he overlooked her scars?"

"Scars!" he muttered derisively. "They are naught but a few pockmarks."

Aimee regarded him a moment in silence. "It is different in a woman, as I am sure you know. I heard she was the most famous beauty in all the land before she was stricken down with the red pox."

Her husband shifted in his seat. "Orde does not seem to mind her mottled skin."

"No, and isn't that strange when, as you say, he does not have a chivalrous bone in his body? I wonder why that could be, my lord," she flung at him in challenge.

Someone down the other end of the table dropped a knife, and at the same time, both Aimee and Kentigern seemed to recall they were not dining alone. They glanced down the table where their hosts and the de Crecys were watching them with interest.

Aimee cleared her throat. She wasn't sure why she had suddenly taken up her cudgels, but remembering the wonderful moments she had glimpsed at Kellingford between Sir Garman and Lady Lenora, she could not bear to hear anyone suggest their bond was anything other than loving. Just because most marriages were not so fortunate did not mean that none were.

Toward the end of the meal, the redheaded musician approached her with parchment and quill in hand to take down the verses of "The Tree, the Moon, and the Lover's Promise."

"I protest," Lady Howard said, raising her voice from the head of the table. "Lady Kentigern should be singing that sweet song for us and not simply reciting the words for your benefit, good Master Jacobs."

The musician bowed. "I confess I did hope that Lady Kentigern might grace us once again with her voice."

"Nay, Mother!" Sir Chaucey cried. "We have the awarding of today's prizes first. I declare that Lady Kentigern should sing at the close of our festivities, not at the commencement."

At that, his brother, Sir Darby, looked up quickly. "Aileen has been practicing all day after taking Lady Kentigern's instruction," he said. "Perhaps they could sing it together?"

"But of course!" Aimee said, interrupting Aileen's stammered protestations. "I was always in the habit of singing that song with my sister, so I am more accustomed to singing it in company." From their brief practice that morning, she knew the other woman's voice was pleasant though not particularly strong. Aileen gave her a happy smile by way of thanks.

Sir Chaucey walked to the front of the dais and cleared his throat. "It gives me very great pleasure," he announced, "to award these purses of monies to the fifteen members of the winning blue team." He announced the names, and Aimee sent an encouraging smile toward Sir Fulke, who seemed embarrassed about receiving prize money when his own performance had been nothing outstanding.

They all clapped as the knights came up the dais to receive their winnings. Sir Chaucey set aside the winner's trophy for The Last Man Standing and two purses for Sir Armand, which would have to be delivered to his tent. "And now for the awarding of the second cup," Sir Chaucey said, reaching for a handsome copper bowl.

"This award is a new one which we will be awarding this year. It is for The People's Champion, the knight who garners the most appreciation from those of us watching in the stands. It is gauged by both the cheers and groans of the audience. This year at Beres Caple, we are unanimous in our decision to award this prize to the one and only Lord Kentigern."

Aimee caught her breath as all eyes in the hall turned to look at her husband, who sat beside her with a thunderstruck expression on his face. After a moment, the shouts of encouragement started, and he swung his leg over the bench and made his way to join Sir Chaucey. If anything, she thought Konrad looked rather more awkward about going up to collect his reward than Sir Fulke had. She clapped along with everyone else and could not help but laugh when some of the knights started drumming their feet on the flagstones.

After thanking them all brusquely, Konrad made his way back to her side, clutching the copper bowl as though it might bite him. She guessed he had never won what amounted to a popularity prize before. His ears looked rather red as he lowered himself back onto the bench.

"What a lovely thing." Aimee beamed at him.

He lowered his voice. "I am sure it would have been de Bussell's had he bothered to show this eve."

"I do not think so," Aimee disagreed. "For it seems to me that *you* are the firm crowd favorite here."

Konrad growled. "Aye, well…" he started but seemed unable to continue. Taking pity on his discomfort, she patted his hand and then rose from her seat to join Aileen Howard to sing their song as the closing entertainment of the evening.

26

On the walk back to the pavilion, Konrad was still feeling out of sorts. He was not sure what had happened over the course of the meal, but the copper bowl under his arm seemed to proclaim him some sort of people's champion. He glanced down at Aimee, who was tripping blithely along by his side.

"As a matter of fact, I do not dislike Orde," he said in the manner of one severely goaded.

"I know you do not," his infuriating wife replied calmly. "You like him. You like him because he treats you as an equal." While he reeled from this piece of wisdom, she carried on. "There are actually remarkably few people you dislike, Konrad. You even like your manservant, who would have been your enemy in the last war. You like him so well you trust him at your throat with a straight razor."

Once again, Kentigern found himself at a loss for words. "He's very careful to avoid my scars," he heard himself bluster in reply. He sounded like a damned fool.

"Why did you not invite any of your fellow knights to our wedding?" she asked, ducking inside the tent before he could answer.

He followed her inside. "Because," he said heavily. "It seems my blindness extends to more than just this one eye." He placed the bowl down carefully. "I did not even realize they liked me here," he added, sounding as confused as he felt.

"Maybe it is not just here," Aimee said softly. She had started to undress. He moved across at once to help her with the lacing down her back.

"Maybe," he conceded gruffly. He remembered how he had been sought out at the palace by the likes of Vawdrey and Orde. Vawdrey had wanted him to hold his baby, for the sake of the gods. You did not let your enemy do that. Was it possible, he pondered, that Vawdrey and Orde were also friends of his? He had the lurking suspicion they might be. Or they could be. If he would just let it happen.

He should just have let a lot of things happen, he realized in a moment of sudden clarity. Instead of stubbornly resisting any changes to his barren, arid life. He had thought Magnatrude an embittered fool for shutting herself up in the lodge house at Bartree, brooding on the past. But had he not been just as trapped himself in snares of his own making?

People wanted to like him. Aimee wanted to love him. Why was he forever swimming against the tide when all he really wanted to do was let it engulf him and carry him along? He was not some static piece of rock, but another living creature, with the same longings and needs and concerns as his fellow men.

"Konrad?" Aimee reached up to clasp his hand which was now lying idle on her shoulder. "Is all well?" She started to turn, but he caught her about the waist and pulled her back against him.

"Aimee," he said tightly and dropped his head to rest it against her black hair. It had too many braids and pins in it, so he started to draw them out.

She was silent a moment, seeming to sense his odd mood, letting him hold her close. "Is something wrong?" she asked quietly.

"I still don't like the way you sing that last verse," he admitted lamely.

His thoughts were whirling too much for him to express himself with anything like coherence. He was astonished by the things Aimee had made him admit that night, even if only to himself.

"Lady Aileen sang it very nicely, I thought."

He grunted, unable to comment on Aileen Howard's performance as he had not paid it any heed. Setting the handful of pins he had removed from her head onto the table, he ran his fingers through the perfumed length of her dark hair, separating the strands.

"Jakeman brought all the furniture back into the tent," she commented, looking about them. "The candle looks like it is about to go out. Let me light another."

"Do not bother," he said. "There is sufficient remaining for us to undress by."

Aimee stepped out of her loosened gown. "Brrr." She shivered, now down to her shift. "Once the sun goes down, you certainly feel a nip in the air."

"Get under the covers," he recommended.

"I will once I have washed my hands." She removed her necklace and set it on the table and then moved to the basin for a quick wash in what must be cold water by now.

"Should I rouse Jakeman to fetch more water?" he asked.

"No," she answered with a quick shake of her head. "I had a good wash before dinner. This will suffice."

She splashed about a bit and then hurried to the bed while he performed his own strip wash and blew out the candle.

When he joined her moments later, they both gravitated toward each other in the darkness, and Aimee gave a contented sigh as he wrapped himself around her.

"How is your body now?" she asked in a muffled voice from his shoulder.

"My body?" He hoped she had not noticed his inevitable reaction to her closeness. He certainly had no intention of making demands of her in the middle of the Howards' meadow.

"Your aches and pains," she elaborated. "From earlier."

He thought about it. "Surprisingly good," he admitted. Usually by this time in the evening his joints and muscles would be protesting. "You did a good job."

"Mayhap I will become indispensable to you given time, husband," she said with a wistful catch in her voice.

His throat closed, and he lay blinking in the dark. How was he supposed to answer such statements? He was not good at making other people feel valued. In fact, he was monstrously bad at it. He lay a moment feeling frustrated with himself. Then he realized something. She gave him opportunities all the damned time. Opportunities he failed to take.

Fuck it. "You already are," he growled and felt gratified when Aimee's arm, which lay around his waist, tightened in a squeeze. She gave another happy-sounding sigh that went straight to his already half-hard cock. Hopefully, she would not realize what was sticking in her hip.

"Konrad?"

"Aimee," he groaned. "We should really get some sleep. I have the joust tomorrow." The trouble was that he was aching in different places now, thanks to her.

403

She lifted her head from his chest. "Of course, if you are tired," she said reassuringly.

He groaned with frustration and then rolled her under him. "If you truly want to know how my body is, I will tell you. It *is* aching, wife, but not in my joints." He ground his hips against hers, letting her feel his hard, aching shaft against the swell of her soft stomach. He wished he had not blown out the bloody candle so he could see her face. Her lovely, beauteous face gazing up at him, with her dark hair spread out behind her. He stared into the darkness but could not make out more than her form.

"Konrad," Aimee breathed, her arms reaching up to clasp him to her. *Thank gods.*

"I'm an unreasonable brute to expect you to do this—to let me rut you in a field," he muttered shakily as he yanked up her shift. "Tell me now if you want me to stop, sweetheart, and I will."

She gasped, though whether it was from his using an endearment or something else entirely he was not sure. He forced himself to halt his progress, resting his hand at her waist. "Aimee?"

"Yes—I mean no. It—it is not unreasonable," she stammered, sounding as though she was striving to catch her breath. She slid her legs restlessly against his, and he had to bite back a groan. "I want you to do that. Here and now in your pavilion."

"You do?" He dipped his head to make sure he had heard her right. "You would tell me if you did not? Aimee?"

"Truly," she urged breathlessly, and her hands slid down his back so firmly, he could not help but buck his hips against hers.

"Yes," she moaned. "I've wanted it since I saw you naked in the tent this afternoon."

Konrad's eyes widened in the dark. He had not been expecting that.

"I wanted to—to touch you here." Her hands slid down over his buttocks and squeezed, drawing a startled grunt from him.

"*Fuck*, Aimee. Why did you not say so?"

She gave a breathless laugh. "Well, I was not sure you would be receptive to such a strange request."

"There's nothing strange about it," he growled, slipping a hand between her legs. He paused to stroke against her nether hair before sliding his fingers through her cleft. Finding her already wet, he grunted again and teased her there, wedging his thigh between hers and toying with her until he could *hear* how wet she was. Gods, he was a lucky bastard. A really lucky bastard.

Aimee whimpered. "*Konrad!*" Her hands roamed over his back again. Her touch felt amazing, and at her touch his body seemed to light up from within, somehow recognizing it as uniquely hers. Maybe he was growing fanciful in the near dark, but no one else had ever touched him with such reverence and obvious pleasure as Aimee. No one else had made him feel as desired as she did. Not even before his face was ruined.

He shifted down the mattress, and Aimee let out a muffled wail of disappointment, her hands landing in his hair. "No, Konrad," she begged in a hoarse whisper. "Not that. I do not want everyone to hear me."

"You think only my tongue can make you scream?" he asked, rubbing his jaw against her soft thigh. Aimee shivered and he could deny himself no longer. "Put your hand over your mouth," he said thickly and lowered his mouth between her plump thighs. It was mere moments before she was squirming and sobbing beneath him.

He did not hold back, sucking and tonguing her tender flesh until she came apart with a muffled shriek that almost undid him on the spot. Instead, he forced himself to pause, breathing raggedly between her trembling thighs as he strove to get himself under control. He concentrated on listening to Aimee's shallow breathing until he could inch back up her body and take full possession of it with his pulsing cock.

To his delight, she looped her arms about his waist as soon as he moved back up, making him welcome. "See?" he teased. "You were nice and quiet."

She gave a breathless laugh that somehow made his chest contract. He wanted to kiss her but was not sure how welcome that would be considering where his mouth had just been. Women could be squeamish about such things. Would Aimee? "Can I kiss you?" he asked gruffly.

The bedclothes rustled, and he realized she was lifting her head to meet his. When their lips met, he felt the tightness in his chest relax, even though his ballocks were starting to throb with increasing urgency. He settled his palms over her plump bosom and lightly squeezed, letting his fingers find her generous nipples, plucking at them lightly through the fabric of her thin shift.

Aimee gave a soft moan into his mouth that made his poor neglected cock jerk. He lifted his mouth from hers to whisper her name and thought he caught a gleam from her eyes even though the interior of the tent was black as pitch. He tugged the neckline of her shift down, exposing her bared breasts to the brisk night air. Again, he regretted the lack of candlelight so he could feast his eyes, but he found her hardening nipples just fine with his hot, sucking mouth.

By the time he had traced the undersides of her breasts with his tongue and rubbed his beard up and down the tender valley betwixt her lovely globes, her legs had parted once more and tightened about his hips with a pleasing urgency.

"Please, my lord," she whimpered, and he would have loved to delay, just to hear her beg a little more so prettily. However, he was already going to spend with an embarrassing haste if he was not careful. Reaching down, he took himself in hand and guided himself where he most wanted to be.

His chest was heaving like he'd run a mile, and as he felt the thick head of his cock engulfed in her tight, wet heat, his eyes rolled back in his head, and he thrust inside her, once, twice, thrice until he was fully sheathed and had let out a yell far louder than he'd intended.

It was he who needed to cover his mouth, he thought dazedly as he slumped over her, striving for breath. *My gods.* "Aimee?" he asked shakily.

She reached up her hands and stroked the sides of his face. More shockingly, he did not feel the need to flinch away. Her thumbs caressed his cheekbones. She must feel the difference between the left and right sides of his face, he thought dimly, but could not bring himself to care.

"I wish I could see your face," she whispered, and for some godsforsaken reason, it made him want to kiss her again. He remained hovering where he was above her a moment, just luxuriating in the *feel* of her. Even her breath on his face gave him gratification, and suddenly he could stand it no longer and had to start moving.

"Aimee," he breathed, and capturing her hands, he bore them to the mattress, pinning them to either side of her head and lacing their fingers together. She arched her back and must have

407

planted her feet on the mattress to propel herself, for she met his thrusts with a vigor that threatened to take his breath away.

"Oh, my lord," she gasped. *"Oh yes."*

Konrad gritted his teeth. It was almost too much. Somehow the darkness made it feel more intense as it seemed to heighten his awareness of how good it was. He was losing himself in her and it felt incredible. For the first time in his life, he did not temper his thrusts or worry that his large body might be overwhelming. His wife had made it clear that she reveled in his strength and power.

"Konrad!" she cried out, and he felt the blood rush in his head, pounding in his ears. "Konrad! Oh, Konrad! *Yes!*"

"Aimee!" he shouted, and fuck, he didn't care if the whole damn field heard them.

27

Konrad woke in the early hours to the sound of light rain drumming against the roof of the pavilion and an unaccustomed feeling coursing through his large body. He lay a moment, blinking in confusion before he got some vague notion what it might be. Contentment, was that it?

Aimee was curled into his side, one arm wrapped around his waist, one curvy leg slung over his as though she were staking her claim on his territory. He had no idea why the notion should make him grin, but it did, damn it. Twice more he had taken her enthusiastically in the night, and he still felt relaxed and mellowed from it.

Shifting onto his side, he turned toward her and brushed the dark hair out of her face. This made her frown and bump her head against his chest. "Mmm. Keep still," she complained. Then she blinked and attempted to sit up with a confused look on her face. He braced a hand against her stomach, preventing her.

"Shhh, it is still early," he murmured. "Go back to sleep."

Obligingly, she settled back against him, but he could tell she had not relaxed into sleep. "Is it raining?" she asked.

"Mmmm," he murmured discouragingly. Then repeated: "Go back to sleep."

There was a moment's silence, then another question. "Will it come through the roof?"

Konrad sighed. "You are not going to go back to sleep, are you?"

"Most likely not," she said, wriggling to get comfortable. "I don't tend to once I have awakened."

He felt her fingers brush caressingly against his side and huffed out a breath. He really should sleep another hour or two. The joust was a demanding event, and he consumed a goodly quantity of wine the day before. Then, too, his sleep had not been undisturbed what with one thing and another. It had been late when they had returned from the hall and then there had been their enthusiastic coupling. It was a good thing their pavilion was a decent distance from anyone else's.

All good reasons to close his eyes again and sleep, he told himself sternly, but then he felt her hand settle against his chest. "Aimee," he warned without opening his eyes. "If you do not go back to sleep, then I will find something else for you to do."

"Such as what?"

"You should have a damned good notion what, after last night."

She was quiet a moment. "I would voice no objection," she admitted, and Konrad gave up on sleep altogether. This time their coupling was lazy and unhurried, and he gazed into her eyes the whole time.

He took care to build up her pleasure slowly, slowly as his own climbed up his spine inch by inch, making his gaze flicker as he bit his lip to keep his strokes unhurried and leisurely, however much the temptation rode him to go faster and deeper and make his possession known.

The steady thrum of rain on the roof, Aimee's hitched breathing, the beat of his own heart, all helped him keep the relaxed pace he wanted, helped him keep in check, until finally Aimee's hands slid from his hips around to his arse. She gripped him there hard. "*Please*, Konrad!" she begged, and just like that, his body surged as though it were hers to command all along. He only had to drive into her hard three times, and they were both there, gasping and groaning and clinging to one another.

He rolled onto his back, taking her with him so she lay half on top of him. He did not want to pull out of her, so he stayed where he was for as long as possible, passing a hand down the length of her dark, tousled hair and wrapping his hand in its length.

"Your mother must have been very beautiful," he heard himself say.

"Yes, apparently so."

"Her people were from the east?"

"Yes. From Samare."

"You have lovely coloring."

"You think so?"

"Yes." He reached for her hand, enfolding it in his. "We tend to be darker in the north than those from southern Karadok, but you are darker still." He ran a hand up and down her lower back caressingly. "I hope our children look like you."

Aimee turned her face to lay her cheek against his shoulder. "And I hope they look like *both* of us."

He smiled. "That is usually the way of things, I believe." They lay silent for a few moments, and then he sighed. He did not really want to go to the blasted joust. He wanted to loll here all day, he thought with faint astonishment. Until this moment, he would have said jousting was his favorite pastime in all the world.

Aimee's hand moved over his chest in swirls like figures of eight. He liked it. Too much. He stared down at her, a vague unease spreading through his limbs. What was he doing here lying on his back and letting her pet him like this when he had a hard slog ahead of him today? A hard slog he was ill prepared for after a night's carousing. He girded his loins, sat up, and cleared his throat. "I need to fetch you some water to clean up."

"What time do you suppose it is?" Aimee asked when he rolled out of bed a moment later. He did not think she sounded as sorry about it as she ought.

"Half five?" he hazarded. "Something like that."

He had a hurried wash in the cold basin and pulled on his clothes. His body protested to this rude treatment after reveling in pleasure. His head might tell him he needed to get ready for the joust, but the rest of him was protesting he should climb back in the bed with his wife.

He forced himself out of the tent. Outside, the rain had stopped, and he saw it had been naught but a quick shower. By the time he returned from the hall with two pails of hot water, the day was bidding to be a fair one. He thought Aimee might have fallen back to sleep as he ducked inside, however, he was wrong. His wife was bright-eyed, sat up, and hugging her knees. She was also chirpy. Extremely chirpy.

Konrad fetched her clothes from the pack and poured the first of the pails of water into the basin for her.

"Were many people up and about at the hall?" she asked cheerfully as she bent over the basin. He grunted and she half turned, lowering her cloth. "Is that a yes or a no?"

"Just kitchen staff," he said, forcing himself to drag his eyes from her pleasing form.

412

She turned back, apparently satisfied by his clipped reply, only to ask moments later, "What time will Jakeman attend us?"

Konrad rubbed his eyes. "About seven."

"So late?"

"Proceedings don't start until nine. What would be the point in his coming any earlier?"

"I suppose that is true," she acknowledged, flinging her hair over one shoulder, and placing the basin on the floor to stand in it now, she had done her upper body.

Konrad cleared his throat and looked away as Aimee completed her wash. To give himself something to do, he fetched his broadsword and the oil rag to give it a quick polish.

"I hope Freda is doing well in Caer-Lyoness without us," Aimee said chattily as she tied a drying cloth about her body.

Freda? She wanted to talk about Freda? He had to think a moment before he could make a reply. "She's a fully grown woman, Aimee," he pointed out direly. "I am sure she will be fine."

"Yes, but in a strange part of the country to her," she said with a frown in her voice. "Did you know her only real friends up until now were household cats? She's so sweet. How old is she, by the way?"

He thought for a minute, lowering his oil rag. "She must number somewhere between forty and fifty," he answered at last.

"I have grown so fond of her," Aimee sighed. "Freda loved how the brooch turned out, you know. She could not have been happier even if it had still belonged to her. She said she thought it had sapphires originally, but they were lost."

413

He snorted. "My uncle likely sold them," he said, setting down his sword as Aimee walked toward the bed. "Freda has always shrunk from hard truths."

Picking up the basin of water, he walked out of the pavilion and emptied it before returning to fill it with the second pail of hot water.

"She's unfailingly kind," Aimee pointed out. She had fetched a comb now and was drawing it through her hair.

He grunted dismissively. He did not want to talk about Freda. He needed to get ready for the day ahead.

"Did she suffer ill health in her youth?" Aimee persisted.

"What?" He looked up from unfastening his tunic.

"It occurred to me that might be why Freda never married," she explained patiently.

"Not that I remember."

"Hmmm." She sounded thoughtful, and it crossed his mind as he stripped down to his braies that here was an opening for him to mention his suspicions that Ankatel had an interest in his cousin as a matrimonial prospect. Then he reminded himself he did not wish to dwell on such subjects. He had better things to be concentrating on right now, such as readying himself for the joust. Resolutely, he set about his ablutions.

"Do you think that Magnatrude will be happy as one of the Queen's ladies?" Aimee asked, lowering her comb.

"So she says," he answered in clipped tones, rubbing soap flakes between his fingers.

"But do you think she will?" she asked insistently.

"If she is," he snorted, "it will be for the first time in her life."

"She has always been dissatisfied with her lot?" she asked curiously. "Never happy? Not even"—she hesitated as though unsure whether it was her place to ask—"when she was betrothed?"

"Not even then," he confirmed. "My sister was contrary and difficult prior to the war. What has happened since was not likely to sweeten her. She even admitted the other day that the marriage would have been an unhappy one."

"Then mayhap this appointment to the Queen's retinue will truly be her vocation," Aimee mused, shaking out a gown of amber satin.

That caught his eye. "What is that?" he asked pointedly.

Aimee looked startled. "My gown, you mean?"

"That is not the gown you are wearing this day."

Aimee's face reddened. "Konrad…"

"You are wearing my colors for the joust, remember?"

She looked instantly guilt-ridden. "I no longer own a gown in your colors," she admitted.

"I told you to get another one made up," he reminded her tersely.

"There was insufficient time for that, husband—" she said, dropping her gaze from his, and he felt a sudden stab of suspicion.

"You did not commission one to be made, did you?" he asked flatly.

Her face flamed. "No," she confessed, staring down at the hands which clutched her gown. "In truth, I cannot imagine myself wearing a heraldic gown like that again by choice. Not since..." Her words trailed off.

"Since what?" he demanded harshly, narrowing his eyes at her. "Since the royal festival? Since I let you down?"

Aimee gasped, then drew in a steadying breath. "Someone tried to warn me that I would look too conspicuous in that gown," she started in a conciliatory tone. "And that I would appear vulgar in it," she said, two spots of color appearing in her cheeks. "But I did not listen."

"Magnatrude, you mean?" he asked angrily. "I will have words with her on our return."

Aimee's face fell. "No, no," she said urgently. "It was not *your* sister. It was mine."

"Yours?" He thought of gentle-eyed Ursula Ankatel and snorted derisively. "Do not lie to me, Aimee."

"I'm not lying!" she flared up. "Except she didn't flat out say it like that," she amended consciously. "But rather softened the blow." At his open skepticism, she lifted her chin. "She explained that a noblewoman may wear something with impunity, where a merchant's daughter may not."

"What the hells do you mean by that?"

"I would have thought it was obvious. I was not born to this role, Konrad. I will no doubt make many missteps along the way, and parading around in your colors like that, so ostentatiously, was a pretty hefty one."

"What was ostentatious about it?" he bit out crossly.

"I went completely overboard with flaunting your crest in the early days of our marriage," she answered with a gulp. "I—you must have seen how I embroidered it on every bare patch of cloth in my trousseau, Konrad! You were kind enough not to mention it, but you must have thought me quite ridiculous!"

He remembered the portcullises all over his bedclothes. "I did not think it ridiculous." He might as well have held his tongue for all the attention she paid him.

"Since then," she continued steadily, "I have observed that ladies of rank rather bear themselves with a quiet assurance than plastering their credentials all over themselves—"

"What ladies of rank? What are you talking about?" he interrupted irritably.

"Princess Una, for one," she answered before correcting herself. "I mean, the Lady de Bussell. She certainly wasn't swathed in pearls and sapphires like me, and she doesn't need them. Her natural dignity is such that no one could mistake her for anything but highly born."

"Bullshit," Konrad interrupted her rudely. "When she was a princess, she was so decked in ceremonial garb she was barely recognizable. She avoids it now because she's likely sick of pomp."

Aimee's expression wavered. "Well, but—"

"How do you think my ancestors seized power?" he demanded. "I'll give you a hint, Aimee, it wasn't through good manners. They simply took it because they were in a position of strength, and none could stand against them. I am damned sure the first Kentigern covered his wife in jewels and vastly enjoyed the spectacle."

"I am sure you speak true, Konrad," she replied after a moment's stunned silence. "But I simply meant that ladies who have been born and raised to the role will not be judged harshly when they—"

"If anyone thinks you vulgar, it is out of jealousy or spite, nothing more."

Aimee stiffened. "My sister has only ever sought to advise me for my own good, *never* to wound me."

He lowered his washing cloth. "Are you saying Ursula called you vulgar?"

"Of course not!" she replied, looking incensed. "She only meant to caution me against appearing foolish and gauche in public!"

He paused a moment, selecting his words with more care. "Your sister lacks your spirit, Aimee, but given time and Renlow's encouragement, she will hopefully grow more spine. It seemed to me the other day that she was already well on her way."

Aimee gasped. "What do you mean? The other day?"

Damn it. He gazed back at her stony-faced, realizing his error at once.

"Have you seen my sister? Since our marriage, I mean?" she persisted hotly. It seemed Aimee could read his expression, for she immediately burst out accusingly, "You have! And you did not tell me!"

He huffed out a breath and looked away. "I know you are used to getting your own way, Aimee, but you don't always get to dictate how things are going to be anymore. Not as my wife. Your sister needed some time to find her feet and that is all

418

there is to it. You are no longer her first concern, and you don't get to tell her how to live her life anymore."

Aimee sucked in a shocked breath. "What? When have I ever…?" Words seemed to fail her.

"Picked out your sister's husband, did you not? As well as your own. Decided she was going to get married the same day as you as well as everything else."

Aimee's eyes widened so far it was lucky her eyeballs didn't fall out. "Ursula admired Sir Renlow excessively—!" she spluttered, but he cut her off again.

"Maybe so, but we both know that's all it would have remained as, if not for your intercession. Admiration. From afar. Nothing more."

Aimee's chest heaved. "Ursula does not have the forthright temperament necessary—"

"Small wonder," he interrupted, folding his arms across his chest. "With you in the same house, running rings around her. It wasn't from Hilda's shadow she needed to escape from, it was yours."

Aimee reeled back almost as if he had struck her. The backs of her knees hit a wooden chair, and she fell onto the seat almost sprawling before she corrected herself, sitting up straight. "So!" she said hollowly. "*This* is what you think of me, then!"

He eyed her a moment, measuring. "Aye. You're a damned managing woman. It's small wonder your father never remarried. I doubt you ever let him."

Aimee shot out of the seat. "How *dare* you! I would never try to impede my father's happiness—"

"That's good, as I think he's steeling himself to take the plunge again."

A struggle waged across Aimee's face. "Say what you will, I *cannot* believe that the Widow Hemmings will make him happy!" she burst out hotly.

"Good gods, no," he agreed. "I shouldn't think she would make any man happy."

Aimee deflated. "Oh. Then…then who did you mean?"

He waved this aside. "It is not your concern anymore, wife. You have other things to occupy you."

"He is still my father!"

"If I did not know any better, I would almost think you had conspired with the Queen to get Magnatrude out from under my roof," he mused.

Aimee glared at him speechlessly. "You must think me bossy indeed if you think that I can bend a *queen* to my bidding!" she said bitterly. "But as a matter of fact, that had nothing whatsoever to do with me!"

"No," he agreed fairly. "You just knew you did not want it to be you or Freda that had to do it."

Aimee stewed on this a moment. "Trude is much better suited to the role than either of us would have been," she pointed out with wounded dignity.

"Agreed. Just as you are much better suited to *your* new role. Even more so when I give you a few children, I daresay, to keep you occupied. And now, if you don't mind, I have a day's competition ahead of me. We cannot have this discussion now. I need quiet to focus. If that is too much to ask from you, then I will go and ready myself in the attendants' tent."

420

Several emotions warred on Aimee's face before she swallowed, nodded, and swung around, presenting her back to him. Well, he supposed he had asked for that. She certainly would not be ogling his naked body this morn.

Konrad finished his ablutions and dressed in silence. By the time Jakeman arrived, the atmosphere in their pavilion had grown sadly oppressive. Konrad flung off to the competitors' area, skulking around the less populated areas while he tried to get in the right frame of mind to compete.

If he had felt a good deal too mellow and benign when he had first awoken, he now felt twitchy and annoyed. In truth, his current mood was closer to his habitual one but for the niggling guilt gnawing at him for being ungracious with his wife. Had he gone too far in defending himself? He had not meant to wound her, just give her something to think about.

He did not usually have to deal with guilt, as he lacked the compunction. He was a tactless bastard at the best of times, and he knew he had not handled things well that morning. Well, all had been fine until the moment he had climbed out of bed. Maybe he should just have stayed in it, he thought irritably. All had been well until that point.

He should have told his wife previously about that visit he had paid to Renlow in town, he acknowledged, picking up a lance and testing its weight, but he had not done so. Mostly because he knew he would have to go into minute detail to please Aimee, and he had not wanted her to dwell so much on her sister and brother-in-law on this trip. He frowned. He had wanted her to dwell on more important things. Namely him. If that was selfish, so be it.

Jakeman arrived some while later to help him into his armor, and it was as much as he could do not to demand his wife's whereabouts. He knew full well Aimee was being collected by

Lowell, who was escorting her to the stands. It had been arranged the previous evening within his hearing. He scowled and Jakeman, glancing up, asked if he had fastened the straps of his greaves too tightly.

He waved away the question irritably. Maybe he should stash his wife at Bartree, away from all the unwelcome distractions she surrounded herself with. He considered the matter as the rest of his armor was assembled. It was hard to imagine Aimee at his family home, for he had not seen her in such a setting.

He conjured from memory a few of the old familiar faces. Ernald, his father's aged steward, old Clothilde, the alewife. Before he even knew it, the certainty crept into his thoughts that Aimee would soon hold them all in the palm of her hand. It would not even be a sennight before she had learned all the names of their children and grandchildren, knew all about their hopes for the future, and supported them in their endeavors.

Wherever he took her, the blessed woman would be worming her way into the affection of others. He snorted, and it was only after Jakeman announced that his horse had been brought around that he realized he had not even troubled to enquire whose name he had drawn for the first tilt, let alone marshalled his thoughts around his strategy for the day.

What in the name of the gods had he even spent the past hour dwelling on?

*

He might have known from the outset that the day would be an unmitigated disaster. The morning passed uneventfully enough. He won all three of his jousts and avoided the majority of his fellow competitors in between. This was not difficult as Symes lost his second tilt and went to join Lowell and Aimee in the crowd. As for Farleigh, he was in a different grouping to

422

Konrad, so their paths did not cross, and he did not catch so much as a glimpse of him all morning.

Still, he could not shake the ill mood that had descended on him. He had spotted Aimee in the crowd from the first and told himself it did not matter that she looked wholly unaffected by their spat that morning. If his eye strayed to that same spot several times throughout the day, he maintained it was mere chance. The last time he looked at her, she seemed to be pointing someone out to her companions. Someone who was not him.

Not that it bothered him.

By the afternoon, the competition had been whittled down to the final forty. By three o'clock, there were only twenty knights remaining. Unsurprisingly, de Bussell and de Crecy were among their number, as was Farleigh. In quick succession, Konrad beat his opponent, de Bussell knocked out Farleigh, and de Crecy advanced with seemingly little effort to the final six.

Jakeman offered him the choice of two lances, and as Konrad deliberated, he said in a low voice, "Your next opponent will be de Bussell, my lord."

Konrad looked up with a flicker of interest. "Indeed?"

"Aye, my lord."

He glanced across to where he had last seen de Bussell lolling against a tree and met his gaze squarely. Sir Armand grinned and raised a hand in salutation. He was having another of his good days. Konrad regarded him thoughtfully a moment before returning the gesture. It was funny to think how vastly your opinion could change of someone in a mere few days.

If de Bussell had performed at Areley Kings the same way as he had here, word would surely soon spread that the curse of his

423

inconsistent performance had been broken. He had only to crown this winning streak with a win at a royal tournament for his fame to spread far and wide.

Konrad set his chin grimly. If he were not to win, he would have vastly favored de Bussell over Jeffree de Crecy. That bastard had said he would crown Aimee tourney queen if he won, just for spite. He scowled and ignored the uncomfortable sting of his conscience which reminded him he had been the one to initiate that particular insult. It had been different back then. At least… No, it had been wrong back then too.

He recalled Aimee's reaction with a grimace. Although that had not been his first transgression as a husband—for he had surely fallen from grace on their very wedding day when he had abandoned her to dispense wedding favors all by herself—it had, though, been the final insult that prompted her to actually withdraw her avowal of love for him.

What if he were to crown her here this afternoon? he wondered. Would that earn her love back? He rubbed his breastplate distractedly with an armored gauntlet, causing a clash of metal. Could such a wrong be so easily righted? Besides, she was barely speaking to him by this point, he thought wretchedly. It would probably serve him right if she dashed the garland to the ground and trampled all over it. Just like she had his heart.

The spear slipped from his nerveless fingers and crashed to the floor.

"My lord?" said Jakeman, hurrying forward to help him retrieve it.

"Hmmm?" Konrad turned to look at the concerned face of his manservant.

"Is all well, my lord?"

"No," replied Konrad heavily. "No, it is not. Are you married, Jakeman?"

"Widower, my lord."

"You are?"

"Yes, my lord."

"You never mentioned it before."

"No, my lord." His discreet servant hesitated. "You see, you never asked."

"No, I suppose I did not." Konrad sighed heavily. He supposed he should try to get his head focused back on the tournament. "Anything else I should know?"

Jakeman's expression flickered. "Er…I'm a father of three, my lord, if that's any interest to you."

"Three?" Konrad was startled. "Good gods, are you really?"

"Aye, my lord."

"Sons?" he asked, curious in spite of himself. "Or daughters?"

"Three sons, my lord."

"Three! Where do you stash them all?"

A smile flickered across Jakeman's face. He coughed. "Your lordship pays me well enough I am able to pay a woman to care for them."

Konrad was just thinking his manservant must find the townhouse a handy location for visiting his offspring when an attendant came panting toward them.

"My lord Kentigern!" he cried. "You are up next!"

*

Konrad was perhaps the only one not surprised when he went crashing out of his saddle and ended up in a heap on the ground mere moments later in the third pass. He lay winded for a moment before raising a hand to flip up his visor and gaze up at the blue sky above. That was that, then. He was out of the running. All he could hope for now was that he had lost to the eventual victor.

He heard Jakeman's low voice in his ear a moment before he registered the mixed reaction of the crowd. "They're sorry to see you lose, my lord," his manservant said, helping him to roll onto his side and then a sitting position. "For all de Bussell's so popular."

Konrad groaned and tore ineffectually at his dented chest plate. Jakeman took the hint and unbuckled the twisted plate. De Bussell had struck him a mighty blow, dead center. "He will be more popular still before the year is out," Konrad predicted in a growl. "Damn him." His words lacked heat, however, and when moments later de Bussell appeared in front of him with his lazy smile, he congratulated him without rancor.

"That's twice you've defeated me in as many days, de Bussell," he grouched. "Next time I see you, I will knock you flat on your arse."

Sir Armand laughed his easy laugh. "I don't doubt it, Kentigern," he answered good-naturedly. "It won't be the first time you have done so."

"Aye, well… just make sure you send de Crecy home with a broken head," he growled by way of reply, and they clasped wrists.

It seemed, however, that nothing was to go Konrad's way that day. He retreated to the sidelines to watch the final joust, only allowing himself the barest glance in Aimee's direction. So far from being devastated by his loss, she appeared to be absorbed in eating a pastry. He smarted, discarding the last vestiges of his armor into a pile at his feet.

Jakeman would return for it presently when he had seen to rubbing down Actaeon. For now, Konrad focused his attention on the field. De Bussell had been given a scant quarter of an hour to recover before the final joust. By rights, it ought to have been longer, but these rural tournaments were not so well regulated as the larger ones. Timings could be, and frequently were, arbitrary.

So it proved this time for Sir Armand. Perhaps the two glancing blows Konrad had managed to deal him contributed to his subsequent defeat at Sir Jeffree's hands, but none could say for sure. All that could be said with certainty was that Sir Jeffree emerged the winner of the joust that year at Beres Caple.

Konrad watched grimly as Lady Howard held up the flowered crown for de Crecy's lance. He hooked it on the end and then directed his white horse toward the lady he intended to honor. Konrad steeled himself for the indignity, but to his astonishment de Crecy did not make for Aimee at all. Instead, he halted before his own wife, Sabina de Crecy, and held the lance steady before her.

She froze a moment in seeming indecision before accepting the tribute and placing it on her own head. For the second tournament in a row, Lady de Crecy was crowned Queen of the Tournament. It seemed to Konrad that she and de Crecy could barely look each other full in the face. Interesting.

His own gaze traveled to his wife, who was clapping politely along with the rest of the crowd. Of course, Aimee had never been aware that de Crecy had vowed to award her the crown in retaliation. She angled her head to say something to Lowell, who nodded in agreement, and Konrad felt his shoulders slowly relax. He winced at the concurrent sensation of pain that shot through his chest. He was going to be badly bruised on the morrow.

He glanced up at the sky. In fact, he thought maybe it would be as well to set off now. It was three o'clock or thereabouts. A five-hour ride back to Caer-Lyoness meant they could be back in their own beds by a little after nine o'clock that evening. Their bed, he amended conscientiously, for he meant to put an end to this separate bedchamber foolishness once and for all.

The notion was a tempting one. He glanced about for Jakeman and saw his trusty manservant weaving his way through the crowd toward him. He raised a hand and hailed him. "Pack up our things, Jakeman. We're heading home."

28

Aimee saw the familiar city walls of Caer-Lyoness looming in the distance and breathed a sigh of relief. She could not wait to get out of the saddle, even though she had been lifted onto the docile Ivy's back from the first, and Jakeman had taken the more spirited Deirdre.

When she had ventured to question this switching of horses, her husband had directed an ironic look her way. "You want to be jolted about by the white mare for five hours, then say so now."

Of course, Deirdre had chosen that moment to aim a vicious kick at a stable hand imprudent enough to pass close by her flanks. He only narrowly avoided injury, and Aimee had hastily assured Jakeman that he could ride her pretty white horse back to the capital with her blessing.

She patted Ivy's neck and admitted to herself that she vastly preferred the quiet brown mare to her own. Maybe Jakeman would do a permanent swap of steeds with her. After all, her father need never know. She directed a surreptitious glance in her husband's direction. He had been quiet on the ride home.

Likely, he was simply tired, she told herself, after the exertions of the day. It had been a disappointing day for him, she reminded herself, for he did not like to lose, however gracious she believed he appeared in defeat. Just because she thought he looked his best in such moments did not mean he enjoyed them.

She sighed to herself, knowing she was still in disgrace with him about the gown. For her part, she still bore a grudge that he had not told her of his visit to her sister's house. Maybe after all, this was what married life was like? A never-ending stream of grievances and injured feelings!

As it was the height of summer, darkness was only just starting to fall as they had reached Lime Street. Being lifted down from the saddle, Aimee was profoundly grateful to feel the cobbled streets of her hometown beneath her feet again. Jakeman took charge of the horses, and Konrad ushered her up the steps to the large black and white timbered dwelling she had not realized she had grown so fond of.

They were met in the corridor by a startled-looking Matthews hurrying toward them. "My lord!" he exclaimed. "My lady! We were not expecting your return until the morrow."

"What of it?" Konrad snapped testily.

"We returned early," Aimee hastily interjected in what she hoped was a soothing manner, noticing Matthews glance back down the corridor. "Is something amiss?"

Matthews looked embarrassed. "No, no, milady, of course not!" he hurried to assure her. "'Tis only that Mistress Freda is entertaining in the dining chamber, and we have not set places for you at table."

Aimee and Konrad exchanged glances. "Please do not interrupt Mistress Freda and her guests," she said, lowering her voice at once. "I, er…I do not currently feel up to partaking of company after our arduous journey." She turned to Konrad. "Perhaps you, my lord—?"

"No," he replied firmly. "No, I need to rid myself of all my travel dirt and dust before I am fit to be seen. Besides, I am currently disinclined for the society of others."

Aimee bit her lip. She knew the guests were likely her father and sister, but she felt unequal to facing them right now. "Would it be unpardonably rude of us to just sneak up to our rooms to wash and retire for the evening?" she asked her husband frankly, her gaze darting longingly toward the staircase.

"No, I think it would be damned sensible," Konrad responded at once. "It is not as though they will be offended or disappointed. They are not even expecting us." He nodded to Matthews. "Have hot water sent up immediately but try to keep our arrival quiet if you can," he specified. "Have it brought to Lady Kentigern's chamber."

Matthews nodded. "Of course, milord."

"I was going to request a bath," Aimee protested.

"Her ladyship can be brought a bath," Konrad directed at Matthews. "But in an hour's time. Actually…" He considered a moment. "Make it two hours."

Matthews gave a bow. "Certainly, milord."

Aimee frowned at this, but as her main desire was to escape to the quiet and solicitude of her own room, she did not concern herself overmuch and instead made for the stairs, divesting herself of her cloak and laying it over a convenient chair as she went.

Konrad was close behind her, so close that she almost shut her bedchamber door in his face. "Oh!" she exclaimed as he followed her inside. "Your pardon, I did not realize you meant to accompany me…" She regarded him with bewilderment as he shut the door resolutely behind them and leaned his back against it, his eyes on hers. "You said you did not feel up to company just now."

"You are not company," he said, pushing away from the door and reaching for the laces at his throat. "You are my wife."

431

"Well," Aimee responded, feeling nettled. "You certainly could not get away from me fast enough this morning!"

"Not true," he contradicted her flatly.

"It certainly seemed that way!"

"I was in a bad mood," he said, pulling his tunic over his head. "Because I did not want to climb out of bed with you. The feeling was an unaccustomed one, living as I always have for the battlefield. I was not quite sure how to deal with it. But now I know." While Aimee reeled from this revelation, he flung his tunic on the floor and started unlacing his chausses.

"Why are you undressing in my room?" Aimee asked with a sudden frown.

"This is no longer your room," he answered coolly, glancing around it like he had never really seen it before. "It is our dressing room."

"D-dressing room?" Aimee stammered in confusion. She found she, too, was looking about the room like a simpleton. She had better snap out of this. "Then where, pray, is my bedchamber to be?" she asked in an attempt to rally.

"You no longer require one," he stated calmly. "As you, Aimee Bartree, belong with me in mine."

She stared at him a moment, unable to draw breath. "Well, but Lady Wycliffe said that married nobles do not share bedchambers," she managed to croak at last.

"I care little for what the Wycliffes think. Or anyone, for that matter. No," he acknowledged with a sudden frown. "That is not true. I care what *you* think." His gaze softened. "I need to start saying these things out loud," he muttered, and Aimee was not sure if he was speaking to her or himself.

The knock on the door startled them both, and Konrad moved away from it as Matthews entered carrying two large pails of steaming water.

"Here you are, milord," he said jovially as he carried them across the room with his heavy tread. He set them down on the floor and turned back around. "Is this enough for now or…?"

"Quite sufficient, thank you, Matthews," Aimee answered. After all, she was to have a bath in two hours' time. Though, why two hours she could not fathom! As soon as the door closed after the retreating Matthews, Aimee started loosening her cuff. Konrad moved toward her and helped her remove her pearls, the love heart brooch, her gold hairnet, and finally her gown, so she stood in just her shift and stockings before the basin.

She sighed as she pressed a hot cloth to her face.

"Sore?" came Konrad's voice behind her.

"A little," she admitted cautiously. "It has been a long day." She turned her head to look over her shoulder as he moved about the room. What was he doing? To her surprise, he seemed to be collecting up an armful of things from the table where she kept her trinkets. As she watched, he gave a shrug and then carried them out of the room, disappearing up the passage.

Was he moving her possessions into his bedchamber? When he returned, she watched him surreptitiously in the looking glass. He stood before the bridal chest decorated with the wedding procession, his hands on his hips, a thoughtful look in his eye.

"What do you keep in here?" he asked, meeting her eye in the glass.

Aimee shrugged. "A medley of things. Take a look, if it pleases you."

It was only when he lifted the lid that Aimee remembered she had thrown the two bags of cheap tokens in there after buying them at the market. The breath caught in her throat, her eyes widening with horror. Pray the gods she had resecured the ties on the opened bag!

As he lifted his scorching eye to hers, Aimee knew she had not. In fact, her last memory of them was haphazardly flinging them in there as she hurried off to place the tin hedgehog on his pillow bearer. Some of them had definitely spilled out. *Curses.*

He cleared his throat. "You owe me some more of these, by my reckoning, wife," he said in a gravelly voice.

Aimee's color mounted. "I suppose I do," she agreed in strangled tones.

Before Aimee's astonished gaze, he stooped suddenly down and picked up the whole chest, bearing it out of the room as though it weighed no more than a cushion.

Aimee stood frozen, immobile before the basin for a full moment before giving herself a slight shake and dunking her cloth back into the water. He was acting oddly to be sure, but regardless, she needed to get clean.

She was still flustered but had completed her wash by the time he returned. Emptying the basin out of the window, she refilled it for him with clean water as he stripped down efficiently to his waist. Then she retreated to her cabinet wondering what to dress her damp, shivering body in while she waited for her bath.

After a moment's deliberation, Aimee selected a peach-colored robe decorated with gold thread which she had not even worn before. Her shift was so damp after her wash that she dispensed with it altogether and drew the silk robe on without an undergarment. The fabric felt so soft and decadent against her

434

skin that Aimee wondered why she had never tried it before. Of course, it would not do outside of one's own bedchamber, but all the same. Inside it, one *could* indulge oneself in privacy.

Turning around, Aimee met Konrad's eyes once more in the mirror. His seeing eye blazed so bright, Aimee was forced to lower her own. Of course, if they were to share a bedchamber from now on, she thought breathlessly, then any indulgences would be shared. Her husband unlaced his crotch and peeled down his chausses.

Aimee coughed and forced her eyes away, busying herself by first selecting a pair of embroidered slippers and then by picking up a comb and tidying her hair. For some reason, speech was beyond her right now, though her tiredness seemed to have slipped away like a mantle from her shoulders.

"Are you finished?" he asked, turning from the basin and starting toward her. Before she had even made her reply, he was scooping her up and bearing her along the corridor to his bedchamber. *Their* bedchamber, she reminded herself as the door closed behind them. He had lit candles already, and she noted he had placed the second wedding chest at the foot of the bed.

"The chest looks well there," she commented with surprise, her eye traveling to the one by the window.

"I want to show you something," he said gruffly, and instead of laying her on the bed as she had half expected, he carried her to the wall cabinet, setting her on her feet there and opening the door.

"That's my trunk," he said, nodding to a battered-looking, studded wooden chest lying on the bottom shelf.

Aimee gazed at it. It was a tatty old thing. "Did you want me to transfer your things into the painted chest?" she asked after a moment of silence.

He shook his head. "This was my grandfather's. It's where I keep things that are precious to me."

"Oh," she murmured. "I see." Though, of course, she saw no such thing.

He held his hand out to her, and she saw the key lying on his palm. "Open it."

Aimee blinked but took it all the same and, kneeling down, set the key in the lock and turned it. It was stiff and took some force. "This is starting to rust from disuse, Konrad."

"I know," he said softly. "I barely use it. Very little is precious to me, Aimee."

For some reason, his words seemed poignant. She peered inside the dark trunk, and for a moment, though, there was nothing in it apart from some old rags.

"You can take it out," he offered, and Aimee reached inside with a puzzled frown to lift out the bundle of rags. As it emerged from the dark interior of the chest, she recognized it was the blue and yellow gown she had ripped into shreds. She almost dropped it.

"So, this is where it went," she whispered. "I looked everywhere."

"I kept it."

"I think it is beyond repair, Konrad," she said weakly.

"Is it?"

For some reason, his question made her look up sharply. "'Tis cut to ribbons," she pointed out.

"I know."

She clutched the maligned dress to her chest, unsure what to do with it. "This is not what I expected," she confessed. "I thought...well, maybe some old jewels or something," she finished lamely.

"Those are all being reset for you." He shrugged. "You should have them in a month or so." Aimee started to turn toward him. "That's not the only thing in there." He forestalled her, and she turned back and peered inside. Seeing nothing else, she reached inside to grope in the corners until she found another scrap of cloth. As she picked it up, something small and hard fell to the bottom of the trunk with a clatter.

Aimee lifted out both objects. One was her dreadful needlework depiction of his horse, Actaeon, and the other was the tin hedgehog. Aimee stared from one to the other in stupefaction. "Of all the things I have bestowed on you, these seem an odd selection," she confessed in a wobbly voice. "Though it's good you like hedgehog, for there are plenty more where that came from," she joked. "Ninety-nine of them, in fact."

"I don't want you to give me any more tokens, Aimee. I want something else now."

She refused to ask what. She was too scared to. "What am I supposed to do with the rest of them?" she asked instead flippantly. "You realize they are so inexpensive, that a mere penny buys a dozen of the things." *That's right, Aimee, let him know they were simply cheap, empty nothings. Don't let him think you have been foolishly pining over him like a lovestruck little idiot. Don't let him think you were placing them on his pillow in the hope of winning his heart.*

437

It was only then she realized he had made no response. She ventured a quick glance up at his face, but it was as stern and impassive as ever. For the veriest instant, she had been afraid she might have hurt his feelings. *Foolish Aimee.* As if she had the power to affect Lord Kentigern in any way. "It's of no matter," she said lightly. "I can just give them to someone else."

"Oh no, you won't." The answer came quickly, and it was in a low, angry growl. He crossed to the bed, sitting on the edge. "Go and fetch me the rest. Now." He gestured toward the wedding chest.

Aimee stared at him. "But you just said you do not want any more of them!"

"Every last one you have bought already belongs to me," he answered in a steely voice. "Go and fetch them here."

Aimee's face grew heated. Silently, she cursed the impulse that had prompted her to buy a bulk lot of them last time she had visited the market. They were so much cheaper that way, and Aimee had always loved a bargain. She hesitated, trying to think of an argument.

"Now, Aimee," his voice thundered.

Reluctantly, she dragged herself to her feet and made for the lacquered chest. Lifting the lid, she retrieved the first pouch of tokens, picking up the four or five that had spilled out and shoving them back into the bag. Her cheeks aflame, she turned and stalked over to the bed with them.

"Here," she said, thrusting the bag toward him.

He reached behind him, patting the pillow bearer. "Do it right," he growled, and Aimee stared at him indignantly.

"You want me to—?"

"You know what I want," he insisted.

With a smothered exclamation of annoyance, Aimee held the bag over the bed next to him and upended it. The silly, flashy little tin medallions spilled out onto the coverlet, as humiliating as an unsolicited confession of love.

Her husband's gaze was riveted to the fall of shiny discs. The last one that fell was stamped crudely with the image of a heart. *As if things could not get any more embarrassing.*

"There," she said, a betraying wobble in her voice.

Wordlessly, he reached down and spread the tokens with the flat of his hand, his gaze roaming over them as though they were runes to be read. Aimee looked at the silly jumble of animal shapes and love symbols and inwardly quaked. Slowly, he dragged his gaze up to look at her. "Is that all of them?" he countered.

She thought of the second unopened bag and tried to brazen it out. "Just how many do you think I purchased?" she answered with a shrug but could not hold his gaze. She saw the flare of realization in his eye and felt her heart thud.

"All of them belong to me, Aimee," he repeated slowly. "Go and fetch them to me now."

Aimee huffed out a frustrated breath. "I hope you realize it was the principle of thrift alone that prompted me to buy so many!" she flung over her shoulder as she returned to the wedding chest and seized the second pouch. She marched them back to him. Her cheeks were scalded with humiliation.

"Here!" she said, holding out the bag. He patted the bed, and Aimee ground her teeth as her fingers fumbled with the strings to open it.

"Is that the last of them?" he asked in a low voice.

"Yes, of course! I only bought a hundred." Her words were ridiculous. *Only a hundred*. She was such an idiot.

Biting her lip, Aimee opened the bag and tipped the contents practically into Lord Kentigern's lap. It was only at that point that she realized how aroused he was. The drying cloth did very little to conceal the fact his manhood was curved straight up from his thighs, full and angry looking. It jerked as the metal disks fell about his lap, and he shivered slightly.

The bag slipped through Aimee's nerveless fingers and fell at her feet. "That's all of them," she uttered.

"You're sure of that?" His voice was so low and gravelly that she had to think a moment to translate his words.

She nodded. "Isn't it enough?" she pushed, feeling mortified, feeling reckless. "I bet you wish they were gold coins," she observed, lifting her chin. "You'd have a king's ransom."

He barely seemed to register her words, and when he reached for her, dragging her down to him, she went with a faint cry. She was half disappointed when he did not roll her under him or bear her down to the mattress at once.

Instead, he held her gripped firmly in his lap, one hand clasped viselike to her hip, the other wrapped in her hair, dragging her face to his.

"Aimee," he breathed deeply. "Ask me what I want."

She swallowed. "I already know what you want, Konrad. You want me to stop being so damned managing. And…and you want me to stop trying to force your hand to make you love me." Her voice broke over the last few words, and she tried to look away, but his hand tightened in her hair preventing it.

440

"No," he corrected her. "That's not it at all." He breathed deeply, as though gathering his thoughts. "It is strange, wife, that you are so bad at guessing this time when you always anticipated my needs so well previously."

That caught her attention. "What needs?"

"Number one, my need for a wife," he answered promptly. "You saw that long before I did."

Aimee regarded him doubtfully. "Konrad…"

"Number two, my need for companionship," he continued calmly. "Yours most of all, and to a lesser degree, that of others." He shrugged. "Family, friends…"

Aimee caught her breath. "You do?"

"Apparently so."

"Oh."

"Number three, my need for your love," he stated in so matter-of-fact a tone that she would very likely have fallen off his lap if his grip on her had not been so tight. A shadow passed over his face. "Sadly, I did not realize how badly I needed that until you withdrew it from me." He glanced away as Aimee stared.

"I was…like that battered old chest of my grandfather's," he said grimly. "The keyhole was so rusted up I didn't think anyone would ever get in." He was silent a moment, and she did not dare speak. "I thought I was a damned lost cause, Aimee, before you came along. I know I have no right to ask this, wife, but I want you to love me again."

"What?" she gasped, almost unable to believe her ears.

"I know 'tis my own fault you do not," he admitted, his voice thick with emotion. "After what I did at the Summer

Tournament, giving that crown to another. I know now that was unforgiveable, and the gods know I have plenty of faults besides that."

He swallowed as his voice grew choked. "But I want you to try and overlook them all. Will you, Aimee?" There was so much longing in his tone that she could only stare and try to catch her breath. "Then I would scarcely care about anything else. Even if I never again lift another trophy."

"But you did win something, Konrad," she managed to tell him through sudden tears. "You won the trophy for the most liked knight. And you won something else," she said in a choked voice. "You won my poor heart all over again."

"Aimee!" His voice was hoarse. "Say that again, sweetheart."

"You made me fall in love with you all over again." Tears were coming thick and fast now, trickling down her cheeks. His grasp on her tightened, but she did not even flinch. "In vain, I tried to guard my heart against you, but it did not work," she sobbed. "If you asked it of me, I would even wear a heraldic gown again. In your colors. To every tournament, if you desired it."

"I do desire it," he growled. "The gods help me, I should never dare make such a request after the way I behaved, but I do desire it."

"Then I will wear it," she laughed tearily. "Though I will need a new one, for that other is not fit to be seen... Mmmf!" Her words were cut off as he crushed his mouth to hers, and for a long moment, Aimee gave herself up to the sensation of being consumed by Lord Kentigern's kiss.

Her heart seemed almost to stutter to a halt in her chest before pounding into life again. She clung onto his massive shoulders

442

for dear life and scarcely noticed when he turned them both and bore her down to the mattress.

"Ah gods," he groaned raggedly against her mouth moments later. "I don't deserve you, Aimee Bartree."

"Ouch!" she cried, and he froze. Reaching behind her, Aimee plucked a bent token from where it had become wedged between her back and the mattress. "These things have sharp edges," she complained.

He gathered her in his arms and rolled onto his back, so she lay on top of him.

"Aren't they digging into you now?" Aimee asked in concern. "Your back is bare."

"I don't mind it," he replied. "My hide's thicker than yours." His hands roamed over the silky fabric covering her back and hips. "Let's take this off," he suggested.

They took it off.

"I meant to be calm and considerate," Konrad panted some time later. "But you reduced me to a frenzy again." He sounded regretful.

"You were considerate," Aimee murmured, running her hands over his hairy chest. "I will never, ever grow tired of this wonderous body," she sighed, making him snort. She reached down to peel off a token which was stuck to his upper arm and showed it to him. "It has left the impression of a true lover's knot on your arm," she said, tracing it with her finger. He turned his arm and glanced down at it but made no comment. "I would give you five of these tokens, just for the pleasure of beholding you naked," she confessed with great daring.

A lazy grin spread across his face. "I would give you ten."

443

Lightly, Aimee pressed a fingertip to the upturned corner of his mouth. She loved seeing his smile. It was everything she had hoped it would be, and somehow more. "Ten to look at me or for me to look at you?" she asked teasingly, hoping to see more.

"Fifty to look at you," he said, his eye kindling.

"Fifty?" She quirked an eyebrow at him and tipped her head to one side. "How much is an *I love you* worth in tokens?"

"One hundred," he responded at once.

"One hundred tokens?" she repeated. "That's a lot."

"Yes."

"How much is it worth…when I take care of you and rub lotion all over your body?" she ventured thoughtfully.

He rolled on top of her, sweeping tokens off the bed and onto the floor with a brush of his arm. "I really like that, Aimee. You know I do. But nothing's worth as much as a hundred tokens, except an *I love you*."

Aimee caught her breath. "Oh," she said. They gazed at each other for a long moment.

"I'm waiting," he said tersely.

Aimee laughed. "Personally, I think it's worth more when it is given freely without prompting!"

"So do I," he growled. "But beggars can't be choosers."

"I doubt you've ever begged for anything in your life," she told him breathlessly.

"Oh, I'll beg if that's what it takes. Do you want that?"

"No," she said quickly. "I love you."

His gaze softened instantly, and they kissed again lingeringly. "I still don't know how I finally made fortune smile down on me at last," he sighed.

She shook her head. "You do know," she insisted. "For I told you what it was that inspired love in my breast."

"My losing," he scoffed, but only lightly.

"Not just losing, but losing *honorably*," she corrected him. "You were pleased for Sir Renlow, and that touched my heart."

"Hmmm."

"Will you let me put lotion all over you after our bath?"

"Gods, yes," he groaned. "But you must let me return the favor, wife."

"I will." She smiled up at him. "But first, Konrad," she said so shyly that he tensed at once. "Would you—would you very much mind saying it to me, please?" she asked, feeling like she might die of embarrassment.

He sucked in a shocked breath. "I told you that I love you!" he thundered. "Didn't I?"

Aimee shook her head. "No, not in so many words."

He looked horrified. "When I told you about that trunk?"

Aimee shook her head again. "You told me that I was precious to you, but you did not actually—"

"Gods, I am a bloody fool!" he said shakily. "I love you, Aimee. So, so much…" Then he lifted her hand and pressed it to the scarred side of his face and held it there, and she finally believed him.

*

After Konrad had gathered up every last one of the one hundred tokens and added them to his chest, they bathed in the tub which had been set up in Aimee's old bedchamber. It was a squeeze, but they both about managed to fit in. Then they applied lotion to each other with many caresses and whispered words of love.

Konrad let her do his face without a murmur, though every time her face came close to his, he seemed to expect a kiss. As for Aimee, she was not at all sure that Konrad would not soon surpass her in the skill. He rubbed and circled all her sore spots until she could think of a saddle once more without wincing.

"I suppose I really ought to practice some more horseback riding," Aimee admitted with a heavy sigh. "It does not really become a baroness to be so bad at it."

Her husband grunted, swinging her up into his arms and making for the door of her old bedchamber. "My robe!" Aimee squeaked, for they were both still naked from their bath. She was not at all sure she would ever be as comfortable with her nudity as her husband was. He caught up a mantle from the chair and flung it over her front.

"There is no one around to see you," he pointed out as he strode down the corridor to his own bedchamber. "We are the only ones with rooms on this floor."

"One of the servants could come along!"

"They would have the sense to avert their eyes," he pointed out, which was probably true.

Aimee raised her head which had been resting against his chest, suddenly remembering something. "Konrad?" she asked as he closed the door behind them. "Do you really think I'm a *managing woman*?"

"Gods, yes," he said, setting her down on the bed and climbing on after her.

"Oh." She sounded as put out about it as she felt.

"I don't mind it personally." He shrugged. "Any wife of mine needs to be able to hold her own. We Bartrees are a contentious lot."

She frowned, drawing down the sheets to clamber beneath them. "What about when you said I was an overbearing sister?" she asked. "Just lately, I *have* been thinking that I probably should not have forced Ursula's hand. Do—do you think she might be unhappy in her marriage with Sir Renlow?"

He shook his head, joining her under the covers. "No, far from it. They both seem vastly contented, all told."

"You—you did not tell me of your visit to them," she reminded him as he drew her close.

He paused a moment. "I thought the subject could likely wait."

"Until we were far from Caer-Lyoness?" she asked with sudden suspicion. "In case I went rushing around there trying to take charge of their lives?"

He gave a muffled laugh against her hair. "If it is any consolation, you have always acted far better toward your sister than I ever did to mine. My decision was not impartial. I wanted you to worry your pretty head *less* about your sister and *more* about me."

"You do realize," she said hesitantly, "that it is probably Ursula and Renlow that are dining downstairs presently with Freda. And maybe my father."

"I do realize it," he responded frankly. "Though I was not so sure you did."

447

"Because I did not go barging in there, you mean?" she asked with a little asperity. "Trying to organize them all to my satisfaction?"

He squeezed her waist. "I know you have done wonders with Freda," he said placatingly. "She is much happier here than in Vettel." He slipped a finger under her chin and gently tipped her head up, touching his brow to hers. "Forgive me for this morning," he said abruptly. "I was a fool.

"When I first woke beside you, I felt good, really good. For the first time since I cannot remember when. Then I started to panic as I'm just not used to feeling that way." He paused a moment, as though searching for the right words. "I knew the earth was shifting beneath my feet, and I was left scrambling for well-trod ground."

Aimee was listening carefully. "You were?" she asked quietly. She could tell he was trying to explain himself to her.

"I was," he agreed firmly. "I realized that things were changing in my life, and nothing was going to be the same again."

"And that panicked you. But now it does not?"

He shook his head. "No," he said, propping his head up on his hand. "Now I am actually looking forward to it."

"What exactly are you looking forward to?" she asked suspiciously.

"Everything," he said promptly. "Even the bloody awful blue and yellow pavilion I have no doubt you are going to commission, and which will be a complete eyesore to all who behold it." Aimee spluttered. "To you sweeping through Bartree Castle, setting the place to rights. To you being at my side." He shrugged. "Always."

Aimee opened her mouth to respond, but it seemed he had not finished. "You have turned everything on its head, wife," he continued in an odd tone. "Everything I thought was important to me…I no longer seem to care about at all."

She reached up to stroke the hair from his brow. "Such as…?" she asked.

"Bartree Castle," he answered promptly. "The north. I don't even—" He broke off, looking baffled. "I don't feel the slightest desire to travel north to see how the restorations are going." The admission left him looking dazed.

She shrugged. "You may feel differently when it nears completion," she suggested. "Or when you have an heir."

His gaze snapped to hers as though that aspect had not occurred to him. "Yes," he growled after a moment. "That may be true." He shrugged. "But even so, I can see us living most of the year in Caer-Lyoness." He directed a searching glance at her. "What say you to that, wife?"

"I have lived in Caer-Lyoness all my life, my lord," she told him with a smile. "That will be no hardship to me. The rest of my family is here."

"Yes, but when you decided to marry me," he persisted, waving that aside, "you wanted to live in a castle, did you not?"

Aimee gazed at him in some confusion. "Not particularly. Why is that important?"

"I want to give you your every heart's desire," he persisted stubbornly.

Aimee laughed. "I just wanted to be with you," she confessed. "I knew you had a castle, so I thought I would live in it one day.

But that was neither here nor there with me, and it was far from the reason I fell in love with you."

His clasp of her tightened again, and he was silent, crossing one ankle over the other. "'Tis the strangest thing to me," he pondered, glancing around the bedchamber distractedly. "But I think I like it here best of all." There was just a hint of accusation in the baffled look he directed at her.

"This house?" Aimee asked. "Or this city?"

"Both are one and the same to me now. If anyone would have ever told me that the southern capital could be my most beloved place, I would ne'er have believed them. But these past few days, nay, this past month has been the happiest I think I have ever been in my life. Because of you." Aimee gazed back at him, but before she could speak, another thought seemed to strike him.

"And Beres Caple is now my favorite tournament," he added, looking thunderstruck. "It's a backwater event for yokels, and I didn't even win it!"

"You did win—" she started to protest, but he interrupted her.

"Because of you. Because we were there together," he reiterated. "It was the best time I ever had. In my whole life. Even though I lost both events," he admitted with a slight shake of his head. "Looking back on it now, I feel benevolent toward everyone there. Even," he added in bewilderment, "de Crecy."

Aimee felt the smile spreading over her face before he had even finished speaking. He sounded so astonished by his own words. "Well," she started, "I think it is only right that Beres Caple is your favorite tournament, considering you are their most popular knight there." But it seemed Konrad had tired of the conversation, for his big hands were grabbing her about the waist and hauling her up the bed so he could rain kisses over her face and neck.

Aimee subsided against the pillows with a sigh. They could talk about it later.

Epilogue

"Oh, that feels so much better," Aimee moaned, then fell disappointingly silent.

"Have you drifted back to sleep?" Konrad asked after a moment. He really should remove his hands from her delectable body. Her delectable *pregnant* body. Aimee had only just started to show, but already he was fascinated by the subtle changes.

Both Ingrid from their household and Old Janet from her father's house had been consulted and had agreed the babe would be born in the spring. He ran his hand over the swell of her belly and told himself he needed to get out of bed.

What he really needed to do was prepare for the melee, not be lying abed unable to tear himself away from his wife.

"Yes," she murmured, her eyes still closed. "Fast asleep."

"Want me to wake you up?" he asked with a groan. Gods, what he really wanted right now was to lift up her shift and have his way with her.

Aimee frowned, her eyes springing open. "Why do *you* sound like you're in pain all of a sudden?" she asked. "I doubt you're saddle sore."

"I'm not," he admitted. "I ache somewhere else entirely." His hands roamed over her plump thighs. Unable to prevent

452

himself, he leaned down to kiss her one shapely shoulder where her shift had slipped down.

"How were you thinking of waking me up?" she asked with drowsy interest.

"With my cock," he answered raspily. "Or my mouth."

Her breathing hitched a moment. She seemed to consider. "I really don't want to move though," she sighed. "My backside is *so* stiff, Konrad."

He snorted. Not as stiff as him. Aimee was still a terrible horsewoman. It should bother him more than it did, he realized dimly. Instead, he just added two days to every journey they made and a ridiculous number of rest stops. "You don't have to," he promised, instead of telling her to stop her whining. He lowered his head, whispering in her ear. "I could just lift your hips and slide right in."

Her eyes sprang open at that, a pretty color spreading over her face. "Konrad!" she murmured in reproach, but her breathing was coming fast. "Well, I don't know. We would have to be quiet," she said, glancing around the fancy pavilion he was now obliged to travel to all his tournaments with.

The blasted thing was blue and yellow with a ridiculous number of trimmings and furnishings. He looked like a court jester emerging from it, but for some reason, he couldn't bring himself to give a damn about that either these days.

Aimee shook her head, a look of determination on her face. "No, Konrad," she said firmly. "I've just recalled that you blamed me for your losing at the Autumn Tournament because your legs were too weak after bedding me that same morn."

Konrad snorted. "You *were* to blame, wife," he said huskily as he swung his leg over her hips, bearing her back down onto the mattress. "You sapped all the strength right out of me."

"So then *why* are you looking now to repeat the experience?" she asked, sounding nettled, even as she slipped her arms about his neck.

"Because," he said huskily before he took her mouth, "I care more about conquering you than the competition these days."

"Hmmmm," Aimee hummed around his tongue. When he drew back, she was panting. "I am not sure I believe you, husband."

"Believe it," he growled, bunching her shift up. "Every time I bring you along, I simply resign myself to another loss."

"What?" Aimee squeaked, sounding dismayed. "Wh-what do you mean?"

"Why do you think I only bring you to one in three tournaments?" he asked.

"Because I make you lose?" She sounded so stricken he almost laughed.

He lowered his brow to hers and gazed into her eyes a moment. "You like losers, remember? That's why you liked me in the first place. You skew all my priorities, wife," he sighed, aiming kisses at her mouth and missing as Aimee stubbornly turned her face away.

"Yes, but I don't want to be your unlucky charm, Konrad!" she insisted, then squeaked as he lightly pinched her nipples.

"You could never be that, wife," he said. "Now give me your lips. I'm hungry for a taste."

She complied so satisfactorily that silence ruled over the tent for a good few minutes. Finally, he dragged his lips from hers. "Wait!" he growled, remembering belatedly his vow to make her tourney queen this day.

"Konrad? *Now* what is wrong?" Aimee panted, her dark eyes glazed and fixed on his mouth.

He frowned down at her. *Damn it.* "You gave me a ten-token kiss when I only wanted a two."

Aimee blinked at him. "Nonsense! You did not specify! And anyway, *all* my kisses are ten-token kisses!" The exchange of tokens had become a great game between them these days. Aimee's one hundred tokens flowed endlessly back and forth between them as a sign of high favor.

He had nearly suffered a breakdown three mornings ago when he could find only ninety-eight of their number remaining to him. Poor Jakeman had had to turn the room upside down to find the missing two.

"Not true," he growled. "Some of your kisses are worth far more."

"Oh?" She looked so smugly pleased by his confession that he felt his heart flip in his chest. He was getting distracted, as always, around her.

"However, that is not the issue at hand," he said, clearing his throat. "The fact is, wife, that I just recalled I am determined to win the joust here at Kellingford."

"Oh?" she repeated.

He could tell she was not remotely interested in the outcome of the competition and frowned. "And make you tourney queen," he finished with import.

Aimee wriggled beneath him, making him catch his breath. "I would rather you made me your queen here and now, Konrad," she breathed, saucily hooking a leg over his hip. "Queen of your heart."

"I have already made you that," he wheezed, even as his hips slid between her thighs. "Have you forgotten what anniversary this is?" he asked, giving his head a quick shake and struggling against his baser instincts which wanted very much to take over at this juncture. He felt his resolve waver. "I need some strength left me for the joust," he said a little wildly.

"Anniversary?" Aimee mumbled, bumping her body up against his in unspoken appeal.

"Kellingford, wife," he said through gritted teeth. "When you saw me lose to Renlow. When you fell in love with me. It was a year ago today."

Aimee's gaze focused on him. "Why, so it was," she said and smiled so sweetly up at him that he was lost.

It was a bloody miracle that he actually did lift the victor's cup that afternoon.

"I have just had a very good notion," his wife murmured to him as she sat beside him at the feast that night. She wore a new gown of yellow and blue, and her neck and fingers glittered with the Bartree jewels. She had left off the diadem tonight to wear the flowered garland perched atop her head instead.

He surveyed her with satisfaction, covering her hand with his. "What is that, wife?"

"I think you should ask Sir Douglas to be godfather to our child. 'Twill console him for the fact Lady Constance has recently become betrothed to James Wycliffe."

Konrad considered this. "I want to ask Vawdrey and Orde," he answered, for he had already given the matter much deliberation. "They will have more idea of what the role entails being fathers themselves or as good as." Orde's wife, Lenora, was due any day now, which was the reason the Twyfords were not at Kellingford this year. "Farleigh, Symes, and Lowell can be godfathers to the next one."

Aimee nodded. "Very well, but I do hope that poor Sir Douglas will cheer up soon," she sighed. "You would have thought that news of Sir Leonard's betrothal would have cheered him up, but he had a face as long as a horse last time I saw him."

Another of Aimee's notions had been the tactful suggestion that Symes approach the bishop in Caer-Lyoness about a dispensation to wed his stepsister, Sybil. It had taken her a full week to convince Konrad to raise such a subject with Symes. Even then, he had only managed it after they had drunk a good few flagons of ale together in The Jennet Tree.

Three days later, Symes had appeared at their door covered in mud after a hard ride up from the country. He looked exhausted but was flourishing a piece of paper in his hand bearing a red wax seal. "She said she'll have me," he had announced unsteadily. "It was not just me. She feels the same way."

His pale face had crumpled at this point, and he had been overcome with emotion, having to cover his welling eyes. Konrad had had to practically carry him into the house before the lad had all but collapsed into incoherence. "I've paid off the bishop," he babbled. "And it's all legal. Sybil is to be mine." Konrad had hurried to fetch Aimee, who would know the right things to say on such an occasion, for he was damned if he knew what they were.

Naturally, Aimee had known just what to do, namely shriek, fling her arms about Sir Leo's neck, and give him her heartfelt

457

congratulations. Symes's expression had changed from profoundly shaken to elated in a moment, and Konrad had been vastly relieved.

Symes's happiness had been complete when a week later Lowell, infected no doubt by all the talk of weddings, had asked for his sister Helen's hand. "That leaves only one sister left at home," Aimee had whispered when they had entertained them all for dinner to celebrate. "Sir Leo's sister Miranda." Konrad had not particularly cared for the gleam in her eye as she had turned back to contemplate Farleigh. If Aimee had her way, the poor bastard would no doubt find himself leg-shackled to Miranda Symes before the month was out.

And it was not only Konrad's friends who were flocking to get handfasted, for not long after their return from Beres Caple, Gerold Ankatel had formally approached him as head of the family to request his cousin Freda's hand in marriage. Ankatel had assured him gravely that Freda was consenting, and he had taken care to secure her affections before taking this step.

To Konrad's considerable relief, Aimee had been delighted by this development, though rather astonished by the match. In truth, she and Freda had grown so close that Konrad had almost worried she would not want to part with her, even for her father's sake.

However, the two women had put their heads together and planned such a magnificent celebration that it made Aimee and Ursula's joint wedding look almost a humble affair. Konrad, who had imagined a timid creature like Freda would have been terrified by such a spectacle, had been astonished to find she took great delight in throwing the grandest wedding Caer-Lyoness had seen in many a year.

At the culmination of the day, Freda had gazed down shortsightedly from the balcony at Ankatel's townhouse, watching the crowd jostling for coins and wedding favors with tears in her eyes. "So many well-wishers, all so very kind," she had quavered, pressing a hand to her thin chest which was now clad in costly silk raiment. "But then, *everyone* in the south is so kind, I find."

Gerold Ankatel had beamed at her and patted her hand. "Well, my dear," he had answered with a flourish. "Who could fail to be kind to one so sweet as yourself?"

Konrad had glanced at his sister, who had the grace to blush. Magnatrude was making an effort these days to be less snappish with her family members. To be fair to her, she was a good deal pleasanter to be around of late. No doubt because she was a good deal happier. Her situation at court seemed to give her a fulfilment in life she had previously lacked.

His sister had been accompanied to Freda's wedding by Unwin, who had been resplendent in the Bartree family colors and looking vastly pleased with himself. When Konrad had descended to their kitchens that evening in search of a servant, he had found the young page sat on a wooden stool, regaling his mother and an open-mouthed Matthews with tales of the palace.

Golda had been the one person who *had* been put out by Freda's marriage, and that was only because she had taken her friend the kitchen cat with her to her new home, and the pantry had been overrun with mice for three days until they had obtained another.

Konrad was just grateful Jakeman remained stalwart and dependable. At Aimee's instigation, he had asked his manservant the age of his eldest son to see if he might wish to join their household as kitchen boy at some future point. Trude and Unwin had taken up their palace quarters and returned to the townhouse only once a month at most. Jakeman had seemed pleased at the idea, and his boy Vincent had since started with them two days a week to ease him into his duties.

Ursula, too, had been happy at the news of her father's remarriage. Seeing how contented the mature couple was in each other's company, it would have been hard for any fond daughter not to be pleased. Freda now attended guild banquets almost every week at her husband's side and was relishing the novelty of being the most important female at the table. As for Gerold, he was loving having someone to indulge, and Freda, who had never been cosseted, was blossoming under his care.

Ursula and Renlow had not been without family troubles of their own, for though Ursula's family gave them the space they needed to start their wedded life, they had soon found themselves besieged by d'Avenants. Renlow's three brothers had descended on them with their quarrelsome wives in tow and had finally outstayed even their mild-mannered host's welcome.

After a month, Ursula had declared none of her in-laws appreciated her husband's finer qualities and were trying to take advantage of him. She had them thrown out on the street by her burly manservant and the door bolted fast against them. Renlow had been very taken aback at first by such warlike behavior from his quiet bride, but as none of his brothers had shown the slightest interest in his well-being for years, he was soon convinced she was the one who had his best interests at heart. Harmony was once again restored to their household.

Aimee had been vastly diverted by the tale and made her pink-cheeked sister tell it several times before she was satisfied, calling in first Golda to hear it, and then Ingrid, who she seemed to think would appreciate its finer points. To Konrad's surprise, the old woman had cackled away and slapped her thigh as though it was a great jest. He and Renlow had eyed each other and exchanged shrugs. He wasn't sure he would ever fully fathom the female way of thinking.

Surveying Aimee now as she leaned in to thank him again for her tourney crown, he slipped an arm about her waist and held her rather closer than good manners dictated, but he found he did not much care. "I have thought of something I wanted to ask you," she murmured close to his ear.

"Hmm? And what is that, wife?"

"How is it that you decide what hostages to take?" she asked. "For I have noticed that you do not drag all your fallen foes to pile them up before Jakeman, only some of them."

He paused a moment, debating how to answer this. "Is it by their raiment?" she asked shrewdly. "Only, I have noticed that the more poorly dressed ones you tend to let go free." He gave a brief nod. "I thought so," she said triumphantly.

He eyed her askance. "It is not by any noble prompting," he started direly. "If that is what you are thinking. I am simply not inclined to go chasing debts all over the countryside from impoverished knights."

His wife patted his chest. "Yes, yes," she said. "Do not trouble yourself. No one knows your nature better than I, husband."

"Aye, well," he said uneasily, for he knew she attributed him with far better qualities than he truly possessed. "Now I have a question for you."

"What is it?"

"How do you like being tourney queen?"

She beamed up at him. "It is wonderful."

"Everything you dreamed it would be?"

A strange expression flitted over her face. "I never actually dreamed of being tourney queen, Konrad," she admitted.

"Just as well," he growled, lowering his voice. "As it will be a miracle if I win another tournament with you present, wife."

Aimee laughed. "Am I really so distracting?"

"Always."

She squeezed his arm. "Do you know what I did dream about?" she asked softly. "Being your wife, and that *far* surpasses my imaginings."

At that, he had to lean down for a kiss. The long table cheered, and when he drew back, he found he was smiling all over his face, both the scarred and the whole side.

"Three cheers for Lord and Lady Kentigern!" cried Sir Roger Kellingford, founder of the tournament.

And as the rafters rang out, Konrad realized that Beres Caple was not the only place he was popular. Not anymore.

THE END

If you want to read more about Karadok, then the next book in the series is Sabina's story:

An Inconvenient Vow

Never did Sabina Burrell imagine that foiling a plot against her sister would lead to her having to wed the arrogant Sir Jeffree de Crecy! She has never met such a loathsome man, and that includes her late, unlamented husband!

Sir Jeffree, raised in the expectation of succeeding to his uncle's title, is appalled to become ensnared in a scheme to discredit his uncle's new bride. The whole thing is beneath his dignity, as is the shameless young widow who denounces him in front of everyone and makes him look a fool!

Jeffree will do anything to salvage his honor, even if it means wedding a woman he despises. Revenge will be sweet indeed, ensuring Sabina pays for what she did. What he does not anticipate is that his own long-prized vow of chastity will be so very sorely tried…

The Favourite

Alisander de Balon, fifth Viscount Bardulf, is a lot of things. Ambassador. Diplomat. Spy. He is also bored as hell at the Argent King's court. His only diversion these days is tormenting staid Jane Cecil, the Queen's favorite lady-in-waiting. Seeing her vexed amuses him more than any royal entertainment.

Jane has finally found her place at court, and it is among the Queen's retinue. All she wants to do is faithfully serve Her

Majesty, something she could do in peace if it was not for the Queen's countryman, Viscount Bardulf, who seems to delight in baiting her!

Neither Bardulf nor Jane could have foreseen the sudden tragedy that leads to their hasty union, and certainly neither of them could have anticipated that they would fall so easily into different roles…that of husband and wife.

If you enjoyed this book, please consider leaving me a rating on Goodreads, Amazon, Bookbub or wherever else you leave your reviews. I would be very grateful.

You can find my website at: www.alicecoldbreath.com where you can sign up for my monthly newsletter and find out what I am up to.

Also, please do check out some of my other stories!
Many thanks, Alice.

www.ingramcontent.com/pod-product-compliance
Lightning Source LLC
Chambersburg PA
CBHW020826030726
47496CB00001B/118